SEVENTEEN SPOONS

SEVENTEEN SPOONS

ESTHER GOLDENBERG

Row House Publishing recognizes that the power of justice-centered storytelling isn't a phenomenon; it is essential for progress. We believe in equity and activism, and that books—and the culture around them—have the potential to transform the universal conversation around what it means to be human.

Thank you for being an important part of the conversation and holding sacred the critical work of our authors.

Library of Congress Cataloging-in-Publication Data
Available Upon Request

ISBN 978-1-955905-83-1 (TP)
ISBN 978-1-955905-84-8 (eBook)

Printed in the United States
Distributed by Simon & Schuster

Design by Neuwith & Associates, Inc.

First edition

10 9 8 7 6 5 4 3 2 1

To our parents and ancestors
and all the people who have come before us.

CONTENTS

PART 1: BEFORE

PART 2: AFTER

CONTENTS

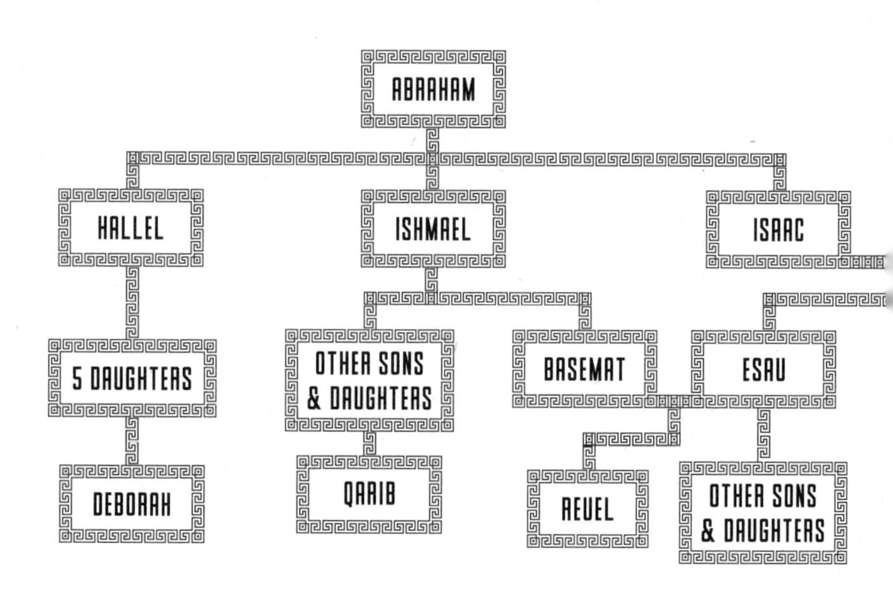
ABRAHAM
HALLEL
ISHMAEL
ISAAC
5 DAUGHTERS
OTHER SONS & DAUGHTERS
BASEMAT
ESAU
DEBORAH
QARIB
REUEL
OTHER SONS & DAUGHTERS

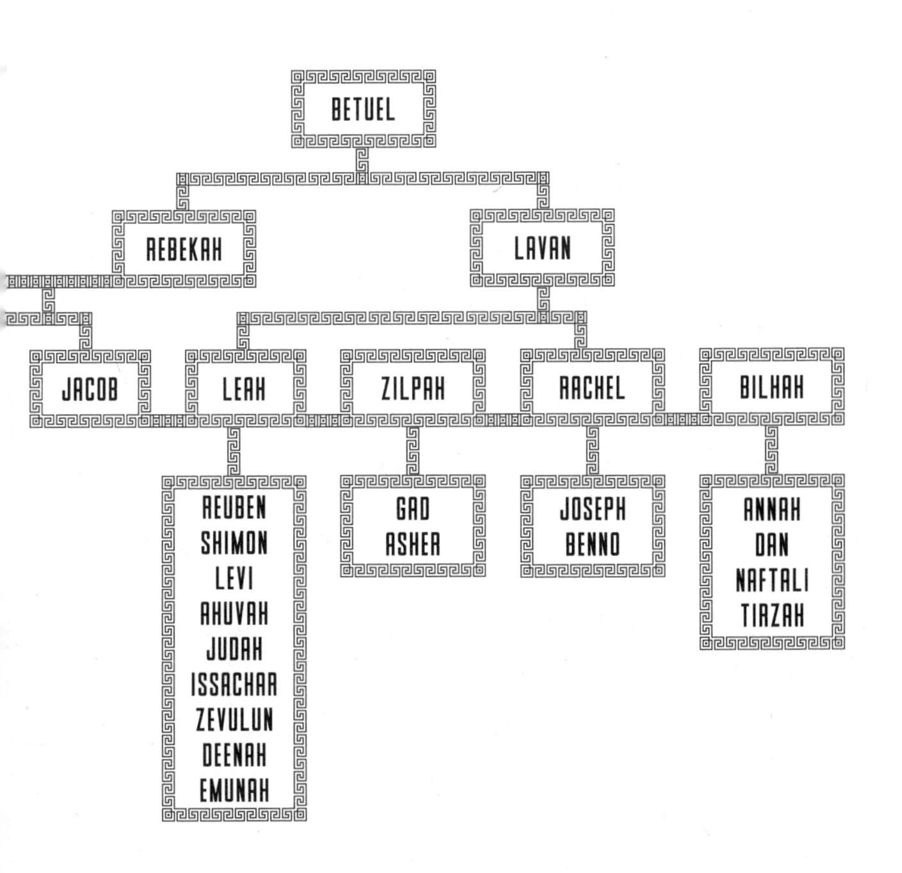
BETUEL
REBEKAH
LAVAN
JACOB
LEAH
ZILPAH
RACHEL
BILHAH
REUBEN
SHIMON
LEVI
AHUVAH
JUDAH
ISSACHAR
ZEVULUN
DEENAH
EMUNAH
GAD
ASHER
JOSEPH
BENNO
ANNAH
DAN
NAFTALI
TIRZAH

By the time my body was placed in my coffin, I had taken over 924 million breaths. I had much to be grateful for. Also, some regrets. But this number impressed me, and I believe the smile on my face was one of pride due to realizing my body had been breathing for that long.

Mind you, this number might not be exact. Perhaps it was 924,134,123 breaths. Maybe it was 923,625,321. Or any number close to those, really. I did this calculation without the aid of my court magicians, nor did I have tools to help me other than my own thoughts. My Physician, who watched me as I climbed into my coffin, had assured me I would not die right away. Rather than panicking about being in a closed space, I began breathing the ceremonial breaths. Eventually, I began counting them.

Each inhale was an opportunity to bring My God into my body. Each exhale was a little bit of me going back out to My God and the world around me. True, the world around me was only six finger-widths of area between my body and the inside of my enclosure, but My God can fit in all spaces. YhWh. That was the name My ancestors used for My God. We usually just said *Yah* or *Elohim*, saving the full name only for ceremonies. This would be my final ceremony. I would certainly use the name.

Inhale. *Yhhhh*. Exhale. *Whhhh*. Inhale. *Yhhhh*. Exhale. *Whhhh*. If I began to feel discomfort, I went back to noticing my breaths.

Inhale. *Yhhhh*. Exhale. *Whhhh*.

When My Pharaoh died, I knew I would be buried too. That wasn't the custom of my family, but I had been an Egyptian for a long time. It was my new custom, and part of the pact of having the privilege I enjoyed as Second-in-Command of all of Egypt. All those close to Pharaoh must be buried with him so that he can take his riches into his next life. I was one of those riches. But unlike his throne and his horses, his horsemen and his other servants, I had power of my own. When the others were given the poison, they were commanded to drink immediately. As Second-in-Command, nobody would dare stop me from keeping mine in my hand, though a guard was assigned to my burial chamber to ensure that I didn't leave it.

The important thing was that this gave me time to make preparations before my death because I knew it was coming. I spoke with My Little Brother, Benno. The idea of calling him My Little Brother made me chuckle. There was a brief time in our lives when I had been able to cradle him in my arms and sing him shepherding songs, and so in my heart, he holds the place of "little" brother, while in fact he grew taller than me by a full hand and fathered more sons.

But Benno, bigger or littler brother, no matter, was my closest confidant in the family. I taught him of the burial customs in Egypt. I told him what to expect: my body would be embalmed like that of My Pharaoh—an honor, really—and placed in a tomb almost as ornate. Pharaoh's mummified body would stay there forever, but I wished for my bones to be returned to the Land of My Fathers when my family made that journey back to the north. That had been important to My Father as well. My death wasn't long after his, so the request was familiar to Benno. I am just grateful that My Father was already dead when my time came. He could not have handled losing me a second time.

I took Benno to the hidden entrance of the tomb that would be mine so that he would know where to go to retrieve my body when the time came. He would not be the first person to rob an Egyptian grave, nor the last, I'm sure. But I instructed him to take only my body and the simple wooden case it was in, no more, no less. I knew it would be no easy task to carry the stone coffin, so it would need to stay behind. This way, the carvings in the stone showing me among the abundance of grain and grapes would remind the Egyptians of what I did for generations to come. The new pharaoh would not object to my body departing, as he would see it as a diminishing of My Pharaoh's riches—an advantage to himself. Meanwhile, my own descendants would have my mummified bones with my likeness painted on the plaster case to remind them of who I was.

I took my last meal with my family the morning before the burial. It was the grandest feast they had ever seen or eaten, and though we were all aware of the morbid reason for our gathering, every morsel that passed our lips was enjoyed. The last food I took in was a date, neither fancy nor dried like others on the table. It was fresh, full of goodness, and perfect just the way it was. As I savored the sweetness, I heard My God tell me that I was the same as that date. Perfect just the way I was. That night, I dreamt of a land so sweet that its rivers were flowing with honey.

Early the next morning, I climbed into my casket and was carried on parade by six men who showed the people that I was lying there with eyes closed and arms crossed. No words were allowed to be uttered, but they bore witness to my exit from this world and my entrance to the next. My vial of poison was concealed in my hand, not swallowed as they believed. For I would do that in my own time. When the parade was over, the men set my wooden casket gently on the stone slab reserved for the Second-in-Command. They sang a song of tribute to My Pharaoh and closed the lid. Though the sun had just risen outside, it was a quick sunset on my life.

"My God," I said silently, my lips moving but no sound escaping them, "Elohim, God of My Father Jacob, God of My Father Isaac, God of My Father Abraham, You have granted me two lifetimes, one in the Land of My Fathers, and one in the Land of the River. They were not without challenges, but You have blessed me manyfold. I ask You now for two more blessings. Please bless My Children with Your presence and their children after them for all generations. And please be with me now."

And then I took that first inhale. Slow, long, filling my body so that it rose almost to the top of my casket. *Yhhhh*. Then my first exhale. *Whhhh*. Slow, long, shrinking my body back down to the bottom. I was lucky; as Second-in-Command, my casket was lined with cushions and soft linens. Even so, I knew while lying there, awaiting my death, I would want to shift my weight and my position and not be able to. I quickly stopped that thought with an inhale. *Yhhhh*. My God is in me. Then an exhale. *Whhhh*. My God is all around me.

This went on for more than a day. I know because although I had no sight and little sound, I was able to hear the distant ringing of the morning bell. I had breathed, and I had slept, and I had lived through the night calmly. I felt strong enough to do it again. Inhale. Exhale. Although the air was already stuffy from my own breath, I was not yet ready to stop breathing. *Yhhhh. Whhhh*. I felt calm. And also a little bored, which was why I began counting my breaths.

I counted my breaths until the next morning. I don't know if I slept. Perhaps I even counted in my sleep. I cannot know. But when the morning bells rang again, the number in my thoughts was 20,009. It was then that I began to be curious about how many breaths I had taken in my life. The exact number will never be known, nor is it important. What was important was each inhale and exhale. Each breath with My God while I could still breathe.

My Physician had once told me that at the time of their deaths, many men spoke aloud about having their lives play in front of them like an act of theater, or perhaps a dream, in their last moments. They saw themselves as babies, youths, and grown men. They saw everything that happened in their lives, even many things which they had forgotten.

That is exactly what happened to me.

As soon as that began, I jolted with horror and opened my eyes. I had written many things for others, and many things had been written about me, but not since my youth had I written anything about myself. That had to be changed. Immediately.

"Guard! Guard!" I called, but he didn't answer. I was sure he was close enough to hear me. He wouldn't leave his post, for he knew he would be risking his own life. I needed to tell him that staying would be an even greater risk. "Guard! My Lord has just reprimanded me for not having written the accounts of my life. He has come to me and told me that I must do it immediately, or He will not allow me into the world to come, and the same fate will befall anyone who prevents His command from being carried out."

The guard certainly thought that "My Lord" referred to My Pharaoh, though it was Elohim who had helped me come to this realization. The young Egyptian would understand nothing of this if I told him, nor did we have time. What he did understand was that I would give him riches from my own body in exchange for him bringing lanterns and oil as well as papyrus and ink.

As scared as he was of retribution from the afterlife, he was also scared of punishment in this life. His shaky voice repeated many times that he was standing beside me with his dagger drawn should I try to escape. It took longer than I had hoped to convince him to open my coffin just enough for me to give him the smooth golden ring from my finger. I promised that it would be his to keep if he would help me. Along with safety from My Pharaoh.

With the ring on his finger, he slid the lid off my coffin. I quickly instructed him to take a golden pendant from my wrist to hire the fastest horseman to bring him to Benjamin the Israelite. Then I took the bejeweled breastplate from my chest. "Give this to Benjamin," I ordered, "and tell him to give you oil and lamps and all the papyrus and ink that he can gather. Quickly."

Now, the guard has returned with all the supplies I requested. His belly and his pockets are full, so he was happy to push aside the lid of the coffin of the one who had filled them. It is with gratitude to My God that I sit in my lit burial chamber with a guard who has completed this errand and has agreed to stay out until the light under the door stops flickering. When he returns, it is of no consequence to me whether he believes that the missing fruit from the silver platter on the offerings table was eaten by gods in the afterlife or me in this one. What is important is that I can now write about myself before I die.

I am Joseph.

Son of Jacob.

Son of Isaac.

Son of Abraham.

These are the stories of my lives.

PART 1:
BEFORE

CHAPTER 1

My birth was on a joy-filled day. My Father had been awaiting this day for more than fourteen years. He always said he had longed for it ever since first meeting My Mother at the well. She teased him that he had just been thirsty and tired and afraid—and relieved—when they had first met that day, and that he would have been happy with any life better than the one he had just fled.

But My Father insisted that wasn't true. Yes, he had left his homeland with the fear that his twin, Esau, was on his heels, ready to attack. But My Father trusted in his god, Elohim, to deliver him safely to the house of his mother's brother, Lavan. What he didn't know was that Lavan had this beautiful daughter waiting for him. The moment he saw her, he was overcome with enough love to single-handedly remove the heavy rock covering the well to show her his strength.

My Mother, Rachel, had not exactly been waiting for him. She was simply out watering Lavan's sheep when My Father, Jacob, arrived. He was smitten with her, but she was too young to notice. She matured quickly with him around, though, and by the time they married, seven years after their first meeting, she was as in love with him as he was with her, and they eagerly awaited the birth of their first son. Me.

They did not know that I was going to take my time in arriving. Sure, My Father had other sons with his other wives. My Mother's older sister, Leah, was My Father's first wife. She had many sons, and in fact, My Father rejoiced in their births and was entertained as they played childhood games and mimicked their elders. As soon as each became old enough, he took them to the field with him and taught them his successful shepherding ways.

The same was so of My Brothers who were born of My Father's other wives, Bilhah and Zilpah. Jacob was always kind to them, the women and the babies, and treated them as well as Leah's sons. He was thrilled and proud to be the father of ten fine young sons. He loved his three daughters as well.

But when My Mother went to My Father—after his many years of needing to work for Lavan due to his uncle's unspoken rules and deceptive ways—and gave him the news that she was carrying a son in her womb, My Father was overcome with joy. It was no secret that My Mother was his favorite wife, his beloved. And while he was kind to all four of his wives, and even loved them, his devotion to My Mother surpassed anything he had ever felt—until the moment he learned that I was on the way. A son from his beloved Rachel!

My Father lifted and twirled My Mother, laughing and crying at the same time. Then he thought better of all that motion and gently set her back on the ground and danced before her. My

Father needed no flute nor harp nor drums to dance. The music was inside his ears and burst out through his feet and his smile.

My Brothers saw all the activity and quickly came to join in the merriment. The older ones, Reuben, Shimon, Levi, and Judah, were nearly the same age. True, Reuben was born first, but Shimon and Levi—the first twins born to My Father—came less than a year later, and Judah and his sister—the next pair—less than a year after that. Those four boys were always quick to separate themselves from the little ones and show that they would be the first to be men. They joined arms with My Father and danced a circle around My Mother. The younger ones just clapped and jumped as young children do. None of them yet knew of the reason but were happy to have a dance. My Mother smiled at the attention and the joy that was around her and the little me that was coming.

When the other women saw the merriment, they knew that My Mother had finally shared the news openly with My Father. The women had already known a baby was on the way. They had watched as the moon grew and shrank and grew and shrank and as My Mother's belly grew. They prayed that her belly would not shrink this time. For seven months, they took on her share of chores. They sang songs to her and rubbed her back and feet. They all hoped as much as she did that this time, a baby would make its way into the world from her womb.

It was after the eighth moon came and went, and I did not, that My Mother told My Father publicly. He had not said a word about the pregnancy until she did. He had also been consumed with fear that it would bring sadness again, not babies. But as soon as she announced that she was carrying me, the dancing began. The women joined the circle, lifting the babies above their heads until they shrieked with glee. My Mother reported that during that dance, she felt me stir inside her, eager to dance with my family.

For the next two months, My Father stayed close to the compound. My Mother laughed at him, reminding him there was still a long time until my arrival. If he went to the far fields, he would still not miss the big day. But My Father could not bear to be so far, so he sent his trusted servant, Kemke, out in his stead. Jacob wanted to return to the tents every evening and tell My Mother stories of the animals and how his son—her son—would one day go out there with him. I heard him tell those stories in a voice muffled by My Mother's body every night until I was born. I don't remember those nights, but I have been told of them so many times that it feels as if the memory is my own.

What does belong to me is my dream. On the night of my birth, I had my first dream. That is something I remember well. I dreamt of seventeen large dipping spoons with long handles. The spoons were all dipping into a well. It was loud with all those heavy metal spoons clanging into each other, but despite all their noisy effort, all came out without having even a drop of water. They then were gathered into a large sack and tossed onto the back of a camel. When I was weaned and my hair was cut and I no longer talked like a baby, I told My Mother of this dream. She said it was impossible. A baby just born does not dream.

But I did.

I ran off from My Mother that day. She thought I was angry, but I wasn't. I was sad. I thought she knew me so well. She anticipated my hungers and desires. She sang songs as she stared into my eyes. I was no longer a baby, but she still sometimes strapped me to her back when she watered the sheep to feel the familiar rise and fall of my breath against hers. She played games with my toes and knew each one of my dark curls by name. But this dream, she did not know about me, even when I told her so. And that made me sad.

I was crying in my favorite hiding place, the crevice in the rock behind the old, twisted olive tree on the far side of our compound. I didn't like to go near the tents of Lavan's sons, in case I might meet up with one of them while alone. But this tree wasn't visible from their area and was at the outer edge of ours. The view of the hills went on and on, but I was close enough to the cooking tent that no wild beast would dare come there.

My Mother knew this to be one of my favorite hiding places, but she didn't come. Which only made me cry harder. And that was how Judah found me: staring into the wilderness and crying like a baby. I quickly wiped my eyes so that he would see I was getting bigger. Not big enough to go out with My Brothers to look after the sheep, but not a little cry baby either.

"It's okay, Joseph," he said. "You can cry."

"I'm not a baby," I said. "I'm getting bigger every moment. I've lost milk teeth already, and I have a haircut like you." I stood as tall as I could.

"You're sure growing," he said, "but I'm still bigger!" With that, he swooped me off my feet and onto his shoulders before I even knew what was happening. I giggled and wiggled up there and was suddenly staring at the same view but from a much higher point. I couldn't wait to be as tall as Judah!

"So, are your problems smaller from up there?" he asked me. "Or do you want to tell me what's wrong?"

"Judah," I asked, "do you remember when I was born?"

Judah laughed. "I remember it, alright," he said.

"Judah," I started again. "I remember it too. I had a dream that night. The very night that I was born. I didn't know what dreams were. I didn't know what sleep was or waking. I didn't know words. But now I know the words. Now I know about dreams. I know I had one the very night that I was born."

Judah was quiet; he just continued walking with me on his shoulders, so I continued talking.

"Judah, the night I was born, I dreamt of seventeen large dipping spoons. You know the sort that bring water to a cooking pot? Like that, only larger. And they were not dipping into a pot; they were dipping into a well. They had colorful stones on them. But strange colors for stones. Not red or white or brown like the stones of these hills. There were stones the green of leaves on the tree, the purple of the hollyhocks, the blue of the sky, even red as blood. And they sparkled like stars. They were the most beautiful dipping spoons one could hope for. But when they dipped into the well, they came up empty. Dry. They were useless and gathered into a sack that rode off on the back of a camel."

"Joseph, you are a wonderful storyteller," Judah said. "Now, would you like me to tell you a story?" I'm sad to say that My Brother's compliment did not feel good to hear. I was telling about my dream, not a story! But I agreed to hear his.

"Joseph, on the night you were born, there was anticipation everywhere. Your mother, Rachel, was in her tent with my mother, Leah, and the other women. They had been in there most of the day. Every once in a while, they would exit in a little huddle. Your mother was held up by a woman on each side while she walked around the outside of the tent. You're too young to know of babies being born, but this is what the women do. They walk when they can to help the baby move. And when the walking becomes too difficult, they go back into the tent.

"Of course, I can't tell you what happens in there. When a baby is being born, only the women go in. When a baby is coming, the women close three sides of the tent, not just two, and the men know to stay away from the fourth side.

"Even so, our father wanted to go in when it was your time to come. He knew it was not his place, but he was so eager for your arrival. Of course, the women kept him out. They didn't need to take care of any extra babies. He was as silly as a man having his first son. He circled as much of the tent as he could when the women went around, just to get close for a few moments. When they went back in, he would run to the top of that hill there. Do you see that one, with the three trees taller than the rest?"

I looked where Judah was pointing. I saw the hill he was talking about and tried to imagine My Father running there from the compound.

"I see it," I said.

"That's where he would go," Judah continued. "He said he needed quiet to speak to his god and hear his god well at this important time. But then he would run back, afraid he'd missed your birth, which of course he hadn't. You took a long time in coming, as babies do. Especially first babies. Our father had everyone wait at the compound.

The sheep took care of themselves that day. We were all happy for the holiday, and in fact, nobody wanted to miss your arrival. It wasn't just our father who had yearned for you. We all knew how much Rachel longed to have a baby. And we all love Rachel."

I knew this to be true. There was something very special about My Mother. People often described her as more beautiful than any woman they had seen. I had spent a lot of time looking into her eyes, touching the sun-kissed skin on her face, and even putting my fingers under her head covering to feel her hair. My Mother was certainly very beautiful.

My Mother's beauty wasn't a physical one. Indeed, she and her sister Leah looked very similar. Of course, Leah's body was rounder after all the babies she had grown, but their faces shared the same features. They both had deep brown eyes with golden flecks. Leah's didn't see as well as My Mother's, but they were just as inviting. They shared the same prominent nose that both My Grandfather Lavan and My Father Jacob had. After all, Jacob was the son of Lavan's sister Rebekah, so it was not surprising that they both had this feature. My Mother and Leah also had the same dimples that showed on the right side of their cheeks when they smiled and the same thick black hair that was almost always covered.

What strangers didn't know was that they found My Mother more attractive than the others because of her inner beauty. She had a joy that bubbled out of her. She always made those with her feel like they were the most special people. She was generous with her attention and affection. Everyone loved her. And everyone knew how long she had waited to bring a son into the world. Everyone was happy for her when it was finally happening.

"Our father had us all doing silly things," Judah said. "He couldn't think. He was like a man taken over by a spirit that was not his own. A spirit that could not make a plan." Judah laughed.

"When he heard sounds coming from inside the tent, he would begin yelling. 'Make a feast,' he commanded one time. 'Where are you going?' he demanded when the rugs were being arranged for the feast. 'We must have music!' he barked. But when Naftali began to play his flute, our father immediately shushed him. There was no calming him down. All day he was like that, and into the evening.

"When the moon rose that night, it was a half-moon. I'll tell you the truth—it was different from other nights. The moon was there and just as beautiful as usual for most of the night. But then, suddenly and to our surprise, a red cloud began to cover it. It was not like the clouds usually in the sky. It was more like a shadow. It came from the left and began to almost swallow the moon. Before our eyes, the redness crept over more and more of the moon until the white of the moon was completely replaced by red.

"Before we could wonder whether it would stay like that forever, we saw that the shadow was still moving, revealing again the white part of the moon on one side, slowly returning it to how it had been for every night, always. The sky that had been dark with the red moon lightened again, and with it, some of the stars were obscured. But just where our compound begins, so did the darkness of the sky and the brightness of the twinkling stars.

"I was too excited to sleep—we all were. I just lay back and watched the sky, waiting for your arrival. Which is why I saw that directly over your mother's tent was the star pattern that makes the large dipper. You know the one, don't you Joseph?"

I nodded. I had seen many different shapes mapped in the stars.

"I was looking at that large dipper and smiling as I imagined it scooping up anything it wanted. It's so big, I think it could hold all these hills! As I was looking, we heard your cry from inside the tent! We all jumped at once! Of course, we are used to having babies around here. Deenah was born just a few months before, and we were happy and had rejoiced, even though she was the third girl, and even though she was my mother's eighth child. She was welcomed like everyone who had come before her.

"But you, Joseph, you were welcomed differently. When we all should have been sleeping, we jumped up with energy and excitement. We were pulled to our feet by the sound of life coming from Rachel's womb. We all embraced each other with tears in our eyes. Even the little ones knew it was important. It seemed even the moon was happy to see you, for at the moment we heard your first cry, the last bits of the moon came back from under its red cover. But nobody was more excited than our father. He dropped to his knees and thanked Elohim. He stood and raised his arms and shouted 'Hallelu Yah!' Then he blew the ram's horn to announce your birth, even though nobody needed to heed the call to come in from the fields since we were already there.

"Shortly after, you and your mother emerged from the tent with the other women. Rachel stood among our tears and smiles and showed us your face and told us your name."

Judah didn't even have to say "Joseph." Just him saying that My Mother had announced my name made me smile. My

Mother said "Joseph" like nobody else. When my name rolled out of her soft mouth, it was like a hug and kiss from a distance. My name coming from her was not just one word but a proclamation to the world that the beautiful boy they had all been waiting for was here at last, and joy could now increase manyfold. Still on Judah's shoulders, I looked at the rolling brown hills and the wide blue sky. There was no wind, and everything was calm. But inside, with only the thought of the sound of My Mother saying my name, colors were bouncing.

"You had already had your first meal," Judah said. "Your face was that of a satisfied and sleepy baby. But other than that, you did not look remarkably different from any of the rest of us. You already had dark brown hair growing from your head. It's curly like everyone else's now, but then it was too short to curl. Your skin was not as dark as it is now, but you had not yet been in the sun to earn the rich brown we all wear. You looked a little sickly. Of course, I had seen babies before, and they were all like that.

"But still, since you came from Rachel, our father brought out a whole pile of rugs by himself—a whole pile at once!—and placed them only a few paces from the mouth of the tent. He didn't want your mother to have to walk far when she came to present you. The rugs were right below the large dipper in the sky. Your mother sat with you in her arms.

"And our father could not contain himself. He began to dance! You know how he is. He always welcomes an opportunity to dance. But this was different. He had more energy than we did! He could not stop smiling! And he pulled everyone into a circle with him, surrounding you and your mother with our joy and laughter and love.

"It wasn't just us young men dancing either," Judah said. He and Reuben and Shimon and Levi had started calling themselves young men instead of boys because their voices had deepened like My Father's. "It was all of us. Your ten brothers, your three sisters, our father, and my mother and Zilpah and Bilhah. We all danced and danced around you and your mother. It was similar to when we heard the news that Rachel was with child, only this time we all surrounded you both. Your mother's face was as bright as the newly lit moon with love and relief. But even when she was too tired to sit up, she just lay down on the rugs, put you on her chest, and slept while we continued to dance into the night."

Newly born, I suppose I was too young to participate in the dancing, but I was almost sad to have missed it. I reminded myself that I didn't miss it. I was there while everyone else danced around me.

"Our father insisted on having a celebration feast that morning. Don't worry. We had another feast for you after your circumcision on your eighth day of life. But our father couldn't wait that long to celebrate. On your first morning in the world, we dined on fresh dates and figs, and we had bread dripping in olive oil and herbs. The finest drinks were passed around.

"Nothing was spared, and nothing could dampen the mood. Even when Lavan came with his sons. They ate until they could barely stand, and then they filled a sack so heavy with figs that they loaded it onto a camel to walk back to their tents. But I'm not sure it was actually *that* heavy," Judah laughed. "You know Lavan and his sons are not used to hard work. Maybe it was just heavy because their bellies were so full."

I laughed. I was not big enough to do the work of a man, but even I could carry a sack of figs. Judah took me off his shoulders and placed me back on the ground. I looked up at him and smiled at the sight of how high I'd been. I reached up to his chin with the thumb of my right hand and rubbed the bottom of it in a little circle. No hair. I did the same to my chin. Also no hair. How did Judah get so wise when he wasn't even a man yet? Maybe I was wise with a smooth chin too. I smiled with the hope.

"I'm glad to see you feeling better," he said. "A good story always makes me feel better."

I nodded. It was a good story. I think that's why the story replaced my dream in my memory for a long time. The next time I thought about that dream was on the day it came true—but that was many years later.

CHAPTER 2

Judah went back to the fields after we spoke. He and the others had their hands full with the sheep. By the time of my birth, My Father had fulfilled his obligation of shepherding fourteen years for Lavan, and he wanted to take his leave. They had made a bargain that My Father's payment would be the spotted and speckled animals of the flock. Everyone knew that their wool was rougher. What Lavan and his sons didn't know was that these animals were a stronger breed.

My Father and brothers were growing our flock, increasing the spotted and speckled sheep and goats that would belong to us, not Lavan. They worked at this for many years. The older brothers became expert shepherds in that time, and I became old enough to go to the fields on occasion. My Father said that I wasn't ready to be a shepherd but that I could come and watch My Brothers and the sheep. I did that during the long days. I learned the songs the men sang in the fields and enjoyed watching the clouds.

Often, the clouds looked like sheep to me. It's a good thing they weren't since they were almost always pure white, and had they been real sheep, they would have belonged to Lavan. Under the watch of his sons, Lavan's flock was growing sicker and smaller. My Father said not to help them shepherd, or we would be stuck in Lavan's service forever.

My Father didn't yet know how long we would stay near Lavan. The two did not get along and spent little time together—something we were all glad about. My Father said he would know when it was the right time to leave, and until he knew, we would continue to grow our flocks and our tribe and live in the land of Haran, camped near Lavan.

It was in my fourth summer that two baby girls were born. First, Leah gave birth to Emunah, and in the next month, Bilhah birthed Tirzah. Nobody thought Emunah would live through her first night except My Father. Her body was the right size, but her nose and mouth and ears were too small for her head. We did not know if they even worked. Yet My Father instructed that every effort be made to help her grow, even with her tongue that was too large for regular suckling. He even announced her birth with a blast of the ram's horn, calling everyone in from the fields to witness the fact that he had fathered another child.

Emunah lived not only through her first night but continued to live and grow alongside her milk sister, even though she did everything Tirzah did much later. With the births of these babies, I was no longer the youngest. I think that was why My Father allowed me to begin occasionally going to the fields.

But the real excitement happened at the end of my sixth winter. That was when My Father announced to us that he had an important story to tell us. He told all of us about it. It's true, yes, that first he told just My Mother and Leah alone, but then he told us children. He even told the younger children along with the older children, his daughters along with me and My Brothers, showing just how important it was that everyone hear and know.

After the day of work in the fields, we had a light evening meal and thought we were going to prepare to go to bed as the sun prepared to do so. But My Father stopped us all. "Children," he said. "Gather round. I will tell you a story. Joseph, my son, come and sit on my lap. Listen well, all of you. This is not a fanciful story, but a true story of what happened to me, and a true story of what is about to happen to all of us."

He began by telling us of his honored parents and his birthplace. We had all heard this story many times before. We knew of his father, Isaac, and his failing eyesight. We knew of his brother, Esau, who had squeaked out of their mother's womb just one breath before him and who had sold My Father his blessing of the firstborn in exchange for a pot of lentil stew. We knew of his mother, Rebekah, helping him to get that blessing from his father, even the trickery it involved. And we knew of his quick exit from his homeland to save his own life, lest his brother kill him in revenge and in an attempt to get his birthright back.

The story always ended with My Father arriving in this northern land of Haran and meeting My Mother, Rachel, at the well. He fell in love and made a deal with her father, Lavan, to marry her after seven years of laboring for him with his sheep. But on the night of the ceremony, My Father said, Lavan secretly wed him to Rachel's older sister Leah. Every time My Father told that story, he laughed and smiled a broad smile at Leah and said,

"That dirty old trickster did one thing right by me. He gave me more beautiful wives than I thought I would get and more strong sons than I ever could have imagined." This always made Leah, mother of six sons, blush with pride.

That was the only story My Father ever told us of his past, but I always enjoyed it and never suspected there was more. But this time, he did not tell that part. For the first time, he told us of his journey.

"My beloved mother, Rebekah, charged me with coming here, to her brother Lavan in Haran, to flee from Esau. She had told my father it was so that I could find a wife from her family. This was also true, but to marry, I first needed to be alive. And so, I left. Many had made the journey before me, but I had never done so. Children, you must know this: it is not shameful to feel fear. Even your own father has felt it. I had the unknown in front of me, and behind me was the impossibility of returning to my home where my brother would pounce on me at his first chance.

"I began my journey and traveled as far as I could on the first day to set a distance between myself and Esau. I walked until the darkness was too thick for me to continue, so I knew that the darkness was also a safety from being found. There was no natural shelter where I stopped, but I went a few steps off the path—enough so that I would not be trampled or seen by anyone coming but not so much as to lose my way. There, I found a rock that was flat and still warmed from the sun. In my exhaustion, I laid my head on the rock and slept.

"While I slept, I had a dream in which my god, Elohim, came to me in a vision. There before me was a ladder that extended from my hard sleeping stone directly up to the heavens. And going up that ladder were angels. Angel after angel, ascending the ladder from here to the clouds. What's more, there were also angels coming down this divine ladder and stepping foot on the very ground upon which I lay.

"It wasn't merely messengers of my god who were there but Elohim as well. In this dream, I heard Elohim's voice in my ear. On that night, Elohim promised me the same promise that my fathers had received: that I would be the one to inherit that land. I . . ."

My Father paused. At this point, the sun had been sleeping for a long time already. There were two small oil lamps burning by the entrance to the tent, but there was not enough light for me to see My Father's face as he paused. I waited, holding my breath, hoping there was more to the story. We all waited; there wasn't a sound among us.

My Father continued. "The promise was that I would inherit that land, I and . . . and *you*, my sons, and your sons after you, and theirs, until we are as many as the dust of the Earth. We will be so large in number that we will burst forth, to the Sea, to the east, to the north, and to the Negev in the south. All the clans will find blessing through me, . . . through *us*.

"Children, that day, my god promised to watch over me and return me safely to my homeland. When I awoke, I was still in awe. I stood the rock that had been my resting place on its end and anointed it with oil. I proclaimed that the name of that place shall be Beit El, House of Elohim, for surely it was, and I had not known it when I had arrived. I thanked my god, and I vowed that day that if indeed Elohim would watch over me and provide food and clothes for me and protect me and return me safely to my homeland, then certainly I would accept Elohim as my god, just as my father, Isaac, had and his father, Abraham, before him."

My Father was silent. In that moment of his silence, we all burst forth with our questions at once. I was so amazed that My Father, too, was a dreamer. I had not known this about him. I immediately wanted to discuss with him the dreams I'd had—dreams of waters I had not seen, and beasts I couldn't fathom, and even dreams in which voices came to speak in my ears when nobody was present but me. But I didn't get a chance to ask him anything at all. Neither did My Brothers. As we began to stir, My Father called out, "There's more." These words were met with a collective gasp from us children.

"Living here has not been without challenges, but my life overflows with blessings. I have four strong wives who have borne me sixteen energetic children." With the tone of his voice, I knew he was winking, even without seeing his face in the darkness. My Father often praised his children for the energy we had when caring for the flocks and the gardens, but he also lamented this energy when he came in tired from the fields and the little ones jumped on him.

"It has been many years since I left my homeland. Indeed, Elohim has fulfilled the promise and then some. Now my god has returned to me in a dream once again, saying, 'I am Elohim of Beit El, where you anointed the pillar, where you vowed a vow to me. So now, arise, get out of this land, return to the land of your family!'

"I have already discussed this with your mothers. They are as wise as they are strong. There is only one thing to do. We will leave this land and return to the land of my family."

Many moments of silence followed as we waited to learn if there was more to the story. My Father took a long, slow breath. I felt the rustling of his sleeves as he raised his arms. "Children," he said, "May Elohim bless you and keep you. It is too late to go to our sleeping rugs in our own tents. We will all lie here for tonight."

I wanted desperately to tell My Father of my dreams. I wanted his council on what they meant. My desire even overpowered my wonder and joy of sleeping together in My Father's tent. But I knew that I would never be able to do this in the darkness and togetherness that night. I would have to wait until morning.

CHAPTER 3

When I awoke the next morning, the sun was already partly up in the sky. My Father and the older brothers, now just beginning to include Issachar and Zevulun, were nowhere to be seen. Surely the older girls had gone with My Mother and Leah to the garden, and the women had taken the babies with them. Four of My Brothers were still there in the tent with me. Dan and Asher were eating barley cakes and olives, looking as tired as I felt, while Naftali and Gad were still huddled in sleep. I got up and joined Dan and Asher in breaking the fast from the night before.

None of us spoke. I don't know their reason, but mine was that I had too many words swirling in my ears. I wanted to speak to My Father about his dreams. I wanted his guidance in understanding my own dreams. The newest happened right before my waking that morning. It was surely because of the story My Father told the night before; I have no doubt. But what did it mean?

In the dream, I saw a man who resembled My Father greatly. He had the same nose, the same chin, the same brow. He walked the same way I was used to seeing My Father walk. But he was greater in size—height and breadth—and every piece of his skin that was visible was covered in red hair. There were five hunters behind him, carrying five bucks.

My Father was in the dream as well. He was not walking in his usual manner, but with a slow skip, as a goat does after it's gotten one leg caught between rocks and then needed to be set free. My Father was also accompanied in this dream. He had five of his finest sheep and five shepherds.

I watched these two men approach each other, but I could not see what happened when their paths met. All I could see instead was a rainbow. The rainbow began where I couldn't see the two men and stretched all the way to the south. Much farther than I should be able to see, but as it was a dream, I could see land covered in gold at the end. Although the rainbow was in the sky, it also appeared to be a path for travel between the two places.

Oh, how I wanted to ask My Father what the meaning was behind this dream! But it was many days before I saw him again. Preparations were being made for our journey. The whole tribe was filled with excitement. Also, some fear, which My Father had said earlier was alright. There was no opportunity for questions. Any time I was near someone older than I, they put me to work. And the same was even true when I was with the babies. I often was left watching them, making sure they didn't get under foot while we were in such a rush.

"Joseph," Leah called. "Where is Emunah?"

"She's right here," I answered. Entering her second summer, Emunah was just beginning to stand by herself, and we were told to help her but not do things for her. But I was eager to be free to participate in the excitement, so I scooped her up and ran her to her mother. Emunah laughed with joy and smiled her bright smile as she bounced along on my hip. "Here you go, Leah," I said. I turned to make my quick exit to freedom, but I wasn't fast enough.

"Take this with you, Joseph," she called after me. She brought a cloth as large as my body and filled with dates. "These have been drying in the sun; they're ready for travel. Bring them to the southern tent; that's where we're collecting all the food for the journey." Leah helped me gather the corners of the cloth and heave it over my shoulder as a sack. I had been to the southern tent already. Of course, I knew that was the gathering place for the food. These dates would be transferred to a large basket that would go on a wagon so that the cloth could be used again.

I brought the dates to the southern tent. "Oh, Joseph," My Mother said when she saw me. She kissed me on the top of my head. And right in front of Issachar and Zevulun! I could feel my face redden as they stifled their giggles. "Joseph, you arrived right on time," she said. "Please help Issachar and Zevvy put those dates in with the others. Then I believe the basket will be full. Afterward, you three go out and inform your father that we will be ready to take down the tents tomorrow."

I had hoped to drop off the dates and not have another job to do, but there was always one more thing to do to get ready. I tried to help Issachar and Zevulun, but they didn't let me. So, I mostly stood there until it was done. As soon as the lid was on the basket, they took off, running toward the pasture where My Father was with the sheep.

"Wait for me," I called, panting behind.

"We don't have time to wait for babies," Issachar called out.

"I'm not a baby," I said. "I'm in my sixth year already!"

"And I am in my eighth," Issachar called behind him, "And Zevulun is almost in his eighth. You'll never catch up."

I tried, but they were right. They were faster than I was. Why did they need to run, anyway? We could have walked together. But as it was, by the time I made it to My Father, the other boys had already delivered the message, and he'd sent them off to tell the older ones. When I saw them departing, I slowed my step. No need to run any longer. I walked with my head lowered, disappointed.

Then I realized that for the first time, I would be alone with My Father! And I would have no task from anyone trying to put me to work. I picked up my step, and by the time I approached My Father, I was running as fast as I could.

"Joseph, my son!" My Father grabbed me by the arms and swung me in a circle around him. "Look," he said. "Take a look at this land. It has fed us. It has fed our flocks. It has provided for us because my god brought me to this place. But tomorrow, tomorrow . . ." I saw a tear in My Father's eye.

"Tomorrow," My Father continued, "tomorrow, we leave this good land for a better one. We leave Lavan's hills for *our* hills. And with us, we will bring the fruits of my labor and my loins." His tears turned to laughter. "Joseph, soon you will see your father's birthplace." He hugged me so tightly I wasn't sure whether I would be able to get loose. But no sooner had he squeezed me than he let me go. He tousled my hair and pointed me to the east and charged me with making sure that Issachar and Zevulun had delivered the message properly. And just like that, my moment alone with My Father ended.

I ran off to where Reuben and Judah were shepherding with Gad and Asher. My Father had the two younger ones stay with two of the older ones at all times. Soon, they would be able to go off on their own, but first he wanted them to learn the ways of the flock properly.

"Here comes the runt," Gad called as I approached.

"Leave him alone," Reuben chastised. "He can't help it that he was the last one born."

Gad and Asher listened to Reuben because he was the oldest, but I still defended myself. "Not the last," I said. "Emunah and Tirzah are younger than I am."

"The youngest brother," Gad said. "You're the youngest brother. Not old enough to be shepherding. What brings you here?"

"My Father sent me," I said. "He wants to make sure you know that we will take down the tents tomorrow and begin our journey."

"Our father already sent Issachar and Zevulun to tell us," Gad said. "We're doing our best to contain the flock so they're ready for tomorrow. The tents are the least of our worries. They have no legs of their own. Now go off on your little legs and return to the compound."

"I had a dream of a man with legs covered in red hair," I said. Gad's mention of legs had reminded me, and I was hoping sharing this strange story would allow me more time with My Brothers. But they just laughed.

I dropped my head and turned back toward the tents. "Joseph," Reuben called after me. I looked up. "Joseph, are you excited?"

"I am," I said. "I've never gone beyond a morning's walk away from the tents. I know there is so much to see."

"I'm excited too," Reuben said. "I've been to sheepshearing many times, but that is a two days' journey to the north. Tomorrow, we go south. I have never set foot in that direction. I'm eager to see the land."

"My Mother has told me that one day, when I am a man as strong and noble as My Father, I shall have my own land there and be the leader of my own tribe on that land," I said.

"Yes, that will come to pass with Elohim's help," Reuben confirmed. "But there is much to be done before we depart tomorrow. We all need to move as quickly and efficiently as we can. So, no more talk for today, understand? When we journey, if you look for me in our caravan, I will tell you of my trips to the north while we travel south. I will tell you of seeing city walls and hearing new words from travelers from far, far away. How does that sound?"

"It sounds good," I said, gratefully. I could not imagine a city or how someone could speak a word that did not exist. But I wanted to try. Reuben sent me off with a squeeze on my shoulder. I'd seen him squeeze the older boys that way. He knew I wouldn't be small forever. Even if no other brother should come, I would continue to grow. One day, I too would be old enough to help our flock prosper in our land.

I started out toward Shimon and Levi to make sure that Zevulun and Issachar had delivered the message to them as well.

Perhaps because Shimon and Levi were twins, they often acted as one person. Though Judah and his sister Ahuvah were twins different in every way, Shimon and Levi only looked different. Shimon grew bigger and wider, his body always showing that he was the older of the two, even though they had shared the womb together. And Levi had hair the color of the sun and skin as white as sheep but covered in brown speckles and spots. He looked like he would fit in perfectly with our new flock. I would never say this to him, of course, for I would not want a beating.

Luckily for me, as I approached the twins, I saw Issachar and Zevvy were still there. Shimon and Levi were pushing them back and forth between the two of them. Then they gave them a final push in the direction away from the compound and doubled over laughing. Good that Issachar and Zevulun had delivered the message and that I didn't need to suffer at the hands of Shimon and Levi.

Returning to the tents, I saw Naftali and Dan loading the food. They were carrying one of the large earthen jars and trying to hoist it up onto a wagon. I was afraid they would miss their mark and it would fall. "A little to the left!" I called out. They immediately shifted to the right. "My left!" I corrected them. My Brothers moved over and were able to load the jar without it breaking or spilling.

I came closer and stood by each wagon as they loaded it, giving them direction so that none of the food would be lost. They loaded barley and olives, dried fruits and almonds. Leah had said to leave the fresh food in the garden until just before departure. One more thing to do tomorrow. I reminded Dan and Naftali of that when they wanted to take a break before loading the wine and oil.

"We'll need lots to drink along the way," I said. "And tomorrow there are the vegetables and herbs to add on, the tents to take down, the rugs to pile, and the donkeys to load up. Go on," I said. "It's almost finished. I'll show you just where there's room on the wagon."

"Rather than showing us," Dan said, "why don't you run off and get us a drink that we can have now. We'll manage the loading." But as I went to bring them drinks, I saw them sit under the shade of a date tree. It was as if they didn't want my help at all.

That night was another sleepless one. My Mother kept the oil lamp burning in the tent while she and Bilhah packed most of our pillows and rugs onto the cart beside it. I wondered about the day that everyone had waited for me to be born. Was this what it had felt like?

At the first hint of light, everyone was up and taking down the tents. The women picked everything from the garden. The younger brothers loaded the donkeys, and the sisters brought fruit for everyone to quickly eat before we left. I said goodbye to my favorite places: the crevice by the olive tree at the edge of the compound, the jagged rock that I pretended was a lion, the flat stones in the now-dry riverbed. It was there that I was surprised by My Mother and Leah talking quietly to each other.

"Do you think it's right that we leave without telling him?" My Mother asked.

"Of course not," Leah responded. "It's not right, but it is still the best choice. You know our father has nothing but trickery and greed in his ways. And we are still his property in his view, though Jacob has fulfilled his work obligations for us both. He will find false words to accuse our husband of taking his flock, when we know it is only because of Jacob that our angry father has anything at all. Finally, we will be rid of him. Is it the right way? No, but yes. It is the right way because of who he is. Do you want him after your son?" Leah didn't even wait for a response from My Mother. "I don't," she said.

"It is best for us to leave now, while he and his sons are at the sheepshearing. They do not miss us now; they will not miss us then. It has always been that way. They send for us when they want something, and they come only to feast at our celebrations and accuse us when they do a poor job themselves."

My Mother slowly nodded. She knew. We all knew.

"Think of it," Leah continued. "Our own land for our sons. That is how many descendants of Jacob there will be one day. Those are our sons, our descendants. That is their land. And what of Rebekah? She lived here once, too, and she chose to go south to marry Isaac. She raised this fine son and sent him to us. Now we will go to her. A mother. Rachel, can you imagine how wonderful it will be to have a mother again?"

"I do miss having a mother," my own mother said. The two of them embraced. "But I will also miss this home. It has been our only one. All the memories . . ."

"The memories will come with us," Leah comforted. "And we don't even need to load them on donkeys." She laughed at her own joke, and My Mother smiled slightly. "We've taken everything important with us, have we not?"

My Mother clutched a small sack tied by a cord around her waist and nodded. The sisters held hands and took a last look toward their father's tents, then turned to look to where their own tents had just been removed. That was when they saw me.

"Joseph!" My Mother smiled the smile that was mine alone. I went to her and let her wrap me in her arms and kiss the top of my head. Nobody was there to call me a baby for doing so. I knew Leah wouldn't mock us. She stole kisses from her babies as well, though mostly only Emunah and Deenah would still let her.

"Joseph," My Mother asked, "Do you like having a mother?" I nodded my head. I certainly enjoyed having a mother very much! It was My Mother who always embraced me in love. It was she who looked at me with welcoming eyes every single time. And her words to me were always kind. She often made funny faces to get me to laugh, and she stroked my cheek when I was sad. "Soon, I shall have one too," she said, "and I think I shall enjoy it as much as you do. And we shall all have a new land. Let us go and begin our journey."

CHAPTER 4

It was very strange to walk back to where the tents had been and find the grounds completely without tents. Instead, it was full of the excitement and chaos of all the people and animals. Gazing upon them all, I imagined they were enough to fill a city. Then I remembered My Father's dream and the promise that the whole land shall belong to us.

My Mother and Leah went to stand beside My Father. The whole tribe was there. My Father, his four wives, his ten sons, his five daughters. I went to stand with My Brothers. Even though they always made sure I remembered that I was the youngest, they didn't push me aside when I joined them. All the manservants that followed My Father's direction in the fields were there, and all the maidservants that helped the women with the garden and the cooking and weaving were there, as were all their children and no small number of donkeys carrying their tents and provisions.

My Father, in one of his shows of great strength, lifted My Mother onto a camel. He then lifted Leah onto the next, Zilpah onto the next, and Bilhah onto the next. My Father took a small flask of oil from around his neck and placed it around My Mother's. That would be used when we arrived at Beit El. Then My Father picked up Emunah and twirled her around and placed her in Leah's lap. Deenah was next and was to ride with Zilpah. Tirzah was twirled and handed to Bilhah. Ahuvah and Annah were older. They could make the trip on foot. As could the mothers and Deenah, but My Father insisted that they at least begin the journey by riding like royalty.

My Father walked over to Reuben and put his hand on his shoulder in the same way that Reuben had done to me the day before. "Reuben," he said, "you are the eldest, the next man after me. I ask you: Are you willing to be the man at the back of our caravan? Are you willing to protect us from behind, if needed, and be the last set of eyes to make sure that none of the flock go astray?"

It was clear that Reuben recognized the honor being given to him. He put his hand on My Father's shoulder and firmly said he was willing and ready.

"When we depart," My Father instructed, "you take the dogs with you, and place yourself at the end of our procession."

Reuben nodded.

"Where are my oldest boys?" My Father called, even though he was looking right at them. The eldest, minus Reuben, stepped forward. "Judah, you will lead the flocks. I'd like you to come to the front. Do not let any of the animals get in front of you and wreak havoc. Take Gad and Asher with you. They are old enough to help." My Father did not address them directly, but they beamed as he told Judah that if he needed anything for the flock or himself, he could rely on them. They had not spent much time in the fields but would take instruction to heart.

"Shimon," My Father continued, "you will take Dan and guard the flock to the east, keeping it contained on that side. Levi, you will take Naftali and do the same on the west. As we travel, we will be organized and courteous travelers. Our flocks will not stray to the left nor to the right. Do you understand?"

Dan and Naftali immediately said that they did. Levi and Shimon stepped forward. As if My Father knew what they would say, he reproached them, telling them that they may not travel together but that each one would take a younger brother and train him. The older four had been to sheepshearing, but Dan and Naftali had not yet traveled with the flock, and they were ready to learn this important skill from their older brothers. Moreover, Shimon and Levi were to spend the time apart rather than stew in bad ideas.

"Issachar and Zevulun," My Father called, "you will walk in front with the women. If there is something needed from a wagon, you will fetch it for them. If a drink is desired, you will offer it to them. You will listen to their every instruction and be the ones they can rely on for anything. Further, you will tend to the donkeys and care for them as they pull the wagons and carry the tents. You will guide the camels and tend to their needs as well. Are you ready for such work?"

From the looks on their faces, they didn't seem happy with their task until My Father called it work. He spoke of it with such importance that they could not think of it as being shoved off with the little ones. Without looking at each other, each of them stood just a little taller, a little prouder, to have a job on this big day.

My Father had offered each of his manservants and maidservants the opportunity to choose between coming with us or staying behind. There wasn't one of them that chose to stay behind. I'm sure none of them wished to be there when Lavan found us gone, but more than that, they knew that My Father would treat them well—he always had. And they knew he would be prosperous—he always was. Each of the men took sons and joined one of My Brothers at their various posts. The women and their daughters went behind My Mother and My Father's other wives. They all seemed to already know where to go without My Father's instruction.

The only one yet without an assignment was me. What would My Father ask me to do? Would he think me too young to help because of my six summers? I shifted my weight from foot to foot as My Father surveyed his clan. He had arrived in this land with nothing. And now was leaving a rich man and the father of many.

"Joseph," he finally called. "Come here, my son. You will walk with me."

I think for just the time it takes to blink, my heart soared out of my body and to the clouds above. I could hardly believe my ears. I may have been the youngest son, but in that moment, I felt that I was the tallest. I felt that I even towered over My Father, so great was my joy and pride. I stood beside him, mute with awe.

My Father put his hand on my shoulder, just like he had done with Reuben only moments before. "Not long ago, your mother worried that I would become too old to father a child before she got her chance at motherhood. I did get older with every summer, but I'm not such an old man that I cannot keep pace with a strong boy." Then he spoke loudly to everyone: all the people, all the animals, the hills and the trees, and even the sacks of food.

"Elohim! You have blessed me as you promised. You have fed me, clothed me, and grown my possessions a hundredfold. What is more, You have granted me this family. Today, we go back to the land that You have also promised me and my sons after me. Thank You for bringing me to this day. Please lead us forward on a safe journey. I ask that You guard us in our departure, guard us in our arrival, and guard us along the way. Do this for me, Elohim, and I will continue to be Your servant, and You will always be my god."

Without any pause, My Father turned and began the journey south, with me skipping and rushing with excitement to keep my place beside him. The camels with the women and children followed after us. Judah, Gad, and Asher made space after the camels. They did not want the sheep and goats to overtake us. But they were not far behind. I could smell them and breathe the dust of their many hooves on the highway, even without looking back to see them.

That day, I wore new sandals that had been fashioned to my feet for this walk. In the first day alone, it would be more walking than I had ever done. But my feet did not hurt, and my legs did not tire. It was as if a wind was pushing me from behind, urging me toward the new land.

It was a lot of walking, though. For two days, we walked along the highway that was beside the river. At first, I was excited to see the river. The girls gasped at the sight of the flowing water, but I had been lucky enough to see it once before when the oldest brothers had felt moved to celebrate something. I am not sure what it was that they were rejoicing about, perhaps just a warm day after a rain, but they took all the rest of us brothers for a trek to the river.

When we arrived, my mouth dropped open at the sight of so much water in one place. Even if we were to spend all day pulling water from the well and filling the drinking troughs, we would not get an amount of water that could compare to this river. My Brothers were not moved. All of them had been there before. They quickly removed their clothing and jumped in.

Even Shimon and Levi, who were often up to no good, played like small children in the water. They splashed each other and the rest of the brothers. Even me! Levi showed me how to blow bubbles in the water with my mouth—and with my bottom! And when I complimented Shimon on the way he was resting on the surface of the water on his back, he offered to help me try it as well.

Shimon knelt in the water and put his hands out for me to lie on. "Just look up at the sky and relax," he said. "I'll hold you here, but mostly the water will do the work." And while he held me, I did look at the sky. I watched as the light darted behind the few small clouds that pocked the blue, and I felt at peace in My Brother's arms. When he wanted to go back to floating himself, I asked for just a little longer.

"Fine," he said, "a little longer, but this time, try it on your stomach." And with one swift movement, Shimon flipped me from staring at the sky to staring under the water; his hands went from under my back to on top of it. And what I saw was beyond anything I could have imagined! There was red earth beneath the water, and little silver fish that I hadn't noticed before were diving into the soft soil below and swimming out again. As they swam out, little bits of dirt were loosened and rose in the water, making it a murky mixture of wet and dry.

I was mesmerized by watching the fish go in and out, in and out of the ground—so much so that I had forgotten to breathe. When I tried, instead of air, I was filled with water. I began coughing, which only brought more water in through my nose and mouth. As I moved to stand on the red earth below the water, I felt Shimon's hands push down harder on my back, bringing me closer to the ground, yes, but aiming my stomach there, not my feet. I struggled to stand but could not get my feet below me due to Shimon pushing on my back. More water entered my nose and mouth. My body shook. My hands reached for the fish simply because they needed to grab at something so I could get out!

Then I felt two hands grasp me under my arms and pull me to the surface. "Shimon!" the voice attached to the hands shouted. "What are you doing?" I recognized the voice now as Reuben's, even though I couldn't move my head to look at him. "Don't touch the boy. What would I tell our father if we returned without him?" Reuben pulled me to the edge of the water and laid me down. I realized the ground was just as red there as it was under the river. I dug my hands into it, threw up all the water I had taken in, and slept from the labor of it all while My Brothers played. I began to keep an even greater distance between myself and Shimon whenever I could.

That day at the river, we had stayed in one spot, not traveling anywhere. I didn't know the river was so much longer than I could see. When my family continued on our way to the south, we walked and walked and walked, and still the river was beside us. I delighted in knowing that there were little silver fish in there, swimming in and out of the red earth. My Father had not spoken to me yet during the journey, and I did not feel that I should ask him about dreams before he even said a word to me. But I was so overcome by the never-ending river that I couldn't restrain myself from speaking.

"Does this river go on forever?" I asked. "It is the most magnificent sight I have ever seen."

My Father laughed. "Joseph, I am glad you can appreciate the glory of this river. But let me show you something. Hold your hand up in front of you please." I did as he asked. "You see this little finger here? The baby one?" I nodded. "That, Joseph, is like the river beside us now. We will walk for the rest of the day. Tonight, we will sleep by this beautiful river, and tomorrow we will walk again. Before sunset, we will come to a city. The city is like this little knuckle right here." My Father traced his finger across the line where my baby finger met my hand. "The morning after, you will see a river that is like the size of your hand and your arm."

I stopped walking for a moment, my mouth dropped wide in astonishment, and My Father laughed again. "Joseph, my son, you are going to see worlds that you have never imagined."

He was right. Though, I did try to imagine a river as grand as the one he had spoken of. I tried and tried. Would it be longer than this one? That seemed impossible since this one had no end. Perhaps wider? This river was admittedly not very wide. It was beautiful and just the perfect width for a river, though I had never seen another. But I realized that while I could probably not throw a rock across it, the men and even my oldest brothers probably could. What if the river were so wide that a rock thrown across would fall short of the other side and splash into the water? I believed I could cross this river in ten steps if I did not slip on one of the rocks along the way. How many steps would be needed to cross a wider river?

Attempts to create a vision of this mysterious river, and the city we would come to on the way, occupied me for much of the walk. My Father didn't share his thoughts with me. Soon, I would muster the courage to ask him about dreams. But for the time being, my waking adventure kept me more than satisfied.

The walk continued just as My Father had said. When the sun began to set, we stopped along the river and ate. We unloaded rugs from the donkeys and laid them in a clearing. There was no need to put up a tent for the night since we would begin walking again at dawn.

We walked all day, and still the river did not come to an end. I was becoming such an expert traveler by the second day of the journey that I was no longer struck by awe at the length of the river. In fact, it no longer felt like the wind was pushing at my back or that my new sandals provided any protection for my sore feet. I was beginning to long for a ride on one of the camels, but my pride prevented me from asking. Instead, I asked My Father about his dreams.

My Father put his hand on my shoulder. "A dream is a special thing, Joseph. I had the dream. I told it. Now I live it. That is all there is to it."

"Which dream?"

"All of them. Any of them. A dream is one way that my god tells me things. It is not the only way. I'm sure Elohim tells me things all the time and I am too stiff-necked to know what they are or do as I'm guided."

"The dreams are messages?"

"Yes, my son, some are messages. Some are merely there. When Elohim sends me a dream that is a message, He also helps me understand the message. Otherwise, I might as well dream of sweet cakes and nights of looking up at the stars. Sometimes, I do that too," he laughed.

"Please tell me one of your dreams, Father. Perhaps I had the same one?"

"My son, every dream is as different as every dreamer." His pause made me think he would not continue, but after a few paces, he did. "I have told you of a dream, remember? When I left the land we are returning to, I was fleeing for my life. I was afraid. When night fell, I thought it was better to offer myself as a sacrifice to Elohim than to my brother. So, I laid myself on a rock, a large rock—you shall see it soon when we arrive in Beit El. You will see it is large enough for a burnt offering. I had no fire and no intention of burning myself. But I did offer myself.

"I put my whole body on the rock, even my head. I did not look around, but I rested it there, vulnerable, should my god wish to take it—take me. Almost silently, I whispered the words that I had learned from my father. The same words that he once recited when he was laid on a rock as an offering. 'Yah is our god, reliable, ever existing, honest, loyal, beloved, kind, mighty, perfect, and good.'

"I hoped that like his, my life would be spared. There was nothing I could do but wait to find out. I breathed deeply. I kept whispering the words and breathing until I fell asleep. I don't remember falling asleep, but I remember dreaming of angels going up a ladder that began beside my head and of others coming down that same ladder and circling around me.

"When I awoke, I understood that I was in Elohim's own house. That is why I erected the stone and anointed it with oil and named the place Beit El. It is there that Elohim promised that He would bring me back safely. Elohim helped me understand that this was the message of the dream."

"So, My God will help me understand the messages of my dreams?" I asked.

"Yes," My Father answered. "When the time is right for you to understand, you will have help. Then you will understand, and you will know."

"I am glad," I said. "It must be that Elohim understands my dream about a hairy red man, because I do not."

"You dreamt of a hairy red man?" My Father asked.

"Yes," I said. "And you were in the dream as well. You two met, each with five men and five animal offerings with those men."

My Father nodded in response but said nothing more. For now, this conversation satisfied me, and I began to get excited about our journey again. It was easy to do, as at that point, the walls of a city were just coming into view over the next hill!

CHAPTER 5

I had been enjoying My Father's company and attention, but when the city came into view, I was tasked with errands. My Father sent me off to tell each group of shepherds that when we got to the city, we would not stay long. The men were to stay with the flocks in the fields, set apart from the city walls and the highway until they received word from My Father. They were to keep a fire at night and watch over the animals so that they wouldn't wander off and so that no beast or bandit would come for them.

My Father had me repeat his words back to him and was satisfied that I remembered. "Now go," he said. "Start with Judah, but tell him to leave the animals under the watch of Gad and Asher and come to me when we stop. Then cross to the east and to the west to tell Shimon and Levi, then tell Reuben. Afterward, come back to me, for the rest of us will enter the city and sleep the night inside the walls."

Inside the walls! Of a city! As if seeing the city weren't enough. As if the river weren't enough. I was going to be spending the night inside the walls of a real city!

The news pushed my feet faster than I knew they could run—my mouth too. Judah was only a short distance behind the camels and met me with a smile when he saw the excitement on my face.

"What is it, Joseph? Are you enjoying this adventure?"

"Yes! Yes!"

"What have you liked so far?" he asked.

"All of it! The sound of all the hoofs behind me, the sound and sight of the river to the side. Did you know My Father said we are to see an even bigger river? And a city! Judah, a city! And My Father has sent me to deliver you a message. He says, 'When we get to the city, we will not stay long. The men are to stay with the flocks in the fields, set apart from the city walls and the highway until you receive word. You are to keep a fire so that the animals don't wander off and so that no beasts or bandits bother anyone. And you, Judah, are to leave the animals in the care of the others and join My Father when we arrive at the city so that you may enter with us.'"

My Father must have thought Judah very wise to allow him into the city as his companion. I reached my thumb up to his chin to feel if he was beginning to grow hair yet, but he still was not.

"What is this you're doing with my chin?" he asked me.

"Judah, My Father trusts you to enter the city with him, and I myself know of your wisdom for I have seen you with the sheep and the other brothers. Yet you still have no hair on your chin. You are just a boy like me."

"A boy like you?" he scoffed. "If by that you mean young and fast, then yes. But I have helped My Father with the flocks and trading in the past. I may not yet have whiskers on my chin, but they will be here soon, and they are not the only sign of wisdom. I will grow them someday. In the meanwhile, I have experience. Now go off and tell the others. Gad and Asher and I will do as our father has asked."

So, I left Judah and went to Shimon and Dan. They were on the east as they were instructed, and they were keeping the flock contained, though it seemed that My Father's manservants were doing most of the work. What I was not expecting was that they had donkeys with them. One was carrying rugs, and the other, food. I realized this was how they got what they needed without leaving their stations.

"Shimon, Dan, we are coming to a city!"

"We can see the city," Shimon said. "We know." Shimon had a way of taking the excitement out of anything that wasn't his idea—or Levi's.

"Well," I said, "My Father has sent me to you with a message." I recited my father's words quickly, eager to remove myself from Shimon's reach.

"Joseph, I've seen a city before," Shimon replied. "You can tell our father I already know how to keep care of the animals outside of the walls."

"Well, I will be inside the walls," I boasted. I didn't mean to. But there were men around. I didn't think these shepherds would allow Shimon to hurt me. I was excited about the city. It was just my excitement mixed with Shimon talking to me as if I were a little baby and the rudeness he showed to My Father as well. Shimon's face turned quickly to anger. When I had first arrived, he and Dan had been walking amicably, but Dan took a step back when he saw Shimon's face. I took several quick steps in the other direction, calling over my shoulder that I needed to run to tell the others.

Running to Levi and Naftali was not as simple as my first errands. In fact, running was not really a possibility. They were at the other side of the flock, which was packed closer than usual but still so wide that I could not see to the other side. Perhaps that was what the river was going to be like. I had to weave my way between the animals as they walked and occasionally nibbled at little greenery popping up in the road. I accidentally stepped on more than one hoof along the way, and more than one hoof stepped on me.

When I arrived at Levi and Naftali, I was tired and reeking of sheep. Not that they could tell, I'm sure, as that was how they spent their days. I noted they, too, had a donkey with supplies they would use when staying outside the city that night, and though they were helping the shepherds, the men were doing most of the work. I delivered my message quickly. Then I fled as soon as the last word left my mouth, not giving Levi any chance to harm me.

To get to Reuben, I went around the outer edge of the flock. I was amazed when I saw him. He was behind all the animals, walking with two dogs on either side of him. The manservants who were with him walked at his pace but a few steps behind. They stopped when he put up his hand for them to do so as I approached. I realized when I saw how the men took direction from him that Reuben wasn't just at the back of our tribe, he was the head of our tribe from that direction.

"Hello, Joseph." He greeted me when I was still a few paces away. "Have you brought me a message?"

"Yes," I said. "How did you know?"

"You were walking at the front with our father. I wouldn't expect him to let you wander without reason, nor would I expect you to choose to do so. You must be here only to tell me something important." He began to walk again, and I did as he did.

"You're right, I am. Soon, we will come to a city. You cannot see it from here, but when I was in the front, I could already see the walls on the hill from where I stood. Soon, you will also be close enough to see. My Father sent me to tell you and the others." I relayed the message My Father had entrusted me with for the final time.

"Thank you," Reuben said when I finished my speech. "You can tell our father that these fine shepherds and I will watch over our animals here as well as we do at home. Please assure our father that we'll keep them safe and contained. And he will surely ask after their well-being. Please take this message back to our father. Tell him that the animals are faring well and will also be ready for the rest."

He sounded so much like My Father. I saw for the first time that he had a dark shadow over his upper lip, and his voice had the depth of a man's. It wasn't just that. He also spoke as if he were a man of importance. With confidence, he had not only accepted My Father's message but sent one of his own. Was this journey changing him too? Or was I only noticing this now?

"Reuben, remember you said you would tell me of your sheepshearing trips?"

My oldest brother's posture loosened with the request. He kept his seriousness but also found his delight. He smiled. "Okay, little brother. We will walk together for one short story.

"When our father tended Lavan's sheep, we often took them to shearing. Our new flock with these spots and speckles do not bring such a good price for their wool, but they have other benefits: their sturdiness and strength as well as their milk and flesh. But the wool of Lavan's sheep could be exchanged for many pieces of silver."

"Reuben, does Lavan have the better sheep?"

"He has the better sheep if all you care about is wool that can be dyed a color of your choice. Our wool is just as warm and just as fine. It cannot be sold for as many coins as the white wool, but it can be used for our clothing and rugs, and it does the job just as well. Lavan thinks he has the better sheep and is up getting them sheared with his sons right now. I do not know how that is going for him. He has not been in years. The men at the shearing are used to us and our cooperative ways, not Lavan and his harshness. I suspect they are not shaving the sheep as carefully or trading as honestly with him because he does not know any better.

"But Lavan and his sons are surely having a good time. Yes, the shearing is a time to remove the wool, gather it in sacks, and trade some of it for other goods. But much more than that happens at these gatherings. There are many men with time on their hands while the sheep are with the groomers, so other men come to entertain everyone with strong drink and food spiced with flavors from farther than our feet will ever travel."

I had never gotten to go with My Father and My Brothers to the shearing. I wondered whether we would travel back this season or shear the sheep elsewhere. Either way, I hoped to enjoy the adventure with them one day soon, and I soaked up Reuben's description as he went on.

"Other men, men who don't even have livestock, come and bring instruments. They are traveling musicians. You have heard the lovely sound of Naftali's flute, but these men play differently. They can play their instruments as well as you or I can sing a tune. And the men play the same tune together at the same time. You must pay them to be a part of the crowd of listeners; that is how they earn a living without having any animals. So, everyone who comes to the shearing pays the musicians, even our father, because the merriment is so delightful and everyone can feel their money sacks filling with the value of their wool. Our father has paid many times. We have enjoyed hearing the music and, of course, participating in the dancing that always accompanies it.

"The walk to the shearing takes two days' time, and, naturally, so does the walk back. But the walk back always feels shorter. On the way there, the landscape is familiar but still exciting because of the passing of the season since our last trip. On the way back, seven days of celebration feels too short and like home and work are just around the bend. And the sheep are all naked of their coverings; watching over them takes more attention while we get used to their new look."

The thought of the shorn sheep made Reuben smile, and I laughed.

After some time, I had a much less funny thought. "Reuben? It's a two-day journey to the sheep shearing? And two days back?"

He nodded.

"And seven days at the shearing?"

He nodded again.

"Reuben? The night that My Father told us of his dreams and the plan to return to the land of his birth, Lavan had left for the shearing that morning, had he not?"

"He had."

"And we worked as fast as we could to gather our food, herd the animals, load the donkeys, and take down the tents?"

"Yes."

"And the day we left? Yesterday? That was the last day of the shearing?"

"Yes."

"And today, Lavan and his sons began the return journey?"

"Most likely."

"And tomorrow, they will return to the compound and find us gone?"

"Unless they tarry, yes."

"Reuben? Will he come after us?"

"I'm sure he will."

I began to shake. Surely Lavan would be mad. Furious. I had seen him that way before. I had seen him throw bowls at rocks and laugh as they shattered and scared us. I had seen him charge at a tent pole, bringing it to the ground and part of the covering with it. Most frequently, I had heard him raise his voice louder than drums and twist his face into that of a monster and spew curses from his mouth that were as hot and damaging as a fire uncontained. I had once even seen him lift his hand to My Mother.

"Reuben, I must go tell My Father! We must prepare!"

Reuben put his arm on my shoulder again. "Our father knows, Joseph." Of course. I had not thought of that. If Reuben knew, surely My Father had told him to expect this.

"What will happen?"

"Lavan will be angry. He will gather some travel supplies and silver so that he can pursue us. All the while, he will tell himself lies of our father cheating him. He will tell himself that our father took his best sheep. He will tell himself that our father is lazy and did not take good care of his animals all those years. He will tell himself that our mothers belong to him and that our father stole them away. He will tell himself that he is sad to not have the children of our mothers nearby."

"But, Reuben!" I could not say any more. None of that was the truth! Lavan's flock never did so well as when My Father tended to it. My Father was known in the region to be a caring and successful shepherd. And now, all the mothers were a part of My Father's tribe, not Lavan's. What got me the most upset was Reuben's words that Lavan would be sad to see the children gone. Whenever he saw us children, he only yelled at us about how worthless My Father was or, worse, told us twisted stories of our father mistreating us, which weren't true, but sounded as if they were.

"Reuben, none of that is true!"

Reuben shook his head. "I know, Joseph. But it doesn't matter. Lavan convinces himself that it is true. This way, he can blame his misfortune on our father instead of taking responsibility for it himself. Lavan could be just as successful as our father if he chose to work the way our father does. He does not want to see himself as a lazy trickster, so, instead, he portrays himself in his stories as our father's victim. It comforts him."

"What will he do when he gets here? Will he hurt us?"

"He will do what he always does. He will yell. He will accuse. He will tell stories that sound true when they come from his calm lips but feel wrong in our stomachs because of their obvious falseness. He will make a mess of our things and of our hearts in the process. He will hurt all our hearts, but not our bodies."

My body shivered as he said that.

"It takes a brave man to strike another, but Lavan is a coward. He only throws blows that he knows will not be returned. When he throws lies, he can say he didn't, even though he did. When he throws punches, he cannot say he didn't. But there will be one good thing when he comes."

"What's that?" I asked, still fearful but now a little hopeful too.

"It will be the last time. Remember that, Joseph. Remember that when he's here. It will be just as awful as the other times, but it will be the last time."

We walked together in silence for a while until we saw the walls of the city appear ahead of us.

"You best get going, Joseph," Reuben suggested. "Certainly, you will be sleeping in the city tonight, and you should arrive at the front of our group."

I gasped. "Reuben? How did you know My Father said that I will sleep in the city?" And then, because I was more curious to hear about cities than I was to hear about how he acquired this information, I quickly followed that question with another. "Have you ever been inside a city, Reuben? What's it like?"

"I have not," he said. "You will have to tell me about it the next time we walk together. Okay?"

I agreed and turned west to walk back to My Father. The flock was too big and close together for me to try to walk through it again, and I thought I would rather pass by Levi than Shimon for a second time today.

"One more thing before you go," Reuben called after me. I immediately went back to his side to walk with him again. I needed to walk as quickly with Reuben as I did with My Father. His stride was that long.

"Joseph, who was our father before you were born?"

The question startled me. What did that mean? Who was he before I was born? Why, he was the same man he was after I was born. Was he not? I thought for another moment. Surely Reuben had a reason for asking me this puzzle.

"I suppose he was Jacob. Jacob, son of Isaac and Rebekah." I said tentatively. "The same as now?"

"Was he your father before you were born?" Reuben asked me.

"Certainly not," I said. "How could he be My Father then?"

Reuben agreed that he could not have been.

He posed another question. "Joseph, how many children were born before you?"

That was easy. The older boys never ceased to remind the younger ones of their order. "Thirteen," I said. "Ten brothers and three sisters. Reuben, Shimon, Levi, Judah, Dan, Naftali, Gad, Asher, Issachar, Zevulun, Ahuvah, Annah, and Deenah were all born before me." I recited this in one quick breath as I was used to doing when any one of them required me to remember that I was younger.

"And who is the father of those thirteen children?" he asked.

"Why, My Father, of course," I said.

Reuben shook his head. "Joseph, I am the firstborn of Jacob and Leah. Leah is my mother; she is not your mother. You are the firstborn of Jacob and Rachel. Rachel is your mother; she is not my mother. Joseph, Jacob is your father. He is my father as well and the father of all the brothers and sisters. It would serve you well to call him 'our father.'" I nodded. I could not speak. Reuben had not made fun of me, but this, perhaps, was worse. I departed with my cheeks red and my head low.

"I enjoyed our talk, Joseph. I hope you will come back and tell me about the city." Reuben tried to mend my heart as I walked away. But I could not face him again yet. I continued my walk back to the front of the caravan.

CHAPTER 6

When I rejoined My Father, he was with Judah, some of our shepherds, and a man whom I had never seen. My Father had just agreed to give the entire flock of sheep that was walking with Shimon and Dan to this man in exchange for one hundred head of cattle and twenty extra camels.

I dared not question My Father's judgment in trading away one fourth of our sheep, but I will admit that coming to the trade as inexperienced as I was, I thought it was a bad deal. That was, until I saw the cattle. I had heard tales of cows, of course, as My Brothers mocked their captivating eyes and spindly, long legs when they got back from their travels each season. But never had I, personally, seen such large, gentle creatures.

Each cow was as tall as a camel yet wider than a sheep. Some were brown, and some were tan. Their hair was short, and Judah said it just grew that way—they had never been shorn. And their horns! I am amazed that the goats did not flee in embarrassment when they saw those horns—some were longer than I was tall!

"What will we do with the cows?" I asked Judah.

"When our father began the negotiations with the trader," Judah explained, "he said that he wanted fewer, more valuable animals. This way, he didn't need to bring as many creatures across the river, but he could still use them for trading. Our father asked the men if any of them had experience with cattle, and Kemke stepped forward and assured us that he could take good care of them. He shall train me as we continue the journey. He said it will be just like caring for the sheep. They are docile, eat the grasses, and give milk. They don't give wool, but just one can feed many people and provide lots of hide."

All the same, when the trader left with a quarter of our flock, replacing it with only 120 creatures, our size and population suddenly looked greatly diminished. To my eye, this didn't seem good. But I didn't have much time to contemplate the situation, as when the deal was done, My Father announced that it was time to enter the city.

For this, he placed me on a camel, just like the women and girls. I did not take offense, however, because he did the same with Issachar and Zevulun, instructed Judah to ride one, and even mounted a camel himself. He then directed Kemke to lead us to the city, and that was how our small group approached the walls and the guard standing on duty at the gate.

"Who are you?" the guard asked My Father.

But My Father did not answer, not right away. It was his manservant who spoke first.

"Sir, this is my master Jacob, son of Isaac, father of eleven sons and head of this tribe."

"Is this true?" the guard asked.

This time, My Father spoke. "What he says is true. I am Jacob, son of Isaac, son of Abraham. My Father was a wandering Aramean. He came from this land and went south on the command of Elohim. There, his fortune grew. Now, my fortune has grown. I am going back to the land of my birth with my four wives and many children, manservants, maidservants, sheep, goats, cattle, and camels. We seek passage across the river tomorrow. Those of us whom you see here, my wives and daughters and four of my many sons, seek lodging for the night. We are shepherds. It would be an honor to partake in the hospitality of your customs. Of course, the animals will stay outside the walls because we do not want to bring animal filth into your fine city."

My father spoke with confidence and prestige and would not let the man of this lowly, sheepless stature look down upon him. I sat a little taller as I was filled with pride to be the son of such a man.

"I would be honored to pay for the use of a room in your city's inn for those of us here. Surely, it would not be wise to leave my beautiful wives outside the walls, subjected to the whims of travelers and beasts. We will not impose on you for long, as we will begin our voyage at sunrise. We need no more than simple accommodations, but I will pay for all we use."

At this, the guard laughed and loosened his grip on his dagger. Which was when I first noticed that My Father, too, had been gripping his dagger by his side.

"Jacob the Shepherd, what will a city dweller do with sheep? We have no room for livestock in here, nor do we want them. Those who cannot pay must set their tents up outside the walls; I'm sure nobody will come and take your precious sheep from you."

"The animals will stay outside the walls," My Father agreed. "My trusted manservant will even remove the camels and take them to the camp that the other men are already preparing. But our voyage must resume with the rise of the sun, and there is no better way for us to ensure an early crossing than to sleep in this fine city near your finest raftsmen. I will need many since my flock is large."

My Father paused and removed a large silver coin from a leather pouch that I did not know he had been carrying under his cloak, against his skin, this whole while. He presented it to the guard. "I will need accommodations as well as a meeting with the most equipped crosser available. We have a hundred heads among us, and even more legs." My Father laughed at his own joke.

But while My Father was laughing, the guard understood the opportunity that was available. He took the silver My Father was holding and began to smile. "Of course, sir," he said. "My brother, Milwan, is the most experienced crosser in the whole city. I will have him meet you at sunrise. For now, please, follow me. It would be my honor to escort you and your family to the inn."

At My Father's signal, we all alighted from the camels, and Kemke gathered them and led them away from the walls. I saw Judah also put away a dagger that I didn't know he had. Once the path was clear of our animals, the guard clasped My Father on the shoulder, patted him on the back, and led him through the gate he had been blocking.

I did not know what to expect from the other side of the city walls. I suppose, in my naivete, I had unknowingly assumed that the inside of the walls would be similar to the outside: hilly, grassy, dusty, perhaps absent of animals since the guard had mentioned that. It turned out that the city was not at all open spaces within walls—it was more crowded than walking between the sheep of my family's flock. Only instead of animals, the city was packed with people and with more walls.

Inside the towering stone outer walls of the city were smaller stone and wooden walls. Walking through the pathways, I saw that some of these walls belonged to shops of all different kinds.

There was a shop filled from floor to ceiling with bowls. Only bowls! These bowls were stacked on shelves and on top of each other. Some were brown and wooden, though not plain. The bowls were ornate with carvings of grapevines—including grapes and leaves. There were also bowls made of ceramic that were painted the brightest, most vivid colors I had ever seen outside of fruits or flowers. Some of these had only one color in various shades, and some of the bowls were painted with scenes.

How do I know this? How could I see these bowls if they were inside the walls that were inside the city walls? The walls had square and rectangular holes cut in them! Right through the holes, I could see the bowls and even an artist working on them. Instead of tent flaps that were open, and instead of tent flaps that were closed, these walled structures were always closed—except where they were always open.

"Joseph, Deenah," Leah called from up ahead. "You must stay with us."

My eyes and delight had been so captured by the bowls that I did not even notice that I had stopped to stare at their beauty, let alone that My Sister had done so also.

We reluctantly pulled ourselves away from the shop and rushed to catch up with the rest. I looked at Deenah and saw the same wonder in her eyes that I felt inside. I took her hand and leaned close and confided in her ear, "I wish to have bowls as beautiful as those one day." Deenah said that she hoped for the same.

As we wound our way through the city streets, I was grateful that Leah called to us. We would have surely been lost forever had we gotten separated. Some of the paths went uphill and circled around several buildings before going downhill again. Some were covered in stones that matched the walls, and some were flattened dirt like the highway we'd traveled along. For those who lived there, perhaps there were familiar landmarks, but for me, it all looked the same. It was only by peeking into the buildings that I was able to see their differences.

And the paths were all so much narrower than the ones we had traveled along on the way there. Had My Father and the guard been joined by one more man, they would not have fit shoulder to shoulder. As it was, Judah even walked a few steps behind the two of them. I thought that was because he was not one of the men, but perhaps it was just because there wasn't room.

My eyes were wide and peeking into the shops as much as I could without getting lost. This was no easy task since I would have gladly gawked all day at each one. But whenever I slowed down, I was bumped by a city dweller. Not as a punishment, but simply because they wanted to pass and I was using too much of the path. But I couldn't help myself when we got to the stall filled with spices.

This one was outdoors. The spice seller had set a table with sacks filled with different spices. More spices than a whole tribe could use in a whole year! More spices than any one garden could grow in a whole lifetime! This stall had caused My Mothers to stop, and we children took that as permission to stop as well. Even My Father stopped because it was clear he would get nowhere.

"Jacob," Leah said. "There are some spices here that I know you would enjoy in your stew and others that would be heavenly with fresh bread and the thick olive oil we have."

My Father listened to Leah as she told him of the plans she had to fill his mouth and stomach with freshly spiced foods over the course of the journey. He listened as she talked about how much his mother, Rebekah, would surely love a sampling of these delicacies when they reunited after so much time. My Mother nodded in agreement, then dipped a finger into one of the spices and placed it on My Father's tongue. He smiled.

As the three of them determined which spices would come with us and how much of each, Deenah spotted a girl about our age not far from the table. Deenah walked up to her. "Is this your father's shop?" she asked.

The girl laughed at My Sister. I didn't understand why until she replied, "Yes, I am the daughter of the spice merchant." Then it was our turn to laugh. It wasn't her words that made us laugh, and I could tell that it wasn't Deenah's words that humored her, either. It was the way they sounded. The words were the same as I had known all my life, but the sounds were all together new.

Judah stepped forward to scold us all. With the air of importance of someone who had traveled to sheepshearing many times and met shepherds and other travelers from different places, he told us that what we were laughing about was called different accents and wasn't funny at all. It was merely a sign that people lived in places where the same words sounded a bit different.

I bowed my head in shame at being reprimanded by Judah—and so shortly after Reuben had corrected me. But Deenah was not bothered, nor was the merchant's daughter. She motioned for Deenah to join her behind the table and then gave her a taste of the fruit she had been eating. Within moments, the two of them were chatting away.

"Do you live in this city?" Deenah asked.

"Yes, of course," the girl told her.

"In one of these containers?"

The girl laughed again. "They're called *houses*."

"Why do you live in a house?" My Sister asked.

"Where else would I live?" asked the girl. "On the streets? In the square?"

"I live in a large, open tent with my mother and Zilpah and brothers and sisters," Deenah explained. "And nearby, Joseph," she pointed to me as she said my name, "lives with Rachel and Bilhah and those brothers and sisters. My father dwells in his own tent. And my grandfather, who we are leaving, also lives in a tent, his grown sons live in their own tents, their wives live in tents with their children, and the manservants and maidservants do the same. We all live in tents."

The girl didn't laugh at this information, but I could see it was strange to her.

"You are like the people who live outside the walls?" she asked us.

"We just got here," I explained. "We don't know how those people live. We live as My Sister just explained. Which of these houses is yours? Which is your father's?"

"We cannot see our house from here. It is around the bend and past the water square, down the hill. We all live in the same house. Me, my father, my mother, my brothers and sisters, my aunt, and my mother's parents. We sleep closely together at night, and when the day begins, we all leave the house to go to our places.

"My grandmother, aunt, and mother usually go to the ovens to bake bread. I have been with them before. The women talk and make bread and take turns using the ovens. It is very loud and busy there. My sister loves to go and hear the news of the day, but I prefer to come here and see all the travelers and city dwellers alike. I just go to the ovens on the coldest days so I can warm up."

Deenah and I had no response to this description of so many new things. Deenah just ate the fruit the girl shared, and I nodded passively. My Father was giving coins to the spice merchant, and My Mother and Leah were gathering spices into cloths. The girl dipped her finger and thumb into a basket of a dark red spice. She took Deenah's hand in hers and spread the spice on Deenah's wrist, pressing down to make it stick to her skin. Then she did the same for me. "This is called *cinnamon*," she said. "My Father gets it from a trader who travels far to the east and gets it from another trader who reports that it is from a small land that floats in the middle of a sea. May it be with you on a safe journey."

Smelling my wrist brought a sensation to my nose and beyond that I had never experienced. It was as if all the world and all the sky opened and created a great, warm space of beauty within me and all around me. My Mother called my name three times before I heard her. I know this because I finally noticed she was leaving only when she said, "Joseph, I have called your name three times already. Come along now so you don't get lost."

I followed the adults along the winding roads and between the houses and shops. I put one foot in front of the other and somehow managed to keep my body with my family. But my thoughts were elsewhere. I do not even know where. Just elsewhere, enveloped in the sensation that was brought to me by the cinnamon. I don't know how long my reverie lasted, but it was abruptly ended when we walked into the inn and my nostrils were invaded by a stench that not even placing my nose in direct contact with my wrist could override.

CHAPTER 7

The night we spent in the inn was the most uncomfortable, loud, smelly, sleepless night of my life to that point. Despite the square window supposedly letting air in and out, I felt as if I were suffocating during every minute. My Father had requested sleeping space on the roof, but the innkeeper insisted that there was none available. We found out he was speaking the truth when My Father offered him two extra silver pieces, then three, and then four, but with no success.

"You need to get here early, my good man, to get space on the roof. But don't you worry, I have a private room available for you and your party. You won't need to share with the travelers from other parts." The man looked us over. I wondered how we appeared to him. What thoughts did he have when he saw so many daughters and young boys and only one older son? Did he realize My Father was an important man when he saw the four wives? The answers to these questions would remain a mystery, but his opinion of Emunah was revealed.

Looking at her in Leah's arms, he said, "My wife had one of those babies. We sent him to the bottom of the river that same day. Are you here to send her to the river?"

My Father clenched his teeth and his fists. "No," he said. He stared at the innkeeper. I thought he might say more, but he didn't.

The innkeeper was surprised by My Father's reaction and quickly changed the subject back to business. "You all look weary," he said. "I will show you to the room I have for you."

My Father nodded, resigned. "It will only be for one night, beloveds," My Father said to the rest of us. He had never called us *beloveds* before, but neither had he ever subjected us to such conditions. "At dawn, we will go to the river to meet Milwan and begin our crossing."

Thus, we were stuck, five adults—six if counting Judah—and seven children—eight if counting Judah—in a room large enough for us to lay skin to skin on threadbare rugs that had been used many times before us by many people. Such quarters made me long for home. Yes, Lavan was there, but so was air. Fresh air. Of course, fresh air was closer than our old compound, but the suffocation did make me realize the enormity of the unknown that awaited me.

After much pleading and moaning, My Father agreed to tell us all a story in an attempt to distract us from our misery. "Children, you are now among the great travelers of the hills. Many men do not ever leave the campgrounds where they were born. My own father, Isaac, has never set foot out of the land of Canaan in all his years. But my grandfather Abraham had seen many lands. He was living not far from our old camp when Elohim spoke to him and told him to travel south. And even before that, he had traveled with his father from the great city of Ur. He settled in the fertile land where we lived until just days ago, and he could have built himself a life and a great name there. Indeed, he did. But his life and his name became even greater when he set forth on the journey to the south.

"We are now traveling that same road. Perhaps he and my grandmother Sarah stayed in this very inn on their way. We will never know; though, I think it is reasonable to guess that his men and animals stayed outside the walls. You are now traveling great distances by the command and invitation of Elohim. You can stand proud . . . when it's morning and time to stand.

"When I left my father's house to journey to Haran, I didn't venture off the highway. Inns and innkeepers require payment, and I had none to give. But I also had with me only what I most needed and could carry myself. I had no donkeys, no carts, no camels, no men. I was a man on my own, prepared to meet the elements. I had no need of an inn. Traveling alone gave me plenty of time to think. Being outside, unburdened and quiet, gave me plenty of space to talk with Elohim. More importantly, it gave me room to listen."

I realized that I had been listening to the sounds of the flock as we traveled, and at the inn, the sounds were different.

"Here in this inn, in this room, where we can hear the babies suckling and everyone tossing and turning, it is noisy. My children, if you are going to hear a message from Elohim, you must be extra quiet and extra attentive. So, be still now and listen, and in the morning, as we cross the great river, one like you've never seen or even imagined, if Elohim spoke to you in the night, you will come and cross with me personally."

My Father was a shepherd, accustomed to the peace and quiet of tending to sheep when they have distance between them. He was a man of tents, not of stone houses, a man of song when rejoicing, and a man of solitude when communing with Elohim. Maybe he was trying to hold our interest, or maybe he was just hoping for quiet. But as I strained my ears and my attention to hear any messages, I eventually fell asleep from the effort.

That night, I had a terribly fitful dream. It was not like my others, which may sometimes be hard to understand but at least are not scary. In this dream, there was a blind ram. It was tied to an altar for sacrifice, but just as the knife was headed for its neck, the would-be butcher looked and saw a boy caught in the thicket. "Come here, my boy," the man said. He took the boy on his shoulders and danced with him. Far away, a woman laughed and then fell to her death. Nothing had pushed her; she was just alive one moment and dead the next. My dream then took me back to the boy who had fallen off the man's shoulders and hit his head on the sacrificing stone.

In the morning, I woke perplexed but more sore, tired, and hungry than curious about my dream; so, I forgot about it for a time. My Father took My Brothers and me outside of the inn to relieve ourselves, while the women went elsewhere. Then we rolled up the sleeping rugs we had been allowed to use for the night and returned them to the innkeeper in exchange for a few olives and a hunk of bread for each of us.

The city that had so enticed me the day before was not yet light and smelled of urine. I was ready to move on. Not that I had a choice in the matter. My Father walked downhill according to the innkeeper's instructions, and we all followed. Deenah and I only stopped to look in one window—it was that of a sandal maker. My feet had never worn anything before this trip but were now well protected in the hide that was covering them, even if a little warm. But these sandals in the window did more than protect from the rough ground and animal mess of the highway; they were also adorned.

As Deenah and I looked in the window, we pointed out different pairs of sandals to each other, each pair being more ornate than the one before it.

"Look," she said, "just look." She pointed, jaw dropped, at a pair of sandals made from leather on the bottom and wool ties around the top. It was laced around a wooden carving that resembled a person's foot so that we could see how it would be worn. The sashes wove and crossed, wove and crossed, almost to the knee. One of the sashes was blue, the other purple, so that anyone wearing these beauties would be seen as someone of great taste and surely great means.

Judah, noticing we were separate from the group, backtracked to get us. "Come on, you two. Don't you want to see the river? It will surely be wider and more beautiful than any of these sandals," he said, though we could see him eying a pair that had strands of leather covered in painted beads wrapping around the wooden ankle. "Elohim created the river, whereas these little scraps were sewn together by man. The river has always been here and will always be. These sandals will only be worn by one set of feet, yet untold numbers of feet will cross the river. So, hurry, come and see the beauty, and do it before our father knows you've been gone."

We followed everyone down the hill, resisting the pull of the windows and the action in the squares as the townspeople awoke and came to the well. I knew in my heart that one day I would go to a city again, and despite its wretched smells, stay there. But not on this day. On this day, other adventures awaited me, and I would turn my attention there.

No effort was needed for that, though, as at the bottom of the hill, there was a city gate like the one we had entered the day before. It was thick and guarded and led to a small turn that then took us to the other side of the wall. And it was on that side of the wall that I suddenly realized there had been a loud sound inside my head yet coming from outside of it. It had grown there subtly without my noticing until I saw the source of that sound: the river.

I am not ashamed to admit that the sight of that river brought me to my knees, and tears gushed from my eyes. I heaved heavy sobs and thought I would expel my bread from the inn, but I did not. My Mother came and put her arms around me. She pushed my curls back and hummed a little song while I wailed.

This seemed to give permission to our whole party to stop and stare at what I soon learned was called the Euphrates River. It was a sight worth taking in, a sight worth stopping for. I had seen a river on the way here, but seeing this one made the first seem as if it were a blade of grass while this one was a whole field. Only this was so much more than a field—it went on beyond the point that the eye could see in both directions. It just went on and on. And the water in it was so beautiful! Not murky from the ground beneath it but clear and shimmering.

I felt at that time something that I had previously only felt in dreams. A familiarity that had no basis in my life. Coming to the river was like coming home, though I had never been there. These thoughts were too much for me to put into words—too much for me to even feel all at once in my little body. And so, I wept with My Mother's arms around me. Even My Father paused. Whether for me or for the river or for the significance of crossing it or in anticipation of the work ahead to do so, I will never know.

As other travelers began to wake and make their way to the river, My Father rushed to the shore to find Milwan. When we caught up with them, he had finished his negotiations and sent Judah to rush the rest of the tribe along. "You're sure?" he asked Milwan. "You're sure you can get us all across today?"

"Honorable Jacob, son of Isaac. I have told you again and again. I cannot cross people and animals who are not here. If your tribe and your flock arrive before the sun has completely risen, I will have enough time to cross them all in the daylight. Look along the bank of the river. These thirty vessels are mine and at your service today. The moon will be almost full tonight, so for some extra silver, I will take anyone remaining on this side after dusk across to the other. But this will only be necessary if you tarry."

My Father nodded. He reached into his purse and removed ten large silver coins. He counted them into Milwan's rough hands. "Ten more when half of my camp is across, and the final ten when the last man steps off your last boat." The men nodded their agreement.

With the money in his hand, Milwan was no longer the serious negotiator. He looked down at me and My Brothers and smiled.

"Have you ever been on a boat as beautiful as this one?" he asked us, though he knew we had not. "You will be the first ones to cross while we wait for those animals to arrive." Then he leaned in and whispered to us, "But you don't take up much space, so if you find it to be as fun as I think you will, then you can hop on one of the boats as they cross back this way and ride back again."

We smiled as we walked across a wooden board to get from the land along the river's edge onto the boat. The boat itself was not large, not this one. Looking down the river, I saw many boats that were the size of My Father's tent and some that were bigger. But this boat was a small one. There were benches on it where we were welcomed to sit. My Mother and Leah sat next to each other, while Bilhah and Zilpah did the same. Babies were on laps, but Issachar and Zevvy and I got to sit on our own bench, as did Ahuvah, Annah, and Deenah.

When we were seated, four of Milwan's men boarded and sat beside the oars. As if they were four men of one breath, they moved the oars in perfect synchronicity. I was torn between watching this beautiful dance and watching the water as it passed beneath us. I set my eyes on the spot where two of the oars entered and exited the water. The men were pushing the water behind us, and I felt as if we were birds flying just above the surface of the water.

This bliss passed all too quickly because in what felt like one blink, we had already reached the other side. Without planning or thinking, My Brothers and Sisters and I all stood and jumped and pleaded, "Again, again, again!" The women screeched as we accidentally caused the boat to rock back and forth with our jumps, and the oarsmen laughed.

"Don't worry, little mothers," one man said. "Morning and evening, we make this trip across the Euphrates River. Back and forth, back and forth. Sometimes, we contain the animals on the larger boats, but the real joy comes in taking first-time riders. I assure you that your children are not the first to ask for more rides; we have yet to meet a child who doesn't. This is why Milwan sent us ahead of the flocks—so that we would be able to cross a few times just for the joy of being on this beloved river. The great god Enki gave us this river for water, fish, exploration, and joy. We will take the children back to the other bank and bring them back here again. Would you like to wait on this side or take the ride again?"

The women were quiet again, looking at each other in words expressed with their eyes that only they understood. Then Leah spoke up. "Surely it would not be right to send our young children across the river without us. We will ride again." With smiles on our faces and gladness in our hearts, we turned our backs to this new side of the river while the men flipped their legs to the other side of the benches to face the bank we were departing from and glide us back to the first side of the river. Then they began rowing back to where we had left My Father.

I do not think my face stopped smiling the entire time. Knowing that I would get at least one more ride, I was able to take in the surroundings less urgently. I felt the smooth ride across the river and enjoyed the sound of the oars pushing the water and lifting into the air to do it again. I saw the birds flying overhead, occasionally dipping into the river and coming up with a fish in their beaks. I watched as the walls of the city appeared to get closer at a pace much faster than they had when we were walking toward them. I did not know of this great god Enki of whom the oarsman spoke, but I thought him very wise to create such a river and silently thanked the men who had fashioned this boat that allowed us to fly across it.

When we returned to our starting position, we all got off the boat. My Brothers and Sisters and I rushed toward My Father, filled with glee and excitement about the adventure we had just experienced. We all spoke at once, causing him to laugh and tell us that he remembered the wonder he had felt so many years ago when first coming to this river and first getting on a boat. I could see the wide, excited eyes of my older brothers as they looked at the river, looked at the boats, and looked at our faces that were unable to contain our delight. In my short life, I had always been the last of the brothers to do things: the last to keep all my milk teeth, the last to have my hair cut, the last to go into the fields with the flocks. Now, I had been one of the *first* to sleep in a city and to ride in a boat.

I spent the rest of the day riding across the river, back and forth, back and forth. I think I sampled each one of the boats. Most of them were much bigger than the first, and I stood packed in with the sheep as they baaed and bleated with this new sensation of having the ground move under them. When they got to the far side of the river, they did not walk down wooden bridges as the people did. Instead, one side of the boat was unhinged from the rest, and the sheep were coaxed into the shallow water to walk the rest of the way.

They were not the only ones who got wet. Milwan insisted that the dogs would enjoy swimming across the river, and he was right. My Father said that each dog should make only one trip so as not to get tired out, but I could see that their bodies enjoyed the adventure of swimming in the water, herding the sheep that floated ahead of them on the boats.

The cows and the camels were the hardest to get onto the boats. The men put ropes around their necks and pulled them over the wooden planks one by one. Milwan said that it was not even worth trying to herd these larger beasts onto the boats. He did this every day and knew that they would not just walk on themselves the way sheep would. And so, his men walked them on, sometimes enticing them with the promise of a bite of fruit when they followed.

Only once in all the crossings of all the thirty boats—back and forth with cattle and camels, donkeys and carts, sheep and goats and people—was there a moment of fear. It was on one of the boats that carried the donkeys. Milwan brought a special helper on all the donkey crossings. This man was to sing to the donkeys as we crossed. "The donkeys love soft singing," he explained. "And they love land. Since we have taken the land from under their feet, we put songs in their ears to help keep them still on the river."

Indeed, the animals, who were willing enough to board the boats but wanted nothing to do with their rocky unsteadiness once on, seemed to calm with the singing. Except one time, when one of the donkeys, spooked by the sound of a bird call above, shook its head fiercely several times, perhaps in the hopes of ridding her ears of this sound. This caused the boat to rock and many of the other donkeys to react. With an inability to run, they began to kick, as if doing so would get them back to land. This rocked the boat. I was on that ride and unsteady, and even with four legs, I saw the donkeys were unsteady as well. One of them toppled over and, in getting up as quickly as it could, knocked another one in its flank, lifting it just enough so that it fell over the edge of the boat as it tipped to that side.

The donkey brayed twice in the water before going under. Quickly, one of the oarsmen jumped over the edge of the boat with a rope. He put the loop over the donkey's neck and attempted to guide it to the shore. The donkey was under for a long time. Eventually, she showed her head, gasped for breath with two loud brays, and sank to the bottom again. Thankfully, the rope was long, and the man could still bring the donkey forward, even though it seemed intent on getting there by sinking and jumping, sinking and jumping, and bobbing across until finally arriving at the other bank long after the rest of us were on solid ground again.

I decided to stay on that side of the river, not wanting to have another ride like that again. Zevvy kept riding, though. I think he took every trip back and forth and was the last one off the last boat.

When most of the flocks and all our tribe had crossed the river, My Father instructed the young men to lead the animals toward Gilead. He set Reuben with the task of leading the tribe in his stead while he settled payment with Milwan and brought up the rear of the caravan. And so, I walked with My Brother, firstborn with firstborn, leading our tribe until the last of us had crossed the river and My Father came to the front again.

CHAPTER 8

Once across the river, we traveled only enough to part from the highway, and then we set up our tents in Gilead. Until this time, we had slept under the stars, but My Father said we would rest a few days, and so we set up camp atop a hill that gave us a view of both where we had left and where we were headed. That night, I shared a tent with My Mother again for the first time since we left. I got to tell her of my travels. I could hear her smile with pleasure at my excitement before she sang me to sleep. I was glad there would be more such nights ahead of us.

Perhaps we should have kept moving, though, because it was in Gilead that Lavan caught up to us. Seeing his face, I appreciated the seven days during which we were free of him, and I hoped we would have many more. Even though Reuben had told me that Lavan would come, it would be a lie to say I was not afraid. I was hardly more than a baby when I learned that Lavan might do anything. There was nothing he thought wasn't his, nobody he thought to be kind to besides himself.

My Father had chosen to set up our campground atop the hill. "Just like with a city," he said, "we can see who is approaching from this position." Which is how we knew in advance that Lavan was here and that he and his sons were climbing the mountain, surely up to no good. When Lavan arrived at the top, he was met by My Father who was surrounded by all his sons. The young men were the strongest, and armed, but I was prepared to bite and claw if necessary. I told My Father so, but he assured me it would not be necessary.

Lavan faced us all with his hands on his hips, ever the entitled one, ever feigning that he was the wounded one. But at least he had to face all of us. I saw a flicker of hesitation in him before he began stating his position.

"What did you mean keeping me in the dark and carrying off my daughters like captives of the sword?" he asked My Father. "Why did you flee in secrecy and mislead me and not tell me? I would have sent you off with festive music, with timbrel and lyre."

I bit my tongue so as not to spit. What a lie! I was younger than the rest, but even I knew that Lavan would never create a celebration that cost him anything, and he had nobody who would do him a favor. He continued to feign affection for us.

"You did not even let me kiss my sons and daughters goodbye. It was a foolish thing for you to do." I remembered the conversation I had overheard when My Mother and Leah were talking. It was a foolish thing to do—had it not been *Lavan* we were leaving behind. And so, it was smart.

"I have it in my power to do you harm, but the god of your father said to me last night, 'Beware of attempting anything with Jacob, good or bad.' Very well that you had to leave, because you were longing for your father's house, but why did you steal my gods?'"

My Father had taken only what had rightfully belonged to him. I witnessed this myself. And why would he even desire Lavan's gods? They were merely clay figures that had no more ability to do anything than Lavan himself.

"I was afraid because I thought you would take your daughters from me by force, but anyone with whom you find your gods shall not remain alive! In the presence of our kinsmen, point out what I have of yours, and take it."

At this, we parted. Lavan followed My Father to his tent to search it first. His was the only large tent. We had set up small tents for this short stop, with each mother having a little lean-to for her and her children. None of the children were willing to leave their mothers to be alone with Lavan while he searched the tents, so we each accompanied them. While I had always enjoyed having My Mother's affection only for me, I wished for brothers nearby even more than I ever had. Soon it would be just me and My Mother and Lavan in the tent. I quietly vowed to protect her and come to her aid under any circumstance, but I was filled with fear at the same time.

Alone in the tent, it seemed My Mother was filled with fear as well. I saw her eyes scan the temporary home. The top of the tent gave us shade from the hot sun, and the lowered sides were down for the same reason, though it prevented a breeze from entering. The floor was uncovered because it wasn't necessary to unpack the rugs for only our short stay here. Most things were still in the donkeys' carts, and the few cushions and baskets and our two pallets that were in the tent were pushed to the side. There was nowhere to hide and nothing to throw. I reminded myself that everyone was nearby, and if that ugly Lavan began to hurt My Mother, I could run past him and get help.

My Mother's face already held the pain of the anticipated visit. Her eyes were tightly shut, her nose and forehead wrinkled with the effort. Her breathing was loud and hard as if she were already in a fight. "Joseph," she whispered.

"I am here, Mother," I said. And I was, directly by her side.

"Joseph, dig a small hole in the earth here." There were no tools, and though she didn't open her eyes to see my pause, she knew my thoughts. "You will need to use your hands. Be quick now. It can be small. If your two closed hands could fit in there, it is enough. But now open those hands and dig. Quickly."

I did as she asked. I would like to say it took my attention away from Lavan, but it did not. I heard him in one of the other tents. His yell was so loud he was possibly heard as far back as the Euphrates. He barked orders mostly, and obscenities, and grunts and growls. I heard Levi's voice: "Look all you want, old man. You will find nothing here of yours. Nothing." This was followed by a short scuffle. As I dug, I imagined Lavan hitting Levi and Leah pulling him away from returning the blow.

When the hole was as big as I thought My Mother expected, I whispered to her that it was finished. This was also the first time I'd looked up since I began my fervid task. My eyes widened with surprise to see her squatting with her belt between her teeth, biting down hard, tears streaming down her cheeks from tightly shut eyes.

What would she do? Was she relieving herself inside the tent? She would never do such a thing! And now, of all times! My fear pushed aside everything else, and I blurted out the words I was thinking: "Mother, this is not the place to relieve yourself!"

She reached out her hand for me, and I went to her. She was trembling with effort and was pushing down with silent screams. She squeezed my hand so hard I thought it would break the bones in my fingers. But soon, she breathed again, long enough to hurriedly tell me that she was not relieving herself. She was birthing.

Birthing?

"Mother, I'll get the women!" I nearly shouted.

"No," she said. "Hush. There is no time. I have done this before; it is almost over. Your father mustn't know. He will blame Lavan for bringing such stress, and he might not be wholly wrong, nor will he be wholly right. We just want Lavan to leave, and I don't want your father to go after him." She stopped talking and breathed hard, loud, fast breaths. "Joseph, you will help me. You are my strong boy. You are my love. You can do this."

There was not much to do. I stood beside her as she crouched at my level and let her squeeze my hand. Again, she squeezed more than I thought I could bear. The effort nearly toppled her off balance, and so I put my shoulder under her to help her steady. This caused her to let go of my hand and lean her weight on my body. She pushed down hard, and I heard the sound of something fall underneath her robe.

My Mother released her breath and took in air slowly. Then she released her grip on me and put her hands on the ground in front of her, her knees down at her sides. Slowly, she pushed herself up to a kneeling position and reached under her robe. Gently, she brought her hands back with a tiny baby girl inside of them. She was perfectly formed, though her skin was too thin and covered in white liquid; her body, too small and not moving. Not even with gentle breaths of sleep. She had a cord attached to her belly that stretched upward under My Mother's clothes. She swiftly cut that cord with the knife in her pouch and held the baby up to her face and bathed her in tears.

"She is my sixth child, Joseph. You are my fourth. I may have only one living child so far, but know this about your mother. I am a mother of many. I have birthed six babies from my very body. I have grown these babies, and I have done the labor of delivering them. And I have been the mother of each one. I have joined the women who have birthed many, and I have held life in me that died inside me. Your mother has held death in her body and lived. Elohim has given me that strength. Elohim has also given me the strength to find joy in each little life. And someday, Elohim will give me the strength to endure the sorrow."

And then she stopped addressing me. Once again, she closed her eyes, but this time, softly. She held the tiny baby on her chest and spoke softly but loud enough for me to hear: "Elohim, the baby you put inside of me, her life is pure. You created her, you protected her, you breathed her into me, and now you take her back. Thank you for all the time that you allowed her to be in my body."

She kissed the baby on the head and held her out toward me. I knew she was inviting me to do the same. I kissed her head as well. My Sister. I kissed My Sister's head and gently stroked her fingers that were as small as ants. Tears streamed down my face as fully and quickly as those on My Mother's as she placed the tiny baby into the hole I'd dug while not knowing it was to bury My Sister.

Then My Mother retrieved the little sack I'd seen her pat when talking with Leah in the wadi. Sitting on the floor, she removed two small clay figures of women with full, pregnant bellies and placed them on the baby's body. "These will be your little mothers now, Little One." And with that statement, My Mother went from mourning to motion. She pushed the dirt back over the little hole, filling it quickly. She emptied a waterskin partially on her hands and partially on the small mound, then used the water from her hands to wipe her face clean.

"Bring me a cushion, Joseph. Soon there will be more blood. It's okay, it will come out easily and won't hurt. But I must have a cushion to sit on for now. My father will be here in our tent before we know it."

With witnessing the birth and death of My Sister, I had forgotten about everything else that was happening. I brought My Mother the cushion she requested and placed it on the tiny grave as she pointed. "Help me up," she asked, and I did. Then I helped her slowly lower herself onto the pillow. She composed herself as if nothing had happened, though I saw blood beginning to stain the cushion and her clothes as she concealed it with her body. She was sitting there when Lavan entered our tent.

Lavan saw my face, smudged from wiping away tears with hands that had been in the dirt. "Coward," he said. "The runt here with his little mother. Standing tall as if you could do anything for her, though your body shakes with fear. Don't worry, little boy. I only came for the two gods stolen from my altar." He began rifling through the baskets, dumping their contents on the dirt, then kicking the empty baskets around the tent. One nearly hit My Mother in the head, but she did not flinch or alter her position on the pillow. Lavan noticed this.

"Have you learned so much disrespect from your husband that you do not even rise to greet your father?" he asked.

"Forgive me, Father," she said, "but the time of women is upon me."

"You mock me," he said. "The women aren't slacking in their duties together. The moon is not new. I know it is not the time."

My Mother reached a hand under her robe and brought it out with blood. She reached the bloody hand toward her father. "If you will please help me rise, I will stand for you," she said. Lavan recoiled and left the tent.

I rushed to My Mother's side and pushed my face into her bosom. Her breath was fast and shallow. She hugged me tightly but released me quickly. "Now," she said, "now is the time to go get Bilhah. Thank you, my love; you were wonderful." Her smile was pained but sincere.

"Mother," I asked before stepping away, "Mother, what is her name?"

"Bilhah," My Mother repeated. "Go and get Bilhah. And not a word of this to anyone else. Remember."

"My Sister," I clarified. "What is her name?"

"She wasn't here long enough for a name," she said. She closed her eyes, exhausted, and shooed me away with her hand.

I ran as fast as I could to Bilhah's tent. She was still there with Naftali and Dan, putting things back in order after Lavan's search. "Bilhah," I said, "My Mother needs you." Bilhah took in my face, and hers immediately changed to a look of concern. She left quickly.

"What's wrong?" Naftali asked.

"My Mother wants Bilhah," I answered.

"Yes, clearly, but why?" Dan asked. "What happened?"

I had a sister, I thought. But I couldn't say the words aloud. I couldn't tell them of kissing My Sister. I couldn't tell them of being a big brother taking care of her only need: a grave. I couldn't tell them anything that had happened. My Mother had insisted. I would have to keep her in my heart only. While they waited for an answer I couldn't give, I decided I would give My Sister a name. I chose Levav because it sounded like *Lavan*, because she had been so brave to have made her entrance and exit in secret from him, and because the name means "attached to my heart"—the place where she would now live forever.

I left Bilhah's tent with Levav in my heart and Naftali and Dan staring after me, empty of answers. I got a waterskin and washed my hands and face as My Mother had and composed myself as she had as well. Everything was over, as if it had never happened, except for one important detail. I had a sister. A sister who I had kissed and stroked and buried in the ground and in my heart.

Hearing My Father's raised voice interrupted my thoughts.

"What is my crime?" My Father barked. "What is my guilt that you have followed me here? You rummaged through all my things! What have you found of your household items? What? Set it here, before my kinsmen and yours. They will decide between us." Lavan had nothing to show for all his trouble. He had found nothing.

"During the twenty years I have spent in your service, your ewes and she-goats never miscarried. Nor did I ever feast on rams from your flock. That which was torn by beasts, I never brought to you. I, myself, made good on the loss, and you exacted it from me whether you took it by day or by night. During the days, the heat ravaged me; during the nights, frost. My eyes got no rest.

"Of the twenty years I spent in your household, I served you fourteen years for your two daughters, and six for your flocks, and you changed my wages over and over again! Had not Elohim, the god of my father Abraham, the god of my father Isaac, been with me, you would have sent me away empty-handed. But Elohim saw me and the work I have done and judged me favorably."

Lavan was not one to back down from strong words, no matter how true. There was only one possibility for him, and that was that he was right. He would talk or fight until he proved this to everyone around him—or at least for as long as it took for him to believe that he was believed. He answered My Father in a harsh tone.

"The daughters are my daughters, the children are my children, and the flocks are my flocks. All that you see is mine."

Everyone paused and looked around. We all saw the same thing: My Father, *his* wives, *his* children, *his* tents, *his* manservants, *his* maidservants, *his* speckled flocks, *his* camels, *his* carts, . . . *his* everything. Everything belonged to My Father. He had worked for every thread.

Lavan switched his tone to attempt to be seen as the honorable one. "What can I do now about my daughters or the children they have borne? Come, let's make a pact, Jacob, you and I, and it will be a witness between you and me."

My Father didn't waste a moment. He began to gather rocks from the hilltop and bid us to do the same. Together, we created a mound the height of a man. We sat by that mound—My

Father and My Brothers and I, along with Lavan and his sons. Nobody spoke; each person living only with our own thoughts. We ate in silence—and quickly, not wishing to add any more to this experience.

When, finally, the last crumbs were eaten, Lavan stood and announced that the name of the place where we had set the mound of stones shall be called Yegar Sahadutta. But My Father thought a better name would be Witness Mound, and he declared as such. I saw Lavan's face admit that this was, indeed, a better name, and he opened his foul mouth and immediately took credit for naming it.

"This place is named Witness Mound," he said, "for it is a mound that is a witness between you and me." He addressed My Father. "It is also called the Outlook. Because here, Elohim will look out between you and me. Know, Jacob, that if you ill-treat my daughters or take other wives besides them, even if I am not there to see it, Elohim will see it. Elohim will be the witness between you and me."

I saw My Father reach out his arm to stop Shimon and Levi, who both wanted to advance on Lavan. They had borne witness to the time that Lavan had come to our camp in search of My Mother. I was a boy of only four summers at the time and had forgotten, but now, the memory came flooding back as if it had happened just that morning.

That awful day, Lavan had come stomping and yelling, hitting the donkeys with his stick, and knocking over jugs and pots, spilling food and beer and stepping in them without care. "Where is my beautiful daughter?" he'd cried out. "Where is she? I am in need of comfort. She must come back to my camp with me tonight and comfort me."

My Father had been in the fields and would remain there for several days since it was lambing time. All the men had gone, but the boys had stayed in camp. I remember the older ones protesting, arguing with My Father that they were old enough to help with the lambing. And My Father had said that was precisely why they would stay at the camp: because they were old enough, and he would not leave the women and children alone.

My Brothers complained the whole time, but it was good that they were there. By the time Lavan reached My Mother, everyone had gathered there along with her. This didn't stop Lavan from reaching out and grabbing her by the wrist. She tried to pull away but couldn't break his grasp. Leah stepped closer to her father and spat at his feet. "Leave her alone, old man. Our husband will return from your fields and not be pleased to find that you have been on his property."

Lavan released his grasp on My Mother's wrist and grabbed Leah by the hair, putting his hand under her head covering to do so. He spat right in her face. "Always jealous of your sister, beast. Then I will take you instead. Your husband will not miss you." He began to pull her with him, but Shimon and Levi were both upon him before he'd even taken two steps. They were so tangled I was afraid that they would hurt each other, but, in fact, it was only Lavan who was knocked out on the ground moments later, while My Brothers kicked him.

"Stop," Leah said. "It's enough. Do not kill that pile of camel dung—his death will only be avenged."

"We will fight whoever comes to confront us, Mother," Shimon said.

"No," Leah had insisted. "Put him in a cart and bring him back to his own grounds. When you get there, should he happen to fall out upon some rocks . . . that cannot be helped." Reuben had gotten a cart, and then he and Judah had helped Shimon and Levi lift Lavan's limp body into it and push it far away from us.

Now, when Lavan spoke as if it was My Father and not he, himself, who was a threat to his daughters, Shimon and Levi broke from the group to relive the pummeling, but My Father stopped them. It would have been gratifying to watch, though, the fear on Lavan's face as My Brothers stepped forward was a measure of satisfaction.

Lavan quickly added to his speech: "Let this mound be a witness that my kinsmen and I are not to cross this mound to you and that you and your kinsmen shall not cross the mound to this side with hostile intent. May the god of Abraham and the god of Nakhor, our common ancestor, judge between us."

My Father swore agreement by the name of his father, Isaac, and turned his back on Lavan, never to look at him again. Lavan and his sons departed down the mountain, and My Father called the women and the girls from the tents. "Tonight, we will celebrate!" he shouted. And because he is My Father, he began to dance. If the melody in his head had words, we did not hear them, but the smile on his face and the joy in his steps brought us all some much-needed relief.

A feast was quickly prepared. On the same mountaintop where we had earlier dined in silence with our tormentor, we now drank barley beer and ate much of the dried fruit we had brought along for the journey. We made pita with not only flour and water and oil but also some of the herbs from the city. Before anyone ate of the bread, My Father lifted it above his head and said, "Elohim, Yah, God of My Father Abraham, God of My Father Isaac, thank You for allowing us to see this day when I am able to feast in freedom with my beloveds. We are able to eat of this bounty because of Your glory."

With that, My Father took a bite of the bread like a dog tearing into a bone. He even added dog sounds and encouraged us all to do the same. My Mother laughed at his playfulness and joined hands with him and Leah, and the three of them had an extra dance to themselves while the rest of us enjoyed the spiced bread.

CHAPTER 9

The morning after parting with Lavan, I was surprised to see Reuben and Judah laughing and joking over breakfast. Ahuvah, Annah, Deenah, and the mothers all sat in a circle braiding each other's hair. Tirzah, with not enough hair to braid, sat on her mother's lap and got it lovingly combed.

My Father was holding Emunah and giggling as she pulled on his beard and laughed. Even Shimon and Levi, though teasing Naftali about his flute, were more playful and less hurtful about it. There was an air of ease and relaxation among us that replaced the fear we had been holding as we fled Lavan.

Leah called me over to the circle of women and girls for a moment to sit next to her. She gave my head a little comb, but really, she leaned over to whisper in my ear: "Joseph, you were strong and brave yesterday. You did a good job helping your mother—my sister. I am grateful." She kissed me on the top of my head, then prompted me to stand. My Mother witnessed this exchange and smiled at me with her hands still in Annah's hair.

We stayed in Gilead for three days and three nights after Lavan's departure. It gave us a much-needed rest and allowed the animals to pasture without being driven. But the three days were more than just a rest—they were like a celebration. Never in my life, never in any of our lives, except My Father's, had we lived without Lavan. We were truly our own tribe, and we reveled in the freedom.

Of course, there was still much to be done, but it was joyful. The women sang as they cooked meals with the new spices from the city, and each night, as we sat to eat those meals, My Father told us another story of his homeland. One night, he told of when there had been famine in the land. "Once," he said, "long before I was born, even before my honored father was born, there was famine in the land. My grandfather Abraham was living in the land with my grandmother Sarah. They had already made the journey that we are making right now, and they had already settled in the land that Elohim had told Abraham would someday be his—be ours.

"But there was a famine in the land. Therefore, my beloved grandfather Abraham and my grandmother Sarah traveled south to Egypt, where there was food. But when they got there, they got much, much more than food." My Father was a seasoned storyteller, so we all leaned in a bit closer as he paused to make sure he had our attention.

"As they got close, Abraham realized that Sarah's beauty could endanger them. I never met my grandmother, but my grandfather assured me she was a beauty. While approaching Egypt, he began to fear for his life. It was one thing to die by famine, but it was another to die by the sword of a jealous pharaoh. You see, Abraham predicted that the pharaoh would find his wife as beautiful as he did and want to marry her. But unable to marry a married woman, he would kill her husband!"

We all gasped as My Father spoke of Abraham being killed by the pharaoh. This couldn't have happened as My Father said since the story took place before the birth of his own father. So, there would be a happy ending, but this fact was forgotten with the suspense of the story. "What did he do?" Dan asked.

"I am glad you asked, Dan. Abraham looked at his beautiful and beloved wife and asked her to please tell the Egyptians that she was his sister."

"But Father!" I burst out. "Why would he profess something untrue to be true?"

"Joseph, my boy," My Father said, "I will tell you what my grandfather told me when I asked him that very question when I wasn't much older than you. This is what he told me. He said, 'Jacob, she was in fact my sister from a different mother, so it was a truth, and a truth that would save my life.'"

"But surely the pharaoh would learn the other piece of the truth," Judah said. It had been what I was thinking as well. I rubbed my chin with my thumb, knowing that neither of us had grown hair in this short time yet still amazed that such wisdom could grow in before a beard.

"He did, Judah, and he was honorable when he learned it. But let me first share with you the wisdom that my grandfather imparted that day. My grandfather said, 'Jacob, she was in fact my sister from a different mother, so it was a truth, and a truth that would save my life. Jacob,' he continued, 'sometimes people believe what they think more than they believe what they see with their own eyes; even among kinsmen.'"

Asher popped up. "Good day," he said to Dan. "I am a trader from the far north. I have come to sell you my sandals, for I will not need them in the north. Would you like to buy some sandals from a trader from the far north?"

"Indeed, I would, good sir," Dan replied. "Such handsome sandals they are, and on such a handsome young man. Surely, you are a fine trader and someone whom I would wish to get to know if only we were able to spend more time together."

This little performance had Naftali rolling on the floor with laughter. Gad walked up to him and said, "Young lad, this is not the way to show respect to others. Sit nicely. You must listen to me now, as you can clearly see that I am your father." This only increased Naftali's laughing.

We never did hear the ending of My Father's story. We spent the rest of the evening light laughing with each other, pretending there could be situations where we did not recognize one another as our very own kin, and telling tales—each one more outrageous than the next.

Storytelling was a wonderful way to pass the time in Gilead. As promised, I told Reuben of the night in the city; he told me of this night outside the walls. Deenah and I sat together and sniffed each other's wrists over and over, trying to get any last scent of cinnamon and retelling of when the girl had given it to us to keep the memory of the smell fresh in our noses. We all ate together and drank together; My Father didn't have to go far afield because there was no far field. Nor was there a garden or a well or looms or much work at all. This made for an unexpected holiday but could also not sustain us for long.

On the third night, My Father told us we would break camp in the morning. He told us one last story on our final night on the mountain. It was the story we had all heard many times, about the angels he had met going up and down the ladder when he'd left his homeland and journeyed to Haran. I fell asleep that night imagining one day when I would tell my own children the story of living in Haran and then leaving it to return to the place of My Father's birth. I imagined telling them of the night at the inn, the day of crossing the great river, and the Festival of Parting with Lavan.

ON OUR SIXTH morning in Gilead, which was the fourth after Lavan's departure, we broke camp and continued our journey. This time, rather than leading the line, My Father sent some of the servants ahead of us as scouts. I still accompanied him as we walked together, and we were still first of the tribe, but My Father thought it best to have the servants see Esau first. That is, for Esau to see them first before seeing My Father.

So, he instructed them to go ahead of us, more quickly than the rest, to meet Esau and tell him that we were coming. Even after voicing his objections to Lavan the night before, it seemed to me that My Father was uncertain about reuniting with his twin. He gave the servants a message. He said, "Tell Esau that his servant Jacob has been with Lavan until now. Tell him that

I, Jacob, have acquired cattle, donkeys, flocks, and servants and that I send him this message in hopes of gaining his favor."

The servants went on ahead of us, and as I saw them disappear in the distance, I thought of My Father making this journey the first time, fleeing from his brother. Now, he was supplicating himself before him. I wondered who this uncle of mine was. Was he like Lavan? Was he like My Father?

"What is your brother like?" I asked.

To my surprise, My Father laughed at my question. "Oh, my son, Esau is my brother. He is like a brother. You have many—surely you know what a brother is like." I gave this some thought. Each of My Brothers were different, except perhaps for Shimon and Levi who had grown in the womb together and had rarely been separated since. Maybe My Father and Esau were like that. Yet Reuben was like My Father already: strong, responsible, good with sheep. And so was Judah, yet he was different from Reuben, even though they shared both a mother and father, as did Issachar and Zevvy. Gad and Asher, Dan and Naftali, they also shared both a mother and father. I had no brother who shared both of these with me, none who shared a sleeping mat with me at night or shared work with me during the day. I wasn't sure I knew.

"I know My Brothers," I said, "but not yours."

My Father laughed again. "Very well, then, my son. I will tell you. Esau and I shared the same womb, but once we left, our lives were different. I wanted to be the first born, but he beat me to it and never tired of showing me that he was bigger, faster, hairier, and older. We kept to ourselves often. I was in the tents studying and was always available to my beloved mother should she need something. Esau was often far afield, chasing after a beast to conquer and bring back to boast to our father. He always won Father's favor, while I never managed to," he sighed.

"But though we were different, we were not always at odds. As brothers, there were many times that we wrestled, fought, argued, and didn't speak to each other. But there were also times when we went on adventures, basked together in the glory of the sunshine, played childhood games, raced up and down hills, and even shared secrets. Joseph, I know you are the only son of your mother, but you see the other children together, so you know what it's like. So it was with my brother and me."

I felt a pang of jealousy. While it was true that I enjoyed not needing to share My Mother's affections or attention, I also missed out on the camaraderie that I saw evident among My Siblings. Gad and Asher had each other—and Annah. Leah's tent was nearly crowded when the young men weren't out in the fields. But even when they were, Ahuvah, Issachar, Zevvy, Deenah, and Emunah had each other. When My Mother slept in My Father's tent, Bilhah moved her sleeping rug closer to mine, but Naftali, Dan, and Tirzah stayed in their area of the tent.

There was a closeness of brothers sharing space that did not exist in the sleeping area that I shared with My Mother. More than once, I had quietly moved closer to them in the night. But they slept huddled together like the dogs, breathing easily, warm and content in the shared place. Naftali and Dan were quiet when I came closer, even though I got the feeling that when it was just them, they spoke more. Still, I was glad for the company and imagined My Father having that company with his brother.

"Tell me of one of the adventures," I asked. "Or one of the secrets you shared."

"Come now, my son. Secrets are secrets. Even all these years later. But I will tell you of an adventure." My Father's voice and feet quickened with excitement. "There was one time when Esau insisted that I go hunting with him. He had been into the fields with me a number of times to watch over the sheep. Not because he wanted to, but because it was lambing time and all of us needed to help. Most of the time, I was practicing my studies, but I learned to cherish the time in the field. I tried to tell Esau that usually, it is quiet there. Mostly, it was time to walk and look at the clouds and be with the land.

"Esau never experienced this since he was so keen on hunting. He began chasing the smaller animals when we were half your height. He was quick and had a good instinct for it. I could have been quick, too, but I didn't want to chase the animals. One time, when we were much older, he took me to look for deer in the forests on the hills. He gave me a set of bow and arrows that he had fashioned just for me. It was not as ornate as the one he carried, but, of course, he used his often. He then spent some time showing me the skill needed for hunting deer.

"We went off together for the day. We walked in silence to the forest. I followed my brother, we didn't walk side by side like you and I are doing now," he told me. "It was important to stay quiet so as not to cause the animals to stir. When we got to the woods, it was even more important to stay quiet. We crouched together, silently, invisible by a big rock, and waited for the unsuspecting deer." My father paused his walking to crouch as he had done that day.

"We waited and waited. And my son, the truth is, I liked it almost as much as I now like watching the sheep. I could understand that my brother enjoyed this quiet time in the woods the same way that I enjoyed my quiet time by the tents. I was content and at peace. And then all at once, Esau stood up and shot an arrow out in front of him, which hit a deer right in the soft spot where the top of its chest meets its neck, and it fell. Everything from Esau standing until the deer falling happened almost faster than I could see. My brother is a skilled hunter.

"And a strong man. He carried that deer back to the campground. He insisted on doing it himself without a hand from me. After all, not only had he shot it himself but this had been the only time I went hunting with him; he always carried the game back himself. Also, I know he enjoyed the moment when he would come close to our campgrounds and see our father meditating in the field but then open his eyes when he felt our presence. A huge smile crossed his face when he saw Esau carrying that deer. 'Well done,' he'd said."

"You are a strong man too," I said. Surely, this uncle was not stronger than My Father. I had seen him carry a sheep or a ram over his shoulders many times, just as he described Esau doing with the deer. My Father could remove a stone well covering without any assistance and lift My Mother onto a camel.

My Father laughed and put his hand on my shoulder. "Yes, my son, I am a strong man too," he said. "Just as strong as my brother. We differ in many ways, but we are well matched in physical strength. I will remind him of this when we meet, if need be."

This pleased me and calmed me. Soon, we would meet this brother, and I had not forgotten that the last time he was in My

Father's life, he had wished to end it. My Father and I walked in silence again until close to evening, when his scouts came back reporting that Esau was coming to meet My Father with four hundred men! This made me fearful again, and I worried that it did the same for My Father as well.

While the messengers stood awaiting further direction, My Father began to shake. This caused me great distress, and I saw that the men were concerned also. "Kemke," he said, and his trusted servant stepped forward from the group of messengers. "Kemke, you must bring me my children. Those who are with the flocks must join me here now. And then you must divide the camp into two camps. They shall be equal in size and number. But all the men in the first camp shall give their arms to the men in the second. We will meet my brother peacefully. I do not wish him to think that I come here to harm him. I do not. But if he is determined to kill, then at least the second half of the camp will be able to defend itself and escape and survive."

We walked on in silence, joined by My Mother and the other women and children who had been a few paces apart from us with the camels. Judah was the next to join us, followed by Shimon and Dan, Levi and Naftali, and finally, Reuben from the back of our caravan. When we were all together, My Father said we would stop there for the night. Unlike in Gilead where we had set up our camp for a few days, and unlike along the road where we had each camped where we were in the caravan, this time, we camped together but without setting up our tents.

The women prepared bread for the evening. No herbs this time, just a simple bread for our meal. Some of us went out to gather wood for a fire, and some went to gather fruit. Ahuvah and Annah brought buckets of water for washing from the nearby stream, and My Father went alone into the flock. A short while later, he came back with a kid. Its neck had been speedily broken, and it lay limp over My Father's shoulders. He spent the rest of the light preparing it over the fire, and as the sun began to set, we all sat down to eat of this sacred meal together.

Before our first bites, My Father stepped away from the flames and directed his commanding voice to the sky. "God of My Father Abraham and God of My Father Isaac, Elohim, who said, 'Return to your native land, and I will deal bountifully with you,' I am unworthy of the steadfast kindness You have shown me, Your servant. Only with my staff did I cross the Jordan River, and now I have become two camps. Save me, please, from the hands of my brother, that is, from the hands of Esau. I fear he may come and strike me down as well as the mothers and children. You have said, 'I will deal bountifully with you and make your offspring as bountiful as the sands of the sea, which are too numerous to count.'"

He then turned to address us. "This meal has been provided to us by a generous god. Elohim has transformed me from one man into a large tribe that will become a nation. My children, I have been blessed with the blessing of my father Abraham, and thus so have you. We will someday be as numerous as the sands of the sea with the help of Elohim. Eat of this bounty in gratitude."

And so, we did. We were as silent as we were when eating with Lavan, but the feeling was a different feeling. At once, I feared Esau and yet trusted Elohim to deliver us from any danger, just as we had been delivered from the danger of Lavan.

When the meal ended, My Father began to chant: "My God is My Strength and My Salvation. My God is My Strength and

My Salvation. My God is My Strength and My Salvation." My Mother rose and brought her drum to the circle. When she returned, Leah did the same, followed by Zilpah and Bilhah, Ahuvah and Annah. With the heartbeat of the drums and the breath of the chant, our bodies were consumed with the spirit of Elohim. Sometime in the night, I fell asleep with these words on my lips, my stomach full, and my thoughts in peace.

In the morning, My Father selected the finest gifts for his brother: 200 she-goats and 20 he-goats, 200 ewes and 20 rams, 30 nursing camels with their colts, 40 cows and 10 bulls, 20 female donkeys and 10 male donkeys. This alone would not make My Uncle rich upon receiving it, and neither would it leave us wanting. But the difference in the size of our possessions was clear to the eye, so the gift was a generous one.

My Father called to his most trusted servants. "Take these gifts to my brother," he said. "Drove by drove, with a distance between each, bring them to Esau. When he asks who you are, where you are going, and whom these animals belong to, say to him, 'These animals belong to your servant Jacob. He sends them as a gift to you, and he himself is behind us.' This way, if I send him gifts, perhaps I will calm him before we meet, and he will show me favor when we do."

He had the men repeat the message before leaving. "Be sure to tell him that I, myself, am behind you," he stressed. The messengers nodded their understanding. The men departed with the animals, group by group, leaving a space between them.

My Father clapped me on the shoulder and smiled into my eyes. "Thank you, Joseph—you and your dream—for reminding me of the importance of giving gifts." I felt my cheeks rise as my face filled with a smile of pride. I was glad I had told him of the dream.

I saw the men cross the animals over the Yabbok, the narrow stream that flowed as a silent boundary between My Father and his brother; we stayed in the camp that day. There was tension in the air as we prepared the animals that were being gifted and watched over the ones that we would keep. All the work being done that day was around these gifts for My Uncle. He would receive them that same day, and our paths would meet the next. As the sun began to set in the sky, we had a quick meal of barley cakes and beer and all collapsed on our mats, exhausted from the preparations and anticipation.

Immediately upon falling asleep, I had a dream. This dream was of two men reuniting after a lifetime apart. One had crossed a great river to meet the other. They fell on each other's necks and wept as one. Tears fell down their faces and left thirty-three marks on the ground at their feet. The ground was made of stone, but the water from the tears turned it to the finest grazing grass for sheep. Eleven sheep ate contentedly of the grass.

How long I slept after this dream I do not know. I was awakened by the sound of My Father's voice when the moon was high in the sky. "Wake now!" he shouted. Not at me but at everyone at once. "Wake and roll your mats. It is time to cross the stream."

We all startled awake at once and began to move to My Father's orders, except for Levi who dared to challenge him. "What do you mean by this, having us wake in the night like thieves? If our uncle means us harm, we will fight him with honor, not flee from him."

My Father faced his outspoken son. Levi was almost the height of a man, but not yet. The two stood face-to-face with Levi's eyes up to My Father's mouth. This mouth was speaking harshly now. "If you wish to act with honor, you will honor your father's instructions," he said and then turned to Reuben: "You will take my wives and my children across this stream to a distance that allows enough room for the animals to follow behind you. Spend the night there."

We all followed Reuben, even Levi, while My Father went back and forth, back and forth across the water with the camels, the cattle, the donkeys with the carts, and the spotted and speckled flock he had worked so hard for. He and all the men made countless crossings to accomplish this. No boats were needed for this stream, and no swimming. In the heat of the summer, it was narrow and shallow, not even as high as my young waist. But there were many crossings needed because of the many animals. Our numbers were still large, even after the gifts My Father had sent to his brother. I was proud to be of the tribe of Jacob.

When the last of the animals were on our side, My Father crossed one more time. We saw him put out his lantern on the far side of the stream, and we made a collective gasp. "Coward," Shimon said. "He will flee from his brother once again and leave us here to be killed or become captives of his enemy. But I will not do it. If our father will not face a man who wishes to do him harm, I will. I will not be known as the son of a coward; I will be known as the man to be feared."

I could not bear to hear him speak of My Father this way. "My Father is no coward," I yelled. "And he will not be conquered by Esau. I had a dream this very night that the two men met and embraced like brothers. Their tears lead to pastureland for our sheep, which grew in number as our tribe became richer and richer."

"Nonsense," Levi said, still angry from his confrontation with My Father, and spurred on by Shimon's words. "What is the dream of a boy compared to a man abandoning his wives and children in the night?"

"We could have stayed in Haran," Shimon said. "Why bring us so far from home just to die in these hills? Lavan was useless. We were the ones who amassed his fortune. We could have continued to do that. Our name would have grown great upon his death when everyone saw that we were to thank for Lavan's success."

"We did nothing for Lavan," Reuben corrected. "It was our father who did that work. He is a hard worker."

"Perhaps," Levi said, "but also a disgrace."

"Silence," Leah said. At that, not another word was uttered for the rest of the night. And I don't think any one of us slept at all.

CHAPTER 10

When the faintest light entered the sky in the morning, we all squinted to see over the land and the stream that were between us and where we had last seen My Father. The water was still, and the land, barren. Did it know that our lives were standing still until we saw My Father again?

As the sky became lighter and the stars faded behind the blue, there was still no sign of My Father. The animals were beginning to wake, and we would need to either move on or set up camp soon. Meanwhile, we all stared into the distance, hopeful and scared at the same time. When this seemed to go on forever, Leah spoke. "Reuben. You are the firstborn son and the head of this tribe if . . . ," she said, trailing off briefly. How could there be an if? We were here because Elohim had promised My Father the land, had promised him a safe journey. "Reuben," her voice was stronger this time. "Go and see what has happened."

"I will go too," Shimon said. "I am secondborn. I will be witness to my father's disappearance."

"Secondborn by a breath," Levi said. "It is as if we are both the secondborn. I will not wait here while you go. I will also go with you and Reuben." Shimon and Levi stood up.

"Stop," My Mother said. "Joseph is also the firstborn son. And he is old enough and strong enough. He will go with Reuben." My father had four wives: My Mother, Leah, Zilpah—Leah's maidservant, and Bilhah—My Mother's maidservant. But Zilpah and Bilhah were only his wives because they had both borne him sons on behalf of My Mother and Leah. As I was the eldest of the favored wife, the one who should have been born first, and as Reuben was the one who had actually been born first, we went together.

Reuben and I walked the short distance that we had traveled in the night. We were quiet for a long time. I had fears in my head about what might have happened to My Father. Or worse—what he might have done. When Reuben spoke, I realized he was having similar thoughts, but he also bore the weight of becoming the head of the tribe. Looking at Gilead ahead of him, he said, "This is nice land. It is far from Haran but only a short distance to the great river. The land is fertile, and the grazing, good. It might be a nice place to settle for a time."

We were so close to the land of My Father's birth, the land that was promised to his grandfather Abraham. The land where My Grandfather Isaac still lived. The one that was promised to My Father and his children—me. I did not wish to settle just outside this land. But I also did not wish to settle anywhere without My Father. Reuben would make a fine head of a tribe—his own, though, not My Father's. Just as I was preparing to yell this at My Brother, he gave out a yell of his own. More of a screech. I followed his gaze and saw My Father lying on the hard ground, just on the other side of the stream.

Reuben and I broke into a run. We splashed across the stream. He was faster than I was, but my legs took me more quickly than I thought them able, and I arrived at My Father's side just steps after Reuben. My Brother cradled My Father's head in his arm. "Joseph," he breathed. "Bring water."

I ripped my waterskin from around my neck and left it with My Brother while I raced back to the stream. I had nothing with which to carry water, so I removed my belt and soaked it in the stream. I noticed that the water was refreshing, a little cool from the night that had just passed. I brought the soaked cloth back to My Brother, and he placed it on My Father's forehead.

I sat next to them and cried silently. I did not like seeing My Father like this, his head cradled like that of a baby, his body broken on the ground, one leg awkwardly to the side. I did not like being awake all night. I did not like hearing Shimon and Levi speak badly of him. I didn't even like being the firstborn, sent to find My Father in this state. I was grateful that Reuben was there, older, wiser, and more experienced in the role. I fell asleep next to My Father.

I awoke when My Father stirred. He moaned with pain.

"I can set that for you," Reuben said quietly. My Father winced and nodded. "Joseph," Reuben continued, "bring me a stick, one at least the length and thickness of your arm." I ran off, grateful for the task, and returned quickly. Reuben took the stick from me and placed it in My Father's mouth, and My Father bit down on it. He then placed My Father's head in my arm and stood up, having me sit where he had sat while he knelt next to My Father's stray leg.

"Look away," Reuben instructed. I saw My Father look up to the sky, so I did the same. I kept my gaze there even as My Father let out a scream that I did not know could come from a man, especially one clenching a stick in his teeth. He sounded like a sheep using its last breath as a wail of suffering after being surprised by a lion. I did not see My Father's tears since I kept my gaze to the sky, but I felt them fall on my wrist and slide down to the earth.

When My Father removed the stick from his mouth, I gathered the courage to look at him again. He was looking at Reuben. "Reuben," My Father said, his voice quiet with exhaustion, "you are my firstborn, my might, the beginning of my strength. You excel in power. You have learned well. Thank you for coming to my aid and setting my leg."

Reuben blushed and bowed his head.

"Come now," My Father said, addressing us both, "help me to stand." We each took an arm and pulled My Father to stand on his good leg. We stayed there as he held onto us and worked to maintain his balance. Then he gently touched his right leg—his injured leg—to the ground. His face turned to a wince, but he did not wail again.

"It doesn't seem to be broken," Reuben said. "It was pulled out of your hip, but I put it back in place. I wish you a quick healing." My Father clapped Reuben on the shoulder and nodded. We walked together slowly, My Father with each of his firstborn sons at his sides and dragging his leg behind him. The steps were small, but each one gave him a little more experience and a little more confidence in walking.

The progress was slow. When we reached the side of the stream, My Father asked us to help him sit on a boulder to rest. We had only traveled a few paces, but, of course, we honored his request. He took off his sandals and allowed the cool water to wash over his feet. He looked back to where we had come from. Following his example, I saw scuff marks in the dirt. I hadn't noticed them before because I had been too busy tending to his needs, but now I could clearly see evidence of a struggle.

"My brother Esau is a hunter. He would not approach his prey with four hundred men but would approach alone, quietly, so as not to startle the animal away. The only thing I could do to prepare was to move all of you. Then I sat alone, waiting. He didn't make me wait long, and he did succeed in surprising me, even though I knew he would come. He jumped on my back from behind, and I felt the familiar weight of the brother I hadn't seen in a lifetime, smelled his familiar scent, and remembered the familiar fear that had so often accompanied me in his presence.

"I took a deep breath, breathing in the strength and promise of Elohim and breathing out the fear. I shook my brother off my back and turned to face him. At once, we locked arms and began wrestling, or we resumed our wrestling from so long ago. We are well matched in physical strength, and we stirred up a lot of dust in our mutual physical struggle. But he hurt me instantly with his words.

"'You are a coward,' he said. This is what he called me. A coward. And he was right. I fled for my life, but he was the one left behind. He was the one who stayed. He told me of the gentle care he has been providing for our father, visiting him often and bringing him hunt, for all these many years. I did none of that. While I longed for my parents and my homeland, Esau looked after them." My Father shook his head in disappointment.

"But even with these strong words, Esau did not stop wrestling with me, nor I him. Perhaps I was a coward to flee from him all those years ago, but I would not do it again. If he would conquer me, he would work to do it; I would not make it easy for him. Thus, we wrestled the whole night. When the dawn was breaking, he pulled my leg out from under me, inflicting this wound. But it did not end our struggle the way he'd expected. I continued to challenge him, even from the ground.

"As the light began to enter the sky, he wished for me to let him go. What a change that was! From complaining that I'd left him to wishing I would leave him again all in the space of one night. My brother always was a man of short view. Other than waiting for a hunt, he had no patience. It was that hastiness that had led him to trade me his birthright for a pot of stew. Here it was again. But I told Esau that I would not let him go until he blessed me.

"Eager to return to his tribe before they found him missing, my brother conceded. 'What is your name?' he asked me. I answered him with my name: Jacob. 'You got that name from trying to take my place, battling me to be first, even holding my heel as we exited the womb. You were always trying to take what was mine. That was who you were when you were last here. But now your name shall no longer be Jacob, but Israel. For in these twenty years, you have built a life apart from me. In that time, you have absorbed experiences from divine beings and human beings, and you have prevailed. You return here no longer the man whom I hated, but a new man whom I shall let pass in peace.'

"My brother spoke deep truth. Even in that moment, I had learned from someone divine and human: Esau himself. All these many years later, I realized what I should have known before: he is as much of Elohim as I am. I asked my brother to tell me his new name as well; surely, he had changed in the twenty years in which he had cared for our honored parents and grown his own tribe, but he would not tell me. He left at once to return to his tribe, and I collapsed in exhaustion. In this place, I have seen the merciful face of my god in the face of my brother. From now on, I shall no longer call this place the bank of the Yabbok river, but Penni-El, Face of God."

Reuben spoke next. "Joseph, run back to the camp and tell them our father yet lives. Bring the young men back here to help carry him so that he may save his strength."

I wanted to stay with My Father in my place of honor as his firstborn son, but I did as I was told. My news was met with great relief as well as concern. My Mother had me tell her many times exactly where My Father was injured and whether he was in pain and could walk. I assured her that he was strong, and I told Leah of how her son had put the leg back.

I brought Shimon, Levi, and Judah down the trail to meet My Father. I saw their faces express shock when they saw him leaning heavily on Reuben as he slowly limped forward, but they quickly ran up to help him. The four young men gingerly lifted My Father and began carrying him back to camp. It was then that I first noticed that he no longer had his staff with him. Certainly, he had set it aside, or it had been tossed aside, in the struggle. Here was a way I could help.

"I will go back to Penni-El and get the staff," I said, proud to be useful and also showing My Father and My Brothers that I knew the name of the sacred place of the struggle. My Father smiled at me, and I ran back to the stream.

Crossing the stream, I quickly returned to the scuff marks beside the water. I saw the imprint of My Father's body where we had found him, but much of the other evidence of struggle was already buried by the wind. Only if one knew what to look for would they know what an important place this was. Luckily, I knew what to look for. I searched nearby for My Father's staff. It was not lying in the dirt or standing against a rock awaiting his return. My Father said he'd known Esau was coming. Would he have hidden his staff so that his brother would find him unarmed? Or so that his brother wouldn't break the staff he relied on for shepherding?

I thought that before running off, perhaps I should have asked My Father where his staff was, but, instead, I walked through the thicket to see if it was hiding there. It was only a matter of moments before I accidentally stepped on the curved end that was sticking out from beneath a large bramble. I took the staff out and held it upright.

How grown up I felt! Holding a shepherd's staff—My Father's own staff—in my hand made me feel like a real man. I checked my chin with my thumb, which was quickly becoming a habit. There were still no whiskers growing, but it didn't make me feel less important. I walked tall and proud with My Father's staff back to the bank of the Yabbok, back to the place that he had named Penni-El, and back across the stream, pretending that sheep were following me along the way.

After leading my sheep for a time, I suddenly got the sense that we were all going astray. This did not look like the way back to where I had started that morning. With My Father's staff in my hand, though, I did not fear. I asked myself what a shepherd would do and decided that a shepherd would turn around and follow his footsteps back to the water. And so, I did. It was upon arriving there that fear began to creep in.

I could suddenly see how easy it had been for me to have chosen the wrong path to follow. Along both banks of the river, there were many places to enter between the hills and many places to climb over them. Suddenly, I could no longer remember which one I wanted to take, much less which of the many options would lead me to My Father. Once again, I asked myself what a shepherd would do, but this time, my answer was that I was not a shepherd, and so I did not know.

I sat on a boulder and cried.

Just as I was running out of tears and the sun was approaching the top of the sky, I heard my name being called. I looked toward the sound. "Reuben!" I called with relief. "Reuben, I thought I would sit by the stream forever, never to see My Family again, left only with My Father's staff as a reminder of what I'd once had."

Reuben laughed at what did not seem funny to me. "Don't worry, Joseph," he said. "If you ever get separated, I will come back for you. Just like now. All right?" I nodded my head in understanding. Reuben took my hand like the hand of a baby, but even worse, he took the staff. Then we went to rejoin the others.

CHAPTER 11

It was time for all of us to meet this new uncle. My Father was no longer nervous, though he was still limping. He had rested after being brought back to the camp, and someone had made him a poultice to place on his hip and a tincture to drink. He walked slowly but seemingly with only a little discomfort.

As the distance between our tribe and Esau's closed, we could see the great number of people approaching. My Father separated his children, assigning each to walk with our mothers. No longer did I walk with him, no longer did anyone ride on a camel, no longer did the brothers watch the herds. This day was entirely different from any other. And while, perhaps, I should have been most alert to the meeting of this uncle, what struck me the most was being the last in line of children.

I was always acutely reminded of my birth order by My Brothers, but I was also favored by My Father. I had just enjoyed many days of his company at the front of the tribe, and now I was sent to the back. This injustice stung my heart like a scorpion sting to the skin. Just as My Father made peace with his brother, I began to harbor a resentment toward My Uncle, for it seemed to me that he was the cause of my demotion.

My Mother distracted me from my disappointment. "I'm not afraid of this man, Joseph, and you needn't be either. On the very first day I met your father, he removed the rock that was covering the well on his own while other men stood there waiting for more men to arrive so they could do it together. But not your father. He had the strength of ten men.

"Not only that," she went on, "but he felt the need to wait for no man. When he needed something, he took care of it. And the same has been true of him every day since that very first. He has taken care of his needs and mine for many years now as well as those of our whole tribe. He has worked hard to do so. It has not been easy. Many nights, I comforted him and reminded him of his strengths and abilities and his pact with Elohim. But it matters not whom he faces today or any other day. We are always safe with him."

We watched as My Father approached Esau, bowing seven times along the way. From my distance at the back of the line, I saw them embrace. Then I saw Gad and Asher and Annah with their mother, Zilpah, unfairly meet him first, bowing like My Father had. Bilhah with Dan and Naftali approached next, little Tirzah holding her mother's hand so she wouldn't run off, and followed the examples of Zilpah and the others.

Next, Leah presented herself to Esau. I could not hear or see her well at the distance I was forced to maintain, but I could easily see the small tribe that was hers alone. Reuben, the eldest, led his brothers and sisters in an orderly line. Even Shimon and Levi took their places without quarreling, side by side and second in the line. They were followed by Judah and Ahuvah. It was easy to forget that they were twins as they were never together. Seeing them walk side by side reminded me that they had shared Leah's womb just as Shimon and Levi had done before them. Issachar was next in the line, then Zevulun, and finally Deenah—a child of six summers just like me, yet she was meeting him first! She carried Emunah on her hip.

Even from my unfair distance behind My Siblings, I could see Esau's body change when he saw Emunah. His shoulders softened, and he looked from Emunah to My Father and back again. I was used to Emunah's unusual features: her wide-set eyes and her always parted lips that made room for her tongue. Everything was harder for her than for the rest of us. She was just beginning to hold her weight on her own two feet, and she said only a few words, most of which were impossible to understand. But those facts were often paled by her joy. Emunah found joy in everything, and it shone through her face and body. Esau reached a finger out to stroke her cheek, and she put her arms up to be lifted by him. Esau lifted My Sister and spun her over his head as she squealed with excitement.

Esau hugged Emunah close to his chest before handing her back to Deenah, and finally, My Mother and I approached him from our distance. As we did, we prostrated ourselves like the ones before us. When I arose, Esau had stepped forward, and I choked on my breath. This man standing in front of me was the embodiment of my dream. Every bit of skin that could be seen was covered in red hair. The hair on his head was red, on his arms, on his legs—all of it red. Other than that, he was the spitting image of My Father, had My Father been a slightly larger man.

I fell to my knees in shock as well as gratitude to Elohim for giving me dreams, even if I did not understand them at the time. I recalled the rainbow that sprouted forth from the place where My Father and the other man—his brother—had embraced in my dream and smiled with hope. Hope for what? I did not know. My Mother thought I was bowing before Esau and pulled me to my feet. "Once was enough, Joseph," she whispered harshly in my ears. But My Uncle smiled.

Esau addressed My Father. "Who are all these people with you?" he asked.

"These are my wives and children that Elohim has blessed me with." My Father introduced each one of us by name, beginning with Reuben and ending with Emunah, who squealed with delight and reached her arms out when he looked at her. But My Father did not pick her up the way he usually did after such a request, for he was busy talking to his brother.

"What do you mean by this whole camp that came out to meet me?" Esau asked.

"I sent the gifts to gain the favor of my lord," My Father explained.

"I have much, Brother," Esau said. "Let what is yours remain yours."

My Father persisted, though, eager to be able to present gifts to his brother. "Please, if I have found favor in your eyes, please accept these gifts, for to see your face is like seeing the face of Elohim. Please accept this gift, for Elohim has shown me favor, and I have everything I need."

Esau needed no more persuasion. He accepted the gifts My Father had sent before us and protested no more. Instead, he offered to guide us on the next part of our journey. My Father declined this offer, saying he didn't want to press the animals and the children at Esau's pace, nor did he want to slow Esau down. It was in that moment I realized we could have joined our two tribes, joined our two camps into one.

Although we had been living next to My Mother's father, I had always thought of Lavan's sons as nothing more than his sons. In truth, they were My Mother's brothers and every bit as much My Uncles as Esau was. What would it be like to camp beside the children of Esau? Would he have a son my age? Surely, he had a youngest son of some age. A boy who would understand my plight. Would Esau's sons be skilled at hunting, having learned from their father, the way that the sons of My Father were skilled shepherds?

I was not to find out.

Esau departed that day and went back to his campground in Seir. We traveled only until the evening, and then we set up our tents. My Father said we would stay there a while, building pens for the animals in the morning, giving the flocks a rest, and pausing our journey until the end of the dry season.

I THOUGHT THAT would be the end of our adventures, but I was mistaken. While it was true that we did not travel for another two moons, our new home was nothing like the old one. The tents were put up, and the rugs and pillows were put in their familiar places. But we had no garden to eat from. Our meals came mostly from the milk of the nursing goats—which we shared sparingly—fruit that was gathered from the wild, and a cow from the herd every few days. Beer was made from the barley we brought with us, but the other supplies were only moderately touched since we would need them later.

The men spent most of the days in the field tending to the animals. My Father allowed me to accompany Judah, whom he trusted to train me well. I spent a whole glorious month with him. He instructed me on all a shepherd must know. Judah taught me what plants the sheep may eat from freely and which they must be steered away from, lest they eat them and get sick. He taught me which bugs I must pick off the sheep and which they may brush away with their own tails if they like.

It was during that time that I learned to use a slingshot. Judah made me one of my own with small pieces of leather and rope. He sewed the ends of the two leather strips together so that they made a cup for the rock, and then he attached the rope. My sling was just as long as his. He told me that even though he was taller, he would not use a longer sling because they made the shot less accurate.

When the pieces of the sling were attached and looked ready, Judah said, "There is one more thing you must do." Then he took his knife back out. Judah used his knife to separate the strands of the rope at the ends. "Joseph, one day you will be strong enough to sling this very fast, and when that day comes, you will want the air to blow through these strands and not push up against a firm ending of the rope, for if that happens, it will make a sound loud enough to scare away the flock and warn the wild beast that you are near."

Once again, Judah had amazed me with his wisdom. "These are just things that shepherds learn, Joseph. Our father taught us young men to make slings and told us about the noise, and now I am telling you. One day, you will teach this to another shepherd. And one day before that, when you are as tall as I am, I will even teach you how to use the end of your staff to help you sling your rock farther. But that is for another day."

We went down to the wadi to gather rocks. We looked for smooth ones, the size that would fill my hand when closed, smaller than Judah's hand. He taught me which ones were too heavy and which were too light, and we left those behind. We carried our small pile of ammunition far away from any of the animals. "If a predator comes," Judah said, "you must be able to defend not only yourself but the flock also. Remember, a lion or wolf has little interest in you but wishes to take the smallest of the sheep so it can easily get away with a meal. It is our job to protect them."

Judah placed a rock in his slingshot and instructed me to watch carefully as he swung it over his head. He said I should pay particular attention when he let the rock fly forth. "I must look at what I want to hit. I look right to the center, as if I could see inside of it," he said. "In this case, it is that date palm over there. You see the point on the trunk that is just about your height? That is the one I will hit." He pointed. "And when the time is right and my hips are lined up, I let the rock loose from the sling and . . ." His voice trailed off and was replaced by the thwack of the rock hitting the tree trunk.

It took me many practices to just get the rock to leave the slingshot when I wanted it to and many more practices to send it in a specific direction. But Judah was patient, continually giving me advice that helped me improve my abilities. By the end of the fourth day, I was fairly confident that I would not unintentionally hit a person or animal, even if I wasn't fully sure that I could hit a wild beast purposefully. Judah assured me that I showed enough skill and determination that I would continue to improve.

That month, I also learned how to shear sheep. Because we needed to leave Haran while Lavan was at the shearing, our own flock had made the long journey in their full coats. They were hot and uncomfortable, and their wool needed to be used for weaving or trading. Although I was the least experienced with the sheep, none of My Brothers were good at shearing either, as they had always taken the sheep to the experts. Nonetheless, we did the best we could and just laughed at those naked sheep with their bad haircuts.

I learned a lot that month with Judah and thought I would have many more such months—a lifetime of shepherding, but I was quickly proven wrong. After only those few days of settling into the new land, it was time to pay a visit to Isaac and Rebekah. I was to meet My Grandparents.

To prepare, My Father took all his sons to the well and had us draw water for washing. Normally, we would bathe in a stream, but the days were hot, and the wadis were dry, and he did not want us to walk far and become covered in dust again before presenting us to his parents. As it was, our tunics were beaten mercilessly to remove as much dust as possible. Levi and Shimon had almost beaten each other after they finished with their tunics because they liked swinging the brooms so much, but My Father quickly put a stop to it.

Leah worked for many days to fashion new belts for everyone. My Father and his wives wore a dark purple adornment around their midsections with beautiful white stitching in lined patterns on the edges. For her own children, Leah made belts that were bright pink and had pomegranates stitched in white. Each belt had nine pomegranates, representing each of her nine children. My belt was the same as that of the children of Zilpah and Bilhah: an undyed gray.

The difference was clear. "Why does my son have an unadorned belt?" My Father asked Leah.

"I mean no disrespect," Leah answered. "I simply ran out of time. But these belts are not the belts of servants. Look at the fine weaving." Indeed, the weaving was of excellent quality and even ebbed and flowed in different sections, clearly in a pattern like birds flapping their wings open and shut again.

"We cannot leave like this," My Father said. We all looked around. We were already in formation for traveling to My Grandfather's tent. The journey was to take less than a day, but we had already spent the morning gathering two fine lambs and an abundance of fruits and wine to bring with us. Those had already been placed in donkey carts, and Kemke had brought twenty camels for us to ride on. My Father wanted his parents to see him approach with his tribe and immediately know that he had done well.

What would we do now if not leave? "Leah, you must at least stitch some ornamentation onto the ends of Joseph's belt." With that, he removed my belt himself and gave it to his first wife. Red-faced, she went to get her sewing supplies. My Father left the rest of us standing next to the camels, ready to go. "Stay here," he said. "I will go and talk to Elohim some more to prepare for this reunion. Come and get me when Leah is finished."

He was gone, and Leah was gone, longer than some of the younger brothers could wait. Dan and Asher began kicking some rocks around with their toes. Gad and Naftali chased each other around the camels. I could see the dust was being disturbed from this misbehavior, but I wanted to join in the fun. I took only two steps in stride with Naftali before he made it clear that I was not welcome in their game. "We would be on our way if it were not for you, Joseph," he said. "Why should you have something fancier than us?"

I felt a tear in my eye as my fingers clenched into fists. I walked away to stand alone. I watched as My Brothers enjoyed the wait by running and chasing each other. Even the older ones, while still standing where My Father left them, laughed with each other in this unexpected time away from their duties. After an agonizing wait, Leah returned with my belt and sent Reuben to fetch My Father. She had used the same thread as she'd used on her own children's belts to stitch pomegranates on mine. So, though my belt was gray, it now had pink fruits and pink fringes. I was quite pleased with it.

When My Father saw the belt, he smiled. It was good handiwork, and though not the same as the others, it was clearly ornate and special. He praised Leah for her skill and clapped me on the shoulder with a huge smile. His expression changed quickly when he saw his other sons covered in dust from running around.

"What have you done?" he asked them, though he didn't leave time for an answer. "Today, we are to meet my honored parents in Hevron whom I haven't seen in twenty years. This is how I will greet them? With children who look like dogs covered in filth? The older boys remained clean, as did Joseph, even though he is the youngest brother. How was he able to do what you were not?" My Father turned to me. "Joseph, I do not know why these boys cannot follow instructions like you. You must keep your eye on them and let me know when they're not respecting me." I nodded. I rode my camel tall and proud while they slumped in disgrace, giving me angry looks. They'd brought this on themselves.

CHAPTER 12

Approaching Isaac's tent, we could see that he was sitting just inside in the shade. The sunlight made it impossible to see anything more than the shape of an old man propped up by pillows. Our camels were only steps away from his tent when My Father ordered Kemke to have them stop walking. Then Kemke loudly announced our arrival.

"Master Isaac, I present to you Master Jacob and his tribe. They will now dismount from their many camels and approach you one by one."

Landing on the ground, it became clear why Kemke had announced us so loudly and made a point of mentioning our camels. Isaac's face was so wrinkled that his eyes were shut as if the lids were sewn together. He would have no way of seeing this event unfold for himself. But his shut eyes were only one noteworthy thing about this new grandfather of mine, and even without him opening them once, it was as clear as a still stream that they were not like other eyes.

Just like Emunah's, My Grandfather's eyes were shaped like almonds and set farther apart than anyone else's. There were lines at the corners showing that his eyes had laughed often, wrinkling his face with a joy that lingered. These lines were also on his cheeks at the creases of his lips, which were parted by his tongue, too large for his mouth.

I was overcome with surprise and questions that flooded through me. Was this how My Father knew to give extra help to Emunah? Did My Father have a father who saw all the joy in the world and who also worked harder than others to achieve it himself? Would Emunah become an old woman with eyes seemingly sealed shut? And soon, I wondered whether she would become an old woman who could not hear well since it had become clear that My Grandfather could not.

My Father approached his father and knelt before him, taking his father's hand and bringing it to his lips for a kiss of respect. With that, Isaac reached his hand to My Father's face, down his neck, and along his arms until the two of them were holding hands. "These are the neck and hands of Esau, but the voice had announced Jacob," he said. "You are a man now." His words were muffled by age and his tongue, but his gladness was clear. His face lit up as he pulled My Father into his chest. I could see from My Father's back that he was sobbing, though he wiped his eyes before standing again.

"Father!" Jacob yelled. "I have returned with my family!"

"You have a wife?" Isaac asked. My Father beckoned to My Mother and the other women. Beginning with My Mother, one by one, they took My Grandfather's hand and kissed him while My Father shouted their names in introduction. In turn, My

Grandfather kissed each one on both cheeks and smiled. When it became clear to him that there were no more wives coming, he asked, "Have you any sons?"

"Yes, Father," My Father yelled. "My god has blessed me with eleven strong sons. Meet Joseph, he is the firstborn of my beloved wife, Rachel." Without needing to be asked, I approached My Grandfather the same way My Father and My Mother had. I kissed his hand, and he embraced me.

"He is small," My Grandfather said.

My Father clapped me on the shoulder and smiled at me. "He will grow," he said. "And he is the youngest. Meet Reuben, my firstborn." I was jealous that Reuben was introduced as the firstborn, whereas I was introduced as the firstborn of My Mother, but I reminded myself that I had been the first to be introduced. Reuben kissed Isaac's hand, and Isaac smiled. The same procedure was repeated for the rest of My Brothers and then My Sisters. Having witnessed Esau's reaction to Emunah, I wondered what My Grandfather might do upon meeting her, but he did nothing different. He could not see her any better than he could see the rest of us.

When these formalities came to a close, Isaac directed us to Rebekah, My Grandmother. "Your mothers will want to see you," he said.

We left the camels where they were. We could see Rebekah's tent from where we stood and would approach on foot. My Father had us line up in the way we would be introduced: My Mother behind him, Leah following her, then Zilpah and Bilhah. I was to go after the women and before Reuben, who was then the leader of the other brothers who lined up by age,

Shimon insisting that he walk in front of Levi because he had exited the womb in front of him. After Zevulun, the girls lined up according to their age, except that Emunah was carried by Ahuvah.

We walked with dignity, following My Father's posture and gait until we saw a woman emerge from the tent. This woman seemed an unlikely match for the man we had just parted from. While he needed to put forth great effort to hear, speak, see, and perhaps even sit, this woman walked like a gazelle who had never feared a lion. She was tall and graceful, and when she walked, she seemed to flow as smoothly as olive oil does down a rich man's chin. As soon as My Father saw her, he could no longer proceed like a head of a tribe he was presenting to his parents but ran to his mother like a little boy carrying both sorrow and excitement and fell into her arms.

My Mother then led the line with dignity, and we followed her as we witnessed the teary reunion between My Father and his mother. When we arrived, he was just beginning to slow his breath again. His face had been buried in his mother's bosom for a long time yet. He was much taller than his mother, but he bent low so she could stroke his back the way women did with the babies. The way My Mother sometimes still did for me. If at first I was surprised that this queenly woman was the wife of the feeble old man, then it was no match to the shock I felt when I remembered that this elegant woman was the sister of Lavan! I could see, though, that the shapes of their noses were the same and the thick darkness of their eyebrows as well.

The introductions were made again, though I needed to wait longer for my turn than the last time because after all the mothers had come forth, My Mother and Leah stepped forward again. "Mother," they said in unison, "we have brought you gifts." They removed the necklaces that were around their own necks and placed them around Rebekah's.

Then Leah presented her with a woven belt that was more spectacular even than the ones we wore. There were brown hills woven onto the belt and yellow specks in black that were clearly the stars of a night sky. My Mother then reached into her satchel for a gift too. She brought out a small whitewashed clay jar of spice from the city. "There is more in the cart," she said.

My Grandmother smiled broadly and took their hands. "Finally, I have daughters here and can be in the company of more women."

At that, a second woman emerged from Rebekah's tent. She was taller than My Grandmother, and her skin, darker, almost as black as her hair. She also walked with importance, and she smiled as she spoke. "Are you not in my company constantly?" she asked.

My Father was so surprised he nearly fell off his feet, but instead, he rushed at this woman the way he had rushed at his mother and landed on her bosom, crying again. "Auntie, Auntie, Auntie, Auntie," he wailed as we all stood silently. None of us children knew who this Auntie was or what we were supposed to do.

Rebekah saw our surprise and offered an explanation. "This is Deborah," she said, as if we were then supposed to understand.

When the reunion was over, I was finally introduced to My Grandmother and then to Deborah. As with My Grandfather, I took their hands and kissed them. They each embraced me.

When Deborah released me, she looked me in the eyes. "You are a dreamer," she said.

How did she know? My surprise and silence were enough to confirm her suspicion.

And later that afternoon, I had a dream. While My Father and Levi prepared the animals for the feast, while the women made broths with the spices and were watched closely by My Sisters, and while the other young men sat with Isaac and the younger brothers ran around in the dust, I stared at the sky. It wasn't long before my eyes were closed and my dreams were opened.

In that dream, ten fish surrounded me, though, I was standing on dry land. I awoke, startled. I returned to the tents and found it was time for the feast. We gathered on the rugs and pillows that were inside My Grandfather's tent. Everyone was wide-eyed and silent as his manservants brought in the meal. Before any food had been tasted or wine had been sipped, Deborah spoke my name loudly.

"Joseph." I startled, then looked at her. Everyone else looked at me.

"You dreamt," she said. It was not a question.

"Yes," I confirmed.

"Tell us."

"I dreamt of ten fish surrounding me, though, we were all on land."

"What were the fish there to tell you?" she asked. Though I had not considered this, I knew the answer immediately.

"They came to tell me that they would follow me to the river."

"Who were these fish?"

Again, though, I had not thought of it before, I spoke the words without hesitation. "My Brothers," I said.

All was quiet. I saw My Father and Deborah exchange glances. I saw Rebekah squeeze Deborah's hand. I saw Asher raise his eyebrows in a question. I heard Dan whisper to Naftali, "I, for one, did not follow *him* to the river, but our *father*. I cannot help that Joseph walked at the front of the line where he did not belong." Shimon clenched his fists.

Finally, My Grandfather broke the silence. "It smells like a feast. Is the meal prepared?"

"Yes, Father," My Father yelled, then brought food to his lips.

With that, we ate and drank of the bountiful meal, and when it seemed everyone would fall over from exhaustion, My Father grabbed My Mother by the hands and began to dance with her. Within moments, they opened their arms and widened the circle, welcoming in Rebekah and Deborah. Shimon and Levi began pounding the ground and their chests, making a rhythm for the dancing. As soon as I saw Reuben move to join the circle, I jumped up too. I danced between My Father and My Mother, and from that moment forward, I was unaware of what anyone else was doing, and I wished for this dance to last forever.

It went on for a long time, us circling the tents under the light of the moon, but not forever. Eventually, My Father brought everyone into a sway. "Thank you, Elohim," he nearly whispered, "for bringing us to this day."

In the morning, preparations were being made for us to leave. My Father promised his mother that he would return again soon. "Return in one month," she said. "The day after the moon is full again. In the meantime, leave your wives and your daughters here with me. It is time for us to get to know each other."

My Father bowed to My Grandmother. He would not speak against her, especially while all the women nodded in agreement.

"One more thing," Rebekah said. Then she motioned to My Mother, who looked My Father in the eye and then spoke directly.

"Jacob, my sisters all have daughters to stay with them. Would you leave me here without a child?" My Mother asked.

My gasp was audible, and my hand jumped of its own accord into My Father's. Surely, he wouldn't leave without me. My training with Judah had just begun. I could not be left here with the women and girls.

Next, it was Deborah who spoke. "Jacob, I have seen the boy. Some men are men of the field, and some dwell in the tents. Joseph is one of the latter. He will learn much here." And at that, my fate was decided. My Father and My Brothers would return to our camp, but I was to be left behind.

No sooner had My Father and brothers departed than My Grandmother took me to walk with her. "Joseph," she said, "your father wasn't always a shepherd; did you know that?" This felt to me like when Reuben had asked who My Father had been before I was born. In truth, he was someone I didn't know, someone I had forgotten to imagine. I had not known my own father as anything other than a shepherd, a father, the head of his tribe. I did not know what to answer My Grandmother, or if I was expected to.

"Your father was born to inherit the blessing of Abraham, and he could not be worthy of that without a strong relationship with his god. Yah, whom your father calls Elohim, has spoken to me; it is because of this that I knew Jacob's would be the line in which the blessing continues. Now he has become a shepherd, and your brothers as well. While you and all your brothers will inherit the land of Abraham, Isaac, and your father, Jacob, you, Joseph, will be the one who inherits learning the ways of walking with Yah. At least for now."

Walk with Yah? I could hardly walk with My Grandmother. Her step was quick, and she knew the rocks and cracks in the paths without looking, while I stumbled over half of them, trying to take in her words as much as I could. She stopped and breathed in and out while looking at me.

"Deborah will be your teacher like she was your father's," she said. "She is an extraordinary person. Learn as much as you can from her. You may call her Auntie. You will call me Grandmother."

"Yes, Grandmother," I said.

"You will learn your lessons and practice them as she tells you. Then you will work with Katib."

"Yes, Grandmother," I said. "I can use a slingshot now. Judah taught me." I wanted her to know that I would be a valuable helper, but she just looked at me strangely.

"Now, go and find your auntie, and ask her what your first lesson is to be."

"Yes, Grandmother," I said, and I walked back to the tent she shared with Deborah. Last night, the women and girls slept there, too, while the other boys and My Father and I slept in Isaac's tent.

How would it be tonight? My steps became slower and slower as I walked toward Deborah. I looked down at my feet so as not to keep stumbling on the rocks until Deborah stepped out of her tent and yelled my name.

"Joseph!" I could hear the impatience in her voice. I ran the rest of the way. Once I was there, she met me with a warm smile.

"Joseph," she said more softly this time. "Joseph, you have a lot to learn, but you are a gifted child like your father was. We will begin your training now. If you are like your father in other ways, you will learn quickly, if sometimes reluctantly. I expect your respect and cooperation. You are only here until the next full moon. We must begin right away."

Being with Deborah was not as scary as being with My Grandmother. She compared me to My Father many times, and such compliments helped ease my sorrow. She also walked more deliberately than My Grandmother, though it wasn't frailty that slowed her pace but something else. It was as if Deborah liked each step so much that she didn't want to leave it.

"Joseph?" She said my name slowly and as a question, though no words followed immediately. I was just going to try to think of what the answer might be when she spoke again. "Did you see the idols on Lavan's altar? Or those of his sons'?"

When my first milk tooth had fallen out, My Mother had laughed and cried and held it for all to see. My Father made a ceremony for me and threw my curls into the fire while he and I marched around it praising Elohim as all My Brothers watched. We all feasted on sweet treats and wine that night. In the morning, Shimon put his arm around my shoulder and addressed me personally.

"Well, Joseph," he said, "you're one of the big kids now. Old enough to do brave things, I suppose." I nodded my head, and he went on. "You're old enough to venture to Lavan's camp now. You could even go right to his altar and take one of the idols and smash it. That's how strong I bet you are. I bet you could even smash an idol."

I was sure that I could. I could carry a whole water jug and even carry Emunah. Once, when I'd thrown an olive pit as far as I could, it hit a small bowl and cracked it. An idol was clay just like a bowl. I was certain I could smash it to pieces. But surely Lavan would smash me to pieces if he saw me. As if knowing my thoughts, Shimon spoke again.

"Lavan has gone to the market," he said. "He will be gone half the day. Plenty of time for you to smash all his idols, but one will be enough. He disgraces our father and Elohim by having those idols. Someone should do something. Someone strong and brave. I would do it myself," he said, "but my duties are with the sheep. Luckily, you are big enough now," he said, patting me on the shoulder. "Let me see where that tooth fell out." I showed him, and he congratulated me again. "You must be the man for the job. For our father's honor," he said.

I told My Auntie this story. Told her I did know of Lavan's idols and had even smashed one myself.

"Were you not worried?" she asked.

"Of course not," I said. Did she think me a baby who did not know the helplessness of idols? "Idols cannot do anything," I said.

"But were you not afraid of what Lavan might do?"

"Shimon said Lavan was at the market, but he was not. As soon as he heard the shattering of the idol, he came running. But I was faster. When I heard his feet, I ran and hid behind some of his sheep. He let them wander unattended and never bothered with them himself. He didn't look for me. He just yelled and yelled, then went back to his tent."

My Auntie nodded. She kept walking, and I with her. "So, you know that in Haran, idols are treated as gods. Here in the Land of Canaan, that is also so. But your father knows that idols are useless, and I am glad you also know. These sculptures are not gods. They cannot do things, make things, or help things. Only Yah can do that.

"Breathe with me Joseph." She took in a deep breath, and I imitated her actions: *Yhhhh*. Then she let her breath out, and I did the same. *Whhhh*. "Yah is the One God," she said. "We call YhWh *Yah*, except in ceremonies or when speaking directly to Yah. We breathe Yah in, we breathe ourselves out, and we become one with the One Who Is.

"Slowly saying *Yhhhh Whhhh* is like slowly saying *Is*: I . . . i . . . i . . . i . . . i . . . i . . . i . . . is." I nodded my head yes. "Yah always Is. Is now, Is then, Is here, Is there, Is in us when we take Yah in, and Is outside us when we breathe out. All at once. Some people have not yet realized this, like Lavan, who hopes that idols will help him. But Yah is the god of our ancestors and of yours." I stood a little taller. I did not truly understand all that My Auntie told me on that first day, but I knew that idols were worthless, and I knew to be proud that My Father knew it, and his father, and his."

"You must begin to talk to the god of your fathers, Joseph. Abraham, of blessed memory, used to talk with this god upon waking every morning. He would begin his day by walking off into the hills and being with Yah before he did anything else.

Your grandfather Isaac used to go into the field every afternoon to be with Yah. He has been many places in this land of yours, always with Yah. Now, he is too old and feeble to go far, but he still goes a few paces each afternoon. And your father, Jacob, talked to Yah every night before sleeping. At least he did when he lived here. I hope he still does, though I understand he calls Yah *Elohim*."

Deborah paused. Maybe I was supposed to say something, but if so, I did not know what. "It is good to connect with Yah each day, but it is better to do so many times each day; especially now, when you will be learning for such a short time. So, you will follow in the footsteps of each of them, reaching out to Yah, even if by the name of Elohim, three times a day." She paused again, and we walked in silence. I was frustrated that this walk was not taking me back to My Father. He and My Brothers would have reached their destination by now, yet I had done all this walking and was still here. I began kicking rocks as I walked.

"Joseph," My Auntie said. "You are frustrated. You are thinking of things that upset you, not talking to Yah. Now is when you must begin. I will leave you here. Look at a view that is pleasing to you, and call out to Elohim like this: 'Blessed are You, God of My Father Jacob, God of My Father Isaac, God of My Father Abraham.' Then breathe Yah into you. *Yhhhh*. Then breathe yourself into Yah. *Whhhh*. So that you may notice that you are together. When you are ready, speak to Yah. When you are finished, return to the tent."

Deborah walked away from me as she said she would. I watched her begin to retrace her steps to the tents. The tents themselves were out of sight from here, blocked by a hill with a large rock protruding from the side. When she turned the bend, there was nobody there but me. The hills were quiet without talking, without feet walking nearby, without the sounds of sheep and goats. The only things in view were the hills and the clouds, the blue sky, and the buzzards flying in it that made me think of the lions that might be nearby.

I needed to talk to Elohim so I could get back to the camp. "Elohim, blessed are You, God of My Father Jacob, God of My Father Isaac, God of My Father Abraham," I said. I breathed. *Yhhhh. Whhhh.* But then what? What was I supposed to say next? My Auntie didn't tell me. I listened in case Elohim would tell me. I listened as hard and long as I could, but I didn't hear anything. So, I said it again, "Blessed are You, Elohim, Yah, God of My Father Jacob, God of My Father Isaac, God of My Father Abraham." And when nothing happened, I said it again. And again. And again.

I said it so many times that the words came by themselves. The ending led right back to the beginning and to the ending and the beginning again. I stood there until the sun was high in the sky. I was thirsty, and my legs were tired. I wondered whether Deborah would permit me to sit down, and I wondered whether I could return to the camp. Had I talked to Elohim? I had said the same thing again and again. Was that what she meant? Was it allowed?

As I was fretting over this, I noticed a new movement to my left. Off in the distance, someone was approaching. I watched the progress of this body until I could make out that it was My Sister, Deenah. I was so happy that I would not be alone anymore! I began walking toward her even as she continued toward me.

"Deenah!" I exclaimed when we were finally close enough. I was so happy to see her, to see anyone. "Why have you come?"

"Grandmother said that Ahuvah and Annah are women now and could stay at the camp. Emunah and Tirzah are too little to come out here alone, of course. So, they sent me," she said.

Ahuvah and Annah were considered women now. I guess it made sense, since the older brothers considered themselves young men. But I wasn't wondering why she was there instead of anyone else; I was wondering why anyone was there at all.

"But why did they send you?" I asked. "Are you to talk to Elohim with me? I was very lonely and didn't really know how to do it or what I was doing. It would be nice to have you for a companion out here in the heat. I don't want to be the only one."

"No, Joseph," she said. "They didn't send me to stay with you; they sent me to bring you back. Auntie said it's time for you to go out with Grandfather."

So, we walked back to the camp together. Along the way, I told Deenah of my frustration at not knowing what My Auntie wanted me to do and not knowing how to talk to My God, and I complained for much of the walk about being the only brother left behind. I learned that Deenah had some complaints of her own. The women were all putting henna on their arms and celebrating each other and their togetherness, and they included Ahuvah and Annah, but not her. She was grouped with the babies, which she found insulting.

"Do you think you can ask Elohim for the women to let me have henna?" Deenah asked.

"I don't know," I said. Maybe louder than I should have. I just didn't know anything about what I was supposed to do, and I didn't like Deenah reminding me of that.

"Well, I know something," Deenah said. "I know I can get to Grandfather's tent before you do." She started running before she even stopped talking and got a head start on me. I ran as fast as I could and stepped into the tent only one breath behind her. "Told you," she said.

"You started running before I knew we were racing," I complained. She did not deny it, nor did she give me credit for my speed. She merely smiled and left me there.

My Grandfather was standing just outside his tent, and I stood next to him. Occasionally, he took small steps like the babies did when they were learning to walk. It gave me the impression that he wished to walk, but it was clear that even standing took much effort from him. I asked My Grandfather whether walking while talking to Elohim was permitted. My answer came in the form of him taking a couple of the baby steps. I took only one step forward to stand by his side again.

We stood quietly together. As I had already stood the whole morning and failed at talking to My God, I wished to sit in the shade of the tent, but I was afraid My Auntie would see me and scold me. So, I stayed beside My Grandfather. When I could stand the silence no more, I confessed to him of my inability to talk with Elohim.

"Grandfather, I tried all morning to talk with Elohim. My Auntie didn't leave me good instructions. She told me the opening words, and I said them. But then I just said them again and again because I didn't know what to do next. All My Brothers are taking care of the sheep; they are becoming good shepherds like My Father, your son. I, too, wish to become a good shepherd, but I was left behind. It seems to be because of my dreams. I have many dreams.

"But Grandfather, I am certain these dreams come from Elohim. And so, I should not be punished for having them. I cannot control them or even understand them. So why must I stay here with the women and girls when I should be with My Father and My Brothers?"

My Grandfather did not respond, and we were quiet again for a while, until I realized my unintended disrespect. "I am sorry, Grandfather," I said, "Of course, it's not only the women and girls who are here but my honored grandfather as well. I am grateful to learn from you." After that, we were both silent. I was still upset that I was left behind, and now I was also upset that I had shown disrespect to My Grandfather. Yet something else joined those feelings. I was grateful that I wasn't only with the women and girls. I was grateful for My Grandfather's presence. As I recognized that, he reached out and took my hand.

"Boy," he said, "What is your name?"

"Joseph," I answered him. "Joseph, son of Jacob." But as soon as I said it, he asked me again.

"What is your name, child?" I told him again. But he seemed not to be listening to me, and then I remembered that My Father had shouted, and so on the third time, I answered him as loudly as I could, and he smiled.

"Son of Jacob," he said, "Where is Elioded?" I did not know where his helper was and did not know what to say to him.

"Please guide me back to my tent so I may rest. I am finished with my afternoon meditation." And so, I did.

I hoped that if My Grandfather was finished talking to Elohim, then I could be too. I did not seek out My Grandmother or My Auntie to ask them. Instead, I rested my head on a pillow in the shade of the tent and fell asleep. I had a fitful dream of a team of ten cattle walking the hills. There was a bee buzzing about as a companion. All appeared peaceful, but then one of the cows gave birth to a sheep and dropped dead. All the cattle and even the bee let out a wail that startled me awake. I jerked to my feet and left the tent for some sunshine.

As I stepped out, My Auntie was waiting for me as much as the sun. It seemed she had been watching me. "You dreamt," she said. I didn't need to confirm this. It was not a question, but an observation. "What was the meaning of the dream?" she asked.

"I don't know!" I yelled. And then I apologized for my disrespect.

"Go and sit in the shade," she said. "Alone. Quietly. Talk to the god of your fathers. Begin the way I instructed you. And then listen. Come back when it is time for the evening meal, and you will tell us of your dream."

I dropped my head in disappointment and walked to the date trees. I sat beneath a full tree and ate from some of the sweet fruits that had fallen. Then I sat and began, "Blessed are You, Elohim, God of My Father Jacob, God of My Father Isaac, God of My Father Abraham." This time, I continued with words of my own. Talking as if My God were listening, just as I had done with My Grandfather before I remembered he couldn't hear. "I don't know what my dreams mean. My Father said they will become clearer, but they don't. My Auntie knows when I have dreamt without me telling her, but then she asks me their meaning." I listened until the evening meal was ready, but I heard nothing.

As promised, My Auntie asked me to recount my dream while we ate. I looked around me. I had the attention of My Mother and My Father's three other wives. I also had the attention of my five sisters; even the little ones were looking at me expectantly. Nodding to My Grandmother and Auntie, I told them of the dream. "There was a team of cows walking the hills. Ten of them. They were accompanied by a bee who was their companion. All was peaceful until one of the cows birthed a sheep then died, then everyone wailed, and I startled awake."

"That's awful, Joseph," My Mother said. "I'm sorry you had such a nightmare."

"What does it mean?" Ahuvah asked.

"I don't know," I confessed. "I have no idea."

"No idea?" My Auntie asked.

"No," I said. "How would I know? The meaning comes from My God, and I have listened but heard nothing."

"I will remember it," My Auntie said, "and maybe we will speak of its meaning another time."

I ate the rest of my meal in silence. The others chatted and laughed and admired the new henna on their arms, but I stayed in my disappointment until I was instructed to take a lantern and sleep in My Grandfather's tent. And so, I left the merriment of the evening and returned to the pillow I had slept on earlier. My Grandfather, who took his meals separately, was already asleep.

I had no dream that night; I had something far worse. Not long after I settled in and closed my eyes, I heard a terrible scream.

This one was not in a dream since it continued even when my eyes were wide open and I was on my feet, my heart racing. I looked around me but saw little in the darkness of the tent. As the scream continued, I realized it was coming from My Grandfather. I rushed to his side. I may have been just a boy of seven summers, but I was stronger than he was and willing to fight off any beast from the body of my fragile grandfather. But when I reached him after only a few steps, it was clear that there was no attacker other than his own dream.

"Grandfather, Grandfather!" I yelled, but he still didn't seem to hear me. I put my hand on his to try to arouse him. He grabbed my hand and pulled me to his chest. He held me there with a fierceness that was surprising from his frail body. As I was there, he stroked my hair and mumbled, "Yah will provide the sheep. Yah will provide the sheep. Yah will provide the sheep." Over and over, he repeated this until he fell asleep, still stroking my hair. I was afraid to move away from him, even when his breath became steady and slow and his chest rose and fell like a soft wind. So, I spent the long night awake, kneeling at his side, bent on top of him, wondering about the sheep, and crying that there were still many days until My Father would retrieve me.

When we took our morning meal, I again spent the time recounting a dream, only this time it wasn't mine. I didn't know the meaning; I didn't even know the content of the dream. Only the effect, which was still disturbing me. But once again, My Auntie was not surprised. Neither was My Grandmother. "He still does that sometimes," My Grandmother said. "You were right to go to him, Joseph. I know he found comfort in you being there. Abraham told me he used to cry out every night before we were married. And then I comforted him each night for years. Finally, he slept calmly until the babies were born. Then the screams began again, of course."

"Of course?" Leah asked.

"Yes," My Grandmother continued. "Because they were children. It renewed his fear, of course. With children here again, the screams began and lasted for several years. I was so lucky to have Deborah." They reached out for each other and held hands. "She helped with the nursing, and after I comforted Isaac each night, she comforted me. He remembers nothing of it in the mornings. I would have been so alone to go through that each night without her."

"But why does Isaac cry out?" My Mother asked.

"And why did he speak of a sheep again and again?" I wondered aloud.

My Grandmother looked at us all. "Jacob never told you of his father's fear?"

We all answered no, as if of one voice.

And so, My Grandmother told us: "Abraham, of blessed memory, talked with Yah all the time. And Yah talked with him. Abraham faced many challenges and trials, but throughout it all, he knew that Yah was always with him and that all was well. One time, Yah told him to take Isaac, whom he loved, and offer him as a sacrifice."

We all gasped.

"Abraham knew that he did not know everything, that he must go and find out, that he must walk through the fear. And he knew that all would be well because he trusted Yah. So, he saddled his donkey and took two young men and wood for a burnt offering, and he and Isaac set out on a three-day journey, following Yah's lead. After the third day, Abraham left the young men at the base of Mount Moriah and climbed it only with Isaac.

"When the two reached the summit, Abraham found a rock on which to perform the sacrifice. Isaac was afraid. He saw they were preparing for a sacrifice and saw there was no sheep. He asked Abraham about this, worried, understanding that it would soon be him on the altar. The whole while, Abraham had been telling his son: 'Yah will provide a sheep.' And at the top of the mountain, he repeated this as he bound his son to the rock."

Again, we gave a collective gasp. I looked and saw that My Mother was covered in tears. Then I noticed that everyone else was too; even I was crying without knowing. We knew the sacrifice would not happen because My Grandfather was only a few steps away in his tent while My Grandmother told us this story. But knowing this did not make the story less frightening.

"As Abraham bound his son, they were both crying, but Abraham kept repeating the words. Isaac began to chant with him. The binding continued as they lifted their voices. 'Yah will provide a sheep. Yah will provide a sheep.' Finally, a voice came out instructing Abraham not to kill his son, and a ram appeared in the nearby thicket. Abraham unbound his son Isaac. He had been sacrificed; that is, he had been used to bring Abraham closer to Yah, but Isaac was not killed. It was the ram that had been slaughtered on the stone, not Isaac."

The story was over; My Grandfather's screams, explained. We wiped away our tears. Now it was My Auntie's turn to talk. "I must show you all something," she said. "But you mustn't move at all from how you are now." We all sat perfectly still. I for one, barely breathed, though I could not stop completely.

"Each of you, feel your own bodies," she said, "without moving." And then, thankfully, she explained more. "Leah and Rachel, you two are shoulder to shoulder, leaning into each other, your hands clenched in fists, your necks tense with fear. Ahuvah, Annah, Deenah, look at how you have reached out your hands for comfort from each other, and look at how your fingers are laced together. From here, I can see the whiteness of your knuckles as you squeeze each other's hands. Your faces are still holding the expression of fear. As is yours, Joseph," she turned to me. "Your hands are clenching your tunic as if it will keep you from falling off a cliff. Your eyes, wide.

"This is the fear that Isaac felt atop the mountain, but it is not the fear that Abraham felt. Abraham felt no fear. He was open to having Yah lead the way in teaching him. It is not serving you to close yourselves tight like this. Relax your bodies. Open your hands. You must let go. Sometimes, holding on does more damage than letting go." We all relaxed our bodies and nodded as if we understood.

"Joseph," My Mother said. "You may sleep here from now on. You should not need to endure that suffering each night."

"You call that suffering?" Leah jumped in. "That is not Joseph's suffering; he is merely witnessing his grandfather's sorrow. We all must experience sorrow, even your golden child."

"He has enough to do," My Mother said, defending me, "with dreams of his own that disturb him, and now he carries the task of communicating with Elohim. He is just a boy."

Leah scoffed. "My Reuben is learning to be the head of the tribe, even taking the responsibility of the rear man in the caravan. Your son has little burden."

"The men help him back there," My Mother noted. "And it is an honor that would have belonged to my son had my womb opened earlier."

"And yet it didn't," Leah retorted. "And my firstborn, as well as my other sons, carry the duty of watching over the flocks. It is they who increase our abundance."

"My son is—" My Mother was going to defend me again, but My Grandmother stopped her.

"Sisters," My Grandmother said. "You are sisters. Stop this bickering. You are here to help each other, not create noise. And you have not learned your lesson from Deborah. Open your fists and your jaws. Allow air in your body. Yah sustains us through the open air."

With that, My Auntie turned to me. "Joseph, it is time for you to go and talk to Yah. Speak without fear. Open your hands. Open your ears. I will send Deenah for you again when it is time to return. And this time, Joseph," she continued, "do not forget that you have work with Katib. Go to him directly after you meditate with your grandfather."

I had almost forgotten that I would be banished from the group, but I rose as I was expected and left the others, slowly walking back to the place where I had tried to talk to My God the day before to try again this day. Sadly, I had no more success than the first time, even though I did as I was told.

When I saw Deenah rounding the bend, I walked to meet her. She smiled at me. "You were brave with our grandfather, Joseph," she said.

"I was scared," I told her.

"Still, you were brave."

"Thank you. You were brave afterward."

"I don't know why our father never told us that story. Maybe he was scared by it too."

"Not that," I said. "I was referring to your bravery when My Mother and your mother were fighting with each other. I was glad when they were stopped."

Deenah threw her head back and laughed. It was a beautiful laugh. "Joseph," she said. "I was glad when they were stopped too. But they do that all the time."

"Really?" I asked.

"Of course," she said, and I believed her because she spent time with the women, and I usually did not. "This was the first time they had a mother to stop them."

"But My Mother always tells me of how much she helped your mother," I told Deenah. I was surprised to hear of this fighting. In our tent on the nights when I was too restless to sleep, My Mother told me stories, usually of how proud and glad she was to help Leah. I told Deenah now.

"When My Father first saw My Mother at the well, he loved her right away," I said. "She was beautiful, of course, and a good shepherdess. She was strong and gentle at the same time. This is what My Mother always tells me. Over time, she grew to love him just as much as he loved her. And she was both peaceful and thrilled that she would become his wife. I don't understand how she could feel so excited at one time and peaceful at the same time, but this is how she tells me," I explained.

"But she loved her sister almost as much as she loved My Father, and certainly she had loved her longer. Leah had been there her whole life. When their mother died, they shared a tent alone together. They never let the other out of sight when Lavan or his mean sons were near. They helped each other.

"And both of them knew that if My Mother married My Father, Leah would never marry. She is the elder daughter and has the wandering eye. Lavan would have to pay a price too high to find her a free man to marry. Better to keep her for himself. Leah may have a wandering eye, but we know that she is strong and wise and an expert weaver in addition to a cook of the heartiest meals." I added those compliments to the story for Deenah's sake. My Mother didn't say them, but she didn't need to. We all knew.

"So, the two of them devised a plan. Leah would marry My Father first. She would wear the marriage gown and a veil too thick for anyone to discover her identity. Nobody would be surprised if she were quiet, and so she was. In the morning light, when My Father discovered that it was Leah he had married and not My Mother, he blamed Lavan. My Mother always shakes her head at this time in the story and says, 'That old man is too thickheaded to think of an idea as grand as that. But, of course, he would never admit that, so he pretended the whole thing was his idea.'"

"Your mother told you this?" Deenah asked.

"Yes," I said. "My Mother and your mother did that so Leah doesn't have to live at the mercy of her father. My Mother says Leah should be grateful to her every day and shouldn't have had all those sons that make her seem so important. I agree with her about all those sons. Just two would have been enough for me, Reuben and Judah. And it would have been nice for them to be born after me."

We had been walking together during this story. When I finished, Deenah told me she had never heard it before. I was surprised to learn that her mother had not told her this story one hundred times as mine had.

"I have a question for you," Deenah said. She smiled and I waited. "Do you think you can run faster than I can to Grandfather's tent?" She was off and running before she had finished the question, and once again, she beat me there.

I told her it was because she had started unfairly before I had, but I wasn't completely sure that was the reason. I discussed this with My Grandfather as we were out in the field, but as I did it more quietly than he could hear, I did not receive any response from him. It was a lot like talking to My God.

Afterward, I remembered to seek out Katib. I was pleased that I would be able to help with the flocks, even if they were not My Father's flocks. I was eager to continue learning to be a good shepherd, even if it wasn't from Judah. Not knowing where to find Katib and the animals, I asked Elioded. He laughed. "You will not find Katib with sheep," he said. "Go to the tent that has the rows of earthen jugs around it. He is there."

And so, I walked to the tent with the jugs. It was not hard to find since they were numerous. I called out and was invited in. I bowed my head to the small man sitting on a cushion by the edge of the tent. "Good day, Katib," I said. "I am here to help you. I have learned what plants a sheep may and may not eat, and I can hit a target with my slingshot." This last part wasn't always true, but it was sometimes true, and I would get better.

"There will be no slingshots," Katib said. "Do you not know who I am?" I bowed to the floor because I did not know who he was and now wondered if I had disrespected him. "I am Isaac's scribe," he said. "It is my job to write down his holdings and his messages. And now, it seems it is also my job to teach you to read and write. Your father was a man of the tents, and Deborah has told me that you are to be as well. I don't know why he doesn't teach you himself, but I am happy to do anything Deborah asks of me."

I rubbed my chin with my thumb. Not a beard, not even a hair. Of course not. I did not even have my second set of bottom teeth. Yet I was to be taught to read, something not one of My Brothers could do!

That very day, Katib showed me strange markings and told me what they meant—markings for sheep, goats, camels, and grain. "We will begin there," he said. And then he took some papyrus from one jar and a reed from another and brought yet a third jar to his side; this one was a jar of ink. He showed me how to use these tools but wouldn't let me touch them. "You may use this stick," he said, and then he instructed me to copy the markings for sheep, goats, camels, and grain in the dirt outside his tent until I could commit them to memory.

It was in this way that over the course of the month, I learned to both read and write the markings not only for those words but for many others. Not all the words, though. Katib assured me that there were many more words to learn but that I had shown a fine start. It was something that made me feel proud, even as

I struggled—especially as I struggled—with my other task of communicating with Elohim.

Deenah continued to race me back to the tent every day during our stay. I continued to talk to My Grandfather each afternoon, having better luck with him than talking with My God, though I kept trying three times a day. Several times, My Auntie took the morning walk with me. She was usually quiet, but her presence made me calmer and more hopeful in my efforts.

I met with Katib daily and struggled with the shapes he beseeched me to learn, successfully mastering some of them. The women continued to paint each other with henna and trade stories of their lives. I sometimes heard retellings from Deenah when she was in the mood to share them. In the month that we stayed there, My Grandfather screamed in his dream only once more, and I was less afraid that time. I let him stroke my hair until he slept, and then I went back to sleep on my own pillow.

When the moon was full again, I knew My Father would arrive the following morning. I was excited that we would be reunited, even while the women mourned the impending separation. Deenah didn't come and fetch me that day. She was busy helping the women prepare a celebration for that night. When I came back to the campground on my own, I could smell the spices purchased from the city wafting through the air. I talked to My God about the pleasing smell and the excitement ahead for that night and the following day. I still did not hear anything in response, but I was so filled with contentment that I didn't care.

That night as the moon rose, the women covered each other in jewelry. Each woman, and even the girls, had prepared necklaces, bracelets, and belts for each other. I suddenly realized that I hadn't known much about how they had been spending their time while I was doing my tasks, but now I could see it with my own eyes. When they were all decked in finery, they took out the drums and timbrels. My Auntie stood, and all the others made a line behind her. Deenah grabbed me off the ground, bringing me with her into the line.

We followed My Auntie out of the tent. The women played their instruments, and they all sang a song in praise of the moon and the light. Their raised voices filled the air with joy. It was in this joy that we danced to a clearing near the tent that had been prepared for this moment. We continued the celebration in a circle around a brass bowl of water in the center. The moon shone in all its beauty above us in the sky and was also reflected in the water of the bowl on the ground in our circle.

Once we were there, the same song continued, but in a call and response form. My Auntie sang out the words, and they were repeated by everyone. She did this for a long time while the drums were still drumming and our feet were stomping, hearts pounding, around and around the circle. After a while, My Grandmother became the one calling out the chant for everyone to repeat. Each woman took a turn as the caller: Leah, My Mother, Zilpah, Bilhah, and even Ahuvah and Annah led the chant. We repeated it so many times as we went around the bowl of light that I easily learned the words:

Sister, Mother, Daughter, and Friend,
You shine with love from beginning to end,
We give You our hopes, our dreams, and our pain,
You keep them safe, until we meet again.

When we finished singing and dancing, we feasted. My Auntie told us one more story. "Long ago, there was no moon. No sun. No stars. No hills. No water. No people. No sheep. No beasts. No bugs. Nothing. And out of the nothing, Yah formed everything. And one day, Yah whispered into the ears of the people. 'Look at the moon,' Yah said, 'it is just like you. Sometimes it shines brightly in its fullest. Sometimes it has shadow. Sometimes you see it. Sometimes you do not. Sometimes it is high, sometimes it is low. She is like you, and you are like her. She is your sister. You must celebrate her and celebrate you.'"

My Grandmother looked at each one of us and smiled. "It was a great joy to celebrate the moon with all of you. Tomorrow, we will bid each other farewell, but my heart has been nourished, and my spirit smiles from our time together. Before the planting each year, you will all come back here. I will have women here with me again."

"And what about me?" My Auntie teased.

"I am always grateful for you," My Grandmother corrected and kissed Deborah's hand. "But for one month every year, I will be surrounded by women—*we* will be surrounded by women. Is that not how it was for you when you were a girl? Do you not want to have that again?"

"You do not need to persuade me, Rebekah," My Auntie said. "I am as happy as you are."

The women all embraced each other in a large huddle. Even the babies were raised in solidarity and joy. My Grandmother reached out her hand to me. "And you shall come, too, Joseph, and continue your studies." I didn't want to leave My Father again, but I was glad to be included in the affection and proud that I would be trusted to learn more.

My Father returned the next day, as promised. I was with My Grandfather upon his arrival. My eyes were closed like his, and though I knew My Father would be coming that day, I did not know when. Then I felt an impulse to open my eyes and look up, and there he was, just barely out of my arm's reach.

When I saw him, I jumped up and nearly landed in his arms. He laughed and hugged me, then pushed me away from his body to look at me. "Joseph, I believe you have grown taller in this month, or perhaps it is that you carry yourself with more confidence. I have already spoken with your grandmother and My Auntie, and they both assured me that you have learned much, but seeing you, I am fully convinced."

With such high praise from My Father, I thought I might burst. But there was more. "Come, Joseph, you will help me load the women and girls and supplies. They will ride, but you and I will walk. And I will show you the parcel of land that I have purchased. It is in the fields of Shechem, and the grass is good. Your brothers and the men have been preparing the campground so that it will be ready for us when we arrive."

CHAPTER 13

When I arrived at my new home the next evening, I was surprised to see it looking so much like my old home. The tents had already been set up, and each was in the same place as it had been in Haran. There was no garden yet, but an area had been marked out for one. The rainy season would begin soon, and the seeds would go in the ground before the rains came.

Not everything was the same as it had been in Haran, of course. The most obvious and most pleasant difference was Lavan's absence. We were also close enough to the city of Shechem that we could see the walls from our land. My Brothers often pastured the sheep just outside the city, and I sometimes went there to check on them and bring word back for My Father. That was the closest I got to shepherding after my training was moved from sheep to writing.

This was our rhythm for some years. Most of the time was spent on our land outside of Shechem. The flocks continued to grow, and our garden and vineyard grew too. Goods were made at the campground and traded at market. I walked the hills and practiced my lessons, the Elohim lessons as well as the reading and writing ones.

Every year before the planting, the women and girls and I took the journey to Hevron. My Father accompanied us so that he could pay respect to his parents. He would kiss My Grandmother and My Auntie, give Katib some silver for his teachings, sleep the night with me and My Grandfather, and then set out on his return journey in the morning. After the next full moon, he would repeat those actions, taking us back with him.

Shimon always made it his business to taunt me just before we set out, "Goodbye, Joseph," he'd say. "Father says it's time for the girls to leave." He didn't believe me that I wasn't one of the girls. On our journeys, it was always I alone who walked with My Father. Father and son. None of the girls. Our conversations, when we had them, were short, but his attention meant the world to me. He often told me tales of sheep, sometimes of what happened when he was watching them and sometimes of funny stories he made up about sheep who could talk and sing and go on grand adventures. He inquired about my lessons and occasionally made references to his own from when he was a boy, but mostly, we walked in silence in each other's company.

I would spend the month with the women awaiting his return so that we could walk together. But I didn't only wait. I sat with My Grandfather. I ran with Deenah. I danced under the moon with everyone else. I walked the hills and spoke with Elohim. And I listened to My Auntie's stories, writing each word for her as she spoke it. It pleased me to see those words written on parchments, knowing that I had been the one to put them there. Between each visit, I kept up with my accounting and my practices and saw the improvement in my skill from year to year and was pleased. So was My Auntie. Only once did she use a stern tone with me because I had interrupted her telling. Even then, she'd told me she would answer my question when I'd finished my task. She was strict but kind, and I enjoyed having her attention to myself as much as I enjoyed having My Mother's.

In truth, I greatly enjoyed my month each summer in Hevron, even though I longed to be with My Father. One time, I was able to have both. After the harvest that had come just before our third summer there, when I was in my tenth year, we all journeyed back to Hevron. The occasion was the gathering of the first fruits, and My Father wished to share the abundance from our land with his own parents. So, we traveled again, our first time doing so as a whole tribe since we'd settled.

This time, it was not a matter of packing up our whole camp, just ourselves and our bounty. My Father was giddy with pride that he would bring so many gifts to his parents. He tasked the sons of Leah with selecting forty choice sheep from the flock and instructed the sons of Zilpah and Bilhah to pack ten carts with fruits and wine. I was not to wander as I wished for prayer that morning, but I was to speak to My God by the gathering place so that when everything was being loaded, I could count it all and write it on a scroll for My Father to present to his father!

My Brothers were much stronger than they had been when they were smaller and we were leaving Haran. The same was true of me, of course. I had grown considerably and now reached My Father's shoulder. All My Brothers were taller than me, but soon, I would be taller than My Mother. I envied the young men for their hairy faces. Not a hair had grown on my chin, but my ability to read and write made me feel wise at times. This was one of those times.

While the carts were loaded, I carefully inspected, counted, and recorded the contents. I wouldn't let anyone too close to me so that they would not bump my arm as I wrote with the delicate reed and black ink. I was sure My Father would not want the scroll blemished. And as this was the first time my writing for him was more than a mere exercise, I wanted to make sure it showed my true skill and ability.

When our procession was ready, My Father made a grand gesture of lifting the women onto the camels again. The girls would all walk alongside them; even Emunah was strong enough to make the journey since it was less than two days of travel, three at the most with all the animals.

Reuben confidently went to the back, assuming his position as leader of the tribe from behind. Judah led the animals; small in number though they were, nobody disputed that they were his domain. I wished to walk with him, perhaps to learn a bit more shepherding since my instruction had been so abruptly halted, but Shimon and Levi immediately followed the sheep and called for the rest of us to fall in line behind them by age.

This time, I did not mind being the youngest, the last, because it put me near Reuben. Ever since I had begun my training with My Auntie and been taken out of the fields, I saw My Brothers only occasionally at the campground, and we had very little to talk about. It took me no time at all to see that they had no interest in my daily prayers; they didn't even think it valuable.

And I could not speak intelligently about the sheep. I had no experience.

But Reuben gave me a warm smile. "So, Little Brother," he said, "do you think we'll share some stories on this journey?" I returned his smile and fell into step with him. My stride was not as long as his, but the difference between our legs was growing smaller as mine grew longer. I stood tall and was by his side when My Father approached us.

"Reuben," he said. "I trust you will not let any of these gifts fall behind you or anything or anyone come at them from your direction." As we were traveling just a short distance for a short time, Reuben didn't have any of the men with him this time, and the responsibility would be his alone.

"You can rely on me," he answered My Father.

"I knew I could," My Father said to him. Then he turned to me. "Come, my son, let us begin the journey." I was to walk with him again, even though we were all together! My joy nearly lifted me off my feet as I passed from the back of our procession to the front. Then, though I did not imagine I could possibly receive more honor, My Father turned to me in front of our tribe and said, "Joseph, you have made this journey a number of times now. Perhaps you should be the one to invoke the prayer before we depart."

And so it was. With my unchanged voice and my hairless chin, I stood beside My Father and said the words that I had heard him say on each journey, changing it only slightly so that I began the way My Auntie had taught me: "Dear Elohim, God of My Father Jacob, God of My Father Isaac, God of My Father Abraham, please lead us forward on a safe journey. I ask that you guard us in our departure, guard us in our arrival, and guard us along the way." My Father clapped me on the shoulder, and we began our walk to the south.

Our arrival was more like our first time in Hevron than the month-long times I usually spent there with the women and girls. I was still expected to do my daily practices, but My Brothers, without duties, were free to roam the land as well as relax in the shade. My Grandfather's tent was crowded at night, so many of them chose to sleep under the stars. I attempted to join the younger ones on the first night, but they sent me away.

"Joseph," Zevvy said, "Why don't you go sleep in our grandmother's tent? That is where you belong." Issachar and Gad laughed, though I saw nothing funny.

When I was going to explain that even when I was here on my other trips I did not sleep with the women, Dan spoke before I had a chance. "Or you probably have important work to do, Joseph. Should you really be here under the stars with shepherds when you could be writing scrolls and saying blessings?"

And just when I was going to explain the importance of writing and the importance of blessings but that it wasn't the time for either, Naftali nodded his head in agreement and spoke before I could. "Look around, Joseph," he said. "There is only room for the six of us men here." I looked around. Six brothers were lying on their mats with the vast wilderness open around them with room for our whole tribe to sleep next to them, let alone just one more.

Asher spoke before I could say anything. "Joseph," he said. "Go back in the tent. Do you really want to stay where you are not wanted?"

Since I had not gotten to say the other things, I thought that surely they wouldn't answer me when I asked why I could not be wanted among them. And so, I went back inside and took my usual place in My Grandfather's tent. The warm breeze stroked my forehead the way My Mother used to so long ago, and I fell asleep, alone.

That night, I dreamt of seven leopards. I was one of them, and the others were chasing after me. In my leopard thoughts, my voice said, "This is not right. I am a leopard just like you," but the other leopards continued to chase me until, finally, they caught me and clawed at me. Before I could see the destruction, I bolted upright and could not sleep for the rest of the night.

At the first sign of the sun, I rose and went to walk. I would begin my morning routine and continue about my day as I usually did when in Hevron. As much as possible, anyway. While I was in the hills, a feast was being prepared. Deenah came and got me, and we walked back to the campground together. I was tempted to challenge her to a race. My legs were longer than hers, and I would be the one to start before she was ready. But I could not muster the excitement and just walked looking down at my feet.

"Come on, Joseph," Deenah said. "Why are you moping?"

"My Brothers don't want me here," I said.

"Is here different than at our camp?" she asked. The question stung me, and I didn't answer.

"Joseph, we've come for a joyous occasion. We have been in this land for three years now. We have harvested a spectacular harvest. Elohim has blessed us greatly. Surely your prayers have had a part in that."

I took Deenah's hand and smiled. She was right, and I had not seen it before. *My Brothers think shepherding is the most important thing, but it is Elohim who provides everything, and I who speak with Elohim—something I had been getting better at each year under My Auntie's tutelage.*

"Yes," I agreed with her. "These three days of feasting on our harvest, . . . we would have no harvest if it were not for Elohim. I wish My Brothers understood the importance of my prayers. I'm glad you do, Deenah."

She smiled back at me and then pointed to the sky. "Look," she said. "Look at that beautiful bird!" My eyes searched over the treetops until they landed on a bird with blue wingtips. As I smiled, Deenah let go of my hand and began running back to the tents. By the time I realized her trick, she was many paces ahead of me and laughing. I might have arrived before her if we had gone the distance to My Grandfather's tent, but she slowed her step and began walking when the tents came into view.

The day passed with more and more smells joining each other in the air around us. Levi was preparing not one, but two kids for the feasting. Wine was being poured, stews were being boiled, and breads and sweet cakes were being made. I missed the quiet of my usual visits here, but the mood was festive now, and I liked that too.

The three days were filled not only with wonderful smells but fantastic tastes. We ate many of the first fruits that we had brought down on the carts. They were enjoyed with song and laughter. There was much dancing and merriment as well as time that could be filled as we wished. Reuben and Judah started a friendly competition to see who was the better marksman with a slingshot. It was impossible to tell which of them had better aim since both could hit a specified leaf off a tree or flower in a bunch. And though my skill paled next to theirs, they allowed me to participate.

Of course, the best part of the celebration was the storytelling. Everyone was happy for a good story, and many were told on that trip. Some were very short, like when My Grandmother said to My Father, "Do you remember that time a cat ran by and spilled your ink and stepped in it, leaving little paw prints on rugs and rocks and everything in between?" There were no details beyond that, but the memory was relived and witnessed and wonderful.

Some stories were longer. Gad told of a time that he and Shimon had snuck down to Lavan's camp and secretly put a dead mouse under his sleeping cushion. He had all our attention as he talked of moving the rug aside and digging a small hole in the ground below it, then placing the rotting flesh there and covering it again. Reuben told of a trader he'd met while watching the flock who was so hungry he was willing to trade anything for some of Reuben's barley cakes. Reuben pulled his cloak aside and displayed a dagger with a handle adorned with a carved sun to show us what he'd gotten. And Leah recalled weaving the cloak she liked to wear at every full moon, explaining how and why she chose each color and placed it where she did.

A new story was created while we were there. When Levi was preparing food, My Father approached him from behind and said, "I see you still like a good meal, Esau." He realized his mistake as soon as he'd made it and said it was Levi's red hair and grown size that had made him think of his brother. But from then on, there was a story of the time that My Father had called his son Levi by his brother's name.

My favorite story was one told by My Grandfather. He spoke loudly so that he could hear himself and told us of his brother, Ishmael. "My brother was much older than I was, and he never let me forget it. How could I forget it? From the moment I was born, he was already nearly a man. But he made it his job to remind me all the time. One afternoon, when he was tormenting me too close to others, my mother noticed this behavior. Ishmael was mocking me, and I was ready to cry.

"My Mother, my beautiful and beloved mother, Sarah, told My Father that he should send Ishmael away. After all, the covenant of Elohim would go through me. And so, he sent Ishmael and his mother, Hajar, out into the desert, and I could relax and feel safe, for there would be no way for him to belittle me any longer."

This story brought me hope, and I secretly wished that My Mother would tell My Father to send My Brothers into the desert so that I would not have to be bothered by them anymore. Of course, what I really longed for was to be one of them, but if they were not going to accept me, perhaps they could leave—whether of their own idea or not.

As it turned out, the only place My Brothers went was back to our land near Shechem. When our three days of celebration came to an end, preparing to return was much faster than our preparations to arrive. No food needed to be loaded on the carts, let alone counted. As I realized that, I retrieved my accounting scroll and ran off with it to Katib. I'd had no lessons during this three-day celebration, so I had not seen him, but surely he would want to see how well I had done at this work.

In his tent, he praised my handiwork. His words were encouraging. "Joseph, you have come a long way since you first began. Your hand is steadier in the writing, your columns are neat, and you have written each word correctly. I trust from your good work that your numbers were accurate. Well done, Joseph. Continue your practicing in Shechem, and we will advance our studies when you return. Perhaps while you are away this time, I will send a messenger with a scroll for you to read and respond to."

A messenger! He would send me a real message, and I would read the scroll! And write him one as well! My ears nearly danced with joy upon hearing such news.

But it was not to be, because that day, when everyone departed for Shechem, I was not with them. As I returned to the animals who were awaiting us, Shimon and Levi were there. The camels were gathered, and the carts were hooked to the donkeys. I guessed that the others were saying their goodbyes as I had already done. So, I waited by the carts, using the quiet to talk to Elohim right there.

I did not think there would be any danger in that. Neither did I think that Shimon and Levi were still of the mind to play the pushing game they had fancied as young boys. I was mistaken. Upon seeing me, they stopped talking and approached me. With the animals behind me and the top of the hill to one side and the bottom to my other, I could not leave without passing by them. I stayed, and they stayed. Levi grabbed my shoulders and pushed me to Shimon, who caught me, turned me around, and pushed me back to Levi. This went on so many times I could hardly see from dizziness. I ceased pleading for them to stop when it was clear that it only made them push me harder.

Luckily, I heard Reuben's voice after a while. "Leave the little one alone," he called to them. They both laughed, though not loud enough for Reuben to hear, especially since it seemed he was just walking by and calling for them to stop, not coming to make them do so. I tried to call after him, but my attempt at a word came out garbled. Nevertheless, it was enough for them to stop pushing me and instead have their fun watching me try to regain my balance. I reached out to steady myself on the nearest cart, but in my dizziness, I bumped into it instead and stumbled right over the edge of the hill.

It was not a steep hill, nor a high one, but the rocks on the side of it were many, and every one of them scraped me on my way down. By the time my body stopped at the bottom, I was lying on my side in a bed of rubble and covered in dust. And the debris did not limit itself to the outside of my body but also got into my mouth, nose, and ears. I coughed to expel as much as I could, but as I did, I found that any movement of my body caused severe pain in my right leg. When I looked at it, I saw it was covered in blood, and a bone was protruding from my skin between my knee and my ankle.

I called out for help but could not utter the word due to all the dust still in my throat. Furthermore, gathering the strength to use a loud voice was also a challenge as I clutched my middle, feeling as if I'd been punched in the stomach. Looking up, I saw Shimon and Levi at the top of the hill and knew I would be rescued.

"Should we go and get him?" Shimon asked.

"Why?" Levi replied. "He is useless. He doesn't help with the sheep or the crops. He is always off wandering, and his neediness distracts our father."

"Surely our father will notice him missing, though," Shimon argued.

I managed to eke out a few words. "He will notice I'm missing," I confirmed. But my effort was rewarded only with a rock that flew from Shimon's hand and landed frighteningly close to my chest.

"Well, I don't want to go down there," Levi said. "And for what? Only to have to carry him back up the hill?" With that, they walked away.

"Come back!" I called after them. "I need help! Would you leave your brother here? What will My Father say of this? Come back!" They were too distant to hear my cries for help, but luckily, they were not in vain. Soon, I heard my name being called.

"Joseph? Joseph? Is that you down there?" It was Ahuvah.

"Yes, yes," I called back.

"Wait there," she said. "I will bring help."

I rested my head and my voice. She would bring help. And she brought it quickly. I heard My Mother's voice and her sobs up on the hill. "Joseph, we are coming," she called down to me. "I am here," she continued. "We are coming." And while I listened to the comforting sound of her voice, I saw My Father and Judah descend the hill as quickly as they could without falling, and soon they were by my side.

When they reached me, Judah immediately removed his belt and tied it around my bleeding leg. I remembered when Reuben had helped My Father with his leg, and I remembered My Father's scream at the time. So, I was not embarrassed when one emerged from my own throat that was filled with pain, though muffled with dust. Then I asked My Father, "Will you put my leg back as Reuben did for you?"

"Joseph, this leg does not simply go back. It is not moved; it is broken," he said. And then, if there was more talk, I could not hear it. As My Father and Brother lifted me, the pain was blinding. I could not see, could not hear, could not stay awake. I only knew that two days later, I awoke on a cushion in My Grandmother's tent. My leg between my ankle and my knee was wrapped tightly in an herb-infused cloth. I could smell the strong scent of the herbs that were seeping into my skin. My Grandmother told me that I had slept most of the two days, only waking from pain occasionally, at which time I was given strong drinks to put me back to sleep.

"I will get Deborah," she said after stroking me just a little more. "She will want to check on your progress."

"There is no time for that," I protested, trying to use my elbows to get up. "Surely, My Father is anxious to get back to the flocks. I mustn't keep them any longer."

My Grandmother came back and smiled at me again, but this one wasn't the same loving look as when I awoke; this one was to give me love to balance the disappointment she would serve me alongside it. "They have already left, Joseph."

"Without me?" I nearly screamed.

"Your mother insisted that they stay an extra day, and she spent the whole time by your side. She saw that Deborah will take the best care of you. There is no better healer in the length and breadth of the land, Joseph. Your father knows that as well, though he still stayed and repeatedly prayed, 'Elohim, please heal him,' until long after the sun set. He will be back to retrieve you before the next new moon." But we had just had a new moon! We had come at the new moon. It was not even half full yet, and it was still growing. My Grandmother saw my disappointment.

"We will take good care of you, Joseph," she said. "And your father has left instructions that messages of your healing be sent to him. Soon, the first one will go out." I dropped my head back onto the cushion. "Rest," she said. "I'll bring Deborah."

My Auntie came in and sat beside me. She put her hand on my forehead and smiled. "I wasn't worried about you, Joseph. You still have a lot to learn and do. You will be with us for much longer."

"But My Grandmother said I am to return to Shechem at the new moon," I protested. This made her laugh.

"How are you feeling?" she asked me.

"I feel strong enough to make the journey home."

"You do?" she asked. She gave me her hand so I could use it to steady myself as I stood for the first time. I had no trouble putting my weight on my left leg, but just touching the right to the ground made me wince in pain.

"Maybe I won't walk," I said. "I can ride a camel."

"Very well, then," she replied. "When we send the message to your father, we will ask him to bring a camel for you when he returns. Until then, you will recuperate here. I will ask Katib to bring your supplies in here so that you do not need to walk and can use this time for your practice. But first, rest," she said, laying me back down as if I couldn't do even that myself.

"The sun is bright in the sky," I pointed out. Even from well inside the tent, that was clear to see. But she didn't allow me to continue the conversation. Instead, My Auntie sat beside my injured leg and began to talk to me about it while moving her hands over it. She took a deep breath in. *Yhhhh*. And released it. *Whhhh*. She did this several times.

"Joseph, inside your leg, there is bone, there is blood, there are muscles. There are pieces smaller than we can see with our eyes open but not too small for us to see with our eyes closed. Close your eyes and imagine, and watch as those pieces bond together, doing their job to heal and strengthen your leg." When I opened my eyes again, it was to the sunrise. I had slept another day.

On my fifth morning, I awoke to see Katib. As promised, we would send word to My Father about my recovery. And Katib offered me a gift. "If you are well enough to sit comfortably without pain so that your hand will stay steady, you may write the message." First the accounting, and now a real message! And to My Father, no less. Certainly, My Father missed me and would wish to know that I was well. I assured Katib I was fine.

In fact, I still had great pain in my leg, but it was lessening. And I was willing and able to ignore it for the sake of writing a message to My Father. I was given my first food since the fall, and that helped me feel strong. I sat steadily with all my tools. I found a parchment that seemed to be a good size for the task, prepared a reed, and kept another nearby just in case. I carefully mixed the ink, making sure not to drop it in My Grandmother's tent and not to leave lumps.

As I raised my hand to make the first mark, Katib stopped me from writing my words.

"This is how a message begins," he said. "You are addressing a man of honor, and so you must say so. He is not just any Jacob, but Jacob, son of Isaac, so you must call him such. These words are coming to him from Hevron, and so you must make that clear at the beginning. Let me see you write the words, 'Honored

Jacob, son of Isaac, a message from Hevron." I did as I was instructed.

Katib then went on to dictate almost the rest of the message.

Honored Jacob, son of Isaac,
A message from Hevron
Your son is awake.
He is healing under the care of Deborah.

Katib allowed me to melt the wax and pour it on the rolled parchment to seal it. I watched as he placed his insignia in the middle of the wax, at once closing the message and letting My Father know who had sent it. He even let me clean the wax off his ring, and I imagined myself having such a ring one day.

When Katib left, I found myself going back to sleep. Somehow, that short lesson had exhausted me. Again, I slept until morning. When the sun rose, I was eager to sit under it, but I could not walk, and I would not crawl like an animal. I punched my pillow in frustration, and the sound woke My Grandmother and My Auntie.

They each approached me with a cup of strong herbs to drink and some food to eat. I drank, but when My Auntie saw my hesitation to eat, she put the food away. My leg was feeling better, though still healing. At the same time, my anger was feeling worse. "I should not be here!" I yelled. "I should be with My Father, My Brothers, My Tribe, in the hills beside Shechem. I should not be here!" This was Shimon and Levi's fault. Though they had not pushed me down the hill, they'd caused my dizziness.

Their little game nearly cost me my life, and it did cost me my place. "I should not be here!" I yelled again.

"Joseph, come here," My Auntie beckoned me. "You may sit on my cushion." I had never sat on an elder's cushion, and that was motivation enough for me to stop my yelling and practice my hobbling. My Auntie sat next to me on My Grandmother's cushion and took my hand in hers.

"Do you remember what I taught you about opening?" I didn't want to open. I was angry. But I answered her question truthfully with a yes. As she continued to talk, she gently opened my fingers from their forced clench one by one. "Joseph, we all get hurt. There is pain, and there is sadness. When we close, we keep those things inside us. When we open, we free them to continue their journey, and then we are free to continue ours. A part of your journey was to fall down the hill and get hurt and get healed."

I didn't like her words, but I couldn't ignore the peace in her voice. My Auntie paused and took some slow breaths, inviting me to do so with her before she continued. "Joseph, you are a spark of Yah. We are all sparks of Yah. You, me, your father, your mother, your grandfather, your grandmother, your sisters, and yes, even your brothers. The trees, the hills, the sheep, the grass, the clouds, the sun, all of it—all of us—are sparks of Yah."

My Auntie was quiet for a moment, giving me time to really think about that. Then she continued on a lighter note, "Joseph, would it not be funny if clouds grew from the ground and rocks floated in the sky?" I giggled at the thought. Indeed, it would be funny. And I would always worry that a rock would fall on my head, though I think I would enjoy bouncing on the clouds if given the chance.

"Thanks to Yah, there are clouds in the sky. They bring us rain and shade. They don't come down to the land to try to give us something to walk on. The river does not say 'I am all wet all the time. It should not be this way. I want to be a mountain.' And if it did? If all the rivers wanted to be mountains, who would hold the fish? Who would help the water flow from here to there?"

I laughed at the thought of all the fish flopping around and asking, "Where are you, river?" and complaining that they were hot in the morning sun. My Auntie laughed with me when I told her of this thought. The smile on her face radiated as she took in my joy. Had that light always been there?

She continued her story. "Joseph, Yah is wise enough to make the rivers wet and the grass grow up, wise enough to make the sun shine and the rocks sturdy. Yah is wise enough to make some men shepherds and some dreamers, some merchants and some craftsmen, some playful and some princes. And some, still, that are all these things.

"Joseph, Yah, who is wise enough for all of that and more, is also wise enough to make a boy like you. There might be some things you do not enjoy—a broken leg, torturesome brothers, being separated from the others. But you are just like you because Yah was wise enough to make you that way. Joseph, do you question that wisdom?"

"No," I said immediately. I did not even need to think about it. Though hearing Elohim talk to me without dreams was still a struggle for me, I had no doubt in the glory that lay there.

"Then you need not be afraid when you get hurt. Wisdom lies there as well, and even if you do not understand it, Yah does. Now, give me your other hand," she instructed, and I did. We sat on the cushions, facing each other; my hands, almost the size of My Auntie's, were still small enough for her to close her fingers most of the way around them.

"Now, breathe Yah into your body, like this." Still holding my hands, My Auntie took a deep breath in through slightly parted lips, and I followed her example. *Yhhhh*. "Next, you will breathe yourself into everything around you—Yah, who is around you—and soon, your breath will be a part of that." She exhaled with a sound as slight as the inhale, and I did the same. *Whhhh*.

"You are doing beautifully," she said. "Now, take your hands out of mine but keep them just above, like a blanket that is about to softly cover my hands. Can you do that and still breathe this way?" I nodded that I could.

"Continue," she said. We sat there together, inhaling, *Yhhhh*, bringing Elohim—Yah—from all around into my body, pausing for a moment and then exhaling, *Whhhh*, sharing the breath that was in me with My God. On and on this went as I imagined my breaths mixing with My Auntie's breaths, with the hills just outside the tent, with the trees on the hills, and with the bugs and the birds in the trees. I drew my breath in from as far away as the sun and moon, and I sent it out to every star. With each inhale and exhale, I felt myself becoming more and more one with all that surrounded me.

My breaths became slower, further apart until I was no longer a boy sitting in a tent, but a rainbow of seven radiant colors in the dark expanse. Where once I had a head, I was now a beam of purple. Where my legs had once sat on the ground, I was a pool of red. From bottom to top, I had transformed into light of every color that blended together with everything. Everything. I was all of it, and all of it was me. We were one. The same. Bright and beautiful, dark and beautiful, everywhere and all.

I don't know how long I sat like that, but when I returned, I felt as if I were taking a breath for the first time and that I needed to practice just that even before I could open my eyes. When I was able to slowly do so and take in the world that surrounded me there in the tent, I saw that My Auntie was looking at me with tears and a smile. Before she had a chance to ask me, I said all that I could: "Wonderful."

"Hallelu Yah," she said. "And now, you know. Now you know who you are. That is you. You are that. All that you felt and knew when you were with Yah. Joseph, you are strong. You are a leader. You are a dreamer. You come from the wisdom and beauty of Yah. You are you, Joseph."

We looked into each other's eyes. I saw a river in hers. I don't know if she saw my colors in mine. Before I could ask her, she spoke again. "Joseph, do you remember when you interrupted me while scribing my scrolls?" I nodded that I did, being extra careful not to interrupt her again. "You asked why your brothers say you're a girl and say it unkindly." I always felt sad when My Brothers did this. And confused. They were trying to hurt me when they said it, but was being a girl such a bad thing? The words didn't match. Sitting with My Auntie that day, I didn't feel sadness or confusion. I still felt my colors. I felt happy being my colors.

"Joseph, what happens between day and night?" I was stunned by her question and had no answer. There was nothing between day and night. Either it was night, or it was day.

"Sunset, Joseph. And between night and day comes sunrise. The air is cooler than the day, warmer than the night. The sky is darker than the day, and lighter than the night. Not every day is the same. A long, hot day in the summer is not the same as a short, wet day in the winter. Every day is different, and every night is different. And every person is different.

"Some people are the first crack of light at sunrise, some are the later sunrise waking the sky to a new blue. Some are the sunset. Some are a long, hot, dry summer day, and some are a wet winter day of wind and rain and seeds soaking in the soil. Some are a night with a bright full moon, some are a night of clouds, and some are a night of stars and stars and stars and stars. So many stars that only Yah knows how many. Only Yah can call each one by name. Yah knows your name, Joseph. You only need to be Joseph."

It hadn't always been easy to be Joseph, but on that day, wrapped in my colors, I at least knew who Joseph . . . who I . . . was, and I did feel like a boy who was at least as glorious as a flickering star. I nodded my head to show that I understood. Then My Auntie closed her eyes and took one more deep breath. She finished by saying, "Hallelu Yah."

When she said that, My Grandmother lifted a timbrel. I hadn't noticed her at the other end of the tent, but I turned my head to the sound and saw her standing there, instrument in hand and a smile that somehow seemed bigger than her whole face. "Did you see that, Rebekah?" My Auntie asked.

Grandmother laughed. "I never see what you see," she said, "Yah has blessed me in different ways. But I saw love and peace, and I felt the love and peace, and I am grateful to have been included in that way," she said. Then she lifted the timbrel over her head and gave it a long shake. She shouted, "Hallelu Yah!"

"Hallelu Yah!" My Auntie shouted next. And then, suddenly, it was a back-and-forth of halleluyahs until I couldn't tell who was the start and who was the echo, but I joined in with both.

THE REST OF my time in Hevron was spent in this elevated connection with My God. My prayers turned into actual conversations—I could speak as well as hear now. It's not that My God used words in the way that I did, but I gained an understanding when I asked my questions and quietly waited. And though the waiting sometimes lasted days, I was no longer impatient since I knew that it would come when the time was right.

As my leg healed, I spent more and more time in the hills. It was glorious to be a part of it all. Out there, it was easy to remember myself as the colors I had experienced with Yah. I sometimes threw my arms out wide, pretending that I was wearing the colors even though I couldn't see them, only the memory of them. It was enough. On the day My Father returned, I was outside with my arms outstretched and my face pointed upward. He called to me from afar, and we met each other on the path. My leg wasn't strong enough to be fast, but I walked easily.

The embrace he gave me that day was different than that on any other. He saw immediately that I had changed, and he told me so. "I am proud of you, my son," he said. "You are the son of my ways. I can see that you are learning from Auntie what I learned from her. She sees things we do not see, knows things we cannot know. Elohim has chosen her for that, just as we were chosen for our lives."

I agreed.

After that, we walked to the campground in silence. I was curious to hear more about My Father's studies when he was a boy, but I also thought there was a chance he didn't know the words to tell me, just as I couldn't fully describe being cloaked in my colors of light.

CHAPTER 14

Returning to the hills near Shechem meant returning to my usual life. Though this consisted of daily opportunities to communicate with My God, it was also filled with challenges that didn't exist for me in Hevron. When My Brothers were watching the sheep, I was jealous of their opportunities. When they were in the camp, I was crowded by their noise, even while being excluded. My sisters worked together with My Mother and the other women to cook and harvest and weave, and every month, they celebrated the full moon. I was not a part of that either. I longed for Hevron.

Indeed, the month each year that I spent in Hevron with the women was a joy. The time I spent alone there didn't feel as alone, and there were other things that added to my day: my meals with the women and girls, sharing My Grandfather's tent, the celebration under the moon, and my studies with Katib. Over time, I learned to read and write in two languages, that of the local tribes and that of Egypt, where Katib had been born and received his training.

The most rewarding honor came during the times in which I scribed for My Auntie. The two of us spent many days together while the story of her life's experiences flowed from her mouth, through my hand, and onto the parchments. My Grandmother sewed each of these parchments together into scrolls that we called The Scrolls of Deborah. My Grandmother had a special earthen jug to hold them all, but sometimes she had me take them out to read to her and the women and girls. There was no need to check my chin for whiskers when writing or reading the story of My Auntie's life. Over the years, though my voice had begun to deepen and hairs had finally begun to grow from my chin, this task had nothing to do with age; the assignment was a gift from My God as a way to prepare me for being the man I was to become. Each time I removed the scrolls to read them, I could see how much my skill had improved since the visit before, and, of course, since I had begun the task as a young boy.

All the visits to Hevron were wonderful, but the ninth, and final, time we went was the best. That was when My Mother had begun to grow a rounded belly. After all the times she had been pregnant but not borne a baby, I felt as if I knew of the anticipation that met me at my birth. I would show this little one what it meant to be loved and cared for.

We were all eager to share the good news with My Grandmother and My Auntie. As soon as we arrived, they saw My Mother and kissed her and danced around her and rubbed her skin with fragrant oils. They combed her hair endlessly and took turns lying beside her and feeding her delicacies. It had been a long time since a baby had entered our tribe; even Tirzah and Emunah were almost old enough to be called women.

On our second night there, I was surprised to enter My Grandfather's tent and find a young man lying on the very same rug that I always chose for sleeping. This had never happened before, and I did not know what to do. Should I take a different sleeping place? Ask him to move? Surely a manservant training with Elioded would not be so disrespectful as to relax in My Grandfather's tent. "Are you a traveler?" I asked him.

The young man looked up at me. "No," he said. "Are you?"

"No." He still looked comfortable with his elbows propping him up on the pillow as he spoke to me but gave me no information as to why he was there or who he was. "Who are you, then? And why are you in this tent?" I asked.

"I am Reuel," he said. "This is my grandfather's tent. I always sleep here when I bring him hunt. Who are you?"

"I am Joseph," I answered. "This is *My* Grandfather's tent. I always sleep here when I come for my studies."

At this, Reuel stood and wrapped his arms around me. I must admit that my first reaction was to consider fleeing, but then I realized it was an embrace of welcome, not attack. "Brother!" he said, patting me on my back. "You must be a son of Jacob! My father, Esau, speaks nothing of him, but I, myself, have always been curious ever since our two tribes met when I was just a boy. Welcome!" I had never been welcomed so kindly as a brother, and I returned his embrace with enthusiasm, copying his back patting and welcoming him as well.

For seven days, Reuel and I lived as brothers in My Grandfather's tent. Each morning, we left to walk in the hills together—me to pray and him to hunt—and then parted with the anticipation of enjoying his catch later that evening with My Grandfather. We laughed together that this was our first time meeting, for I had been to Hevron every year, and it was his practice to come four times a year. "My father used to make the trip," Reuel told me, "to visit his own father and bring him sustenance. But his responsibilities are great as the head of our tribe in Seir, and Grandfather no longer is aware of who brings the meat. So now, My Father comes only once each year but sends me to honor his father."

Reuel was a skilled hunter, and we feasted every night. My Grandfather always thanked him for the food, addressing him as Esau even though he was so much younger. I enjoyed having my meals with Reuel. In the days he was there, we seemed to never stop talking when we were together. We shared laughter that we had never met before as well as stories of our own tribes and our hopes and anticipations about one day combining them. "I have many fine sisters," he said, "I see you have, as well. Think of the tribe of Isaac if his sons reunite and we live as one large tribe!"

We shared many talks and walks in our time together, but we kept returning to the idea of combining our tribes and seeing each other again. On his last night in Hevron, I dreamt of many dogs, too many to count, coming together on a road. There were no sheep for them to shepherd, no prey that they were hunting. They just walked separately, walked together, and then walked separately again. I told Reuel of my dream when we awoke.

"What does it mean?" he asked.

"The interpretations belong to My God," I responded. "But often, it seems that the animals in my dream represent people in my life."

"Then I hope this means we shall come together again soon," he said. Of course, I did not know on that day that this would be the final time I spent a month in Hevron, so I was as hopeful as he was that we would meet there again. Reuel politely parted with My Grandfather and then went to do the same with My Grandmother and My Auntie. We walked some distance into the hills together before we embraced once more, and then he turned toward Seir. My heart was full.

TWO NIGHTS AFTER Reuel left, we celebrated the full moon, and the following morning, I led the women back to our land near Shechem. I was old enough to do this now. My Father did not need to leave his flock and duties when I could help so easily.

Not much was worth remembering or noting once we had settled there, as most of it had been the same. We watched the flocks, grew grapes and grains, wove baskets and tales. Occasionally, the quiet was punctuated with market days or sheepshearing. Of course, I walked the hills and talked to My God, and I got better at hearing Elohim sometimes but even better at not minding when I didn't. Mostly, it was the steadiness of one day after the other.

I missed it later: that reliability, the comfort of quiet. The small pleasures. I later felt that I hadn't spent enough time appreciating that period when things were calm—when I wandered the hills and had my dreams looking at the clouds, when the barley grew and we harvested, when we dug wells and drank plenty. It felt that we were as settled as we had been in Haran, except without the fear of Lavan on the backs of our necks.

Not every moment was a dull one, of course. After all, it had been nearly ten years that our tribe camped by the city of Shechem. The young men were married and brought wives to our clan. Sadly, some were women they had brought from local tribes, and none were sisters of Reuel. There were the celebrations of the harvest festivals and the hot winds of the dry summers, but there was little that came as a change, whether expected or unexpected, and, therefore, little stands out. It was simply life as we knew it.

There was one piece of that period that didn't stay with me but did come back to me as a memory later, when all the changes began. We had been by Shechem five years already, long enough to no longer feel awe when looking at those city walls in the distance, and long enough to plant vineyards and pick the grapes. We all helped, even the babies, who were still called that even though they had already lost teeth by the time of that particular harvest.

I complained about it like everyone else, but the truth was that harvesting the grapes was one of my favorite times of year. My Brothers took turns coming in from the fields; most of them ignored me, but Reuben and Judah always shared a few words. I loved putting my hands around the fresh fruit and pulling it gently from the leaves, and the vines provided a bit of shade from the sun.

And, of course, there was the dancing on the grapes. While many tribes left this to the women, My Father so enjoyed his dancing that there was no way he could keep the rest of us from participating. My Father would come back from the flocks, wash his feet, and jump into the trough with whoever was in there. I always tried to be washed and stomping by the time he came in from the fields, but if I wasn't, I hurried to catch up.

Most of My Brothers thought this beneath them already, but I was never one to pass up time to be with My Father—and never one to miss out when he was in a joyful mood. I wasn't the only one. The girls and the women were there, of course, and some of My Brothers did come from time to time. I was so busy having fun, though, that I didn't even regret not having that time to myself with My Father.

One evening, when preparing the grapes for the blessings, and after a particularly rousing and spirited song that My Father had improvised, Deenah and I were still laughing after washing the grape skins off our feet, and we were still laughing while walking back to the camp. We were having such a good time that we decided to take a detour and relive the joy. We veered from the path and down to the wadi where we pretended that the low water was the juice made from grapes.

"Grapes, grapes, it's time to smash the grapes. Wine, wine, we'll turn them into wine. Drink wine, one day we'll drink the wine," Deenah sang, mimicking My Father with a broad smile on her face.

"Burp, burp, and then we'll burp and burp," I picked up where she'd left off. She had a better memory for songs than I did, so I may have changed the words a bit to see if I had the gift of song like My Father. It was easy to do because all I could think of was how I could make Deenah continue that wonderful laughter of hers. Every note rang with pure joy and was worth a thousand songs.

"Burp, burp, then we'll burp and burp," I repeated, and I was rewarded with more laughter.

"Joseph, you're hilarious. One day, surely, you will bring great joy to everyone."

"I'm happy just bringing great joy to you, Deenah," I said.

She blushed and smiled but stopped laughing.

"Really," I said. "I love to hear your laugh." I reached out and tickled her just to hear that laughter. And she did laugh, and she tickled me back. Soon, the two of us were laughing and rolling in the shallow wadi, tangled in tickles, oblivious to the water and everything else until we heard a sharp voice that brought us to a halt.

"Joseph! Deenah!" It was Reuben standing above us, already bearded and yelling with authority. We both mistook him for My Father. We stood quickly and looked up at him.

"How many summers have you now?" Reuben asked.

"Eleven," we both said.

"You are too old to be frolicking together like this. A boy and a girl should not be as close after ten summers. You're too old for this."

"But Reuben," I said. "We were laughing and having fun. And I've seen you frolicking with Bilhah. You are a man, and she a woman, and both of you far exceed ten summers. Why must we stop?"

"You're too young to understand," he said, then he walked away from us.

Deenah and I were perplexed as to how we could be too old and too young all at once. We didn't understand at the time what we had done wrong, but from Reuben's tone, we knew it was something, so we kept a distance between us from then on, spending time together only when with others until we would go back to Hevron.

We saw very little of each other outside of Hevron. I easily forgot about that day until more than five years later when Deenah called me to take a walk with her. "I'm going over by the city," she said while we were in the camp with others around. "It wouldn't be right for me to go myself. Would you come with me, Joseph?" I went.

We walked together in silence for some distance. We walked toward the city, then veered away, and Deenah led me down a steep hill and under an outcropping in the hill. We stopped at the mouth of a cave. She sat and pulled me down with her.

"Where are we?" I asked. "Is this safe? I have no slingshot with me; I can't protect us from a lion."

"Oh hush, Joseph," she chided. "Elohim will not let a wild beast nor any other harm come to us. Especially now, when things are so wonderful."

"So wonderful?" I asked. I wasn't sure what was so wonderful this moment as opposed to the moment before or the months before, but Deenah's world had changed, and mine was about to as well. She put her arm through mine and took my hand in hers and whispered even though there was no person who could possibly hear us even if we were to yell.

"Joseph," she said. "Joseph, the most wonderful thing has happened. Do you remember when we left Haran and came to the city?" I nodded. Of course, I remembered. "And do you remember the spice merchant and the wonderful wares in the windows?" I had since encountered more people than I ever had in my first six summers. I had seen people at market with all manner of clothes, crockery, and different skin colors. There were traders who came from the north—much farther north than Haran—who had skin as pale as clouds and traders who came from the south—much farther south than Egypt—who had skin as dark as a starless night. But even with all that wonder, I would never forget my first exposure to the world I'd seen in that city ten years earlier.

"Joseph, yesterday there was a festival in the city of Shechem."

"Yes," I said. "I know."

"I wanted to go. To see the city and how they were celebrating. I had so many things in my imagination and yet knew there must be even more than I could imagine. And I was right. I saw spice merchants again, not just one but two, though they both had mostly the same spices at different prices. I stopped and smelled each one until the merchant asked what I would like to buy. When I said that I had no coins, he shooed me away."

"Well, who was with you? Did he not have money?"

"Joseph, I went myself. At first, I'd been with some of the girls from the city whom I had met at market, but we quickly lost each other inside the walls."

I was silent. Stunned. A young woman walking through the city alone? What was she thinking? I would have gone with her. I would have loved to go with her! She wasn't the only one who had been excited by the city. As if to answer my thoughts she said, "Joseph, I cannot wait around for my brothers to come away from the sheep to take me if they please. It was a festival for one day only. I was not going to miss it. And it was not dangerous," she added at the end.

"Now, listen to me. Do you want to think about how dangerous it wasn't, or do you want me to tell you of my adventure? I brought you here so I could tell you."

I nodded. Of course, I wanted to hear.

"I told you of the spices. There were also merchants selling other wares, but I didn't stop to admire them. I simply strolled by as slowly as I could manage. I saw the sandal seller with shoes in patterns I could not dream of. The leather was tanned and adorned with linen that tied the sandals to the foot. Even the linen was adorned with beads. I overheard the seller telling a customer that the beads were fashioned out of shells from the great sea. Oh, how I wanted to reach my hand out and feel one, but I didn't dare after what had happened with the spices."

"But I got lucky the next time I came to a stop. A merchant selling tea had boiling hot water that he could pour over any kind of dried leaves. Leaves whose shape and aroma I could not name despite all my years in the garden. The merchant's wife offered me a cup of hot tea! 'Here,' she said, 'taste this one. It will be like nothing you've tried.' When she saw my eager eyes and my hesitation, she added, 'It's free. The first cup is at no cost.'

"And so, I drank. And she was wrong. It *was* similar to something I knew—the cinnamon! Do you remember?"

Of course, I remembered the cinnamon. Deenah saying the word brought the memory of the smell right back into my nose as if I were smelling it at that moment. I smiled and held her hand like we had that day. "You drank it?" I asked. "Tell me."

"I drank it, Joseph, and it was delicious. Cinnamon wasn't the only ingredient. The other was something I didn't know. But all together, the taste warmed my insides while also exciting my tongue as if it were preparing to dance. The woman saw how much I enjoyed it and asked if I'd like to buy some.

"I felt bad, so I told her, 'I'll come back later with My Father, and we will buy this tea,' I said. I had almost said 'with my husband,' but the word *father* came off my tongue, and I believe now that was a gift from Elohim because of what happened next."

Deenah was quiet. I could see she was breathing in the moment again, but I was eager to hear what happened next. I squeezed her hand and looked at her, the Deenah whom I had shared my childhood joys with—and who had done the same with me—but then we had grown apart. Here, we were together again. I felt the rush of happiness that her laughter had always brought me even though she was quiet.

I shoved my shoulder against hers playfully. "Nu," I said, "tell me. This sounds like the best part. Don't tease me—share it with me."

"Yes," she said. "Yes, Joseph, I brought you here to share it with you. To share all of it with you. After I said I would return with my father, a man whom I had somehow not noticed before said, 'There is no need to wait. I will buy the tea for this lovely maiden. I will buy her as much tea as she would like.'"

"The merchant's wife was more surprised by this than I was. Not that I wasn't surprised, which, of course, I was. But I quickly learned why she was so surprised when she said, 'Yes, of course, Prince Shechem. The lady may have whatever she chooses, and I hope you will choose as well.'"

At this point, Deenah stopped again, but I was grateful, as I had now joined in the surprise. "Prince Shechem? The prince?"

"Yes," she said. "A prince. The prince. Prince Shechem. Prince Shechem. Dear Shechem . . . And Shechem said that I may choose any teas I like. He addressed the woman and asked that she package up whatever I chose as well as seven additional kinds of tea. And the funny thing was that there were eight kinds of tea, so he had intentionally made it so that I would get to have some of each. The woman began scooping generous amounts from each sack and placing them in their own smaller sacks of cloth until she finally handed me several bundles that were awkward to carry since I had no basket. And so, Shechem, after paying the woman more coins than I have seen at one time, helped me to carry them.

"'These teas smell delicious,' he said to me. 'You chose well. You are clearly a woman of wisdom as well as beauty.' I felt my face flush with heat, and I didn't know whether to look away from this compliment or toward it. Joseph, Shechem is a beauty as well. He is as beautiful a man as you are. His eyes held the depth of all the wells from here to the great river, and his hair was as dark as charcoal, but, of course, not rough. Nor was his face rough. He was old enough to grow hair, yet his cheeks were smooth."

I instinctively rubbed my chin with my thumb. After sixteen summers, my face finally had hair. It was not yet long like My Father's or brothers', but it was a beard I wore with pride. Still, the habit of checking my chin for wisdom had remained even when the smoothness had left.

"But what really kept me looking at him," Deenah continued, "was the way he was looking at me. He smiled broadly and took me in with his eyes politely, curiously, not possessively. 'Would you do me the honor of coming back to the palace and sampling these teas with me? I have a fine kettle to prepare the water and cups that, before I saw you, I thought to be the most beauty I would ever see in my lifetime.'

"I would have laughed at his attempt at poetry, but I saw him to be sincere. I have witnessed men appreciating Rachel's beauty, and I see the same beauty in my own mother. And do you remember that Abraham said Sarah was a beauty as well? For the first time, I thought that maybe I possess some of that same beauty in me."

"Of course, you do!" I exclaimed, surprised that Deenah did not already know this.

"I walked with him through the winding streets of the city until we reached the center. A palace, indeed! We walked through a gate and into a courtyard you would not believe exists, Joseph. Flowers growing in rows according to their colors, and behind them, a polished stone sculpture of a man standing with a raised sword. There were paths inside the gate made of stones, but not because the ground was rough—they were laid there deliberately. They were flat stones that were easier to walk on than the most packed dirt paths. And on the other side of the courtyard, we entered into Shechem's chamber."

When we had wandered the city up north together as children, on our way from Haran, Deenah and I had seen many wondrous things together. As she talked, I imagined that I had been beside her in the palace, not hearing of it later.

"Of course, he lives indoors; no tents were in view. His house was bigger than I even imagine our grandfather Abraham's tent to be and bigger than all the dwellings of the city—even bigger than the inn where we once stayed. There were doors on each of the four walls that I learned led to separate chambers still within the same house. The rug on which we stepped, I can only imagine, took years to weave, and my mother is the best weaver I've ever seen. Her talent is indisputable."

Here she paused, as if I would ever dispute such a thing. I would no more question Leah's skill with the loom than I would My Mother's with the meals. Leah had a talent for choosing colors and creating patterns with the wool that were creative and unique. Among all the tents we've seen, we have never seen anyone with rugs as fine as Leah's.

"This rug, it was red, but not only red. It had dark red and light red and other shades of red in between. And while that might sound plain, it wasn't. There were shapes woven throughout—all in red. But the glory of the rug were the likenesses of elephants, a large circle of large elephants surrounding a baby elephant in the middle. Oh Joseph, elephants are the funniest creatures! At first, I did not believe Shechem when he told me these animals were real, but as he continued to tell me tales of them, I began to accept that there are simply more creatures on the land than I could ever imagine."

At that, I remembered My Auntie once talking of a hippopotamus. She had me write about this animal in her scrolls, but she also told me about the beast. Large and purple, living in the river, eyes peeking above the water, and mouth wide enough to open and swallow a man at any moment. Even when she told me the words, I could not imagine what this hippopotamus looked like, and now I wondered whether it might be like an elephant.

"Not even you with your vivid dreams could imagine such a funny-looking animal, Joseph. It is not really red, that was just in the rug. Shechem told me that a real elephant is gray and the size of four camels. Shechem says each leg is as wide as he is, and the tails are thin, like a donkey tail, with a little tuft of hair at the end. But the strangest parts of these beasts are their ears and their noses. Their ears are like the flap of a tent, and Shechem said they do flap them to keep cool. And the trunks! Shechem told me this is the proper name for their noses. Their trunks begin on their faces, higher than the height of a man, and extend all the way down to the ground, where their nostrils can smell the grasses and then choose which ones to grab and pull to their mouths with these long noses."

At this, Deenah fell to the ground laughing. Oh, that laughter! She went on all fours and used her arm to simulate a nose—a trunk—looking for grass. "Look at me," she said. "I'm an elephant." And she laughed and laughed, and her laughter was contagious. I joined her on all fours, pretending to be this mysterious animal along with her. We played like that for many moments before we locked our trunks together and began wrestling. This only made us laugh harder. We rolled around at the mouth of the cave, one on top of the other, then the other on top again until we finally unlocked trunks and lay side by side on our backs, gasping for breath from all the giggling.

"One day," she said, "I would like to see a real elephant. Not just one woven into rugs."

But I was no longer thinking of elephants. "You smell nice," I said, inhaling her scent fully for the first time.

"Yes," she said. "I will tell you the rest of the story. Shechem had his maidservants pour us tea and then leave us alone. We drank, and he told me stories of elephants and a fruit called *persimmon* that he said he will feed to me the next time we meet. And everything changed when he told me of his second time eating a persimmon. He said they are deliciously sweet, sweeter than dates, perhaps, and he loved them above all other fruits. And when he saw one perched on his father's table, he grabbed it and took a bite.

"But he was little at the time and didn't know about ripened and unripened fruits, and he learned the hard way. He bit greedily into the orange-colored fruit and found it to be alarmingly sour. As he told me the story, he made the same face that little Shechem must have made when he'd first made that innocent mistake, and I could not help but laugh. I caught myself, apologizing, 'Please forgive me, Prince Shechem,' I said, worried that I'd offended him.

"'You needn't call me that,' he said. And strangely, in that moment, we both realized that he did not know my name. 'I am Deenah, daughter of Leah and Jacob,' I said. And he took my hand in his and said, 'Deenah, daughter of Jacob and Leah, never quiet that beautiful laugh on my account. I have only been blessed to hear a little, and I already love it more than persimmons.' Which, of course, made me laugh again.

With that memory, Deenah laughed yet again, and I got to hear the sound that I've always loved so much.

"After that, Shechem spent a large amount of time doing whatever he could to make me laugh. He made the sour face again, pretended to be an elephant, and made a complete fool of himself doing anything for a laugh. And it worked. My laughter was genuine, and I enjoyed every moment. Part of my joy came from seeing his and knowing we were both outside of our duties, whatever they may be, just covered in smiles.

"When he could think of no more silliness, Shechem presented me with a bottle. 'Open it,' he said, and I did. It was a bottle of fragrant oil. I would describe it to you, but you are smelling it now."

I had hardly realized that I was holding Deenah's hand close to my face, taking in the lovely smell of her skin.

"Joseph, he asked if he could put the oil on my hands, and I said yes. He poured some into his own large, soft palms and took my smaller hand into both of his. I was briefly embarrassed about my rough callouses against his smooth skin, but any shame melted away as I looked into his eyes and felt his fingers alternatingly caressing and pressing on my hands. He did this for a long time before stopping to get more oil and asking permission to put it on my feet. Of course, I consented.

"Shechem sat before me with one of my feet in his lap and the other in his strong hands. He rubbed each one with the attention he'd given to my hands. I felt as if my whole body could melt into his hands, and I know he felt the same because as he finished with my feet, he asked whether he could put oil on my legs. Joseph, I couldn't even speak—my voice was not at my own command. I took his hands into mine and placed them on my legs to show my eagerness. As I did, I saw his eagerness in the form of a small tent arising toward the bottom of his short cloak."

Through Deenah's words, I felt what she had felt. With my eyes closed and the fragrance in my nose, it was as if the prince's soft hand were on my own legs. I was the eager one now. Though my tunic was longer than the one she'd described Shechem as wearing, mine was just as erect. I quivered as Deenah went on with her story.

"'I would like to take my tunic off,' Shechem said. 'And yours, if you will allow me the pleasure of putting oil on every piece of skin that is the beauty who is Deenah.' As he did so, I was experiencing such unknown pleasure that I could not form words, but sounds came from between my lips of their own making. And I wanted more. I poured some of the oil onto my own hands and reached out and put it on Shechem's strong chest, rubbing the wide muscles between his shoulders."

As Deenah said those words, she reached her hand to my chest, and though without oil and on top of my tunic, her touch elicited a sound from me that must have resembled the one she had made in the palace. As Deenah rubbed, she continued the story of her time with Shechem, and from that moment, she used her hands on my body in the same way she had done earlier with him and placed my own hands on her body, showing me where Shechem's had been. I will never remember her words since I was too absorbed in her touch to hear them. I could only follow her body's signals and mine until she finally guided me to enter her, saying, 'And then he entered my body. It hurt for just a moment, but he was gentle, and I met his every move.'"

"Am I hurting you now?" I asked.

"No," she whispered.

Our hips moved as one body, each of us experiencing our own ecstasy together until we dropped in exhilarated exhaustion.

The moment I fell asleep, I dreamt that My Sisters and the mothers were birds flying south as the weather got cold. They were strong white birds soaring beautifully in formation as one flock. And right behind them was a tenth bird. This one was white with blue wingtips and smaller than the others, and though she was following along, she was not merely flying but also singing. For the rest of the night, I slept with Deenah's body lying next to mine and the bird's beautiful song in my ears.

CHAPTER 15

Deenah and I stayed in our embrace throughout the night and into the morning. It was the most perfect oneness. I told Deenah of my dream, and she didn't laugh at me. I was so glad to be back with my confidante, my playmate, with whom I had now connected in a way more brilliant than I had ever imagined. "Joseph," she said as the sun rose. "There is more to my story."

I felt myself getting excited with these words, and I wondered what the prince had done next. I buried my lips into her neck, sucking gently below her ear.

"Not that kind of more," she said, though she moved my hand to the softness of her belly and moaned a little. I marveled to myself that there was now a sound I loved as much as the sound of her laughter. We didn't speak as we repeated the actions from the night before, though we did so much more quickly. In barely the blink of an eye, she'd opened her legs to welcome me.

We rocked only a few times before panting and screaming and collapsing.

I would have gone back to sleep, but after catching her breath, Deenah began to speak again. "Joseph, listen, there's more to my story. When I was with Shechem, it was just like this. A miracle, nothing less. I became one with his body, and he with mine, and it was glorious. We stayed in our embrace all night and into the morning, just like you and I did, and then we entwined again in the morning."

Earlier when I'd heard Deenah speaking of her experience with Shechem, it had aroused desire in me, but now it was arousing jealousy.

"Joseph, Shechem has professed his love for me. He told me all through the night in soft murmurings and loud moans of his desire to be with me. And I desire him. I want to combine my body with his again. I want to live in the city, in the palace. You will come and visit us and see his funny rugs and fancy cups."

I was quiet, and a long time passed.

"Joseph, today, the king, Shechem's father, will come and ask our father his bride-price for me."

"Whatever it is he names, I will work double to pay it!" I shouted.

She covered my lips with hers, and we locked in an embrace.

"Come," I said. "I will tell My Father now."

"No," she said, surprising me once again.

"No, Joseph. You and I will not marry," she said. She removed herself from my embrace, though she did not retreat from my hand when I held hers.

"Why not?" I demanded.

"Joseph, have you ever thought of marrying me?"

I confessed that I had never given it any thought until a moment ago. My Father would choose a bride for me when he deemed the time right. I hadn't thought of choosing my own, though now the thought consumed me.

"Well, I have thought of marrying you. You are my love. That is why I wanted to bring you here. But we will never marry. No matter the bride-price, it will be for Ahuvah. She is Leah's eldest daughter, and you are Rachel's eldest son. The two of you were always meant to marry. If you took me to wife, I would be your second wife, and I don't want that."

Ahuvah. Judah's twin, yet a girl. Certainly, I saw her at feasts, but even in Hevron, we were never together because she had always been with the other girls and women when I studied with Katib or My Auntie and slept in My Grandfather's tent. Was Deenah right about this? Was this what the women discussed while I prayed? "Not so," I demanded. "Just look at My Father. He has always loved My Mother more than your mother. Even if I must marry Ahuvah first, I will marry you the following week, just as My Father had with My Mother, and you will be my favorite."

"Joseph, my own mother was the second choice, and Ahuvah is my sister. My mother and Rachel have suffered in this competition, and I do not want that for myself. I hope that if you love me, you would not want it for me either. I never would have imagined that I would marry Shechem. I didn't even know him just days ago." Deenah paused and pried my fingers from my tight grasp of her hand. "Do not hold on to me, Joseph. You must open like our auntie taught us. You will marry Ahuvah, and she is wonderful.

I want that for you." After a moment of quiet, she added more softly, "And for her."

I could not answer. We stood and left the cave, climbed back up the hill, and walked back to the campground. I thought of the days when we used to run to My Grandfather's tent as quickly as we could. But on this day, I was walking as slowly as I could. Ahuvah? She was a nice girl. Of course, My Father's eldest daughter would be saved for me. But I would speak to him. He would understand my love for Deenah, remembering as he would the way he himself had married a woman other than the one he loved. I vowed to find him in the camp. But when we arrived, there was already a feast being prepared for welcoming Shechem's father, the king, Hamor.

Reuben saw us approaching and met us. "The king is here," he said, "to discuss a marriage between Deenah and his son. He says that his son has already known Deenah and loves her and wants her. Where have you two been?" Deenah and I looked at each other but offered no answer. Reuben shook his head and walked away.

We all gathered in My Father's large tent. Two lambs had been prepared, and cushions had been set out for our guests. My Father sat at a small table opposite King Hamor and Shechem. I sat on My Father's right side, and Reuben, on his left. My other brothers sat in a circle around us, and My Sisters and their mothers and mine sat in a circle around them. My fists opened and closed beneath the table. I did not want to look at Shechem due to rage over what he had done with Deenah. But I couldn't look away from his beauty.

Shechem was just as Deenah had described him. Strong, handsome, important. My thoughts turned to the two of them touching and caressing and rocking and, worst of all, laughing and moaning together. I could not wish it hadn't happened because would Deenah have taken me to the opening of the cave if it hadn't? To the opening of . . . her? I did wish I had been there, though, or, if they must be together again, that I would be there the next time.

My Father poured wine for himself and our guests and then for me and Reuben and then instructed me to pass the jug to Shimon for further distribution to the others. There were no manservants nor maidservants present for this meeting. Only family. Family and the intruders.

As I handed the jug to Shimon, I could see that he was as upset as I was. Had Deenah rocked with him as well? Looking around, I saw that all My Brothers and Sisters were upset too. And Deenah had told me that she'd come straight from the city and gotten me, so that could not be it. "Shimon, why are you so upset?"

"Joseph, this man has defiled our sister. He has lain with her before marriage, and he is not of our tribe. This is the reason we have all left the fields to gather here. Are you not upset about these things?"

"Of course, I am," I said. For I was.

When the wine had been passed around, it was King Hamor who spoke first. "My son Shechem longs for your daughter.

Please, give her to him in marriage. Intermarry with us. Give your daughters to us, and take our daughters for yourselves. You will dwell among us, and the land will be open before you to settle, move about, and acquire holdings in it."

Shechem spoke next, and his passion for Deenah was impossible to ignore. "Do me this favor, and I will pay whatever you tell me," he said to My Father, My Brothers, and me, looking at each one of us in turn. And when he locked eyes with Deenah, his voice softened, "Ask of me a bride-price ever so high, as well as gifts, and I will pay the price you name, only give me the girl to wife." He smiled at her. I turned and saw Deenah blush.

I recalled My Auntie once telling me the story of when Father Abraham had tasked his most trusted manservant with finding the right wife for Isaac. Of course, he'd found My Grandmother, Rebekah. Rebekah's father and brother had asked her if she wished to go; they had let her decide. Would it now be up to Deenah to choose this prince and a life of tea and oils with this man in his palace? She had already spoken her desire to me.

But she would not get a chance to speak it to the others. It was Naftali who spoke first. "Father, Deenah is to be my wife. Do not take from me this beauty. She is strong and wise like her mother and will be a fine mother to my sons." I understood now what Deenah had known all along. As the first son of his favored wife, I would have the privilege of marrying My Father's first daughter, Ahuvah. Perhaps Annah was promised to Dan, the eldest son not born of Leah, and so Deenah was to marry Naftali. The thought of Naftali lying with Deenah caused me to choke. Even if she were not to marry Shechem, I saw that she would not marry me.

"Quiet, Naftali," My Father said. "We have already discussed this. I decided to take Shimon and Levi's counsel on the matter." Shimon took this statement as permission to speak.

"We cannot do this thing that you ask," Shimon boldly told King Hamor. "We cannot give our sister to a man who is uncircumcised, for that is a disgrace among us. Only on this condition will we agree with you: every male among you must become circumcised. Then will we give our daughters to you and take your daughters for ourselves, and then we will dwell among you and become as one tribe."

"But if you will not listen to us," Levi added, "we will take our girl and go."

These words pleased the prince and his father. They vowed that upon returning home, they would circumcise each other as well as all the men of the city. Shimon and Levi smiled broadly, but I was close enough to hear Shimon whisper to his twin that the king was an ass. My Father didn't hear this. He was satisfied with the arrangement and called for the servants to bring in the feast that had been prepared. Shechem and his father, Hamor, were merry, and My Father was pleased. After the meal, he even asked Naftali to bring out his flute. My Father danced a happy jig even though Naftali's tune was a somber one. I heard the pain in his music, as it reflected my own feelings.

Deenah was escorted out of the tent with loud ululations from the women and handed off to a beaming Shechem. She took with her no maidservant nor cart of possessions. Shechem would provide everything she needed and more, he had assured us. The two of them chastely walked side by side without even brushing fingers, though we all knew they had touched before. This truth was more than I could handle. I turned my back and walked away from the newlyweds, believing I would never see Deenah again. While the others resumed their duties, I could only sulk. I stayed close to the tents but spent my time alone.

Three days later, Deenah was back. There was no feast announcing her arrival as there had been for her departure, nor did she return with her beloved. She was brought to our compound kicking and screaming with what was left of her voice. Shimon had her by one arm and Levi had her by the other, and they were alternating between carrying her when they could and dragging her when they couldn't.

"Deenah!" I exclaimed. "What is happening?"

"Joseph, get these beasts off me!" Her hair was wild, and her eyes, even more so. She was covered in filth, her tunic torn, looking more like a beast than Shimon and Levi, though I knew they had no hesitations when it came to cruelty. As I rushed toward them to pull Deenah away, Shimon pulled his dagger out and the sight stopped me. "Unhand me you filthy, despicable murderers!" Deenah cried. She spat on Levi and kicked Shimon in the shins, but still, they did not release her.

"Joseph, with you as my witness, I curse these butchers!" She looked up to the sky and roared a voice so distant from her usual one that I would not have recognized it had I not heard it coming from her body. "You have both spilled blood and will pay with your lives! Shimon, you have made women and children into captives. One day, you, too, shall know what it is to be a captive. Levi, you have taken me from my beloved and now you are even depriving me of the very land that was his. You, too, shall never have land of your own."

She stared each of her brothers in the eyes with looks that even scared me, though I was merely the witness. Shimon and Levi dropped Deenah on the ground and walked away. I ran to her side and attempted to hold her, to comfort her, but she pushed me away. The noise had brought Leah from the garden and My Mother from her tent. My Mother's belly was rounder every day, and it was difficult for her to walk much as the time for her to birth My Brother got closer and closer. Yet her strength was fully present as she and Leah helped Deenah to her feet and coaxed her to her mother's tent.

It wasn't long before I learned why and how Deenah had returned. Shimon and Levi bragged that they had slaughtered every last man in the city while they were incapacitated from their circumcisions. Of course, they could do no such thing—even with the help of My Brothers and their manservants who had come to their aid. There were hundreds of men in the city, and I knew My Brothers were lucky to have made it out alive at all. But while the men of the city recovered from their circumcisions, it had been possible for My Brothers to get inside and kill the men of the palace, catching them unaware. While fleeing, they'd burned enough homes to create chaos and a diversion to make their getaway with enough goods, unarmed women, and livestock to increase their riches and boast that they'd done far more than they had.

After dropping Deenah to the ground, Shimon and Levi had gone back to lead their brothers home with the bounty. As they approached, My Father waited for them, watching as they led the women and children—most still wailing—and the many sheep, camels, and donkeys pulling carts nearly overflowing with rugs and pillows and jugs and baskets full of food. Shimon and Levi bowed low before My Father, then they each reached up and handed him a golden ring, one from Hamor's finger and one from Shechem's.

My Father took the rings, examined them, then threw them into the dust. "You have brought trouble on me! You have made me odious to the inhabitants of the land, the Canaanites and the Perizzites. My men are few in number. If those tribes unite against me, my house will be destroyed!" He went on to both yell and mumble words about being outnumbered, his growing tribe being attacked by larger ones, and all his seed being ground to dust. He threw up his hands in the faces of Shimon and Levi and accused them of disgracing him in front of Elohim and neighbors and ending his line.

But they answered him calmly, "Should he benefit from taking our sister?"

My Father growled and stormed off to the hills. Never had I seen him so angry.

CHAPTER 16

My Father came back from the hills with a plan. "We will go to Beit El," he said. "When I fled Esau, Elohim appeared to me there. Elohim has now instructed me to return there as I flee—as we all flee—for our safety. The men of Shechem have no doubt already uncovered what happened and are merely waiting to recover their strength enough to come after us. Did you think some burning houses would be enough to drive everyone out of the city for all time? No, they will be back! Rid yourselves of the alien gods in your midst. Purify yourselves and change your clothes. We will build an altar to Elohim, who answered me when I was in distress the last time."

The four women whom Shimon and Levi had brought from the city of Shechem brought their idols and earrings to My Father, and he buried them. We set out on our journey, and we were not pursued, something for which we gave great thanks when arriving at Beit El.

My Father then erected a pillar and called me to his side. "Joseph," he said. "You are my only son who has not participated in this death and destruction. For your morality, you shall stand with me as I offer my thanksgiving to my god. Here, we will pray together, my son, and beseech guidance." At that, he anointed the pillar.

I dropped my head so My Father would not see the embarrassment rising red in my cheeks. Instead, he saw humility while I bathed in the shame and sadness of the real reasons I hadn't been in the raid. I could not tell him I had been left out once again. I could not tell him I was mourning when My Brothers went to attack. And I certainly could not tell him that losing Deenah was the reason for my sorrow. So, I let him think I was deserving of this honor, even though I was not. We closed our eyes and stood there like that for the remainder of the day while the rest of the camp surrounded us with their bodies and their stares.

At dusk, My Father announced, "My god has deemed me worthy of hearing and has said I am to be called Israel from now on. The tribes in this area will have heard of the sins of the sons of Jacob. But they shall not attack me in revenge, for I am not Jacob. I am Israel." He anointed the pillar once more, and we all dispersed.

I followed My Father and quickly caught up to him. My legs were long like his. I was no longer the little boy who had to work hard to keep up with him. I was a man. Big enough to have long strides, old enough to love Deenah, bold enough to speak my desire to My Father.

"Father," I said. He looked at me. "Father, Deenah is back now, and I wish to marry her." My Father said nothing. He just continued looking at me and I continued talking. "I wish to marry her, Father. I wish to marry Deenah, not Ahuvah. But I know you wish me to marry Ahuvah. I will marry them both, if that is what is most important to you. So long as I can be with Deenah. That is what's most important to me." Still he said nothing.

"Father, I love Deenah. I'm not upset that she went to marry the prince. None of My Brothers will want her like this, but I do. I have nothing to give you, but I will work for you . . . for seven years. Yes, just as you worked for Lavan for seven years in order to marry My Mother. And I'll work another seven for Ahuvah if you wish me to marry her first. Just please, don't make me wait as Lavan made you wait. I wish to marry Deenah now."

My Father stopped walking. He stood still for a long while, looking up at the hills ahead of him. When he finally turned his gaze to me, he sighed and said, "You are right, my son. Ahuvah should marry. Not you, of course, but now. Yes. And Annah, too."

Not me, of course? This stunned me to stillness just as My Father began to walk with speed and purpose. I almost asked him what he meant by that, but decided I could simply be happy that he wasn't requiring me to marry Ahuvah. "Thank you, Father. I shall be glad to only marry Deenah. And I will care for her and provide for her and bring you many descendants through her. Just as Elohim promised you."

"What?" My Father asked. "Hush now. Stop distracting me with this nonsense about Deenah. It is too late for her to help us. But Ahuvah will marry, and Annah, too. We must move quickly now, there is much to do. Go find my wives and send them to me in my tent at once." He nearly ran back to his tent.

My legs carried me almost as quickly to My Mother. I felt certain she would help me to understand what was happening. Certain she would help me to marry Deenah. But I was wrong. Because even though I entered our tent with tears on my face, I dutifully delivered the message from My Father first thing. Then without helping me to feel better at all, My Mother asked me to help her rise and she went to collect the other women and gather in My Father's tent.

Before the sun set on the third day, four brothers were wed to women they had brought back with them from Shechem and two of My Sisters—Ahuvah and Annah—were wed to Perizzite men. My Father said we would have alliances now and be safer. My Mother and the other women hugged each other and cried and cried. Except for Deenah. She wouldn't leave her mother's tent, and she wouldn't speak to me when I sought her out. So I went to talk to Elohim instead. *Why did My Father dismiss me? Why did My Mother not comfort me? Why did Deenah hide from me?* Although I asked questions, I received no answers.

For many days the mood in our tribe was mixed. The men were happy to have wives and about the prospect of becoming fathers. The women were sad and reassuring themselves that they would see Ahuvah and Annah again—the distance wasn't as far as Haran. I kept my eyes raised above the mountains, hoping for help from My God. My thoughts were with Deenah in her mother's tent, even though she would never allow my body to be there. It seemed life would continue like that forever until the day that My Mother approached me, smiling widely, with an assignment.

"Joseph," she said. "My Son. My beauty. My pride and the delight of my life." She smiled at me and ran her fingers through my curls as she had done when I was little. She even stroked my beard and laughed at the sight of it. Her large smile made the wrinkles on her face jump, and I realized that My Mother looked older than she used to.

"You are a grown man now, but you will always be my little boy, all my joy, walking in your body." I smiled. "It has been such a miracle to be your mother. All I ever wanted was more of you. And now, finally, I shall be a mother to another. I hope he will be just like you. The time will come soon for this little boy to exit my womb and enter my arms. Joseph, I want Mother to be here, and Auntie. I want their strength and love beside me when my time comes. Go, go to Hevron and ask them to come. Bring them back with you so that I may have their company and comfort."

I kissed My Mother. Of course, I would do anything she asked. I would have left immediately, but Leah instructed me to prepare camels for them to ride on and donkeys to pull carts with their belongings, should they wish to bring things. "And you must take a gift for your grandfather," she added. "I will speak with Israel about it, and you will leave with the first morning light."

I woke early the next morning. It was decided that I need not bring the animals and carts, for My Grandfather would have plenty for our journey back to Beit El, and I could travel faster without them. So, I carried only enough provisions for myself for the short trek, the gift for My Grandfather, and My Mother's desire that I hurry so that we could return before the birth.

My Grandfather expressed gratitude for the gift My Father had sent, but it came with an invitation to visit My Father's camp—his son's tribe—that My Grandfather declined. I decided that since My Grandfather still denied My Father favor even though he'd tried so hard to gain it, I would not grace My Grandfather with my presence. I still held anger toward My Father for not allowing me to marry Deenah yet, but I began to soften toward him as I felt the sting of his own father's disapproval toward him. I slept my last two nights in Hevron under the stars instead of under the covering of My Grandfather's tent.

During the two days I spent there, My Grandmother and My Auntie were busy with preparing for the journey. My Auntie sent me to fetch Katib and then sent the two of us together to bring Esau to the camp. While we walked toward Esau's camp in Seir, my thoughts were filled with Reuel. Would I see him? Would we greet each other warmly? Would we laugh together? And when I had fully felt the joy of what might come, I began to dream of My Brother. Finally, I would have a real brother all my own. A brother who would be, like me, from My Father and My Mother. A brother who would share My Mother's tent with me. He wouldn't always be a baby. One day we would dine together and talk with Elohim together and sing together and laugh together.

My dreams were interrupted by Katib telling me of his life as a boy in Egypt. He had lived by the river, he said. When I asked him about the hippopotamus I had heard about from My Auntie, he confirmed that he had, indeed, seen one—though, thankfully, only from afar. He had also once been tasked with writing the news of a hippopotamus that had eaten a rower who'd gotten stuck in the reeds and had jumped out to free his boat. It was one of the saddest and also one of the most interesting things he had ever been hired to write. I, not yet a married man, had already scribed The Scrolls of Deborah, which was far longer and more important than any of Katib's work. So, while he talked, I listened to a few words but mostly looked at the hills, hoping to see Reuel. I also talked to My God. If we were to make the journey there and back in one day, we would need to move quickly, and I would not have time to go elsewhere for my prayers.

When we arrived in Seir, Reuel was not there. Esau told me that he was out hunting. He also told me that Reuel had reported that I had been a pleasant companion during his time in Hevron and that he hoped to see me again.

"Joseph?"

"Yes, Uncle?"

"Do your brothers hope to see you again?"

None of My Brothers had ever said these words as Reuel had. And while Reuben and Judah were kind to me, even they seemed content to be out in the fields without me, never seeking my company when they came back. The others avoided me as well, and, when we were together, made a point of teasing me or belittling me—or worse. I was sorry that I could not answer My Uncle's question with a yes.

"Joseph," he continued. "From the moment of my birth—from even before—I was the bigger one, the stronger one, the fastest one, and the first one. But your father was the chosen one. I could not change what came from Yah, but I did not like it. In my anger and jealousy, there were many times I wanted to hurt your father, even though he was the chosen one. *Because* he was the chosen one."

I nodded my head. I was not sure what to say. Katib said nothing while the three of us walked. As he was my teacher of words, I decided to follow his example. We made the rest of the journey in silence. The next words I said were "Yes, Grandmother" on the following day when My Grandmother requested my help in the final preparations for our walk to Beit El.

The journey back to Beit El was much shorter than my usual return to Shechem, even with the women riding on camels. So, it was not long before we met up with Leah, who had walked out to meet us. She offered to guide the camels the rest of the way, allowing me to walk ahead and have quiet time with My God. Emunah had been placed on lookout, and as soon as she spotted me, she and Tirzah came running. The women were reunited, and I didn't see them again until a few nights later when the moon was full.

When the women of our camp danced under the full moon each month, I was not there. But when My Grandmother and My Auntie were there, it was understood that the celebration would happen just as it did in Hevron. That night, there was a bowl of water and a circle of women, drums and song, and something we had not done before: each one of us had a turn to thank My Auntie. The women slept together on the cushions under the stars. Even Deenah was among them, leaving her mother's tent for the first time since her return from Shechem, but I went to sleep in my tent.

It was only once morning came and Tirzah entered my tent to awaken me that I began to understand why we had each praised My Auntie. "Grandmother is calling for you," Tirzah said. "And for Father as well. I will wake him and meet you."

I went to help My Mother rise since she was full with the baby and had difficulty on her own, but then I remembered she was already with My Grandmother and My Auntie. I met My Father along the way. He was running with urgency. He'd known, and My Mother had known, what I was about to learn.

My Auntie was lying on a cloud of pillows with her head resting in My Grandmother's lap. Emunah was gently moistening her dry lips with olive oil. All the women were there. Even Deenah had remained or returned. I smiled at her, happy to see her even under such circumstances—especially under such circumstances—but she turned her back to me.

I noticed that Emunah and Tirzah were softly humming the moon song. The others noticed and joined in. Tears stained My Grandmother's face and ran down her neck. "She has said her goodbyes to all of us," Grandmother said, addressing My Father. "But I know she would wish to bid you farewell."

My Father took My Auntie's hand and kissed it. I followed his example with her other hand. She looked at each one of us, and a small smile curved her lips ever so slightly. Then she closed her eyes again. I did not know what to do next, but Leah rose and escorted me and My Father out of the tent. "I will tell you when she is gone," Leah said. "Pray for her comfort." I did. I prayed fervently for My Auntie's comfort until I heard a long wail that at once sounded like My Grandmother and also didn't. And then I prayed for my own.

Never had more of my attention been focused on talking to My God. I used every lesson My Auntie had taught me. I began by addressing Elohim. I sat in silence, moving from myself to part of the all, using my breath to do so. Inhale. *Yhhhh*. Exhale. *Whhhh. Yhhhh. Whhhh*. Until finally, I was still. "Thank you, Auntie," I heard my voice say. To my great surprise and delight,

I heard her answer, "You are welcome, Joseph." I was comforted in the knowing that she was still with me. When I finished my prayers, I went to the camp and finished My Auntie's scrolls of her life by writing about her death.

My Father would not allow any of the manservants to dig the grave for Deborah. He searched out the most beautiful tree and dug a hole beneath it himself. The women had washed her and covered her skin in fragrant oil and henna one last time before wrapping her in one of Leah's most beautiful rugs. They gently lowered her into the hole My Father had dug, and he and My Brothers covered her softly with soil. Then the women sat and cried there for three days while white blossoms fell from the tree and adorned My Auntie's grave. Only when their mourning was complete did My Grandmother rise and tell My Father we may continue on.

On that same day we left Beit El, and when we were still a far distance from Efrat, My Mother's labor began. There had not been a baby born in our tribe since Tirzah and Emunah, both of whom were nearing marriage age already. There had not been a living baby born from My Mother in the sixteen years of my lifetime. Soon, that would all change, and our camp, which had just begun to move again, made no complaints when we stopped for this occasion.

A tent was hastily assembled, and the women flocked to it. I kissed My Mother's hand and her belly as she parted with me to go deliver My Brother. I joined My Father in madness as we waited and waited and waited. The day turned to night, and the night was the longest of my life. Soon, I would have a little brother. Soon, I would hold him in my arms. I would no longer be the youngest, but I would not treat him as I had been treated, nor would I allow the others to do so. I would protect him and play with him and teach him what I knew, even if it wasn't shepherding.

"Blessed are You, Elohim, God of My Father Jacob, God of My Father Isaac, God of My Father Abraham," I said. I said this so often every day. I knew how to with ease now, with practice. But this time, I said something I had never said before: My God, thank You for bringing us to this day, the day of the birth of My Brother." Thus, I prayed and prayed until finally I heard the tiny sound of a tiny voice come from the tent.

My Father and I jumped into each other's arms and hugged. He squeezed me, patted me on the back, lifted me off the ground. He had always called me the son of his old age, but he did not seem old to me. Even in that moment, when a son was born to him at an even older age, he still was strong enough to lift me off the ground in joy. Once he'd set me down, he sounded the shofar, and all the brothers awoke and greeted us with smiles. Each brother hugged My Father, and each one patted me on my shoulder, even Shimon and Levi. Zevvy, who had always enjoyed his few months of seniority over me, congratulated me on no longer being the youngest.

With my face hurting from all the smiling, I waited eagerly for My Mother to exit the tent and tell me the name of My Brother. My Father was beside me, doing the same. As the waiting continued, My Father's face showed a hint of worry. "He must be a hungry baby, must be having a feast on his first day," he said. I nodded.

But a moment later, we could no longer disguise our worry in jokes or smiles. It was not My Mother who emerged from the tent, but Bilhah. Her face was streaked with tears, her voice barely above a whisper while she presented the baby to My Father. "His name is Ben Oni," she said. "Rachel lived long enough to give him that name: the son of my suffering. She suffered greatly in his birth. She no longer suffers."

"No!" The scream pierced the air and went on and on and was followed by another and another. "No!" It was not until a hand rested on my shoulder that I discovered the screams were my own. Deenah had come from the tent and held my hand. "Joseph, we did everything we could. The baby came out feet first. The midwife saved him. My mother cradled your mother as the blood spilled from her. We could do nothing to stop it. We tried. We tried. We tried. I am so sorry, Joseph." Deenah held me in a secure embrace and allowed me to cry on her shoulder.

My Father stormed to the tent where he was met by Leah and his own mother blocking his entrance. All three of them were wracked with sobs, but when My Father tried to push past the women, they were strong enough to hold him off. "Boys!" Leah yelled, and right away, Shimon and Levi, who were not boys but big men, stronger than My Father, gently turned him away and lowered him to the ground instead of allowing his limp body to fall.

I do not know what happened next. Deenah had somehow returned to the tent without my knowing. In the morning, I found myself in the spot where I had cried the night before, and I cried again. My Father was too bereaved to dig a grave for My Mother, but the sons of Bilhah loosened the ground beneath a carob tree while their mother cared for My Brother. He was fed to his satisfaction, not even knowing My Mother was gone.

The women stayed in the tent preparing her body, and in the evening, they brought her out wrapped in a blue and orange blanket to which Leah had added gold to the fringes. I could not see My Mother, but I wondered how she could be small enough for little Bilhah to carry her to her grave. Leah could not walk there on her own. She was supported by Tirzah on one side and Emunah on the other, even though their bodies, too, shook with sobs. Deenah held on to My Grandmother.

Bilhah placed the blanket with My Mother's body in the hole in the ground. Leah dropped to her belly and hugged the dirt that now held My Mother. Yes. I would do the same. If that is where My Mother is, then I will be as close as I can. I crawled on my belly until my fingers reached the end of the grave. Even when Dan and Naftali had covered her body with the desert dirt, enough tears fell from me, from Leah, from My Father, from Bilhah, from My Grandmother, and from all the others that the ground could have been fertile enough to grow a second tree there. But instead of new life, it held death.

We wailed for three days and three nights. I was given bowls of broth and barley cakes. I don't remember who brought them, only that each one was taken away still full. On the third day, Leah rose and took my hand and told me we must move on. My Father heard her words and rose. He ordered that the camp be packed and prepared to move soon, but not yet.

On his eighth day of life, My Father circumcised My Brother next to My Mother's grave, which was on the road to Bethlehem, where we had stopped our travels the day she'd died. Leah instructed her sons to prepare a feast even though we could not muster the strength to celebrate. "My sister's son will not enter this world to only sorrow," she insisted, though she was as filled with it as anyone. But we ate.

At the end, My Father proclaimed that My Brother's name shall not be Ben Oni, but Benjamin. "He will have a strong name," My Father said, "and we shall not be reminded of his mother's suffering every time we utter it." But I called him Benno in honor of My Mother's choice.

After the feast, we left. In less than a day's time, we got only as far as Migdal Eder. Nobody had the strength to move on, and so we simply stayed there. The camp was not all put up, but as days went by and things were needed, they were unloaded from the carts and then kept out. For more than a month, we lived like that, neither here nor there, walking in shadows, still deeply feeling the loss of My Mother and My Auntie. We did not know how long we would be there, and nobody questioned it. We would stay until we had reason to leave.

That reason came before we could have possibly been ready. I was praying on a hillside with Benno in my arms. I had taken to bringing him with me in the mornings so I could feel his breath against mine. While I was out there, Elioded came into my view. When we were together, I introduced him to my baby brother. "Congratulations," he said, clapping me on my shoulder and giving the baby a smile. When I told him of My Mother dying during childbirth and My Auntie's death just before, his compliments turned to condolences.

"Come," I beckoned him. "You have surely come to see My Grandmother." I brought him back to the campground and handed My Brother over to Bilhah when we came to her. Bilhah's face clouded when she saw Elioded, and she called out to Tirzah to fetch My Father. Then Bilhah followed us to My Grandmother's tent. My Father arrived there just as we did. He saw Elioded and dropped his head, walking into the tent. Moments later, I heard the sounds of My Father's wails once again. Elioded came out and informed the rest of us: My Grandfather Isaac had died.

This news prompted us to pack up our disheveled camp and go back to the tents of Hevron. My Father called to Kemke to lead us, and he rode a camel. The journey was somber. After the losses of My Auntie and My Mother, we had little strength left. Hearing of My Grandfather's death, though less surprising, was more than My Father could suffer.

I walked alongside him for some of the trip, telling him that I was still talking to Elohim, even in this time of sorrow. I kept my hands open, and I breathed deeply. I knew he had learned these things, but he was not doing them. I prayed almost all the time along the way. It helped me to keep my feet moving. I was filled with sadness like he was, but there was something else besides my sadness, whereas he seemed to have only despair.

When I saw My Grandfather's tent in the distance, my heart sang for the beautiful memories that returned with that sight. And then broke when it remembered the reason for our return. So this was the way I walked until we got there, alternating between happiness and sorrow with almost every step. Arriving at the campground, My Father instructed all his wives, sons, and daughters to join him in his father's tent.

Elioded and the others had already prepared My Grandfather's body, and it was no longer on his cushion in the place where I had grown so accustomed to seeing him. We all sat around on the rugs, and a meal appeared before us from somewhere. I could hardly remember the first time we'd all gathered in that tent. It had been for a much happier occasion. As if he shared my thoughts, My Father spoke of this.

"When we first gathered in My Father's tent, it was for a reunion after many years apart. Soon, there will be another reunion. Esau will arrive. I am surprised we got here before he did. Many years ago, when my grandfather Abraham died, my father and his brother Ishmael came together to bury him. I remember the day. I remember seeing Ishmael's tribe. I remember my father bringing his father into the Cave of Makhpelah for burial. This is what sons do: they bury their father. This is what brothers do: they come together for the sake of their father.

"You will see this burial. You will all remember it one day when it is my time to be buried, except Benjamin, who is too young. You will watch me bury my father as I watched him bury his, and thus you will know what to do."

"And they will know how to bury me, when my time comes!" Leah yelled. "Because they saw you bury my sister by the side of the road instead of in the burial ground she deserved!"

My Father did not respond. He was too tired for more. Without ceremony, he put his head back on a pillow and went to sleep. Leah and Tirzah led Rebekah back to the tent she had shared with Deborah for all those years. Deenah and Emunah followed. I quietly took myself to the pillow that I had slept on so many times in My Grandfather's tent and lay there awake for some time, wishing I could go with the women and wondering why My Father had not buried My Mother with honor.

That night, I dreamt twice of My Grandfather bound on the top of Mount Moriah. In the first dream, he was a young man. His eyes were shut tight, his fists were shut tight, and he was curled with his knees to his chest as he recited, "Yah will provide the sheep," over and over, panic growing in his voice with each repetition. The second dream was similar, but in this one, My Grandfather was an old man—as he was when I had known him. He was still being bound on the sacrificing rock and repeating the same words. But in this dream, he was relaxed. His eyes, hands, and body were open. His words weren't pleading; they were simply stating what was.

At first light, I awoke and stretched. I knew My Auntie would say: "You dreamt." I was eager to tell her of the dream. Tell her I understood her teachings about opening and that here they were again in this lesson from My Grandfather. Tell her I would be open to My God flowing through me. I bounded off my pillow with excitement of spreading this message and headed for My Grandmother's tent. I was nearly there before I fell to my knees remembering that I would not be able to share this news with My Auntie. She wasn't there. My Mother wasn't there. This memory hit me as if a boulder had fallen on my head and knocked me senseless.

There on the ground, my body was wracked with sobs. My wails woke the women, woke the men, woke the sheep and the camels and the hills themselves. Oh, how every part of me wanted to curl into a ball and hold myself tight. Perhaps if I were small enough, this pain could not find a way in! But the memory of My Grandfather crying out in his sleep as an old man forced me open. I pried my fingers apart and placed them on the ground to keep them that way. I opened my eyes wide and stared at them. I opened my mouth and inhaled the air of Hevron and expelled my supper from the night before. I breathed and I breathed and kept my eyes open in the morning light, forcing myself to see and be in all the pain.

"Grandfather, Auntie, come back," I cried. "Mother! Mother! Mother! Mother, come back!" This I pleaded again and again, though I knew they would not. "Come back." When I had said it as many times as I could, I changed my words to prayer. I began with My Grandfather's: "Yah will provide the sheep." I was in need of no sheep, but seeing the vision of calm that was on My Grandfather's face in the dream after he'd accepted that his god would take care of it helped symbolize for me the surrender I must give. My God would take care of me. I repeated and repeated and repeated those words, just as he had.

My body was exhausted, and I collapsed to the ground completely. At this, Tirzah emerged from Grandmother's tent and came and helped me up. She helped me walk to the tent where I was given a pillow to rest my head and water to wet my lips. I called out for My Grandmother, and she held my hand. "Grandmother," I said. "I understand Auntie's teachings." She smiled and squeezed my hand, and I fell asleep.

When I awoke the second time that day, the tent was empty. I took my walk out to the hills as I had done every morning on my yearly visits to Hevron. I breathed deeply and recited the words that were as familiar as the air: "Blessed are You, Elohim, God of My Father Jacob, God of My Father Isaac, God of My Father Abraham." And then I talked, and I listened. Nothing was different from all those many times I had done it before. The hills were the same, and the shrubs were the same. The sounds of the animals in the distance were the same, and the air was the same. All was the same, except I was different.

CHAPTER 17

Deenah didn't come and get me that day, and I didn't meditate with Grandfather. And so, I was still on the hills when Esau and his tribe came into view. I went back to the camp and informed My Father of their approach. The two brothers hadn't seen each other since our arrival in Hevron from Haran. This reunion was less formal, more subdued than the one we had witnessed all those years ago, and there were tears.

Esau kissed his mother's hand and bent to whisper a few words in her ear. She nodded and hugged him. And then the two brothers gathered their father's body in the ornate cloth in which it was wrapped and gently placed him on a stack of blankets in the back of a cart. The two of them walked in front of the donkey that pulled the cart, and all the rest of us followed. My Brothers, My Uncle's sons, their wives, their sisters, My Sisters, . . . all of us intermingled as if we were one tribe for that day.

I had only one purpose: to find Reuel. When I saw him, I learned that finding me was his hope as well. Once we were together, the funeral procession became a wonderful day. Overjoyed to be reunited, we talked the entire way. I told him of the recent deaths and the birth of My Brother. He listened attentively and told me of his marriage to a princess from a tribe in the south that would happen the following month. It wasn't just the big events that we discussed, though, but also our pleasure at having our tribes together for that day. We even joked around as I had seen My Brothers do with each other. I savored our time walking side by side.

When we reached the Cave of Makhpelah, My Father and his brother removed My Grandfather from the cart and carried him inside. What happened in there, we did not bear witness to, but when the men emerged, their necks were streaked with sweat, their faces with tears. Esau raised his voice and addressed us all. "Our grandfather, Abraham, bought this Cave from Efron for four hundred pieces of silver when Sarah died. It was the first piece of land he owned in this place that Yah promised him. That promise was made to Isaac after Abraham and to my brother, Israel, next."

"With our father's death, his land must go to the rightful heir." He turned to My Father. "Israel, I will return to my land in Seir, and you will settle in Hevron, where our father's camp awaits you. May you live long in the land that Yah swore to our fathers and to your descendants. May you have rains in season so that you may gather in your grains and new wine and olive oil. May you have grass for your flocks. May you eat and be fulfilled."

My Father spoke next. "Esau," he said, addressing his brother but doing so loud enough for us all to hear, "may you be fruitful and multiply. May you be the father of many princes. May Elohim bless you and watch over you." The two men nodded to each other, Esau kissed My Grandmother's hand, and then his tribe, including Reuel, followed him to Seir, while we followed My Father back to Hevron.

CHAPTER 18

Once we had settled in Hevron, My Father left the shepherding to My Brothers. Occasionally, he wandered the hills, talking to Elohim. I saw him and even heard him once, crying out in disappointment and anger about the death of My Mother. Mostly, he kept to himself. After we had been in Hevron for a couple of months, he called me to his tent. This was unexpected, and I did not know what to make of it. I did not wish to keep him waiting, but I also wanted to properly prepare. Except for baby Benno, all My Brothers were in the fields caring for the sheep, and so I could not ask them whether they had gotten a request such as this or what to expect.

Upon entering his tent, I bent and kissed his hand as I had seen him do with his own father so many times. A smile on his face showed me that this pleased him. He inquired about my practices, wondering whether I was still doing the work that My Auntie had taught me. Again, I pleased him by stating that I had. "And your dreams?" he asked.

"They continue," I told him. "Each one, as unique as the last. I am certain they contain messages, though I usually fail at understanding what they are. Still, they amaze me. Only six nights ago, I dreamt that I was wrapped in the river as if it were my cloak. In places, it was a bright blue, as the water is when it's calm, and in other places, it was white, as the water is in the wind. Between the calm waters and the flowing waters, the river sparkled in golden sunshine. The calm and the wind wrapped around me, and I was inside the river."

My Father nodded and was quiet for a moment. "How did you feel, Joseph? When you were in this river?"

"Proud," I said. "I was proud that the river had chosen me. And I felt one with it, as if I was always meant to wear the river." I hadn't shared a dream so openly since My Auntie had asked me about them, and I was glad to be having this moment with My Father.

Again, My Father nodded and was quiet before speaking. Then he stood, and I stood, and he clapped me on the shoulder. "Joseph, my son, I will call the others in from the fields for a feast. Return to sit beside me when we are all gathered." We exited his tent, and he blew the ram's horn, and with that, I was dismissed.

I returned to My Father's tent when the feast was ready as I had been told. Levi no longer assisted My Father in preparing the animals for slaughter; he now took that over himself. At My Father's request, he had prepared two kids to have a soft and pleasing texture. A stew had been cooked, and pitas lined platters, indicating that there was an abundance of food. Jugs of oil and fig wine had been brought in for the occasion—though none of us yet knew what we were celebrating.

We were all assembled in My Father's tent. All except one. Deenah had not emerged from My Grandmother's tent since we had settled here. When I sought her there, Leah sent me away and told me not to come again. My only chance to see Deenah was if she would come out. It seemed she would not be present even for this grand celebration. My Father recited a blessing, thanking Elohim for the abundance we were blessed with and for bringing us safely to Hevron and allowing us to dwell in the land of his father. We all ate and drank and did not need to be coaxed into a celebratory mood. Not since Benno's birth had there been merriment in the camp.

Some of My Brothers had taken wives, but there had been no celebrations. The women had come from Shechem, and My Father's anger still burned. We had gathered to mourn the deaths of My Mother and My Auntie and My Grandfather, but our losses were so great that there hadn't been merriment. I was glad My Father was creating a ceremony, even if I didn't know the reason. We would learn our reason for gathering in due time. Although My Brothers spent little time with me, Reuben and Judah always inquired after my health, and I was glad to eat with them.

When the final morsels had been consumed, My Father clapped his hands several times. Naftali rose with his flute, prepared to accompany a dance, but My Father motioned him to put it away. My Father wanted our attention so he could speak. It had been a long time since we had heard a story, and we all sat attentively at his feet as we'd done as children. Benno was the only child there, and, having not yet uttered his first word, he was too young to understand.

"When my honored grandfather Abraham followed Elohim to this land, he was promised that his children would inherit it. Yet at the time, he had no children. Nevertheless, he continued to follow the ways that Elohim told him. When there was famine here, he went down to Egypt, but he came back.

"Once back in this land, when my beautiful grandmother Sarah was still barren, she gave her handmaid to Abraham, and he fathered a son with her. That was Ishmael. But thirteen years later, Elohim opened Sarah's womb, and she bore my father, Isaac. When he married my mother, Rebekah, she, too, was barren. Many years passed before she conceived. Then my brother Esau and I were to share her womb, fighting over who would be first to exit."

It was the same story My Father had told countless times. But it was nice to hear it again, nice to hear him talking and not just praying or crying.

"And while I tried to be the firstborn, it was not Elohim's plan. My god's plan was for me to be second *and* for me to inherit the blessing of My Father. And so, it was. The blessing that came from Elohim to Abraham did not go to Abraham's first son, Ishmael, but to my father, Isaac. My own father's blessing did not go to his first son, but to me.

"You have met my brother," My Father continued. As a group, we had seen My Uncle twice. The first time was the meeting on the return from Haran that would be forever etched in our memories. I had seen him again when My Auntie had sent me to get him, but the second time for everyone else had been just recently when Esau had joined My Father in burying Isaac. Although he had not come with his entire camp, he was an impressive force, and those with him were a band of strong men, skilled hunters all of them, and equally strong women who were as good at cooking and weaving as our own women.

"My brother is mighty, and his people are many. Yet he was not the one who carried Abraham's blessing, I was. I am. I did not earn this blessing; I did not even buy this blessing with the stew I prepared for Esau so long ago. As I have aged, I've come to realize that I was chosen for this blessing. It was my god who had made this choice for reasons I do not understand, nor are they mine to know.

"When I fled from this land and went to Haran, Elohim promised to protect me. And I promised to return. We both kept our promises. We returned to this land ten years ago, and in that time, we have seen the fulfillment of Elohim's promise. All this land, abundant with grasses for our flocks and soil for our crops, is ours to settle."

It was good to hear this reassurance from My Father since he had so recently been so angry about my brothers' violence at Shechem. I noticed we all sat a little taller, a little prouder.

"I don't know why Elohim made this covenant with me, but I know how," he continued.

We waited in silence.

"Elohim made this covenant with me, with my father, and with my father's father when we were quiet, listening, and following what we'd heard, even when we didn't understand. I learned to do this from my father's example, from my grandfather's teachings, and from Deborah's example. They are all gone now, but their ways remain. And Joseph has been practicing them."

My Father turned to me now. "Joseph, do you speak to Elohim?" he asked.

"Yes," I said. I spoke to My God every day now, always.

"Does Elohim speak to you?" he asked.

For this, I needed to pause. Elohim's speaking to me was not the same kind of speaking as my kind of speaking. There were no words, but there were glimmers of understanding that had gotten stronger over the years. I had tried many times to ask My God for things, only to get no response, yet there were also many times that I was aware of things that could only have come from My God, including my dreams. And so, I answered yes to this question.

My Father rose from his cushion, and so everyone rose. "Joseph, my son," he said, "you are the son who carries on this wisdom and this connection for our tribe. I am proud of the work you have done these ten years. You are a light for all and should be dressed as such."

With that declaration, My Father reached behind his pillow and presented me with a cloak like no other. The cloak was made with fine threads and had stripes going around it. The stripes were in a pattern, a wide blue stripe followed by a narrow white stripe, then another blue, another white, and one more blue, and one more white. Each blue and white stripe was separated by a fine line of gold thread. I immediately recognized it as the river from my dream made from a material I could wear.

My Father dressed me in this cloak, holding it with his own hands as I placed my arms into the magnificent sleeves and then wrapped myself in it fully. It was the length of my whole body, stopping just above my ankles so that it would not be soiled as I walked. He handed me a belt that matched the blue of the cloak, and I tied it around my waist, closing myself into the majesty of this garment, into the majesty of the river.

My Father took me in his arms and kissed me first on one cheek and then the other. Then he took me by the hands and began dancing with me. Our feet stomped the rugs that lined the floor of his tent, and our arms swung together. He let go and lifted his arms above his head, swaying them back and forth, and I copied his movements. Then he put his hands down by his knees and shook his fingers loosely, and so did I. As with all My Father's dances, this one went through his whole body. But the joy was most evident on his face. The proud smile filled me with elation as I danced with My Father inside a circle of My Brothers.

It was only after My Father and I stopped moving that I noticed My Brothers had not been dancing around us at all, but merely standing. Their expressions did not match our joyful ones, but were cross, surprised, and sad. None of them congratulated me. And when My Father said the final prayer, thanking Elohim for the food and this day, none of them bade me goodnight—even when I did so to them. This was disappointing to me, but my mood could not be dampened while wearing the river.

In the morning, I dressed in my new cloak and left my old tunic aside. I went to find My Brothers before they returned to the sheep because I had some good news for them, news that would help them understand this gift I had received from My Father so that they could rejoice in it along with me. That night, I'd had two dreams in which My God helped me to understand that this was the right thing, and certainly My Brothers would understand once I told them.

Gad was the first brother I saw. "Gad," I called after him. He did not turn around, though. "Gad!" I called louder and quickened my pace. "Gad, I have some good news for you," I said as Judah came out of a tent. "Judah, you too," I said. "Judah, I had a dream last night, and you were there. You too, Gad. You were all there; even My Father, and even little Benno." I told My Brothers who had gathered to listen to the news. I smiled at them. Certainly, they would be pleased.

"Listen to this dream I had. I dreamt that we were all working in the field, binding sheaves. Suddenly, my sheaf stood up, stood up tall and remained upright. Then your sheaves gathered round and bowed low to my sheaf."

The words had hardly left my mouth before Dan growled at me. "Do you think you will reign over us?"

Issachar echoed him. "Do you mean to rule over us?"

And suddenly, they were all asking at once. "Do you think you will reign over us? Do you mean to rule over us?" Over and over, they asked. Louder and louder, they got. Closer and closer, they came. It was clear that their intent was the opposite of the sheaves. I could not argue with a dream. I could not argue with a message from Elohim. I tried to defend myself.

"That was not the only dream," I yelled over their questions. My Father, too, had come out of his tent to see what the noise was. I addressed him over My Brothers. "I also had another dream, where the sun, the moon, and eleven stars came and bowed before me." My Father would understand. He was also a dreamer.

"What is this dream you have dreamt?" My Father asked. "Are we to come, I and your mother and brothers, and bow down to the ground before you?"

I was speechless. It did seem clear that this was what the dream was telling me. And it seemed fitting with my new royal cloak My Father had gifted me. I had not expected his sternness of voice and manner or his surprise. Why was he not happy for me? Proud of me? While moments before I had felt sure that these dreams would enlighten My Brothers, I now saw the angry faces of ten men around me, close enough for me to feel their hot breath.

Suddenly, My Father blew the ram's horn, though we were all right there. "Back to the fields," he said, and with his own staff, he began walking to the hills for the first time in a long time. My Brothers stayed and stared at me a bit longer, then dispersed and returned to their duties. But as they left, I heard Dan whisper to Gad, "We go back to work as King Jo wears his royal robes and relaxes here." I sat on the ground, breathing deeply, releasing the fear that had gripped my body. It was slow to go.

The following month was one of confusion for me. Each morning, I walked away from the bustle of the campground to pray. My lips began by uttering the words that My Auntie had taught me: *Blessed are you, Elohim, God of My Father Jacob, God of My Father Isaac, God of My Father Abraham.* And then I spoke from my heart. For many days I asked and asked: Was the dream wrong? Did I understand it wrong? Was I not meant to wear this cloak?

I sat with my eyes closed, breathing slowly and listening, until the sun was high in the sky. Then I moved to the shade of the date trees and began again. When the sun went down, I closed my prayer and returned to the camp. I took my meal of bread and oil and bid goodnight to the sun. I asked that if I were to dream, I would have My God's help in understanding the dream or that

I would not dream at all. I got no help in interpreting dreams, but my second request was answered. I dreamt no more.

Some days later, My Father asked me to go look after the welfare of My Brothers and bring word back to him. They had left to pasture the sheep by our old fields outside of Shechem and had been gone longer than expected. I did not want to revisit the land where the city had been attacked and, worse, my heart. And My Brothers had shown me their bile when I'd received my coat. I did not wish to help them or even face them. What would they do without the sound of My Father's horn to send them away?

"Father, what shall I do if they still mock my dreams? And me? They left me only when you blew the ram's horn. What if they wish to harm me and you and the shofar blast is not there?"

My Father was quiet for a long moment. Then he answered. "They are your brothers. They will do you no harm. And I must know why they have not returned and how the flock is faring."

My Brothers surely could do me harm, but not all of them. I reminded myself that Reuben and Judah were My Brothers and had always been kind to me and that the others listened to them. And I could not deny My Father. "I am ready," I told him, then left the valley of Hevron to search for My Brothers and bring a report back to My Father.

The journey was an arduous one. The hills were familiar and even inviting. The way was well known to me from the many times I had made the trip after our months with My Grandmother and My Auntie. But the thoughts that accompanied me tortured me along the path. Why would My Father send me alone to My Brothers? He himself knew the venom one brother could hold for another. He himself knew the danger of being in the presence of one angry brother. What about ten? Why would he do this to me? Had I done something to lose his favor?

But upon arriving at the fields, My Brothers were nowhere in sight. I thanked My God for sparing me a confrontation with them. I would be able to return to My Father and tell him that I had completed my assignment and that it was no fault of mine that My Brothers were not there. I was doubly glad to leave the area since everywhere I turned, there were signs of our having lived there for so long. There were trash heaps that marked where the cooking tent had been. There were the wells we'd dug for ourselves in addition to the ones further out that we'd used for the flocks. And I came across holes in the ground that had held the poles where our tents had been standing for years. Our garden was now growing itself the best it could.

I also faced signs of our hasty departure and the reasons for it—shards of jugs broken in the battle, a stray earring, a child's sandal. It was a torn and bloodied rug scrap caught on a rock that felled me to my knees just outside the city walls. What had I done in coming here? My head could not hold the pain of this terror. I dropped to the ground, clutching my ears with my hands so as not to hear my own sobs. I wailed loudly but also quietly whispered, "Deenah, Deenah," for my heart broke again and again.

When my voice was finished with this lamenting, I sat quietly. I closed my eyes and opened my fists. The sun was high, but the city wall brought me shade. Soon, I would return to My Father and tell him that I had not found My Brothers. But first, I would need to sit quietly and restore myself. I would need to breathe in Elohim and become a part of the breaths again. *Yhhhh. Whhhh. Yhhhh. Whhhh.*

When I was calm, I arose to search once more for My Brothers. With the city wall to my left, I looked northward. I felt a sudden hand clasp my shoulder from behind, and a man's voice greeted me. "What are you looking for?" he asked.

I turned quickly, then upon seeing his face, I bowed low to the ground. "Esau," I said. I was tempted to ask My Uncle why he was there, but as he was carrying his bow and six arrows, and as he was my elder, I used the opportunity to ask for directions instead. "I am looking for My Brothers," I told him. "I must have erred in my journey. Can you tell me where they are pasturing?"

"I see you have a new cloak," he observed. I smiled. "A gift from your father, no doubt?"

"It is," I confirmed.

"And he gave one to each of your brothers as well?" he asked, though he seemed to know the answer.

"No, Uncle."

"Your brothers have gone from here. I heard them say, 'Let us go to Dotan.'"

I thanked him, though I was sorry my journey would be continuing.

"Joseph," he said. "Were your brothers jealous when you received this coat?"

"Yes," I said truthfully. "But some time has passed and certainly allowed their hearts to be open again." I hoped this second part would be as true as the first.

"Is that how it is with brothers who have been looked over?" Esau asked. And for that, I had no response. My Uncle clapped me on the shoulder. His hand was firm and strong like My Father's, though every bit of skin was covered in that red hair of his. As I turned toward Dotan, I felt my stomach jump with nerves.

I traveled for the rest of the day, stopping only when I had found a good place to sleep for the night. In finding a rock to rest my head, I was reminded of My Father's dream of the ladder when he had fled his brother so many years ago. I wondered whether I would dream now since I wished to flee mine but instead had to seek them. But I awoke in the morning having slept a restful sleep. I continued my search.

It wasn't long before I spotted our sheep and My Brothers with them. In the distance that I'd covered from the moment I'd seen them from afar, I rehearsed what I might say to them. Should I apologize for the dreams Elohim had given me? Should I pretend to no longer believe my cloak to be both special and deserved? Of course, these were falsehoods, impossibilities. Still, I tried many different words on my way. But when I arrived, I did not get a chance to say any of them.

Issachar approached me and put his arms around me. I thought for just a moment that it was a welcoming embrace, but I quickly learned that it was not. In fact, he used this position to strip me of my cloak! In one movement, I was standing in front of My Brothers as naked as the day I was born. Shimon and Levi came to my sides, and each took me by an arm. Issachar dropped my cloak to the dust and followed behind while Dan and Zevulun blocked my way from the front.

"What is happening?" I yelled. "What are you doing?" I struggled against My Brothers, but I was no match for them.

"Come on little dreamer," Naftali said. "Don't you know? Didn't you dream about this? We're putting you in a pit to die."

"What?" I yelled. "What? No, this is not right! Would you kill your own brother? What of My Father?"

As I asked that, Gad kicked me in the knee, and I buckled over. "Don't worry, King Jo," he said. "Our father has eleven other sons. He will not miss one."

Eleven! "Benno!" I shouted. "Don't take Benno's one brother from him!"

I made my body as heavy as possible. I pleaded with them for my life, but I could not stop them from pulling me across the ground. "Judah!" I called out. "Reuben!" But they did not come to my aide.

"Don't!" Reuben had yelled at the others. But when it was clear that they would not take direction from him, he walked away. I cried out for My God and was suddenly kicked to the bottom of a pit. Thankfully, it was empty—no water in it. Had it rained recently, I would have drowned as soon as I fell. I was given my life for a little longer.

"Help me out!" I screamed; but nobody did. I stood in the bottom of the hole and did the best I could to breathe as I had practiced so many times. It was meant to be a way to connect with My God, not a way to keep me alive, but I felt an urgency to calm myself since there was nothing else I could do. I pried my fingers open and placed them against the wall of the pit to keep them that way. Never did I want to be smaller, but I required myself to stand and breathe. In my quiet, I could hear My Brothers eating a meal at the mouth of the pit.

"Should we toss the boy some bread?" Asher asked.

"Let him dream of bread," Levi answered to great laughter.

"Let me out!" I yelled up to them, and they laughed even louder. I took a rock and gripped it with all my might. I threw it up toward the mouth of the pit and waited for it to hit a brother—any brother. But it didn't even make it to the surface. It slid back down the wall of the pit, and I had to move aside so that it wouldn't hit me. I took it again in my hand and used it to write on the wall: the body you have found here belongs to Joseph, beloved firstborn of Jacob and Rachel. I did not fall into this pit. I was pushed by My Brothers who had a feast while they left me to starve to death!

I let the rock go from my grip. *Breathe*! I told myself. *Breathe*! I closed my eyes and leaned my head against the wall of the pit. Inhale, *Yhhhh*, I bring My God into my body. Exhale, *Whhhh*, I connect what's in me with My God. Inhale. Exhale. Inhale. *Yhhhh*. Exhale. *Whhhh*. My breath tasted of the soil surrounding me. My naked body shivered with cold. Voices in my ears asked me over and over, "Will I live, or will I die? Will I live, or will I die?" I tried to overpower those voices by commanding myself to breathe.

"My God," I said quietly. "My God, this breath that You have given me is pure. You breathed it into me, and You keep it here. One day, You will take it from me. But for now, as long as that breath is in me, I am thankful to You. Blessed are You, God of My Fathers Abraham, Isaac, and Jacob, who breathes life into me."

As I finished my prayer, I felt warmed by a light that was not from the sun, but from inside the pit. It was making me warm, warmer, warmer yet. Was this My God, or was this my death? The light was all around me, through me, in me. My body shook, and I screamed. As I did, a rope came down into the pit and hit me on the head. Dan was at the top of the rope. "Grab on," he said. I thanked him, and I thanked My God as I was pulled up from death into life. At the top of the hole, I collapsed on the ground.

"Get up," Shimon said as he kicked me in the ribs. "We're not done with you yet."

"Leave him, now," Judah said. "I will take him from here."

"You will steal from us," Levi accused. But Judah simply stood tall and stared at Levi, daring him to question his honor again. Issachar and Zevulun joined Judah in the stare. Levi backed down. He knew Judah's honesty was beyond doubt.

Judah took a blanket from the back of a donkey and draped it over me so I would no longer be naked in the desert. He put his arm around my shoulder and steered me away from the others. "Thank you, Judah," I said. "I knew you would not let them harm me, your brother. My Father would be devastated."

"Our father will be devastated," Judah said.

"Yes," I agreed. "Especially after Shechem. He will also be angry that his sons would commit such a crime against his own son. But he will be proud of you for bringing me back."

"I am not bringing you back, Joseph." I stopped walking, shocked, but he nudged me to continue moving forward with him. "Joseph, they wanted to kill you. They will try again. Look ahead." I lifted my eyes. I saw a caravan approaching that I had been too busy to notice. "I convinced them to let me sell you to the Ishmaelites. They were satisfied that they would be rid of you and get some silver in addition, and so they agreed to take you out of the pit rather than leave you to rot."

"Judah," I said. I paused. I could not find the words to express this terrible betrayal. Maybe I should have known to expect such a thing from Shimon and Levi, but not from Judah. What would become of My Father when I didn't return? Of my new baby brother? Of me? "Judah," I said again, not knowing what else to say. As it turned out, I did not have time to say anything more because the Ishmaelites approached and Judah turned his attention to them.

"Peace be upon you," he addressed them. "I see you have many fine goods. You are traders?" Judah clearly already knew the answer. The men were on the road to Egypt, where they would sell their worldly goods at the highest price. The man at the head of the caravan nodded and dismounted from his camel. Judah continued, "Men, I have here a strong lad that I wish to trade for silver." The Ishmaelites looked me over. I dropped my head.

"Sixteen pieces," one of them said.

"Twenty," Judah replied. He nodded his head back to My Brothers. I saw them standing there, watching me being sold. All but Reuben. He always promised he would come back for me. Where was he now? "We are ten men," Judah went on. "We will not agree to anything less than two pieces of silver each." And then he added, "And a measure of salt. The boy can read."

"Twenty," the Ishmaelite agreed. He dropped the coins into Judah's hands and passed him a satchel of salt, which Judah discreetly put into his tunic. Tears streaked my cheeks.

"Joseph," Judah called me softly. I forced myself to look at him. Judah was a leader among the brothers. Though the fourth oldest, he was more decisive than Reuben and not reckless and destructive like Shimon and Levi. He was as strong a man as any, a fine shepherd and a righteous man—at least until this day. He resembled My Father, though he wore Leah's eyes. He looked at me with those eyes while bringing his thumb to stroke his chin, where a thick beard was growing long. "This is the safest way. It is the only way. May Elohim protect you and keep you."

With that, My Brother turned his back on me and walked away. I moved to run, but two Ishmaelites were quickly upon me, bringing me to the ground. "I am Qarib," a man standing over me said. "If you were a trader, you would already know that, for my reputation goes several paces before me. But since you do not know me, I will tell you: I value my goods, and I do not let them get away for free." Qarib walked away, and the two men who had tackled me tied a sack over my body, covering me from my head to my knees. With that, they lifted me and tied me to the back of a camel the way they would with any goods.

In the sack, slung over the camel, I bounced and bounced. My head ached, my body ached. My eyes were drained of all their tears, my throat felt as hollow as a reed. I was filled with shame that in the course of one day, I'd gone from being cloaked in a grand garment to covered in a sack and thrown over a camel like any material good. I was supposed to be walking the hills in splendor, but, instead, I was nothing but an item to trade, bump, bump, bumping along.

And so it was that along that desert road, my limp body against the hindquarters of a camel, my mind lamenting my sudden decline, I remembered the dream from the night I was born. The dream of seventeen spoons dipping into a dry well. The dream of them being thrown into a sack and carried off on a camel. My God had finally given me the understanding I had longed for. The precious cargo wasn't ornate spoons—it was me. And the spoons themselves were not the seventeen loved ones who had surrounded me on the day I was born but the seventeen years that had passed since. That dream had been a message for me that I now finally understood, and it helped me understand my other dreams all at once.

"Thank you," I whispered to My God. "Hallelu Yah."

I whispered, "Hallelu Yah," again and again. With each move of the camel's hindquarters, it was another "Hallelu Yah." Again and again, over and over, coursing through my whole body until it overtook me completely; then I wiggled until I caused myself to fall from the camel, feet first, and land on the ground.

I sat myself up and put my hands above me and tore a hole in the bottom of the sack, which I was then able to push my head through while pulling down on the sack. In that moment, I felt as if I possessed the same strength My Father had when he'd pushed the cover off the well single-handed so many years ago. Thinking of My Father brought me no worry. I knew with certainty that Elohim would watch over him.

With my head out, I could breathe the fresh air again and see the sun, the sky above me, and the beautiful hills stretching out into the distance. Looking down at where I landed, I saw an energetic little bee drinking nectar from a vibrant purple hollyhock, and my whole body filled with bliss. For a moment, the Ishmaelites approached me, but with a reverent look in their eyes, they stopped and just stared. After my head, I pushed my shoulders through the bag, then my arms. I pulled the sack down to my waist so that it would cover my bottom half instead of the top.

Although I was still covered in the sack cloth, I felt like I was wearing nothing less than the cloak of Elohim. My real cloak. I felt the colors of this cloak, the very same upside-down rainbow from the day in My Auntie's tent, looping around my body, at once surrounding me and being me. I put my arms out wide to my sides, raised my hands and my face and my chest to the sky and spun in circles and sang out to My God.

"Hallelu Yah! Hallelu Yah!" I sang. I danced and danced like that—with my arms wide open, taking in the sun and the land, the trees and the sky—one with all of them and more. And I shouted and sang to My God: "I am learning! I am strong! I lead! I dream! I live! I am here! I am Joseph! Hallelu Yah!"

CHAPTER 19

I have hardly slept since I began writing these scrolls. The only light is from the oil lamps, and without the sun, I don't know when the day turns to night. I write until my eyes begin to close, then I lie in my cushioned casket. It is so much smaller than the bed to which I have grown accustomed, but it is cozy and almost feels like I have loving arms wrapped around me. When I awaken, I eat and drink from the stores of riches that are here in my chamber to be used in the next life. I've been using an empty jug as a chamber pot. I'm grateful that the lid can seal so tightly. Someone will have quite the surprise when they open it. Embalming is a smelly process, so the stink will be just one of many that day. I'm glad I don't need to smell it as I write. That would be a great distraction. More than half the oil has already burned, even though I extinguish all but two lamps while I sleep. I must record the stories of my time in Egypt before it runs out.

• • •

THE WALK TO Egypt was blissful. My kinsmen, the Ishmaelites—for they were my kinsmen—were surprised to see me so calm, content, and even happy. I was the one who woke them each morning, eager to continue the journey. Every morning, I walked with My God closer and closer to the destiny I had dreamt about. I helped My Cousins load the donkeys, draw water, pitch tents, . . . anything they needed. And my scribing was useful when it became clear that they had not been keeping a record of the goods they'd been delivering. My accounting helped them get a much higher price in the markets of Egypt than they would have otherwise. Qarib invited me to stay with them to continue trading and traveling far and wide.

The truth is that I was tempted by the offer. I enjoyed my time with the Ishmaelites. I enjoyed hearing their stories of our great-grandfather Abraham and my own grandfather's brother, Ishmael. I enjoyed the hospitality of these men and the adventures of the travel. I enjoyed walking and talking with Elohim and seeing the other travelers we met on the highway. I even enjoyed reminiscing about walking from Haran to Canaan as a young boy. I would have been happy to continue exploring the world with them had I not had a destiny to fulfill, one that was calling me louder and louder the closer and closer we got to the river.

Or so I thought for the two months of walking in the desert. The hills were so beautiful. Looking ahead from afar, they always seemed as if they were covered in a blanket of brown. Yet at close view, every step on the path was full of life. Little bushes still had blooms from the rains a month before, and mice and lizards scampered out of the way as our feet approached. Deer grazed in the distance, and the eyes of big cats shone in the light of our campfires at night. The Ishmaelites took turns guarding our little camp by the fire, two men each night. I always felt protected from those cats.

I worried briefly about being attacked by thieves. We were traveling with a large amount of goods, even half of which could tempt the richest of bandits. When I mentioned my concern to Qarib, he just laughed. "We are the men that others worry about," he said. "We have developed a reputation, and all the traders on this route know us. They know we will deal fairly with anyone who has something we wish to buy and harshly with anyone who tries to take without trade."

I saw this come to pass only one day after I had told Qarib of my worry. A band of men approached us from the south. They had a caravan of camels, each one more burdened than the one before it. Their donkeys pulled carts of what seemed to be plundered, broken goods. No attempts were made to maintain their wholeness or any beauty they once had. The men's heads were covered in scarves; they were dressed well while they were followed by slaves, naked or in rags.

Six of those travelers broke off from the rest, who stayed a short distance behind, watching. Qarib took four of his brethren, three with spears and one with a bow and arrow. He then handed me a dagger and allowed me to come and meet the men with him. As we approached, each of those men drew a dagger from their robe and held it high. The Ishmaelites remained calm and continued walking until we were just a few paces out of their reach.

"We wish to make a trade," the leader of the band announced. "You will give us your goods, and in exchange, we will allow you to keep your lives." At those words, he and his men raised their daggers high.

Qarib spoke to the man softly. "My friends," he said, "one day, the earth will be changed, and the heavens too. You must watch for this day, when all will appear before Allah—the One, the Supreme. On that day, you will see the wicked bound together in chains. Their bodies will be clothed in tar, their faces covered in flames. Do you wish that for yourselves? Allah will reward every soul for what it has committed. We reject your trade, but I will give you three pieces of silver and *your* lives in exchange for the slaves you have mistreated. What do you choose? Surely Allah is swift in reckoning."

"You are Ishmaelites?" To answer, Qarib swiftly moved his spear across the hands of the traders, knocking their daggers to the dust almost before I knew what was even happening. While I wondered whether perhaps Qarib could ever teach me this by putting his arms on mine while I held the spear, five of the traders stood still, and the leader went back to get his slaves. He quickly returned with two tired women and four naked boys covered in scars and presented them to Qarib. He turned his back to walk away, but Qarib called him back and gave him the three pieces of silver he'd offered. Calmly, without fear, Qarib returned to our group, and we followed closely behind. When we returned to the carts, there were clothes, water, and food awaiting the slaves. I praised My God for allowing me to be in the care of such kind men.

In addition to being honest and protective, Qarib was also a man of many words, and he often shared those words in the form of stories. We always knew when he would tell a story, be it long or short, because he would ask: "Has a man even lived if there is no story that tells of his life?" On the day that he'd bought the slaves, he asked his opening question and then went on with this story:

"Long ago, when my blessed great-grandfather Abraham left the land of his birth, Allah brought him to the land of the Canaanites. And Allah promised, 'Those who bless you shall be blessed, and those who curse you shall be cursed. And if you are grateful, I will certainly give you more. But if you are ungrateful, surely my punishment is severe.' So, you see, I show my gratitude to Allah by helping His people live better. In my camp, nobody is beaten or starved. The people bless me for it, and thereby bring more blessing upon themselves."

That same day, I told the Ishmaelites of walking to the land of Canaan with My Father. I told them of how My Father gathered his whole household and how we traveled over the hills and across the river and through the valleys until we reached My Grandfather Isaac's tents. The pain from My Father sending me into the hands of My Brothers was still sharp, but I had to tell a story, for I could not have My Ancestors be men who did not truly live. I did enjoy Qarib's attention while I spoke.

Thus, we traveled to Egypt. My captors-turned-cousins bought and sold wares and did well on their deals—even better with my accounting assistance. We told each other stories, and we dreamt under the desert stars for forty-four nights. On the forty-fifth night, we slept by the riverside.

Oh, to have reached the river! I heard it before I saw it and asked Qarib what was the source of that strange sound.

"It is a river," he said, "but not just any river. You could have seen one hundred rivers, Joseph, and still not have seen anything like this river. *The* River. It is the source of all life in Egypt. They do not need rains, for they have The River to water the soil and grow the grain."

"I have seen such a river," I said, thinking back to the awe of coming to the river in the north.

"Not like this one," Qarib tried to assure me. But I did not believe him. I may have never been to Egypt, but I had traveled, and I had crossed the great river, and I was excited to arrive at this one. But when we did get close enough to see The River, I learned that Qarib was right. Even the great river in the north looked like a child's spit compared to this. And though I was filled with awe, I did not admit to my ignorance. I kept walking along with the others until my excitement was irresistible.

The land was flat by The River, the hills behind us. Qarib said we would set up our camp not far from the edge of the water, and while the men were busy relieving the donkeys of their loads for the evening, I discarded the sack that had become my tunic and pushed past the reeds and into The River. I splashed with delight, not able to quiet my joy.

"Joseph!" one of the men called out to me, and I waved. Then other men gathered around him, and they watched me playing in the water. I blew bubbles out of my bottom and giggled with delight. I called them to come in and splash with me.

"Come out, Joseph!" they called to me. The sun had not yet gone down, and the water was fresh and enlivening. I considered floating on my back, but I was not yet brave enough to leave the worry of being flipped to my front, and so, I splashed more. I tried to throw the water to them to entice them to join me, but I couldn't get it farther than the reeds.

Then Qarib joined the other men and also called me to come out. But that was not all he said. He said, "Joseph! Come out! A crocodile!" And he pointed behind me.

A crocodile? I thought. I had heard the word from My Auntie when she'd told some of her stories of The River. She tried to tell me about this animal, but I could not imagine it. Now would be my chance to see one. My curiosity caused me to look quickly in the direction that Qarib pointed. As soon as I did, I saw eyes the size of my fists just above a long snout and a mouth full of knife-like teeth. I squealed and ran out of The River as quickly as my legs could take me, thankfully, quickly enough. When I looked back, the crocodile was in the same place, but I was safe on shore.

Though I was safe from the crocodile, at least, I could not avoid the laughter of my fellow travelers. They flung their arms and legs in all different directions and ran around looking over their shoulders. Their mocking was so funny, I couldn't help but laugh at myself and join in the dance. Qarib brought me my cloak. "Ah, Joseph," he said, still with levity in his voice, "did I not tell you that The River is the source of all life?" I could not help but laugh with him. After that, I only went in The River until it reached my knees—and in places where the men told me it was safe.

We did not have many dips into The River because by the time we got there, our journey together was nearly ending. Qarib asked me several times to continue with them, to do their accounting and be one of their tribe. "You would be well cared for," he said, and, of course, I knew this to be true for they had treated me well on our journey. But I knew that my place was in

Egypt. Elohim had brought me here for a reason that I would later learn, and I could not leave before that.

And so, Qarib made sure that I was sold to Potifar, a wealthy man in Pharaoh's court who was reputed to not beat his servants. When others offered Qarib coins in exchange for my services, he declined until Potifar made an offer. He nudged me and quietly whispered, "Salaam Alaikum, Joseph." I hugged him, which caused everyone to stare—the traders, Potifar, and Qarib himself, but I'm not sure I could have turned to my next task without doing so.

CHAPTER 20

In Potifar's house, I quickly became trusted and essential. He was wealthy and honest in business and could see my sincerity in wanting to help him run his household efficiently. Even in my first days there, I had many opportunities to be grateful to Katib and My Auntie, My Mother and My Father, and all those who had contributed to my learning. The many lessons in reading, writing, and speaking other languages brought me quick advancement in Potifar's house, and I enjoyed a place of honor and prestige.

While I took stock of Potifar's assets, I was able to admire the grounds. For many days, I had a guide with me. He was somewhat of a guard, put there to watch and ensure that I was only counting and accounting, not taking. He was clean shaven, as I now was, and wore a simple short kilt and unadorned sandals—as did I. Looking at us from afar, we were clearly two servants. Nobody could see at a glance that I was far more educated than he.

But Potifar was different. His sandals were threaded with blue beads on leather straps that reached almost to his knees. The skin of his legs above the straps glistened with the shimmer from the beads. His kilt had a golden belt at the top that gave his dark skin the illusion of being a mirror. And the gold chain he wore around his neck with the large circular red stone hanging from it showed everyone near and far that he was a man of significance. He walked with the posture and confidence of such a man. I admired all of this about him, and strove to do the same, even if my attire immediately shouted that I was not the same.

I felt that my training and education prepared me well for the position I held in his house. This involved much reading and accounting as well as buying materials and directing workers. I was the one who chose the colors that would adorn the walls that Potifar would see in his travel to the next world. I purchased the supplies that became ladders and supervised those who stood on them. I was the one who personally put the writing on the wall for him to follow on his journey to the next life.

Over the years, Potifar would come on occasion and admire the work and watch me as I supervised. Of course, I could see for myself that the work I did and the work I oversaw were both excellent. I wasn't growing a flock of sheep or wealth for My Father, or even for myself, but I was helping Potifar prosper as My Father had once helped Lavan. Only Potifar appreciated how my work benefited him. One morning, when he saw all that had already been completed under my watchful eye, he gave me not only a smile or a nod or a few words of praise, as was his practice, but spoke to me at length. "You bring me great pleasure," he said.

"Joseph, I know the work here is not yet done, but I trust that you will continue to do good work here. I will be a very successful man in the world to come thanks to you."

I felt my face turn warm with his words of praise. I smiled with pride, though I quickly removed my smile when I saw his eyes cast down and his head shaking. "What is it, my lord?" I asked him. "Have I disappointed you? I can change whatever you like!"

"No," he said. "You have not disappointed me. I am sad because the greatness I will enjoy will only be in the next life. If only I were to have more of your help in this lifetime, I could be just as successful now."

"My lord," I said, "I will help in any way I can."

Potifar took my face in his hands and smiled. Then he embraced me! "Thank you, Joseph!" he said. "Thank you! Please, come to my chamber when the sun has gone down."

When darkness set in, I wove my way through Potifar's house to his personal chamber. I knew the house well but had not been in any of the private chambers, especially that of the master. When I arrived, I stood in the doorway and waited to be called in. I did not need to wait long.

"Welcome, Joseph," Potifar whispered, taking my hand and leading me in. Together, we stood just inside the doorway. A little light shone in from the lamps in the hall, but beyond the entrance way was only darkness. "Thank you for your dedication to me. You have surely seen that dedication and compliance can help a person get great privilege here in this house."

"Yes," I confirmed. "It is known far and wide that Potifar treats his servants well. That has been my experience all the while I've been here. I will continue to help you in any way that I can."

Potifar nodded and congratulated me on my wisdom, then complimented me on my education. "You are a fine scribe, Joseph," he said. "And the hands of a scribe are steady and strong, yet not cracked or calloused from hard labor." He took my hands and felt my palms with his fingers to confirm his suspicion. My heart fluttered and my breath quickened at the touch of his hands on mine.

"Such hands will be very helpful," he said.

"What is your struggle, my lord?"

"It is my wife, Zulaika," he said quietly. Then he paused and stepped closer, such that when he spoke again, his words were mostly breath that landed directly on my face. "I trust you with these private words, Joseph. It is shameful. But I shall tell you because I believe your willingness to serve me."

"Yes, of course," I whispered. What an honor to be so trusted and brought to such a private moment with a man of such importance.

He was so close that I could feel his body relax with my assurance. "Thank you," he said. His voice was so quiet that it was mostly just a knowing that he'd said it. He walked forward a couple of small steps, and as there was already almost no room for a breath between us, I backed up a couple of steps until my back was pressed against the wall.

"Thank you, Joseph," he whispered again. Potifar put his right hand on my shoulder, his thumb on my neck. His left hand was on my waist as he leaned to my ear. "She mocks me, Joseph. My wife, she mocks me. It is because I have not planted a child in her. This is her doing. She is conniving. She doesn't entice me. Still, she could divorce me if I do not plant my seed in her. Even if it is her fault. But you," he said, with his chest pressed against mine, "you and I, our bodies are made the same way, and I shall use yours to show you how to help me on mine, and then you shall."

With that, he slid his hands down my chest until he got to the top of my kilt. He stroked me softly a few times, then pumped his whole body against mine. He grew hard against me, and soon, he had one hand around me and one around himself. He let out a soft moan of pleasure, and so did I.

Without stopping his movement, Potifar took my hands and placed them where his had been. "Like this, Joseph," he said. "You do what I was doing." And neither my position in the household nor my own desires would let me do otherwise. We continued like that, hands together, bodies together, breath together, until the pleasure was so strong I thought I might die from it.

And then, Potifar left.

He walked away from me, into a darkness where I could not see where he had gone. But I soon heard. "Open your legs, woman." Those were the only words. The rest of what I heard was grunting, moaning, and finally, releasing. And with his sounds, I completed my pleasure as well—silently and with a large portion of shame for the mess I'd made in the darkness of my master's chamber. I quickly cleaned myself with my kilt and put it back on. I had not been dismissed, but when I heard the snoring, I allowed myself to silently retreat to my quarters.

THE FOLLOWING DAY, Potifar came again to the tomb to check on my work. This time, he expressed so much satisfaction and appreciation that he declared I had earned myself a greater stature in the house, one that came with a private room. He instructed me to follow him there, which I did. The room was small, but it had its own window and an oil lamp, and the narrow sleeping cushion was plump and covered in linen. It was nicer than any place I had ever slept.

"Thank you," I said.

"You deserve it," he replied. "You are skilled and faithful, and you should be rewarded." He lingered for just a moment before adding, "You did well last night. You must get back to your duties as overseer, but come again to my chamber when the sun goes down tonight."

That was the beginning of my working every day and many nights for Potifar. I still had some time to sleep, but he requested my presence after sundown as many nights as not. I enjoyed our time together since it always began with high praise and was always followed by pleasure—until the moment when he would leave me and get in bed with his wife. Then there was my humiliated walk back to my bed.

On the loneliest of those nights, I sought out My God. "Why?" I asked. Yah answered me with the full moon. I had walked under the light of the round moon many times, but on that night, I remembered that I could talk to her.

Sister, Mother, Daughter, and Friend,
You shine with love from beginning to end,
We give you our hopes, our dreams, and our pain,
You keep them safe, until we meet again.

Had the women really been telling the moon all about their hopes and dreams and pain? I had heard the dancing and drumming. I had participated in the dancing and the drumming. But I had never spoken to the moon. That night, returning to my chamber after pleasing Potifar, I told the moon of my pain. I reminded her that I'd once wanted to watch Deenah and the prince. But now, now I was finding the watching painful. Not watching so much as hearing, but still painful. A lonesome pain.

The following month, when the moon was full again, I thanked her for having held my pain. At least I was not alone in it. And I told the moon a hope. I hoped that I would not be so lonely. I hoped I could have celebrations with someone like I'd had under the moon so long ago. The moon was as silent as My God is when I don't understand the messages. But I was glad to have her keeping my hopes and pains safe until the next time she was full.

The moon held my pain as it darkened and lightened each month, month after month. But then, something changed. It happened after I'd whispered my wishes one night to Potifar in his chamber. "Don't go, my lord. Stay here with me. Or come with me to my chamber. Do not think it beneath you. I will make it magnificent for you."

I was afraid of what he would say, what he would do, but I was also hopeful. "Joseph, my wife has no children. She will leave me, and I will be humiliated. I've withheld nothing of mine from you—except when it comes to her. For I must give her a child. That is why you are here, remember? To help me." I said no more.

During the days, the workers submitted to my requests, and during the nights, I submitted to Potifar's. Until the morning after I had made my request of Potifar. His wife Zulaika crossed my path in the garden, and she called to me after she'd passed.

"You are Joseph, are you not?" she inquired.

"I am," I confirmed, proud that she would know of me, until I understood why.

"I can see you better in the full light of the sun," she said. "My head turned to follow you as you walked, as I'm sure everyone's does. You are even more handsome than I realized. Of course, in the dim light of the lamp by the wall, kneeling on the floor and so focused on yourself, it is hard for me to get a very good view of you."

My face burned. I had been helping Potifar for more than a year. In all that time, I had never seen his wife in the darkness of the chamber. I had assumed she hadn't seen me, either. But now as she stared at me, apparently not for the first time, I saw her. I saw that her skin glistened at least as much as her husband's. Her hair was long and danced down her shoulders. Her tunic was tight and queenly. I averted my eyes as quickly as possible, and I turned to walk away. She grabbed me by the wrist. "I have not dismissed you," she said. "I cannot see well from the cushion, but here," she stroked her fingers across my chest, "here, I can see why Potifar enjoys touching you. I am enjoying it too." She ran her fingers down my stomach. I tensed and looked around.

"Nobody is here but us, silly boy," she said. "But privacy would be nice. Go. Walk from here to your room. I know you have received your own room. I shall follow you at a distance."

I didn't know what to do other than follow her orders. And so that is what I did, and that is how the master's wife came to be in my servant's quarters. The last words she said before coming to my cushion were, "Potifar leaves you to bring yourself to pleasure, but I will take you all the way there." And she did. Then she took a brief rest, got dressed, and left.

That night with Potifar, I was aware of his wife watching us. She was as silent as she always was with Potifar, though she had made many sounds of pleasure with me. I still couldn't see her, but my skin prickled with the new knowledge that she could see me. And when Potifar left me for her, I didn't feel so alone knowing she was watching me. It was only much later that I learned the reason I didn't hear Zulaika was because she usually wasn't there.

Zulaika never approached me in the garden again, but she did make frequent visits to my room. They were always before the sun was up, and they were always filled with excitement and pleasure for both of us. When I returned from my overseer duties on those days, I would find a new trinket in my room: a precious stone, an embroidered pillow, a sweet treat, a golden scarab, and once, even a small tapestry depicting the eye of Horus and attached to the wall.

One morning, when we were warm in each other's arms, she told me that while she was sickened at the thought of Potifar's seed being planted in her, she would welcome mine. It was as if her words woke me from a dream. "Zulaika, no." I stood quickly. I could not have my master's wife bear my child! What had I been thinking?

"Don't worry," she said, trying to bring me back down beside her. "He is not a smart man. He would not even know. He would just be glad that I wouldn't leave him." She paused for a moment.

"Though, I could, you know. He hasn't given me a child. I could leave him. Would you like that?"

She must have thought me as much of a fool as her husband. Did she really think I would believe that she would leave her status to live in my servant's quarters? Quarters that would immediately be taken from me by Potifar if he knew I shared them with his wife?

I was prospering in Potifar's house, but I became nervous. For the next few days, I talked with My God only about Potifar and Zulaika. What was I to do? I received no answer that I understood, but I kept asking and asking throughout each day and night. This distraction nearly caused a tragedy when a worker fell from scaffolding that had not been properly secured. His leg broke when he landed, and my master needed to pay for someone to replace him. That night, he still called me to his chamber, but he was not pleased with me and was rough with my body. When he left for his cushion, I went to sleep outside instead of in my room. Zulaika was not happy when she went to my quarters the next morning and found it empty.

Although Potifar's anger eased, my fear of further mistakes did not, so I did not return to my room, ever. I worked all day and focused on my responsibilities with a clear mind thanks to sleeping well under the stars every night. Until Zulaika found me in the hallway retrieving supplies one afternoon. "Come with me, Joseph," she said.

"I cannot," I replied.

She stepped closer. "Joseph," she said more softly, with her warm breath in my ear, "come with me. It has been too long.

Do not avoid me. Do not avoid our fun. Do not deny me my satisfaction."

"I must return to work," I said, quickly running off to do so. I sometimes dreamt of her touch, but I could not have it again.

The next day, Zulaika sought me out again, finding me with my workers and requesting my assistance in front of them. I had no choice but to step aside with her. We walked to the part of the house where nobody was working.

"Lie with me," she said again. She said it softly, looking me first in the eyes, then all the way down my body.

I forced myself to refuse the invitation. "I cannot," I said. "I am working all day out here and then serving Potifar many nights. As you know. I cannot leave my duties, no matter the pleasure of doing so." I hoped that the words would not anger her. I continued to explain my position. "With me here, my master gives no thought to anything in this house. Everything he has, he has put in my hands."

She giggled and reached out, putting her breast in my hand. I didn't retract my hand right away, but I forced myself to do so soon. "He wields no more authority in this house than I do, and he has withheld nothing from me—except you, his wife. How could I then do this wicked thing and sin against Elohim? I cannot make mistakes in my duties again. Elohim has favored me in giving me this position. I wish to keep it."

She took a step back and spoke harshly. "Joseph, you are handsome and strong, and I enjoy our time together. I know you do too. But do not think you are the first or that you will be the last. You may have been brought here by Elohim's will, but you stay here only by mine."

I did not know how to respond to this or of what she spoke. She looked at me and laughed. "Joseph, if I cannot enjoy you, then Potifar shall not either. You must make a choice about whether you will continue to have power here or whether you will be replaced."

My thoughts were many and conflicting, but I had no time for them and no time to genuinely make the choice she spoke of—one I did not understand. I did not know that our conversation was ending with her next words, "Lie with me!" My hesitation to even respond brought events that I did not anticipate.

She grabbed my kilt from my body, leaving me naked in the hall. "Guards!" she called. I ran. I ran as quickly as I could to try to get to my room. But she did not follow; she no longer wanted me to lie with her. "Look!" Zulaika called to the guards who were approaching. She held my kilt high for everyone to see. "Look! Potifar brought us a stranger to toy with us. This one came to lie with me, but I cried out. And when he heard me calling with my raised voice, he left his garment with me and got away and fled outside."

I could still hear her screaming as I crossed the garden and fled to the safety of my room. I did not know what to do, so I just stayed there. As the sun was setting and I was questioning whether I was to go to Potifar or not, he came to me, flanked by two guards. He left them outside and entered my room alone. He hadn't been in there since the day he'd gifted it to me.

"Joseph," he said. "Joseph, your hands are so supple, your body so firm. I wish to feel them one more time." Thus, he did. Potifar laid me on my back on my cushion and touched every part of me. He was finally with me in my chamber. And he stayed with me there. It was just as wonderful as I had hoped and as magnificent for him as I had promised. But it would happen only the one time.

"Stand up," Potifar said after catching his breath. I stood. "Now, I shall have to find someone else, Joseph. I so enjoyed you. But I have no other choice." Potifar left my room, and the guards, one on each side, took me away.

CHAPTER 21

I sat on the dirt floor of the prison with my head in my hands, trying not to feel sorry for myself. Here I was now, stripped of my garment and thrown into a pit for a *second* time. A second time! I told myself over and over that the first time had worked out well. When I'd been removed from that pit, I'd been able to wear my true coat of colors. I'd been able to feel the love of my honored Auntie Deborah. I'd been able to understand my dreams! And yes, these were all true and wonderful, but here I was again. I thought it had worked out well the first time, but *this* was how it had worked out now. *This* was well?

It took me seven days of crying on the ground and refusing food to finally lift my head toward the light coming in from above. When I did, I was struck by the beauty and brightness of the sky. And in that one glance, I both berated myself for not looking sooner and smiled with the pure joy of seeing the world—even from this viewpoint. After that, it didn't take me long to believe the words I'd been telling myself. Yes, this would turn out well.

My renewed energy could not have been more timely, for it was while I was still reveling in being alive and able to see the sunshine that an old man came and deposited a bowl of broth at my side. "Eat quickly," he said. "No more lying around for you. Atsu has dreamt again, and we're all to assemble in the courtyard."

"Atsu?" I asked.

"The warden," he said. And then, with no further words, he left to deliver the bowls that remained on his tray. I sipped my broth as slowly as I was able. When I saw the other men quickly consuming theirs, then leaving the bowls behind with haste to get outside, I thought it best to follow. Outside, the world was even more beautiful than it had been shining through the hole into my cell, and it was all around me and through me as I breathed in the light and fresh scents.

There weren't many prisoners. I counted ten, including myself. Most of the men were assembled in a line a few paces away. I joined the line and saw that they were facing the man who must surely be the warden. He looked to be a little older than I was, perhaps a man with young sons. His arms and legs were strong, and his face, smooth like all the Egyptians in important positions. I touched the stubble starting to grow on my own chin. I had awaited that hair for many years and wore it with pride in my homeland. But I had been in Egypt long enough to begin to feel shame about any hair on my body.

I noticed the warden's appearance, but what was most striking about him was his confidence and calmness. He directed the prisoners with firm command but, at the same time, with compassion. He did not lord over them as he had them fulfill his strange requests. "You two," he said as he took the first two men from the line. "Come and stand here, just like this. Clasp hands with each other. Yes, that's it." He had them face-to-face, each man with an arm stretched out in front of him at shoulder height and another at waist height. "Now, make the area as clear as can be," the warden said. "Your arms are acting as a window. Do you understand?" The men indicated that they did.

I did not.

In a whisper, I asked the man next to me what was going on. He rolled his eyes and whispered back, "The warden has dreamt again. Whenever this happens, he calls us all out here to act his dream so that he may examine it from many directions. He wishes to know the meaning. He's rarely satisfied, yet we repeat this ridiculous indulgence every time."

"You," the warden called to me. "You are new. Welcome. It will not be as bad here as you think. To show you that, you may sit here, in my seat. In the dream, I was looking out of this window." I sat and looked out the window the two men had made with their arms. I stayed still while he called two other men to be on the far side of the window. Each was to get down on all fours and imagine himself as a lion. He instructed the lions to frolic.

"No, that's not quite right," he said. "I remember now that the dream began with one lion. I was gazing at the lion, admiring his prance and his stance. Then the lion stopped and gazed at me. Do that. . . . No, no, don't gaze at me, gaze at the me in the window. Yes. Then, while the lion and I were looking into each other's eyes, it suddenly turned into two lions. They were both young males. It was just one lion, and then suddenly, two. Like when Horus was born from Osiris, except they were father and son, and these lions were brothers."

The men did their best to display this while I watched through the window of arms before me. The warden then gave them instructions to frolic. "Don't go far," he said. "I could view both lions through my window for the entire dream." As the two paced and pounced on the dirt like lions might, the warden watched through the window with me. "Yes," he said. "They did all manner of lion-like things. They walked like kings, focused, fierce, and confident. They were a pair, there to protect each other as well as play with each other."

I watched the men wrestle like cubs, sometimes using their hand-paws to bat each other gently in the face, sometimes pinning each other to the ground, but all in play. They dusted each other off, and the warden seemed pleased with this. They walked in wide circles, sometimes toward each other, sometimes away, but always with eye contact and a plan that was clear to them, if not to everyone else.

"Well done, men," the warden called to them. "I believe that you are lions when I watch you. I do not recall the exact movements of the lions in my dream, but your display of teamwork and playfulness certainly captures their spirits. Go on." I watched the men pretending to be lions until the sun rose nearly overhead. By this time, the other men, those not reenacting the dream, had long ago lost interest. They were wandering the grounds or resting in the shade. The warden seemed aware of their choices but more focused on the lions. He took a turn sitting at the window and took a turn as each of the lions. But after spending the morning like this, his frustration was clear.

"Enough," he said. "You all may go. I'm no closer to understanding the dream than I was this morning."

No sooner had he finished talking than the men who had been creating the window with their arms relaxed and shook them out while walking away. The "lions" got up off their hands and knees, wiping dirt and pebbles from both, and went to pull water from the well. I suppose I could have wandered away, but I didn't know the place and had nowhere to go. So, I stayed and watched the warden pace and mumble to himself about the dream and his disappointment. He noticed I was still there and once again said aloud what he remembered of the dream.

"I was sitting at a window, looking out. And outside were the two lions who had been one. Young males. A person would be wise to be cautious in such a situation, but I didn't feel the need. There was no threat. The two were busy playing and frolicking, even while maintaining a clear presence of authority and confidence. I watched in wonder, almost in jealousy for the life these two had. And I know it was a long life, for in the dream, they changed from youths to mature and, finally, to old lions. I know it is a good dream because I am looking out the window, and the Book of Dreams lists that as a good omen. But it says nothing of what I saw through the window." He paused for a while.

"I have a good position here. I am grateful for the salary and what it enables me to provide for my siblings and our mother. And this is a good prison. Nobody here is dangerous. The worst offenders were thrown in here for having turned down Zulaika's advances, as you presumably did."

Of course, the warden would know my reason for imprisonment, but I had been so busy feeling sorry for myself and then being caught in the drama of the dream that I had forgotten to remember that. I found comfort in knowing that I was jailed with harmless men. And I could see a kindness in the warden in addition to someone who did his job well.

"If you'd like," I offered, "I can tell you the meaning of your dream."

"What?" The warden was stunned, as if it hadn't occurred to him that he wouldn't need to choose between figuring it out himself or going without knowing.

"Surely Elohim knows the meaning of this dream, as all dreams come from Elohim. Would you like to know the meaning?"

"Yes," he responded.

I cleared my throat and said aloud, for the first time in the presence of anyone other than my teachers, the words I said three times daily: "Blessed are You, Elohim, God of My Father Jacob, God of My Father Isaac, and God of My Father Abraham." Then I spoke to My God, allowing the warden to hear the rest of the words as well. "This man has had a dream, and he feels the importance of it but does not understand it. Please, help me interpret the dream for him." And then I was quiet, and so was the warden. When I understood the dream, I thanked My God and shared the explanation I had been given.

"You are correct that it is a good dream," I began. The warden smiled. His smile contained both relief and gratitude. "In the dream, although you felt that you were looking at the two lions, you were also one of the lions. The you from right now was looking into the future, where you saw yourself as a man of importance playing with another man of importance. You two will keep each other safe and protected and be joyful."

The warden had tears in his eyes, and he patted me on the back several times. "Thank you," he said. "Thank you, thank you. I have had many dreams that I have tried to understand, and to have the interpretation is such a relief. It is a resolution. It is an ease of all the worry. I cannot fully describe the feeling."

"I understand," I said. And I told him of the clarity I'd received when I was being hauled off on the back of the camel. The warden laughed as he drew little pictures of the scene on the dirt while I spoke. He admired me for waiting seventeen years to learn the meaning of the spoons and the dream, even if I wasn't waiting by my choice. He still acknowledged me for doing so. For the both of us, it was the first time we'd spoken with anyone about our dreams in such acceptance and freedom.

And in that space of acceptance and freedom, we shared other stories openly. I told him of My Brothers and My Sisters, of My Father and My Mother, of My Auntie and My Teacher. I told him about Reuel and Qarib and many of my dreams. In turn, he told me of his mother, of his father who had held the position of warden before him, and of his older brother who had already had a more prestigious position when their father died and so sent him, the second son, here to watch this jail. He told me of longing for a wife but being unable to bring one here.

We talked like this throughout each day. The prisoners all enjoyed considerable freedom as long as we stayed within the grounds and spent the nights in our cells. So, Atsu was free to talk, and so was I. Only a few days had passed before he told me his deepest wounds: being cast out of his home when falsely accused of stealing, being fondled by his uncle and ridiculed for it, and nearly falling to his death from a ledge he'd been blindly led to by some other boys.

Though I could see he felt shame for having had these moments in his life, I felt nothing but gratitude toward him for telling me about them. I didn't view any of it as shameful. And in turn, I was able to tell him some of my deepest wounds: being cast out by My Brothers, finding a place among the girls, losing my beloved Deenah, and being with Potifar and his wife. What a relief it was to say the words of my life to someone who did not mock me. He actually praised me as he had about my spoons dream and as I had for him about his stories.

Thus, we continued for seven days, telling each other of our stories, our lives, our loves, our losses, and, of course, our dreams. On the eighth day, it was my turn to do the duties in the prison. There were ten men incarcerated and the warden. I learned on the eighth day that each man has a weekly turn to bring the food, sweep the floors, and clean the messes. I finished as the sun began to set and found Atsu waiting for me at my cell.

"I have missed you, Joseph," he said. We embraced warmly even though it had been only one day spent without talking to each other.

"I have missed you too," I said honestly.

"Come with me," he invited. "We did not get to talk all day. Let us say all the words we would have said in the sunlight by the light of the lamp in my quarters."

The warden's room wasn't much nicer than my cell. His was above ground, and so the light, when day, would stream in through the window rather than from above. He had two chairs and a sleeping cushion that was on a pallet instead of on the floor like the prisoners'. He had a lamp and plenty of oil, a table, and a bowl of his own. We sat in the chairs and did tell each other all the words we might have said during the day. We talked until nearly dawn, at which point we felt we still had more to say but were simply too tired to do so.

"Sleep here tonight, Joseph. That is, if you want to."

I did.

We lay down side by side on his cushion, making two bodies fit in the area made for one. From the outside, we may have looked like two lost kittens, huddled together for warmth and survival. But on his mat, what it felt like was us coming into life together in the same womb. I wondered whether this had been how My Father and his brother had felt before they fought for blessings, and I thought of all the years in which I had longed to share such closeness with my own brothers but had always been rejected. In Atsu's arms, I felt my neck and shoulders relax. I thought of the way Reuel had welcomed and embraced me. For the first time since sharing a tent with My Mother, I felt something even better than pleasure. Peace. I felt my colored cloak of light covering us both, and I exhaled into a deep, and safe, slumber beside My Brother.

CHAPTER 22

After that first night, there was never any question that I would share Atsu's room. On occasion, we were up talking until the dawn nearly broke, but as we were spending the days together in conversation, there was little need for that. Life in the jail became different than it had been before. Not only for Atsu but for all the inmates as well.

Atsu had always been a kind and compassionate warden. But he had also been pressed by burden and worry since all the responsibility for these men had been on him alone. There were never any riots, or even complaints. Though all the men there had been banished from prestigious positions, they actually had more freedom in jail than out. Unlike the lives of servants in the fine house, the only work that needed to be done in the jail was to take care of the food and shelter needs of the jailed. Two of the men had landed there the way I had: by refusing to pleasure Zulaika. They were happier, though, with their freedom in jail than they were with their confinement in the fine house. The other men were equally content to live their lives in the sunshine and garden, sleeping under the ground's coolness each night and helping to maintain the jail. In many ways, they preferred it.

That preference got even stronger as the jail got more efficient and friendly with my help. While I loved every talk I had with Atsu, we also made sure to include the other men in the joy. I had confessed to Atsu that I had been left out of the kinship My Brothers had shared in my youth. When he asked about some of the things I wished I had experienced, I told him of how My Brothers sometimes raced or wrestled. I told him of Judah teaching me to use the slingshot and my instruction being cut short. I told him of watching My Brothers trying to be the one to throw the rock the farthest or pee on a lizard while it tried to outrun the unexpected rain shower.

Much to my delight, Atsu suggested that I arrange to do these things with the men. And to my even greater delight and surprise, the men agreed. And so, as the days moved into weeks and months and years, I organized games and singing and stories that everyone looked forward to and greatly enjoyed. Only once was there a bit of a scuffle. It was the first wrestling match I had ever participated in. Though I had seen My Brothers tumble through the dust, I had never been included. So, when the elbow of a large man named Anum landed on my nose with more force than I expected, I was not prepared.

Blood flowed from my nostril as easily and quickly as water streams down rocks in a river. Touching my hand to my face revealed almost enough blood to quench a man's thirst were he to drink it. I was stunned by the redness and the amount. Anum quickly got off me and apologized. Though I was unshaven and dressed in old clothes like the other prisoners, I had been effectively running the prison alongside Atsu for many months. Anum was clearly afraid. I, however, was not.

I wiped my hand off on my leg and used it to clap him on the shoulder. "Thank you, Anum," I said. "Thank you. You have given me an experience My Brothers never did. I truly know what wrestling is like now." I left him there stunned while I went, giddily, to wash off my blood. Atsu accompanied me to the water and helped me stop the flow of blood by inserting an old cloth up my nose. By then, he knew me so well that he didn't repeatedly ask me whether I was suffering. No, his smile was nearly as big as mine, almost as happy for me as I was for myself.

I was extra joyful for the rest of the day, and my time talking with Elohim that evening, while always peaceful, also contained more bliss. That night, I dreamt of eleven sheepdogs. They worked together to guard the flock, and they slept at their various posts at night. In the morning, before herding the sheep, they got together to eat the feast of leftovers from their master's table the night before. They fought over these scraps even though there was plenty. They licked their wounds and then went back to work.

I awoke when the dream ended. I heard My Auntie's voice in my ear saying, "You dreamt," and I smiled at the sound of her sureness and sweetness. As a boy, I believe I would have understood the dogs in that dream to represent myself and the ten other men who had become a pack with me. As a man, I understood that Elohim was the only one who knew the meaning of the dream. Though the sun had not yet risen, I gently woke Atsu.

"Atsu, I have dreamt. I will go outside and talk with My God early this morning so that I may learn the meaning of my dream."

He smiled at me. "If you wish to tell me what you learn, I am eager to listen," he said.

I rose and went into the crisp air that was outside before the morning sun. Many stars still filled the sky, and I had a sudden memory of dreaming of eleven of those stars and the sun and the moon. Now, here was eleven again, only dogs. "Blessed are You, Elohim, God of My Father Jacob, God of My Father Isaac, God of My Father Abraham." I breathed deeply and told My God of my dreams. I asked to be told their meaning. And then I listened. The sun rose and shone brightly on my face before I heard my answer and then felt as if it were shining right through my whole body once I did.

I went to seek out Atsu, eager to share this dream with him since we shared everything. I didn't have to look long at all, as he was waiting for me nearby. His smile was an invitation to talk.

"This is the meaning of the dream," I began. "The eleven dogs represent eleven years. The working together, playing, fighting, sleeping, . . . this is all dog behavior. It was showing that dogs behave like dogs, just as people behave like people and brothers behave like brothers. The dogs do not remain angry with each other when they fight. They forgive. In eleven years, I shall have the opportunity to forgive My Brothers."

"What do you think of that?"

"There is more," I told him. "I have not yet told you of another dream I had many years ago. Atsu, it is hard to believe I had forgotten this dream. Of course, you know of My Brothers throwing me in the pit and selling me to the Ishmaelites. I have told you. I forgot, until dreaming of eleven dogs, that before they put me in the pit, I had dreamt of eleven stars. I dreamt that the sun, the moon, and the eleven stars were bowing down to me. This angered My Brothers, and even My Father. They interpreted the dream to mean that they would all bow down to me one day.

"And today, I asked for Elohim's interpretation. The bowing was an expression of gratitude. The dream was telling me that in thirteen years, I would be in a position to help them all, and they would be grateful to me."

"How?" Atsu asked.

"I don't know," I said. "But I understand now that the celestial bodies were marking time. And eleven of those thirteen years have passed. Meaning I shall get to find out soon." I paused for a moment, not certain whether I wanted to share one more thought with Atsu. But then I continued. "Atsu, My Father asked whether I thought that he and My Mother and all the brothers would bow down to me. But My Mother died long ago—even before the dream with the sun and the moon and the stars. Now I know those were years, not people. But . . . but Atsu, I have been thinking of Deenah with every full moon. I think of her dancing under it, giving it her hopes and dreams and pain. And so, when I see the full moon, I think of Deenah. Now, I wonder whether she will come and we can be beneath the moon together."

Atsu put his hand on my shoulder. He had nothing to say about that sorrow or hope. I had no more to say about it either. "As for the dogs," I went on, "Atsu, I do not question My God's interpretation. But I do wonder about this forgiving in eleven years. The dream has already taught me so much, as did Anum. You know I hold no anger toward Anum for my bloody nose—even though it hurt." I rubbed my nose. It still hurt a little, even the next day. Atsu nodded his understanding.

"I don't think I would like to wrestle again. I tried it, and I am grateful to know what it is. But if I were to wrestle with Anum again, and if he were to cause me pain again, I would understand, just as I did last time, that he was not trying to cause me pain. He was simply wrestling. That is how wrestling goes. And through that wrestling, and the pain, I received an experience that was valuable: I was included, truly included. What if, through My Brothers' cruelty toward me—which was not all the time—I also received an experience that was valuable? They helped teach me that something that looks like the ending may be a new beginning."

"It does seem that you've had new beginnings after endings, Joseph. Maybe even more than I can remember." He quickly listed my leg injury and my learning from My Auntie, being sold into slavery to begin a new life in Egypt, and being thrown in jail to begin a new life with him—a true brother. I was washed with our love. Every pain had been worthwhile for leading me to a brother.

"Atsu, why must I wait another eleven years to forgive My Brothers? They were merely doing what brothers do. And they were helping Elohim bring me to you."

"I don't know why you must wait, Joseph," he responded. "Are you sure that the dogs were another eleven years, and not the ones that have already passed from your other dream?"

"I am sure," I replied. "The dogs came to give a new message. Though eleven of the thirteen years have passed since my celestial dream, My God has given me a new message with the dogs. But My God has not given me the explanation for why I must continue to wait."

"Perhaps, if your heart is ready to forgive them, you can do so now, and if you need to do so again in eleven years, it will be that much easier for having done it once already."

"Yes," I said. I did not think I could withhold forgiveness even if I tried, just as I could already forgive Anum for injuring my nose again if we were to wrestle again.

"And Joseph," Atsu added. "I would not question this god of yours. I have seen the help that Elohim has given you. But as with all gods, Elohim can only speak to you in a way that you can understand, isn't that so?" He didn't wait for a reply but went on. "As with any man, if the god sends a message in a way the man cannot receive, it is worthless. So, Elohim tells you things that you can understand."

"You're right, Atsu, of course." I had never thought of it before, but, of course, if My God were to speak to me in a language of the people of the sea, I would not know these words. And while Elohim's messages to me carried few words at all, I grasped Atsu's meaning that there were other ways I might not understand that Elohim would not use to speak to me, for they wouldn't work.

"In that case," Atsu went on, "I would like to offer another explanation for the waiting eleven years until forgiveness."

"Please," I said eagerly.

"Perhaps another eleven years need to pass before your brothers are able to forgive *you*."

Atsu was right again: I did not understand.

• • •

I REMOVED WRESTLING from our list of activities, but we enjoyed many other games together. And the men enjoyed no longer having to act out Atsu's dreams, as Elohim always provided me with an interpretation to share with him. The other men occasionally came to me with their dreams as well, and I became one who was honored as a dreamer instead of ridiculed as one. The most important dreams that Elohim helped me to understand while I was in jail were those of the Pharaoh's chief baker and chief cupbearer.

These two men had displeased the Pharaoh and were brought to our jail. Although we were already full of our ten men, an inspector had come by and had noticed that there was an empty cell—mine—without noticing that Atsu's room now housed the both of us. A second mat was put into my cell, and it was designated for the cupbearer and baker.

I had been the last prisoner to join this band of men. We were all happy to have new faces and stories to incorporate into our lives. But these two would need some time to adjust to their new circumstances. On their first night in the cell, they each dreamt disturbing dreams. When they awoke, they had barely blinked before they were advised to tell me of their dreams.

They came to me distraught, still struggling in the suddenness of their imprisonment and the unknown meaning of their dreams. I gave them a smile I hoped would set them at ease and shared with them the words that I knew would bring relief: "Surely, Elohim knows their interpretation. Tell me."

Pharaoh's chief cupbearer spoke first. "In my dream, there was a vine in front of me. On the vine were three branches. It had barely budded, when out came its blossoms that ripened into grapes. Pharaoh's cup was in my hand, and I took the grapes and squeezed their juice into Pharaoh's cup and put the cup in Pharaoh's hand."

I thanked the man for telling me. "I will now go talk to My God," I said. I walked the grounds as I did three times each day. The land here was so different from the one where I had dreamt my dreams as a boy, but Elohim was everywhere, and when I called out with my traditional prayer, and listened as I was accustomed, I was provided with the interpretation. I then returned to where the chief cupbearer, and the rest of the men, were eagerly awaiting me.

I closed my eyes and spoke the interpretation given to me by Elohim. "This is its meaning. The three branches are three days. In three days, Pharaoh will pardon you and restore you to your post. You will place Pharaoh's cup in his hand as you had done before when you were his cupbearer." I paused. I knew there was more to tell him, though he already had the meaning of his dream. "Remember me when all is well with you again, and do me the kindness of mentioning me to Pharaoh so as to free me from this place. I was kidnapped from the land of the Hebrews and didn't do anything, yet they put me in this pit."

The cupbearer nodded his agreement and embraced me with relief. Indeed, we all knew that in three days, we would come to the end of the year, and the five-day celebration of the Pharaoh's birth would start. Pharaoh and his court would have a grand party until the new year began, and certainly, he would want his most reliable helpers increasing his joy.

The baker felt quite good about this interpretation and eagerly told me of the dream he had dreamt. "In my dream, there were three open weave baskets on my head. In the uppermost basket were baked goods for Pharaoh, and birds were eating those—out of the basket that was on my head."

I had received the interpretation of this dream before even hearing it. Elohim had shared the words with me, and I would therefore share what Elohim had entrusted to me with the baker, even though I knew the baker would not like what he heard. "This is the interpretation. The three baskets are three days. In three days, Pharaoh will lift your head off you and hang you on a wooden pole, and birds will eat the flesh off your body."

The baker began to shake. He shook and wailed and vomited on the dirt. There was no consoling him, though the cupbearer tried. When it seemed he had exhausted himself to sleep, he sprang from the floor and ran to the gate to escape. Nobody chased him, as there would be no escape. The stone walls surrounding the grounds were taller than three men. The wooden gate was just as tall and thick and only opened from the outside when there were deliveries.

The baker sat on the ground with his back against the wall and his head in his hands. Nobody could rouse him from this position for the next three days. Food was brought to him, but he ignored it. The mood among the other men was just as somber. Though there was the cupbearer's good fortune coming soon, nobody spoke of it except for Atsu and me in the privacy of our room.

"What will become of us?" he asked through tears. "Joseph, make no mistake, I am happy for you that the cupbearer will mention you to Pharaoh and increase your good fortune. But I will be terribly lonely. Terribly, terribly lonely."

We embraced and washed each other's faces with our tears. I could not stand the thought of living life not by his side. Not since Reuel had I loved someone so freely and been so accepted and enjoyed. Atsu had taught me to hold those memories of Reuel with fondness. I was confident that I would cherish my memories of him as well; I just didn't want to do so without him. I did not want to leave My Brother. But I could not ignore the message of Elohim.

For three days, we dug deep to tell each other stories that we might have forgotten. We brought up memories of our time together. And we were quiet, like everyone else. We waited. I was certain we must trust Elohim. "Remember, last time I was thrown into the pit," I told him, "it worked out well in the end."

"Yes, for you," he said, pouting.

I could not help but smile.

"Yes," he admitted. "For me too."

On the third day, guards returned to the prison and escorted the cupbearer away and carried the baker out. We heard the sounds of merriment for five days and nights. Music and drumbeats filled the air. We enjoyed some dancing of our own in the prison while we went back and forth between trusting Elohim and dreading our separation.

As it turned out, we needn't have worried about being separated. Another two years passed before the cupbearer remembered me to Pharaoh, and only then did our lives change forever.

PART 2:
AFTER

CHAPTER 23

In the second month of the Inundation Season, on the third day of the second week of the month, when the sun was still low in the sky and our breakfast was just put away, the gate opened, and two guards entered the compound. Men came in on the first day of every week to drop off food and supplies and any important news. On the first day of the first week of each month, Atsu was allowed a morning to visit his mother, and so on those days, the gate was opened and closed twice. The only other time it had opened off schedule was when the cupbearer and baker had been briefly added to our jail and then removed. We all quickly and curiously gathered to learn the reason for this visit.

Atsu approached the guards. "Welcome, sirs. I am at your service."

One guard unrolled a scroll of papyrus and read from it. "By word of the Pharaoh. I have dreamt a dream that neither the dream book nor my magicians can interpret. I am told there is a Hebrew by the name of Joseph who can interpret my dream. Send him to me at once."

We all stood in silence. Atsu had never received word from Pharaoh before, but he handled it brilliantly after just one breath of silence. He addressed the guards. "The man you speak of is here," he said, "and indeed, he has helped many to understand dreams. He will be bathed and shaved but has no garb that is appropriate for wearing before the king. Come back with clothes when the sun begins its descent from the top of the heavens, and he will be ready to help Pharaoh."

When the gate closed, the men surrounded me, whooping and cheering and patting me on the back. The air was crisp with the excitement of something new and the honor of one of them being requested by the Pharaoh. They danced me over to the well. I removed my own clothing and stood while my nine fellow prisoners each took a turn dumping a bucket of water on me. When they had finished, Atsu took a turn and then refilled the bucket and handed it to me to douse myself.

I held the bucket high over my head, said a prayer of thanks to Elohim, closed my eyes, and splashed myself in the face with the contents of the bucket. I shook my head, letting water fly from my long hair and beard onto my companions, getting them wet too. Then the bucket was filled once more and brought to the sunshine in the middle of the field, as was I. Atsu must have said a few words to some of the men, for there was a chair there for me to sit on, a large jug of oil, and Atsu's shaving kit, and suddenly, he and I were the only ones there.

Atsu took the blade from his kit. He sharpened it after every use, so it was ready to go. I thought of my first day in Egypt when I had been sold to Potifar and had my hair removed. Those men had been rough, and every speck of my skin radiated red with pain. I'd been regularly shaved by them after that point, but the consistent hair removal had made it easier each time. It was just the initial elimination of my long, thick hair that had been so brutal.

I closed my eyes now, ready to endure it once again. But Atsu gently called my name. "Joseph," he said. I opened my eyes to look at him. He was looking me directly in the eyes but then moved his gaze to my beard. He stroked the length of it with a smile. "I shall miss this thing," he said. "I will miss the way you stroke it when you think you've said something particularly wise. I will miss the way you stroke it when you think I've said something wise. I will not miss the things that get caught in it."

Atsu laughed gently, then moved his hands to the hair on my head. "These knots will be better off buried in the dirt or burned in the fire," he said. "I remember when you first came into this jail; you were as smooth-shaven as I—as any well-positioned man in all of Egypt. I look forward to seeing that man again, even though this hairy beast is the brother I've grown to love. I shall miss you, Joseph. And I am also happy with you."

With that, Atsu took the blade to my head and cut my hair close to the scalp. Even his sharp blade required some effort, but soon, the nest of thick black hair was on the ground, and what remained on my head was short and soft. Atsu put his hand through it and laughed. Then he performed similar surgery on my beard. He didn't use any unnecessary force. He would not. Of course.

Atsu dipped his left hand in the oil and poured it from his palm to my scalp. "You shall live the greatness you are meant for,

Joseph." He said this while gently rubbing the oil on the top of my head. Then slowly, carefully, he began shaving that short hair. I hardly noticed anything but the gentle movement of his hand massaging the oil into my scalp.

"Atsu, you speak as if we are parting forever. We don't know that to be true. The pharaoh has asked for my help with his dream. I will learn the meaning from Elohim and report it back. And what will happen next? Will Pharaoh be pleased and send me back here without punishment? Will he be displeased and banish me right back to jail? Atsu, I cannot think of all the possibilities, but never seeing each other again is not one of them."

"Joseph, of course, I don't want that," he said. My head was clean-shaven, and he was massaging oil on my chin and face. "I don't know what will happen. But I know you are destined for greatness, and I am the warden in this jail. I have no trinket to give you to remember me by, but I am encouraged by the knowledge that I will never forget you, and so I know that you will not forget me. Although we will be apart, we will continue to do what we have always done: we'll let time pass and do our best. We'll heal, learn, and grow. We will be in the hands of the gods, and all will be well."

I could not answer him, for his blade was at my cheek. If he cut me, it would look bad for me—and I know he would never desire such a thing. Further, if he cut me, it would reflect poorly on him—which I would never want to happen. I sat quietly, appreciating his gentleness, and fiercely trusting Elohim to not separate us forever. Certainly, another way would show itself.

Once I was clean, smooth, and anointed, we awaited the guards' return in silence. We had said everything we could. All that was left was to wait and see what would happen next. But until it happened, we would sit together.

When the sun began its descent, all the men gathered to bid me farewell. The gate opened, and I was presented with a fine linen loincloth with golden threads along the bottom and first-rate leather sandals that would keep the Pharaoh's floors clean when I was presented to him. I saw Atsu's approval in his smile. He was genuinely happy with me. And we were sad together.

"Be mindful with this one," he said to the guards. "He is well favored by his god and adept at dream interpretation. He should be treated with respect and honor for his skill. He is loyal and will be of great help to Pharaoh."

I looked back at my beloved brother and mouthed the words *thank you* over my shoulder. I then walked toward my destiny as I was escorted through the large gate and out of the prison saying, "Blessed are You, Elohim, who frees the captives."

PHARAOH SAT ON his throne, erect and royal. I prostrated myself before him exactly as I had been instructed. My nose touched the very ground where his feet would step, and my hands were splayed on either side of me. I waited in that position until I was instructed to rise. Once that permission was granted, I still directed my gaze to the floor.

"Leave us," Pharaoh instructed his guards.

The two men went and took posts by the entrance we had used. I saw there was another doorway at the back of the chamber. Two other men stood there with their backs to the pharaoh.

"I have had a dream, but no one can interpret it," he said. "I have heard about you. It is said that for you to hear a dream is for you to interpret it."

"Not I," I corrected him, "but My God will answer this question for Pharaoh."

And so, he told me his dream.

"In my dream, I was standing on the bank of The River, when suddenly, seven healthy, good-looking cows came out of The River and grazed on the reed grass there. Just as suddenly, seven more cows came out of The River after them! They were thin and sickly looking. Never had I seen such ugliness in all of Egypt! Then, . . ." Pharaoh paused and shook his head, like a man who still couldn't believe his eyes. "Then those ugly cows ate the first seven cows! The strong and healthy ones! But when they had consumed them, one could not tell that they had consumed them, for they looked just as sickly as before. Then I woke up."

I nodded and opened my mouth to tell him that I would bring his dream to Elohim and return when I learned the interpretation. But before I could speak, Pharaoh went on. "Then I dreamt of seven ears of grain. They were full and healthy and growing on a single stalk. After them, there were seven ears of grain that were thin, shriveled, and scorched by the wind. The thin ears swallowed the healthy ones!"

Again, the pharaoh shook his head at such a strange thought. I dared not speak, as perhaps he still wasn't done. And in fact, he did go on, but not with more details of the dream. "I have told my magicians, but none has an explanation for me." Pharaoh looked at me now, expecting me to speak.

"My God, Elohim, is more powerful and more knowing than any man or magician. I speak with My God three times each day. I need a quiet place to do so. I have asked and been granted dream interpretations before, and surely, your dream has a meaning I can learn and tell you."

Pharaoh called to the guards that were at the back exit of the room. He instructed them to escort me to his private courtyard and leave me there undisturbed but to stay to lead me back once I had heard the interpretation. This was how I found myself walking toward a field of flowers. This was like no field of flowers I had ever seen. It did not go on and on over hills or valleys, but it still took up as much room as three, or possibly four, of My Father's large tents. Instead of one color of flower, there was a circle of red flowers inside a larger circle of yellow flowers inside a still larger circle of purple flowers. And instead of the flowers going on as far as the eye could see, the edge was clearly marked by bricks surrounding these circles that made a wide path for walking around the flowers.

I instinctively started doing just that. I left the guards at their post and walked around this majestic circle. I could not stop staring at the flowers. It was as if the colors wanted to enter my eyes as fiercely as the fragrance was entering my nose. It was only after walking once around the circle in complete awe that I had a momentary recollection that I was there to talk to My God. But I was quickly distracted by noticing that there was even a path that entered the flower circle itself. It was well hidden, as it was as narrow as my feet placed side by side, but definitely an intentional path since it was made by purple tiles.

I entered the circle.

Careful not to veer off the path to the right or the left, I followed the purple tiles into the purple flowers. One foot in front of the other, I slowly moved forward. As I did, my thoughts floated to My Mother. I saw her opening her arms to a baby boy who was being delivered inside of a large rainbow—my cloak! My real cloak of colors! I saw myself running around our family compound in Haran, naked and free, laughing at a bunny that hopped faster than I could catch it. I saw myself being laughed at by My Brothers and then saw myself by My Father's side with his arm on my shoulder.

As I continued my walk, the tiles changed from purple to yellow, and I was on a narrow path inside the yellow flowers. There, I saw myself in My Auntie's embrace, her strict, but always warm, smile filling my body with confidence and pride. While I walked, I saw my body change from that of a boy to that of a man, and I felt Deenah's hand around mine, loving me exactly as I was and then letting go and walking away from me. And while she walked off in one direction, My Father approached from another and cloaked me in my blue and white coat. *The river.* My brothers had helped me get to the land of the river by selling me to the Ishmaelites.

I saw myself on the back of the camel, and I heard My God say my name in a voice that could only belong to Elohim, and I understood my dreams. I saw myself floating over the desert with Qarib and landing in Potifar's house. I saw Potifar and his wife handing me over to Atsu so that I could know a brother, and know myself, so well. And as I felt that peace, I saw that I had walked not only over the yellow tiles but also over the red ones, through the red flowers, and to the end of the path.

Although, it wasn't really the end. For where the red tiles stopped was at a circle of white tiles. This was the innermost part of the circle, and this flowerless section could not be seen from the rim. It was the perfect size for sitting, and so I sat. I breathed in the flowers—their aroma, their colors, their light and power and glory. I breathed it all in. *Yhhhh.* And released myself to join the beauty. *Whhhh. Yhhhh. Whhhh.* Soon, I spoke to My God.

"Blessed are You, Elohim, God of My Father Jacob, God of My Father Isaac, God of My Father Abraham. God of these flowers, God of these colors, God of all awe and wonder. Thank you for giving me this life. Thank you for guarding me and watching over me. Thank you for bringing me to this day." I sat quietly in this rapture. I don't know how long I sat, but it was long enough to feel the flowers glide out of their roots and float around my body. Long enough to watch them change from flowers to light and from red, yellow, and purple to the full spectrum of colors of my coat, cloaking me in their brilliance as I sailed in it through the sky, past the darkness that lies beneath the stars and past the stars themselves, into a pure light.

When I opened my eyes, the sun had nearly disappeared from the sky. The colors of the flowers were still vibrant, and the path could still be seen. I stood and thanked My God for allowing me that experience, and then I asked that I could know Pharaoh's dream, for I had just remembered that that had been the reason for my coming to this courtyard.

As soon as I set foot again on the red tiles, I began again to see visions of myself. This time, I was not in memories of things that had already happened but in memories of things that were yet to happen. I saw Pharaoh placing a scepter in my hand and a ring on my finger. Then, at once, I saw the land of Egypt covered in crops that grew and nourished the people with abundance. As I continued to walk, I saw the crops wither and die and saw myself distributing food from what had been saved. I saw myself holding three babies. Mine. I saw My Father falling on my neck. I received a gift, and that gift was a young queen bee and a hive of shepherds. My Brothers also received a gift, and their gift was large, healthy flocks. And just before I took the last step off the last purple tiles, I saw myself and Pharaoh walk into a pyramid, I only a few small steps behind him.

Once back on the bricks, I walked directly to the guards. "I am ready," I said, and they escorted me back to Pharaoh.

Pharaoh was sitting on his throne exactly as I'd left him. Whether he had stayed there the whole time or left and returned, I would not know. I prostrated myself before him again, and he quickly instructed me to rise and speak.

"Pharaoh's dreams are one and the same. Elohim has told Pharaoh of what is about to happen. The seven healthy cows are seven years, and the seven healthy ears are seven years. It's the same dream. The seven lean and ugly cows that came after them are also seven years, as are the seven empty and scorched ears of grain. They are seven years of famine.

"These words I have told Pharaoh, this is what Elohim will do and what Elohim has shown you is going to happen. The next seven years will be great, abundant years all over the land of Egypt. After them will come seven years of famine, and all the abundance in the land of Egypt will be forgotten. Hunger will cover the land. Those seven years of plenty will be all but forgotten due to the heaviness of the famine.

"As for Pharaoh having had the same dream twice, it is to show that the matter has been determined by Elohim and that Elohim will soon carry it out. Now, Pharaoh must look for a wise and prophetic man and put him in command over the land of Egypt. Pharaoh must take steps to appoint land overseers and organize the land of Egypt during the seven years of plenty. Gather all the food in these coming good years, and let the grain be gathered under the decree of Pharaoh and stored in the cities. Let that food be a reserve for the seven years of famine that will come to the land of Egypt so that the land may not perish in the famine."

Pharaoh listened attentively as I shared the interpretation of his dream as Elohim had it shared with me. This included more than the meaning, as there were also instructions. When I finished speaking, Pharaoh smiled and released a long exhale. He stood from his throne and spoke to the guards and courtiers who had been in the background this whole time. "Could we possibly find another man like this one? Who so clearly has the spirit of Elohim in him?"

Then Pharaoh descended from his throne and stood in front of me, face-to-face. "If what you say is true, and if Elohim has made all this known to you, then there is nobody as prophetic and wise as you. Therefore, you should be the man to oversee this action. But I cannot have a servant, a prisoner, rank so highly in Egypt. You must shed the man whom you used to be and return as someone who can be entrusted to be my vizier. If you can do this, it shall be so."

I knew the challenge Pharaoh was placing before me, but I did not hesitate. Elohim would guide me and support me and use me to protect the land of Egypt. I was certain. I nodded my acceptance.

Pharaoh went back to sit on his throne. "Guards, escort the dream interpreter to a chamber where he may spend the night."

The two guards who had brought me from prison approached. Yet before they were close enough to touch me, I prostrated myself to the ground one more time. "Pharaoh, if I am to be such a trusted servant of yours and an official of the court, I must certainly have a guard of my own at all times, is this so?"

"You may have one," he responded. "Choose whomever you like, and your needs will be his duty."

"I choose Atsu, the warden from the prison. He is experienced and upstanding and will ensure that nothing bad befalls me and that, therefore, nothing bad will befall the Pharaoh. Furthermore, this will benefit you, My Pharaoh. For Atsu has been loyal his whole life and has trained others to be as well. You can leave him to entrust the position of warden to one of the other men and rest assured that you will not need to search for a replacement for him."

And so it was that Pharaoh's two guards briefly went separate ways. One went to fetch Atsu, and the other brought me to a chamber twice the size of Potifar's with a large bed in the middle that could have held all my prison brothers at once. By dawn, it held me and Atsu and the tale I told him of my day in the palace. We slept only briefly before we were brought a plate piled with fresh fruits that gave me a taste of the sweetness that was about to come.

The next week was filled with meetings and instructions preparing me for my role as vizier. Six men were appointed to my appearance. First, they took me to a private pool of the Nile that came into the palace. I learned there were more than one of these: one for the royal men, one for the women of the harem, and one that the others in the court were allowed to access. Each had water that flowed in from the river and was surrounded by reeds. Once I was clean to their satisfaction, they gently shaved my skin smooth (on a daily basis) and covered me in fragrant oils. They created my new wardrobe of royal attire as well as my garb for the ceremony that was to come in just a matter of days.

I was to wear a golden kilt with a golden belt as well as gold bangles on my wrists and ankles. My feet were sandal-less, as I would be carried on a litter and would walk only on rugs for the ceremony. For my head, I received a blue and gold striped crown noticeably smaller than My Pharaoh's but equally as beautiful. And my neck held such a weight of gold strands dangling with jewels that it was a struggle to keep my back straight.

I was taught how to hold my head as I walked, just how far behind I was to stand from My Pharaoh—ten paces—and when to walk, sit, stand, and bow. I was given a scroll with words already upon it and was required to practice reading it several times even though the content was brief and simple: "I accept these honors and responsibilities and vow to serve faithfully."

As the sun rose on the tenth day following my entrance to My Pharaoh's court, my presence was officially announced. The word had been spread that the new vizier was not someone who had moved up in the ranks of the royal family or staff, but someone new. A large crowd of curious onlookers had already gathered long before the official trumpets had sounded, announcing the beginning of the ceremony.

I was led through the halls of the palace in my stately clothes, walking behind My Pharaoh and his staff and flanked by Atsu and three other guards. When we reached the top of the first flight of stairs, My Pharaoh climbed into his litter and was taken down to the next landing. When he was seated on his throne, I was lifted into a smaller, but similar, carriage and brought to the landing, where I was to dismount.

My Pharaoh's throne was to my left as I stood in the middle of the landing, facing the people who congregated on the ground below for as far as one could see. The throne itself was draped in purple linen so as not to be too hot. My Pharaoh also wore purple. It was woven through his golden kilt and dripped down in tassels from the bottom. When he sat, it was difficult to distinguish what was his throne tapestry and what was his garb. My throne, which was only slightly smaller than his and to my right, at the other end of the landing, was draped in white. But before I sat, I was to stand on display before the people while My Pharaoh announced me.

A scroll was unrolled before him and held high by a helper. The words were recited in My Pharaoh's strong, deep voice that echoed off the marble and down to the people: "This is Zafenat Paaneakh," he said, using the name by which I would be known in Egypt. "He is a revealer of hidden things; he is my vizier, my right hand, my most trusted servant. I appoint him, with the blessings of the other gods, as overseer of all the food, supplies, and trades in this land. No one shall be above him but me." The scroll was then closed and removed.

The trumpets sounded their blasts again, and I knew that as my cue to turn toward My Pharaoh and prostrate myself upon the ground in his direction. The people below followed my example. We all stayed in that position until My Pharaoh sat upon his throne. I knew that as my signal to rise and face the people. Another staircase was still between me and them, as they were to know that our position was higher than theirs in all ways. I looked down upon this crowd and waved with my right arm as I had been instructed. Then my scroll was brought to me and opened for my reading. "I accept these honors and responsibilities and vow to serve faithfully," I announced. And then they all prostrated themselves before me—all but My Pharaoh.

At the sound of a gong, they rose and watched me walk to my throne. While their eyes were on me, mine were on the rugs beneath my feet. I had already felt the softness of the fabric as I stood before the nation, but the walk across it was even more pleasurable to the touch. And as my feet traveled the length of the landing, they walked over the colors of the rainbow. For where I had been standing was at a meeting point between two rainbows woven into the rugs; they connected the two thrones such that as I approached mine, I was walking on my personal rainbow.

If it were not for the lovely feeling of the fabric beneath my feet, I might have thought myself floating, for it felt that the time to cross the landing took much longer than expected. In that time, I enjoyed the softness on my feet, admired and wondered at the mastery of the weaving, and was reminded of a story that My Mother had first told me as a boy all the way back in Haran.

"Joseph," she said and pointed to the sky, "look." It was the first rain after the end of my fourth summer, and My Mother pointed to a band of colors in the sky. "That is a rainbow," she said. My hair and arms were freshly cooled from the rain shower, and my toes enjoyed brief moments of squishing in the wet soil. It had not rained much that morning, but it was enough for streaks to appear on My Mother's face where the drops had rinsed some of the dust away. "Rainbow," I said, repeating the new word and staring at it with My Mother until it disappeared.

Later that night, on the mat in our tent, My Mother told me the story of the rainbow. "Long ago," she said, "most people were wicked. Then there was a great flood, rain for days and nights and days and nights, so many you cannot imagine—forty! It rained for forty days and forty nights, and there was a flood that washed away all the wicked people. But the good people survived on a boat. And when the flood ended, Ishtar painted a rainbow in the sky as a promise that the world would never again be destroyed by a flood."

The first time My Mother told me that story, I flooded her with questions: Who is Ishtar? What is a boat? Where is this boat now? And where is Ishtar? Who were the wicked people? What had they done? Who were the good people? My Mother's answer to each question in turn was the same: "I don't know." So after I had asked all my questions, all I could do was laugh at the thought of My Mother not knowing these things. A mother not knowing something! I found this as unlikely, and therefore as funny, as if a donkey were to open its mouth and talk.

My Mother took to telling me that story often, just so she could hear my laughter. I never did tire of it, even as, over the years, some of my questions got answers. But what I loved most about the story was that Ishtar had made a promise and symbolized it with a rainbow. If Ishtar could do such a thing, certainly My God could as well. Thus, I began to see the rainbow not as Ishtar's promise of not destroying the wicked world but as Elohim's promise of building the good one. It was rare that I saw a rainbow in the sky, but when it happened, it was a reminder of Elohim's promise.

That day in Egypt, the rainbow was not in the sky but on the ground. I walked upon it before the king's court and subjects, and at the end of the rainbow, I finally sat upon my throne. This was the moment I had been waiting for my whole life: the moment that I became the most important man in all the land. Oh, if only My Mother could have seen me on my throne on that rainbow!

The ceremony concluded with trumpet blasts and drums whose music felt like thunderclaps moving through my body. When the sun reached its height, My Pharaoh was given a large goblet of wine to drink. As prescribed, he drank ten sips, and then his cup was brought to my lips to drink after him. The gong sounded one final time, and we were carried off to the sound of the crowd cheering for My Pharaoh, their deity, and for me, their ruler.

CHAPTER 24

The ceremony was followed by feasts and festivities through the night, and in the morning, my work began. I was immediately set to task accounting, planning, and directing the food production and storage in all of Egypt. I traveled the land, managed the resources, and answered to no one save My Pharaoh. My Pharaoh was pleased with my service and rewarded me in many ways. Of course, my chambers were nearly as lavish as the king's, and the respect I garnered in the palace was second only to his. Now, he'd sent a message to inform me that Ah-seenat, the daughter of the priest of Ohn, was mine to take as a wife. I thanked the messenger and sent him away so I could speak privately with Atsu.

Atsu had his own chamber adjacent to mine. It was not as luxurious as that of the vizier, of course, but as spacious as his old quarters five times over. He recently took a wife, who was the sister of one of the palace chefs, and was enjoying his time with her in their shared bed. She would also come and find him while he was at his duties and sneak him a small treat or kiss if he nodded his permission, which he always did. I knew he was quite happy with his wife. What I told him came as a surprise.

"I do not wish to marry her," I said.

"Do you know this woman?" he asked. "Is she a disgrace?"

"No," I said. "I do not know her, and I don't wish to. I wish to marry Deenah."

Atsu put his hand on my shoulder. "Zafenat," he said, first reminding me of my new identity, "you may continue to love Deenah for as long as you like. But she is not here, and you are not there."

"And what if Ah-seenat sends me to jail?" I asked. But even before I finished the question, the fear had left me. Going to jail had been wonderful before; it could be wonderful again.

"Well," Atsu said, "going to jail was wonderful before. It could be wonderful again . . ." Atsu often gave voice to my thoughts. Then he added, "Even though I don't plan to return with you." We smiled. "In any case, she cannot send you to jail. She is not your master's wife. She will be your wife. You are the master."

At my wedding feast, My Pharaoh spared no expense. We had tables and tables of melons, orange ones, green ones, and even yellow ones. He brought in countless bottles of wine from his best vineyards and cakes so sweet that a fig would bow its head in shame by comparison. But the musicians were my favorite part of the day.

Six men stood in the center of the room on a platform that had been raised earlier that morning. Two were with flutes, and two had stringed instruments. One played on a drum twice the size of the rock that used to cover the well by our camp outside of Shechem. My Father had never worked to push that rock, for by the time we'd moved there, he'd had many sons and manservants to do that for him. But as Shimon and Levi grunted and groaned, he'd repeated the story of falling so deeply in love with My Mother that he'd become able to remove the Haran well rock on his own.

During one such retelling of this story, when My Father had looked away from the well for a moment toward the call of one of his workers, I saw Levi kick some dirt in his direction. That was Levi, always full of disdain and disrespect. Did he not wish to follow in My Father's path and love someone as much as My Father loved My Mother?

I wished I would be able to love Ah-seenat that much. I couldn't bring myself to wish I would love her as much as I loved Deenah, but I did want to love her. And I could not hide my joy that I might soon lie with someone again. Atsu was wonderful, but we'd never touched each other in the way that Zulaika and I or Potifar and I had. We never had those kinds of pleasures.

Now that I was vizier, I had access to the harem, so I would not need a wife. But I told myself that surely My Pharaoh had selected a wonderful wife for me. Look at this magnificent feast he was throwing in my honor! A feast of one day was little compared to a wife of one lifetime. *She will be a good wife*, I told myself. *She will.*

And she was. For almost two years, we enjoyed each other, loved each other. She was not Deenah, but she was beautiful, and she was kind. She listened to me and did not laugh at my ideas. She held tightly to her Isis but welcomed My God as well. She adorned herself in the clothing provided to her because of her status, and her skin smelled of the holiest oils and was smooth and a pleasure to touch.

And from our very first night together, when she'd been brought to me after the wedding feast, she enjoyed my touch. She had been so afraid at first because she'd been told of the pain and of her duty. But she did not know that I had been told of pain and duty by Deborah and Deenah and had learned of it myself from Potifar and Zulaika. Never would I inflict that on anyone, least of all My Wife, the woman who would bring me sons. She cried and relaxed and let me hold her and touch her, and our bodies found pleasure together.

Even when she was pregnant with our sons, we paraded our beauty for each other and smiled and laughed and shared sweet treats and sweet touches. When My Son, Menasseh, tore her skin on his exit, I heard her wails from the courtyard where I paced impatiently. And when the midwife reached inside her to pull My Son, Efraim, out, the scream that came from her body tore through mine and brought me to my knees.

"Please, Elohim, please save My Wife!" I was so shaken that I had neglected my opening words, but I quickly came back to them out of habit: "God of My Father Jacob, God of My Father Isaac, God of My Father Abraham, please, please, Elohim, please save My Wife!" This was the prayer I repeated until the midwife came out and told me that they had stopped the bleeding. They told me that My Wife slept in the painless stupor of the poppy juice and that I was the father of two sons.

I fell on her neck in gratitude and removed the gold band I was accustomed to wearing around my ankle and gave it to her.

"I cannot accept that," she said. "I have already been paid."

"This is a gift," I told her. "A gift, please, take it." I walked to the table of food that had been arranged for me to eat in the courtyard while I waited. I had touched none of it. Even before the screams, I could only think of the last baby born—Benno—and how the birthing had been too much for My Mother, how the blood had been too much for the midwife. I gathered all the uneaten food into one of the baskets of cookies. "And take this, too, please." I forced the basket upon her. I did not have enough things to thank her with for saving the life of My Wife and bringing me my boys. Only when I saw her leaving with these gifts could I go back to My God with a new prayer.

"Blessed are You, God of My Father Jacob, God of My Father Isaac, God of My Father Abraham for saving the lives of my family and sustaining us and bringing us to this day."

I brought Ah-seenat a new maidservant, Ebbo. Ebbo was to be by her side and tend to her every need and wish night and day. Ebbo was a strong woman, fit for carrying two babies at once and tending to My Wife. And her very name reminded me of Deborah. *My Grandmother would be pleased*, I thought, and shed a tear for her for the first time in years.

In the days following the birth of My Sons, I felt something I had never felt before. Even as the man who ran all of Egypt, I had not felt the importance or honor that I felt in being the father of two sons and the husband of a woman who had birthed them and lived. And so it was with unspeakable pride that I had Menasseh and Efraim brought to me on their eighth day of life so that I could bring them into the covenant that My Grandfather Abraham had made with My God, that his son Isaac had continued with his sons, and that My Father Jacob had continued with me.

Oh, the morning had been pure ecstasy! I had sharpened the knife myself. A knife that I had chosen from all the tools in the palace. The blade could split a hair, and the handle was embedded with a sapphire scarab. The sun in the open courtyard where we sat among the flowers—just the three of us, my two sons and me—reflected light off the knife, making it sparkle like the stars. It fit perfectly in my hand, and when I watched my hand close around it, I saw My Father's fingers.

Truly, the only thing that could have made the moment better was if My Father himself had been there to witness it. I longed to see him. I longed to contact him. But what would I say? That My Brothers had sold me to traders, but now I have risen to rule Egypt? Come and see My Sons? Yes, yes, I suppose that is what I could have said. But my dreams had told me that Elohim had other plans. Whatever those were, I would not interfere. I would wait for our reunion.

I called on Elohim again, thanking My God for the birth of My Sons. Little bundles in blankets, little faces with brown eyes full of wonder and full lips dripping with milk. I whispered in their ears that they were now the sons of the highest-ranking man after Pharaoh but that they would grow into even greater honors, for one day, they would inherit land. My Land. Their land. The land I had walked to from Haran, the land I had left when I'd been sold, the land My God had promised to My Father and to me and now to them.

And with that promise fresh in their ears, I completed the covenant with a quick and careful swipe of the blade for each boy. The extra foreskin on each penis fell to the ground, and only one drop of blood spilled with it. The air was filled with the music of their strong wails, and I held each one in an arm and danced with them, singing the way I imagined My Father had when it had been my turn so long ago and so far away.

I knew then that it was the right thing to do. I never had a question or a doubt. But Ah-seenat never accepted that. And so it was on that day, the day I had taken My Sons to Elohim that she took them away from me. Their cries had brought her hobbling to the courtyard, hair askew and legs still limping from exhaustion. Ebbo tried to support her, but when Ah-seenat saw the knife, she yelled to her, "Leave me! Get my babies!"

Ah-seenat stood just a few paces away, moving closer with blood running down her leg and fire in her eyes. "No!" she yelled at me while Ebbo removed Menasseh and Efraim from my arms. "No!" Her voice was not her own, but the sound a crocodile would make if it spoke.

I rushed to My Wife. "I would not harm My Sons," I said. "I welcomed them into the covenant of My Forefathers."

But she did not hear me. I could not even hear my words over her yelling, "No!" That was all she said. She stood over me, and every time I opened my mouth, she yelled "No!"

She did not hear me remind her that I had never hurt her—would never. She did not hear me plead for her to understand. And when I stopped talking through my tears, she stopped yelling and walked away.

Atsu suggested I let her be for a while. He had become a father two years earlier, and his wife had borne him a second son just a month before My Sons had been born. I trusted his experienced advice even though it hurt to be separated from My Wife and My Sons. But when I called for Ah-seenat after a month, she came to my chamber only to say that if I called for her again, she would send the curse of Isis upon me.

Then she raised her right arm above her head. I thought she would strike me, but it was her words that attacked me, not her hand. “I have placed seven bangles on this arm. One for each day on which my sons were whole. I will wear them always, and if you hear them, you will know that I am nearby and that you should turn and go the other way.”

CHAPTER 25

When My Wife left, I became lonely in the nights. I longed to smell her and caress her. Even just to lie beside her and hear her breath in the same bed had been a comfort and a joy. Now, she was gone, and My Sons with her. Sometimes, I watched them from afar. I saw them crawling, then standing, then running and chasing after salamanders and each other. Only from afar, though, and only on occasion did I watch them because each viewing brought me so much pride and pain at once that it was hard to bear. I knew that, given my position, it would be in my power to banish Ah-seenat and reclaim My Sons, but I could not bring myself to do such a thing. Though I did not love her in the same way I had once loved Deenah, I did love her still. I could no more wish ill upon her than I could on Atsu. I could take no satisfaction in having My Sons near if it meant I had taken them from their mother who I knew loved them with the ferocity with which My Mother had loved me. And so, I focused on my work.

It was not difficult to keep my attention there. In the years that followed the birth of My Sons, there was much to keep me busy. After all, I oversaw the distribution of sustenance for all of Egypt. I presided over all the requests for food, those that came from as close as the dried banks of the Nile and those that came from as far as Damascus in the north and Kush in the south.

Most men wanted provisions for their families and their tribes and were willing to trade anything for the opportunity to live another year. But some came with intent to spy out our land and attempt to conquer our stores for themselves.

Nine days a week, I received these travelers. I heard their pleas, listened for their motives, and traded Egypt's excess grain for more wealth for My Pharaoh. When the first men came from Canaan, I knew it would not be long before My Brothers would appear before me. I knew of the earlier famine when Abraham had gone to Egypt to live and not starve to death. He did live, and he left Egypt a wealthy man. The land he returned to now belonged to My Father and My Brothers, but what good would it be to them if they died of starvation?

I confided in Atsu that I thought My Brothers would be coming for grain soon. We had discussed this at the beginning of the famine as well. Elohim had provided me with the interpretation of my dream from years earlier, and Atsu and I had talked of it many times. The sun, moon, and eleven stars signified the number of years that would pass before I would be in a mighty position to help my tribe. Thirteen. In fact, it had been thirteen years from the time of the dream until My Pharaoh crowned me his vizier.

When in the prison, I had dreamt of the eleven dogs. My God had helped me understand that that was a dream about eleven years. I had spent the first two of those years in the prison and then seven years of plenty overseeing Egypt. Now that we were in the second year of the famine, the eleven years of my dog dream were coming to a close. *Soon*, I thought, *I would see My Brothers and My Father and my beloved Deenah again.* Deenah must certainly have been the moon, for My Mother had died even before the dream had been dreamt.

"What will you do when you see them?" Atsu asked.

Once, I had answered this question by telling him I would fall on My Father's neck and kiss his hands and feet endlessly. Once, I had answered that I would tell My Father that I would not chastise him for sending me into the arms of My Brothers, for it had landed me this position in Egypt. Another time, I told Atsu that I would stand tall and proud next to Reuben, for even if I was younger than the others, I was still a firstborn. Once, I told Atsu that I would tell the brothers that he, Atsu, was now a better brother to me than all of them combined. One time, my answer was that I would rush to baby Benno and scoop him into my arms even though he would no longer be a baby, but a young man. And every time, I told Atsu I would gently approach Deenah and tell her I have always loved her.

"What if the moon was not Deenah?" Atsu once asked me.

"If not Deenah," I asked, "then who?" But Atsu had no answer.

The part of the dream with the moon, the Deenah part, intrigued and excited me. It was not our custom for the daughters to stay with the tribe; they were to go off with their husbands. Had Deenah remained unmarried after Shechem, secluded in her mother's tent, still not coming out? Had she married one of the brothers after all? I was curious about the details of her life, but mostly, I was grateful for any reason to be able to reunite with my love.

This time, when Atsu asked me, I admitted to both of us that I didn't know the answer. What *would* I do when I saw them again? And what would *they* do?

One evening, two months after the first Canaanites had arrived, my guards announced that the final group of petitioners that day were from Canaan. Then, in walked ten men with their faces covered in long beards and their bodies covered in wool and with belts I immediately recognized as Leah's best weaving. My breath caught in my throat, and I smiled at them proudly.

Until that moment, I had not realized that what I really expected to happen was for My Brothers to rush at me with relief and gratitude for finding me in this position and for finding me alive—for finding me at all and for finding me to be the greatest distributor of food and wealth in all the land! I still believed that they must have suffered some remorse for what they had done to me in the heat of their pride and anger. I sat, awaiting their relief, their atonement, their joy.

Instead, as I sat there on my high throne flooded with anticipation and excitement, embarrassment, then sadness, then anger set in while they bowed their faces to the floor before the vizier. They did not even know their own brother. By the time I permitted them to rise, my face was composed.

I asked where they came from, as I asked everyone who entered to request provisions. I always knew the answer because the guards told me before anyone set foot in my presence. But I always asked to see who was the leader, who spoke up. I asked in my Egyptian tongue as I always did. My translator translated the question for the men, . . . for My Brothers.

"From the land of Canaan," Judah replied.

"To buy food," Shimon added.

"You are spies," I accused. "You are many men banded together who come to see the nakedness of the land and find a way to steal."

They tried to convince me otherwise. "No, my lord." It was Zevvy speaking. Oh, how he would have angered so many years ago to know that he would one day call me "my lord." But he showed no anger nor sarcasm. "My lord, we are hungry brothers with hungry wives and children at home. We have come for food, not to harm you."

"I have money," Levi added. "To pay for the food." Money. *Were any of the coins the same as the ones they had gotten when they'd sold me?* I wondered. I silently thanked My God for the selling. For allowing me to know Qarib and arrive in Egypt and prosper. If I had not thanked Elohim, I think I would have thrashed at Levi in anger when he mentioned the money.

"Whose money is it?" I asked. "Is it yours? You are ten men. Why does only one of you say the money is his?"

Reuben stepped forward. "Your servants were twelve brothers, the sons of one man who lives in the land of Canaan. The youngest is now with our father, and one is no more."

I waited as patiently as possible for the translator to speak between turns. I looked over each one of My Brothers in the meantime. Then I repeated my accusation. "It is just as I told you: you are spies. And this is how you will be tested. As surely as Pharaoh lives, you will not leave this place unless your younger brother comes here. Send one of you to get your brother; the rest of you will be confined here so that your words may be tested, to see if you are telling the truth. If you are not, then as surely as Pharaoh lives, you are spies."

With that, I turned to the guards and had them take the men to the chamber where I had once slept when I first arrived in the house of Pharaoh. I did not even wait for the translators to explain; I just sent them along so that nobody would be in the room with me other than Atsu.

When everyone left, I slumped in my chair, my *throne*, and wept into my hands. Atsu placed a hand on my shoulder and waited for my face to dry.

He didn't need to ask the reasons for my actions, as I volunteered them as soon as I was able to speak. "I just didn't know what to do," I said, still sobbing quietly. "They didn't recognize me. I never thought they wouldn't know me as their brother. All my thoughts of reuniting with them were crushed when they weren't glad to see me—didn't even recognize me! I did the only thing I could think of to keep them here longer."

Atsu stood beside me with his hand on my shoulder for a long while as I wept. When I cleared my face, he said, "Zafenat Paaneakh, perhaps they didn't recognize you because you are not the same man—the same boy—that they last saw. You are not a little brother pleading for your life at the bottom of a pit, but second-in-command of the greatest land for months in all directions! You are not counting sacks of barley cakes being loaded into the wagons of a small tribe, but feeding all the tribes that come for the grain that you have saved. Maybe they didn't recognize their little brother because their little brother is not here. An important man has replaced him."

I was grateful to Atsu for reminding me that I had achieved the status that was always meant for me. And while I was truly pleased to have achieved that goal, I was not sure I wanted to no longer be Joseph. But was it too late? Was it even an option?

I slept little that night. I had my guards turn away everyone who came asking for food the next day, instructing them to wait so that I could see them another day. And then I went and did the very thing I had accused My Brothers of: I spied. I walked the paths outside the chamber where My Brothers were guarded. I had Atsu with me, not trusting myself to be alone, not knowing what I might say or do.

What I did was pace. I heard a word here or there from the chamber, but mostly, they were quiet. This went on for seven days. Finally, when I could tolerate the sleepless nights no longer, when watching them alternatively eat the feasts I sent and pull out their hair lamenting the food their father would not receive, I had them brought back to stand before my throne.

"Do this, and you will live, for I fear Elohim," I told them via my interpreter. "If you are honest men, let one of your brothers be held here under watch while the rest of you bring rations back to your starving households. *And* you must bring me your younger brother so that your words may be verified and you don't die."

As soon as they heard the translation, they turned to each other. Asher spoke first. "We are being punished on account of our brother," he said. "We looked upon his suffering and ignored him as he pleaded with us."

The others nodded in agreement as they wiped their eyes. Naftali spoke softly. "This is why distress has come upon us here."

Reuben addressed them all. "Did I not tell you, 'Do no wrong to the boy?' But you did not listen. When I went back to pull him out of the pit, you had already sold him to traders. *You* were traitors! Now comes the reckoning for his blood."

Reuben had gone back for me! I could not hold back my tears at hearing the words they didn't know I understood. I bolted from the room, Atsu at my heels. Outside, I fell into his arms.

When my breath was steady again, he asked what I wished to do.

"I will send them back," I said. "Just as I informed them. And I will keep one behind as I said. At least in this way, I know they will return one day. And I will send them with the food they need and return the payment they brought. Further, they shall receive provisions for their journey. I shall include a scroll with an accounting of everything in their sacks. Perhaps then they will realize that I am the cause of their good fortune."

"Zafenat Paaneakh," Atsu said, addressing me and then pausing for permission to continue. Of course, I always granted him this permission. It was rare that he even made such a formal request, a sure sign that he was going to say something I might find displeasing. "Zafenat Paaneakh, you are a man and a father, a clean-shaven Egyptian lord. You are speaking the local tongue and covered in jewels. These men think their brother Joseph died many years ago. Perhaps they aren't thinking that the ruler before them is that same boy. Joseph, maybe they will only know that you are their brother and the cause of their good fortune if you tell them." Perhaps he was right, but I was not prepared to tell them something they should have already known. They should have known their brother. They should have known me.

Atsu went to see to my plan, and I returned to My Brothers. "Who is the eldest?" I asked. This amused me, for they had asked me in my youth to recite their birth order so many times, and now I was asking it of them. Reuben immediately stepped forward.

"You shall return to your land," I said, "watching over the others as you travel." Yes, Reuben would lead this time, from the front.

"Who is the next eldest?"

Shimon stepped forward.

"Certainly, there were times when you wished you were treated as the firstborn," I said. "Now, you shall be. You will stay here, and we shall see if your brothers will come and retrieve you from captivity." I instructed the guards to tie him up and remove him from the group. He was taken back to the chamber where he had just spent the last seven days. Only Levi bade him goodbye as the rest of them were escorted back to their donkeys and carts to leave Egypt.

THREE MONTHS PASSED after My Brothers had left Egypt, and still they had not yet returned. The journey should not have taken them this long. Why had I not seen them yet? Atsu had many ideas to consider in response to my question, but he told me repeatedly that his most truthful answer was that he simply did not know. I believe that after a while, he tired of my obsession over the issue, and that was what led him to suggest that I go and ask Shimon.

Though Shimon had spent his time in Egypt in a beautiful chamber and fed like a guest of the king—hardly the life of a prisoner—he hadn't been allowed to wander outside his walls and courtyard or to see anyone other than his appointed guards, who never spoke to him. I suspected that he, too, would be eagerly awaiting the return of My Brothers, so I followed Atsu's suggestion.

I had Shimon brought to my court. I was gratified to see him kneeling before me. Shimon. On the ground. Before me.

"You may rise," I said, when I'd gotten my fill. "Why have your brothers not returned yet?"

When my words were translated for him, he responded that he didn't know.

"Liar," I accused. "You men came before me and swore that you are brothers. Surely, it is like I said: you are spies. You came to view our land and our storages. If you were truly brothers, you would know these men well and be able to answer my question."

"It is not so," he defended himself. "We are brothers. But I am here, and they are there. Do you know what your brothers are doing?"

It took all my strength and patience to wait for the translator to say his filthy words in my new tongue. Then I shouted, "Insolence!" for him to translate back.

Shimon smirked.

I banged my fists on the throne, and he smirked again. Then I noticed how tightly my firsts were clenched, and I began to loosen them. I loosened my whole body and calmly looked him in the eye.

"If you cannot think of where your brothers are, I will help you," I said. "Why might they tarry? What would keep them from returning?"

"Our father will not like your demand to send his youngest son here. He watches over the boy like a child watches the last sweet on a plate."

"Surely, he would not let the whole tribe starve to death—including the boy—out of his desire to keep him close."

"No, he would not," Shimon answered.

"Tell me about the boy," I prodded.

"He is young."

"You said he had a brother who is no more."

"Yes."

"What became of him?"

"He was attacked by wild beasts."

I gasped. "Oh my. What happened?"

"I told you. He was attacked by wild beasts."

"What happened before that?" I asked.

"Before that, he was the favorite son."

"What made him the favorite?" I asked.

"He was the most favored by our father."

"Foreigner! You are saying nothing. Tell me of this boy."

"I have told you."

He wasn't smirking, nor was he apologetic. He was simply stating the truth.

"Tell me as if you were telling your sons of him. Tell me the details you share with them in stories about their tribe. A man has not lived until stories have been told about him."

"I have told you." He repeated. "You have heard everything that my sons have heard about the boy."

"And sisters?" I asked. Would he tell me anything of My Sisters?

"Yes."

"Yes, what?"

"Yes, I have sisters," he said.

"Where are they?" I asked. Even if My Sisters had been married into other tribes, surely, he would know of their whereabouts.

"Married," he said, and so I knew they would be a part of their husbands' tribes now, and my heart sank. "Except one, who became the nursemaid of a brother's wife."

I could not bring myself to ask which sister had stayed with the tribe. I needed to trust the dream that Elohim gave me of the sun and moon and stars. It is Elohim who determined the number of stars in the sky and in my dream. It is Elohim who calls each one by name. Surely, the same is true of the moon. I felt comforted that I would someday see my beloved Deenah again, for Elohim also heals the brokenhearted.

"Tell me about yourself," I prodded.

"My brother Levi and I should be leading our tribe. We conquered a whole kingdom once, killing every last man and making our tribe rich. We are brave and strong and swift to right wrongs and grow our property and might."

I enjoyed hearing this exaggeration. All these years later, Shimon would have people believe that he was mighty enough to conquer a whole city. Long ago, he had slain the men of one family and taken a few women, and still he was telling a story that he thought made him mightier, telling his little story to the mighty vizier of all of Egypt.

"Tell me of this," I said.

"I told you."

"Tell me in the way you tell your sons in stories."

Shimon paused before slowly saying, "I have told you what I have told my sons. I have said to them many times, 'Levi and I should be leading our tribe. We conquered a whole kingdom once, killing every last man and making our tribe rich.'"

"This is all you have told your sons?" I asked. "This is what they know of their father?"

"Yes," he responded.

"Tell me what you know of your father," I instructed.

"He was a shepherd. Now he does nothing during his days."

"More," I demanded.

"I have told you what I know," he insisted.

"You know nothing!" I yelled.

And although the translator did not yell, Shimon knew my anger and frustration. He did not match it; he responded quietly, but not bashfully: "I know that I am stronger and braver than you and that if you were not so high and mighty, I could do away with you in one blow."

I gripped my throne to hold myself back as the interpreter translated. The moment the last word left his mouth, I jumped off my dais and onto Shimon's chest, sending him to the ground with the force of my weight. I then struck his nose with my forehead, bashing it until bloody with one blow and secretly thanking Anum for having taught me that skill. Shimon was still bound and surrounded, so nobody intervened, perhaps also from the shock of my actions. After the blow, I was finished with him. I stood and commanded that he be taken to the jail.

As soon as they left, tears streaked my face.

"Are you hurt?" Atsu asked me.

"Yes," I said. "A good father tells stories to his children, tells them of his own father and mother, tells them of his own life. Has a man even lived if there are no stories told about him? Shimon has not told his sons about My Father or about me. And I have done no better than he has."

He put his hand on my shoulder. "You have told me, Zafenat, and you can still tell your sons." I nodded. Perhaps he was right. Perhaps I could. After I finished shedding my tears, he asked whether I would like to hear good tidings.

I nodded.

"You just wrestled with your brother. *And* you won."

CHAPTER 26

The next morning, I called for My Sons. They entered my chamber with erect backs and eyes focused. Menasseh approached me first, as he was the firstborn, bowed his head and said, "I am here, my lord," before taking a seat to my right. Efraim followed his example, though his face was less stoic. He parted his lips in a nervous smile, showing the space in the top of his mouth where his new set of front teeth had not yet appeared. Did Menasseh already have his? How had I missed this?

With my boys flanking me, their tutor nodded approvingly and left us alone. "My Sons," I said. And then I left a long pause. A pause in which I did not say how wrong I had been to separate myself from them. A pause in which I could not admit aloud that I had let my shame in disgracing their mother lead me to hide my face from them as well. A pause in which I did not even tell them that I had watched them from afar so many, many times. And a pause in which I still could not tell them of Joseph, the boy who had grown to be the man they sat beside. They waited patiently for my next words that were so slow to come.

"We will sit on the floor," I said. Neither of them moved. I arose to gather cushions from the spots where they lay merely decorating the podium on which our chairs sat. They rose when I did, but stood, stunned, until I had arranged the pillows on the floor, sat on one, and invited them to sit facing me. I smiled at them, but received only questioning looks in return.

"I will tell you a story," I said, "a story from the north about a great man who came from the other side of a great river—not The Great River, not the Nile—but another river far, far away, across many mountains and valleys and streams and plains. This great man came from a land where sheep are more abundant than crops and where men let the whiskers on their chins grow to touch their chests." At this detail, Efraim laughed, and I rubbed my chin and felt its now familiar smoothness from daily shavings. It had been so long since I'd considered that hair a sign of wisdom; I had forgotten myself.

I laughed with Efraim, and both boys softened their posture a bit, opening to this new experience of hearing a story from their father.

"Many years ago, there was a man who came to Egypt, all the way to this great land, from far, far away. As I said, he came from the other side of another river, and so he was called 'The Other.' You might think that he'd left that land because this one is so superior. However, he did not know that at the time. He knew only that his god, Elohim, had told him to go."

Elohim. It was the first time I had said the name of My God to someone else since becoming Zafenat Paaneakh. When I left

Joseph behind, I had left so much. I vowed silently, with My Sons as unknowing witnesses, that I would find the balance. I would return to Elohim and my teachings. I would return to being Joseph as well.

"Elohim promised The Other that he would become a father of many. Abraham," I said. Then I paused and repeated it. "*Abraham*. This is how one says 'Father of many' in the language of the north. Say it after me: Abraham."

"Abraham."

To hear My Sons say the name of My Forefather caused tears to begin to well in my eyes. I quickly stopped them before the boys were able to question me and then continued my story.

"Abraham was married to a princess. He took her and his nephew and all their possessions and left the land of his father and followed the word of Elohim and was brought to the land of Canaan. There, Elohim took Abraham to the top of a mountain and blessed him, saying that he would be the father of so many children that they would be as numerous as the stars in the sky and the sand on the land."

I paused and cracked a small smile. I pictured my own father as he had paused for us to grow our curiosity. I looked each of My Sons in their sparkly brown eyes and asked them with a raised eyebrow, "Would you like to know the funny part?"

Thankfully, my storytelling had been powerful enough to let them momentarily forget their training in formality. They happily bounced on their knees in anticipation, squealing, "Yes, yes," in chorus.

"The funny part about this promise of being a father of many is that Abraham's wife, the princess, Sarah, . . . *Sarah* is how you say *princess* in his language from the north. . . . "

"Sarah," they repeated, not knowing they were uttering the name of their own matriarch.

"Sarah," I continued, "was barren."

They gasped. And I laughed. Sarah's barrenness wasn't funny, of course, but because I already knew of the laughter that bubbled up in her when she learned that she was finally no longer barren.

"My Sons," I said. "It is easy to think that this is the end of the story. But it is only the beginning. Elohim followed through on that promise. Another time, I shall tell you of Abraham and Sarah's visit to Egypt, of the son eventually born in their old age, and of their grandchildren and great-grandchildren who are numerous and living in that promised land. Would you like that?"

"Yes, my lord!" they said in one voice.

Their enthusiasm was great, but my heart was fallen. "My Sons," I said. "Menasse. Efraim." I looked each in his eyes as I said his name. "Your tutor has instructed you well. You are the sons of the Second-in-Command in all of Egypt. You hold great stature because mine is even greater, second only to Pharaoh himself. Yet to you, I am not only 'my lord.' I am your father. That is an honor of the highest value. From now on, you shall address me as 'Father.'"

"Yes, my lord!" they said again and immediately corrected themselves. "Yes, Father!" Menasseh smiled at the sound of it, and I was able to see that one of his top teeth was nearly grown in and that the other only halfway. My children were still little. I was not too late to be a good father to them, even if their mother would never speak to me again.

"Come," I instructed. "Help me replace these cushions and then sit on your chairs like good students. I will summon your tutor and inform him that you shall be returning to my chamber. He will not be pleased to hear that I will take you away from your studies, so I will not. You will need to rise early and still answer to him after our story time. Do you understand?" They did. I rang the bell, and the tutor entered, bowing before me.

"In three days, we shall have a full moon," I said. "Beginning at that time, you are to bring My Sons in here to me before sunrise. They shall have instruction with me before meeting with you. We will do this every morning until the next full moon."

"Yes, my lord," the tutor said.

I turned to My Sons. "Menasse, follow your tutor to your studies now. Efraim, follow your brother and tutor to your studies."

They departed obediently with their tutor and returned three days later. As planned, from full moon to full moon, we met every morning. Every time the tutor left us alone, My Sons gathered the cushions and arranged them creatively on the floor. We sat as My Father and his sons had sat, only this time, I was the one who had wide eyes and ears directed at me. I entertained them with stories of Isaac's birth and his near death at his own father's hand. I told them of Jacob's skill with sheep and Esau's with hunt. I told them of the brothers who'd killed the king of the faraway land of Shechem and the beautiful girl who'd cursed them for it. I told them of the beloved grandmother who had been born in Haran and of the wise auntie who had been born in Egypt. I told them of the love of Rachel and of the boy who had been thrown into a pit. The only thing I did not tell them was that these stories were about me. But it was good enough.

It was better than I could have hoped for. From full moon to full moon, we were together every morning. Me and My Sons. We would do the same the next year and the next and the next. Thus, the stories would be told—and heard—and Joseph and Jacob will have lived. And eventually, My Sons learned not only about the man whom their father had been . . . but that I was that very same man.

AFTER THE FIRST month with My Sons, I wanted to apologize to Ah-seenat She had carried and birthed these beautiful boys. I had left her alone all these years at her request, but only because she was angry at me. I knew she didn't want me to call for her to come to me. So, I sought her out to deliver the apology.

When the sun had gone down and I knew she would be retiring to her chamber, I walked through the palace to meet her there. Many nights, I had walked under the moon with gratitude to Elohim for my position, my advantages, and mostly, My God's presence and help. This night, I was finally remembering to feel those things toward Ah-seenat. As I got closer and closer to her chamber, I got more and more excited about our reunion.

The moon was already in the sky, but some of the last sunlight was still coming in the window when I arrived at her chamber. She was already lying in bed, her back against the cushion, her hair surrounding her head, black, shiny, and gorgeous. Her eyes were closed, so I was able to pause and appreciate her beauty unnoticed, which I did. She was naked, and though I could only see the top half of her, I enjoyed seeing her beautiful breasts rising above her chest. She had a smile on her lips, and I wanted nothing more than to kiss her and smile together.

I quietly approached the bed so as not to disturb her. It was after only a few steps that I was close enough to see her lower body, which had been obscured by the curtain when I had stood at a farther distance. Her knees were raised, and there between her legs was a head! I gasped in surprise, and my noise alerted them to my presence. They both looked at me, Ah-seenat from her pillow, and Ebbo, her handmaid, from between Ah-seenat's legs. I took another step closer, but Ah-seenat used her hand to shoo me away, then placed both her hands on Ebbo's head and guided her back to where she had been.

I rushed out of her chamber and into the open air and the darkening sky. Without planning to, I began walking to the garden, then running. When I got there, I lay face down in the flowers and sobbed. When my body could shake out no more tears, I stood and wiped the dirt off my face, grateful for the dark of night and emptiness of the garden. I returned to my chamber, washed myself, and called for My Wife.

Ah-seenat's guards escorted her to me almost immediately. She was not dressed or adorned the way a woman would normally be when called to her husband. She had not prepared her hair or skin with oils—at least not for me. But she had taken the time to put on her bangles, and I heard her entrance even before I saw her.

"What is it?" she asked as soon as the guards left. "I told you not to call me here."

"I called you to apologize," I said. "To apologize for the babies who had nearly ripped your body apart, to apologize for circumcising them according to my old customs and not according to the Egyptian customs, and to apologizc for not making amends sooner. I have missed you, Ah-seenat I have missed you greatly."

"Go on," she said, "I will not call for Isis to get you just yet."

"Ah-seenat, I have missed you," I said again. "I have missed your smooth skin and your warm kisses. I have missed your hand on my chest as I sleep. I have missed your comforting voice and your patient ears. I have even missed hearing your bangles jingle."

"So, you are sad and lonely without me?"

"Yes," I said. "Yes, exactly. I have thought of calling one of the servants in here as you did. But I could not bring myself to bring that pain and suffering on them."

"You think I bring pain and suffering upon Ebbo? Did you not see and hear her pleasure?"

"I did," I said.

"And you have Atsu—it is no different."

"It is entirely different," I said. "Atsu is not at my command; he may leave at any time but does not wish to. And we do not lie together; we never have. We are both married men and have not shared a mat with each other in years. We share our secrets, we comfort each other, we praise each other, and, together, we build ourselves into better people. We are brothers."

"Well, Ebbo and I are not brothers; we are lovers. And I do not wish to lie with you again, so I would like to take my leave."

"Why, Ah-seenat? Why?"

She softened her voice for just a moment. "We had a nice time together before, Zafenat. But I do not wish to have any more babies. You know that. Take another wife, or go to the harem, I don't care. I won't leave you for it."

"I can send you away, you know," I said. "For refusing to come to your husband."

"Don't do that," she replied. "I have not called Isis to come and get you, but I will do so if you try to send me away from Ebbo and my sons. They are good boys, aren't they? I know you have told them stories in the morning. They enjoyed it. It's harmless. You would wish to do it again, I imagine. We have lived all these years apart, and we can continue to do so." Before I could open my mouth to respond, she turned and left my chamber.

In the morning, I postponed interviewing travelers who came for food so that I could have private words with Atsu.

"I don't know what to do," I began. "There are too many thoughts all at the same time."

"It will be all right," he reminded me. "Just speak them one at a time. Tell me all of them, and then we will do whatever we need to do to help."

Just hearing his voice calmed me, as always. I told him the ideas that were competing for attention.

"Until yesterday, I wished that My Wife would forgive me," I began. "I wanted her back, but now I'm not even sure I do. I can banish her. She can leave me, but I don't think she will. She would have to go back to her father and brothers, but her life is better here . . . as long as I leave her alone. And she will curse me if I don't. I don't wish to be cursed.

"Also, she was coupling with Ebbo, her handmaid. And she likened it to me and you, though I think it is more like when Potifar and Zulaika called me to them. Ebbo has no choice but to obey. I have not called any servants to me in all these years because I did not wish to inflict that confusion on anyone, yet perhaps I could have been having pleasure as Ah-seenat has been. Instead, I have had nobody but myself to provide that. Why would I deprive myself while she is not?"

I paused to take a breath, and was going to go on, but Atsu spoke before I could. "Zafenat," he said. "You have taught me so many wise things. Among them, you have introduced me to Elohim. And you have shown me that you can breathe your god into your body and breathe yourself into Him. And whenever I have seen you do this, you have the knowing that Elohim has: you know that all will be well."

He began to take deep breaths, and though I still had many thoughts plaguing me, I closed my eyes and followed his lead in breathing the way that I had once taught him. *Yhhhh*, we inhaled together. *Whhhh*, we exhaled together. Even after only one time, I felt Elohim's presence. But we sat in this way until my heart slowed, followed by my mind. When I opened my eyes, I saw Atsu smiling at me.

"Are you ready for me to say a few words?" he asked. "Or do you have more on your list of complaints?" I chuckled. With the presence of Elohim and My Brother, I already felt much better. I told him I was ready to hear his ideas.

"I do not think you should banish Ah-seenat. Two days ago, you didn't want to banish her, nor two weeks, two months, two years. Nothing has changed other than your desire to now lie with someone. So, perhaps you should do that. You can easily afford a second wife, and the vizier has privileges at the harem. You need not bring in a servant. I do not know whether Ebbo wants to lie with Ah-seenat, but she says this is true, and you heard and saw her seeming to enjoy it. And Ah-seenat is not leaving her in shame the way Potifar left you. As for you and I, what does it matter whether Ah-seenat thinks we lie together though we don't?

"I have observed you for years, and you have shared with me your deepest thoughts and feelings and have been kind and compassionate when I have done the same. Zafenat Paaneakh, I tell you the things I believe to be true, but you are not only vizier, you are my brother. I respect what you will choose to do, and I will help you. Whatever it is."

CHAPTER 27

I did not banish My Wife but took a lover. His name was Kalos, and he was lovely. He had been one of the waiters who had served me for over a year, and I had seen him eyeing me. I had eyed him too. He was young and afraid when I first requested he be brought to my private chamber. But he quickly learned that I would not hurt, shame, or sadden him. In fact, I offered him one hundred pieces of gold and told him they were his to keep whether he stayed with me or took them and never came back. I would not coerce him to stay any more than I would Ah-seenat.

Kalos decided to stay, and as he became more comfortable, he also became more joyful. He danced in delight with every trinket I gave him, and on the occasions that we dined together, he not only regaled me with the details of his adventures in the palace, but he asked me of mine. We had many nights of pleasure in my bed, but what I enjoyed even more was simply lying with my skin up against his and falling asleep with someone beside me.

Kalos did not leave me even when I took Selet as a second wife. He understood that as the vizier, I needed to have a wife. She wanted children, and I agreed to give her those. I wanted privacy, and she agreed to give me that. I rarely called for her. Lying with her was a part of my duties, and Kalos knew that. He did not begrudge me my job even though he knew I enjoyed it. He knew he had my affections. Or so it was until Selet became pregnant.

I was eager and excited to father another son. I would know this one when he was a baby and a young boy with small teeth. He would not be my firstborn or even the firstborn of my favored wife, but I would tell him my stories. I would let him walk beside me, and he would smile at me in appreciation. I spoke of this often to both Atsu and Kalos. I traced Selet's belly and whispered it to her and My Son.

But My Son was born too soon. There had not yet been enough moons. If he'd had a breath, I was not there to feel it. But his mother was. She wailed and wailed, and there was nothing I could do to help her. The midwife dealt with the blood and Selet's tears, but I walked alone with mine. I thanked Elohim for not letting me cause the death of My Wife, and I vowed to never plant another seed in her. I buried My Son Soaf in a tiny golden coffin. When My Wife recovered, she pleaded with me to plant my seed in her again. She begged me to let her carry another son for me. But I could not risk his life like that, or hers. I never went to her again. I didn't leave her either. The fact that she did not produce a son for me was due to me, not her.

I was satisfied with my life as vizier, and busy. The number of people asking for food only increased over the months as stored food was eaten and livestock was diminished after it was turned to meals for the starving. In Egypt, we still had an abundance of everything—including an abundance of beggars.

Eventually, the famine grew so strong in Canaan that My Father was forced to face the death of his tribe or allow his youngest son to travel with the others back to Egypt. Of course, My Father would not allow his children to perish, so I was expecting him to send My Brothers back to me. Yet, it had taken him so long that I had begun to wonder.

Eventually, they came before me: ten men in their best robes, with bags of money and pleading lips. Shimon was released from the jail when the others finally returned. I asked Atsu to tend to the eleven of them. I asked him to oversee their care, to bring them water to wash their hands and feet, to arrange food for their animals, and to invite them to eat in my chamber. I continued my work, albeit rather absentmindedly, until the meal was prepared. Then I came and met them.

In preparation for my arrival, they had laid out the gifts and the money they had brought me. I looked upon them as if with two sets of eyes. The vizier saw trinkets, nearly worthless attempts at art and fancy compared to what I had become accustomed to. But the boy who I had been, who had seen and loved the tents of Jacob, was impressed. There were baskets tightly woven and jugs expertly shaped and painted along with thin golden bangles and weavings that made me feel at home.

They bowed before me. All eleven of them. There they were, the eleven sheaves bowing before me. Soon, soon, they would become the eleven stars, and the sun and moon would be with them. I asked after My Father. "The old father you mentioned," I said, "is he still living?"

As soon as the interpreter translated, Reuben stepped forward. "Our father, your servant, lives."

I looked at each one of them in turn. I had instructed them to gather around the table, pointing at a seat for each one, arranging them in age from oldest to youngest. Surely, then, they would know it was me, for who else would know their birth order? But when I got to My Brother Benno, who would sit in the last seat, I was so full of emotion I could barely stand. "Is this the youngest brother you spoke of?" I asked. When they said what I already knew to be true, the words, "May Elohim be gracious to you, My Son," passed my lips. I almost said "brother." My tongue was acting of its own accord, as were my eyes, which were welling with tears. I exited the room quickly to compose myself.

We all ate separately, of course. It was not fitting for an Egyptian to eat with a Hebrew—especially an Egyptian of my status. But I placed myself where I could see My Brothers, and even hear them, for nobody knew that I could understand their words. And I also made sure that My Brother Benno received five times everyone else's portion. I enjoyed watching him enjoy the bounty that I'd provided.

Even after sharing these quarters and this meal, My Brothers did not know me. I did not understand why Elohim was placing us together but would not allow them to recognize me. I gave instructions that they be packed with their grain and their returned money once again. I also had a guard add my own personal goblet to Benno's sack. Perhaps he would recognize that such a gift would come only from a brother, and then he would come back and embrace me.

But he did not. Even after they had ample time to travel and check their sacks, they did not return. "Atsu," I said, "you must go after them. Please."

"Zafenat," he said, "I will do what you say, but is this what you want? For them to be chased down and dragged back?"

"I don't care how they come back," I said. "I just want them back, want Benno back. The others can go. Quickly, go after them. Ask them why, after all I had given them, all I had done for them, they have repaid my goodness with badness. Raise my cup and challenge them, saying: 'Isn't this the cup that my master drinks from and also uses for divination? You've done a terrible thing.' And then bring him back to me."

"Zafenat?"

"Let them know the feeling of being chased! Let them know the fear of someone else being bigger than them! For once!"

I had not meant to yell, and I apologized to Atsu as he left to begin this errand.

They had not gotten far, for I was still where we'd parted when they returned. Instead of bringing only Benno, all My Brothers were once again bowing before me. To my surprise, I was tiring of it. But there they were, and with their clothes torn, no less. Bowing, mourning, groveling, crying. I shook my head. "Don't you know that a man like me knows divination?"

How many times had I told them that? How many times had they shunned me for my dreams, for my learning, for my gifts? And Elohim had been with me the whole while. Elohim had guided me my whole life, had made me wise, even when I was a boy. I stroked my chin. It was as smooth as the day I was born.

Yet there I was, the leader before all these men with beards that signified only age and not wisdom.

Judah asked, "What can we say to my lord? How can we prove our innocence? Elohim has uncovered our guilt. We are guilty, and we know it now. We will now be your slaves, the one with whom the goblet was found as well as the rest of us."

My Brothers had acted as one when they'd thrown me in the pit to die, and then again, when they'd sold me. They surely were guilty! But not of this crime. And Benno had been a baby and had not participated. He was the only one I wanted. "Far be it from me," I said, "to do such a thing. Only the one who had the cup shall stay and be my servant. The rest of you, go back to your father in peace." I turned my back to walk away and dismissed them. Perhaps I had misunderstood the dream about forgiveness. Time had passed. I had no feelings left for these men who did not even know me.

But Judah stopped me with a bold gesture. He approached me. Nobody walked toward me without permission, but he did. A guard rushed to stop him, but then Judah stopped before he reached me. He was close enough to speak quietly and have me hear him. The interpreter, who until that point had been making all our conversations longer by translating each word, did not do so for this part, for he did not even hear Judah.

In a quiet voice, Judah said, in the language of My Father, "Pardon your servant, my lord. Let me speak a word into my lord's ears. Don't ignite your anger against your servant, my lord, even though you are equal to Pharaoh himself. My lord asked his servants: 'Do you have a father or brother?' And your servants answered my lord: 'We have an elderly father, and he has a young son, born to him in his old age. His brother is dead, and he is the only one of his mother's sons left, and his father loves him."

Oh, how My Father loved My Mother. And me. And now Benno. I had not felt that love in so long. I had built my new life and had unknowingly let the memory of that love slip away. Judah was still talking. He told me of the misery My Father had felt when he believed I'd been attacked by a wild animal. He told me how devastated My Father was to have only one son of My Mother and that he could not lose that son and live.

And then Judah, who had changed everything when he had saved my life and sold me, changed everything again. "Please," he beseeched me, "let me stay here and be your servant in place of the boy. Let the boy return with his brothers." He had not let *me* return with My Brothers. But that had been for the best. Of course, I'd wanted to, though. What would Benno want? I didn't have time to consider it because Judah had me thinking of My Father with his final, quiet words: "How can I go back to My Father if the boy is not with me? Please, no, do not let me see that misery befall My Father again." He bowed his head in respect and request, then lifted it and looked me in the eyes. Slowly, he raised his right hand and stroked the bottom of his bearded chin with his thumb.

I shouted to my attendants, "Leave my presence!" And with a few footsteps, I was left alone with My Brothers. And I cried so loudly that surely they could hear me even outside, but I did not care. For did Judah himself not tell me long ago that I could cry any time I needed to? And had I not heeded and thrived on that advice for all the years since? And now, here he was, reminding me of his wisdom.

"It is me," I shouted in my native tongue. "I am Joseph!" I needed to get them to see beyond the vizier, beyond Zafenat Paaneakh. "Come closer," I said, "I am your brother Joseph, the one you sold into Egypt. Now, don't be distressed or angry with yourselves for selling me here. It was to save lives that Elohim sent me ahead of you. For two years now, there has been a famine in the land. And for the next five, there will still be nothing to plough or reap. But Elohim sent me ahead of you to save your lives by a great deliverance." I gestured to the wealth in the room, including their food sacks that still lay on the table by the entrance."

All My Brothers stood still. Silent.

"You see? It was not you who sent me here, but My God. Elohim made me second only to Pharaoh, made me lord of Pharaoh's entire household and ruler of all Egypt. Now hurry back to My Father and say to him, 'This is what your son Joseph says: Elohim has made me lord of all Egypt. Come down to me; don't delay. You shall live in the region of Goshen and be near me—you, your children and grandchildren, your flocks and herds, and all that you have. I will provide for you there because five years of famine are still to come. Otherwise, you and your household and all who belong to you will become destitute.'"

They all stared at me. "You can see for yourselves, even My Brother Benno can see—Benjamin, as you call him—that it is really I who am speaking to you." I stroked my chin. "Judah knows," I said. Judah nodded. I placed my hand on his shoulder and smiled. He took me in his arms and wept. Then each brother came and embraced me—even Shimon and Levi. Benno stayed the longest in my arms, and when we separated, I told him of the last time I had seen him and how I had carried his whole body, not even one year old, in my arms and had sang to him.

I addressed them all again, "Tell My Father about all the honor accorded me in Egypt and about everything you have seen. And bring My Father down here quickly."

Even My Pharaoh supported the plan. For when he heard that My Father was to come to Egypt, he released many carts and drivers to go and carry him and his wares—should they wish to bring anything. My Pharaoh told My Brothers that they could leave their belongings there, for they would be replaced in Egypt with everything they needed—including the choicest land for grazing.

So, My Brothers departed with ten male donkeys loaded with the best things in Egypt and ten female donkeys loaded with grain and provisions for the journey. I also sent them all with new clothes and money, five new outfits for Benno and three hundred shekels for him alone, and instructions for them not to quarrel along the way. I thought of the long trek from Haran to Shechem. This would be so different. My Father would travel like a king. I was not to go and get him, for I was needed in Egypt, of course, but soon, I would welcome him.

WHAT A WELCOME I gave My Father! When his arrival was close, Judah came ahead of everyone else to inform me they were near and learn the way to the land I was gifting them. This time, he did not need to beg for or buy food, but he was escorted directly to my chamber where we feasted together. Judah told me of the sorrow that had befallen My Father when he thought me dead and how he, himself, had been weighed down with misery. He told me of the deaths of two of his own sons, feeling that their deaths were surely Elohim punishing him for what he had done to My Father.

"But you saved my life, Judah. The other brothers would have left me there to die," I reminded him. Still, he shook his head.

Together, we left the palace accompanied by my guards and with servants bearing gifts. My chariot was brought to me, and Judah and I rode north to meet My Father. He was not riding in one of the carts sent by My Pharaoh but was walking at the head of his large tribe, his tall shepherd's staff in hand and chin held high. "Stop," I ordered my driver. All was stillness.

Judah placed his hand on my shoulder. Tears welled in my eyes. I left my chariot and began to walk to My Father on foot. As I got closer, I could see that he was an old man now. "Elohim, God of My Father Jacob," I whispered, "God of My Father Isaac, God of My Father Abraham, bless this meeting between us." The light between us looked truly blessed. It shimmered over the land and warmed my feet with every step. And then, My Father took me in his arms and released all his tears upon my neck.

"My Son," he said. My Father had his hands upon my shoulders and was looking at me. I was as decorated as the pharaoh himself, and more handsome by many accounts. I was taller than My Father by nearly a head, so in this position, he had to look up at me, and I had to bend my head down to look into his eyes. It took him a while to meet my eyes, though, as he was admiring the coat I'd had made for this reunion. It was finely woven and blue and white, with gold stitching between each stripe. Because I had access to all of My Pharaoh's riches, I also had blue stones added to the collar. I wore it to remind My Father of the coat he had given me.

"I thought a wild beast had gotten you," he said. "But it was Elohim. Elohim got you and brought you here to feed and save us all." My Father let go of my shoulders and bowed before me the way he had done before his brother so long ago. When he rose, he said, "Your mother would have been delighted beyond measure to see you like this." Then after a moment of thought he added, "Although, I suppose your mother always did see you like this. Well done, my son."

I invited My Father to step into my chariot with me. Together, we rode to the land of Goshen, where I would ensure his food and his prosperity, and that his flocks had the best grazing land.

CHAPTER 28

I had not smelled the odor of flocks of sheep in many years, and I decided on that day that I did not miss it. My Father and his shepherding sons carried on with their work, and I, mine. It was my practice to spend several days each week seeing travelers who were seeking food. Often, the process took from dawn until dusk. Each group came with their own language, their own needs, their own stories, and their own offerings of trade. I took the job of assessing them and making deals that would benefit My Pharaoh very seriously. Atsu always stood to my right, and I often consulted him. Translators were always present. Guards were always at the door unless they were escorting unruly traders away. Everyone in the court knew the importance of this process, and I was never disturbed.

Until the evening when I was disturbed.

When a group of Hyksos left, having traded silver for grain, there was the normal pause before another group would be escorted in. During that quiet, I heard my guards arguing with two other guards who normally held a post at the gate.

"Nobody is to disturb Zafenat Paaneakh. Egypt has the grain for all the nations around us. He is growing our land and our might in trade. Nothing is more important."

"Yes, I understand," I heard a gate guard respond. "But the Israelite woman won't go away. We have told her all day every day for a week already. Now she is refusing to eat and refusing to drink until she is allowed to enter."

"So, let her refuse," I heard.

"We *did* let her," was the response. "She has gone three days without food or water. We tried to remove her, and then she began kicking and clawing at us and shouting. She was causing a scene, and those around jeered at us for beating a starving woman. Translators came and said that she is repeating this over and over: 'For the Love of Deenah, I must see Joseph. For the Love of Deenah, I must see Joseph.'"

I gasped.

"Let her in," I said.

The guards looked at me. They had been unaware that I'd heard their conversation. I repeated myself. "Let her in. I will not need you; you are dismissed while she is here. Only Atsu will stay." Nobody moved. "Go on," I said. "Leave us. Direct her here. I will see her."

The guards left. Atsu put his hand on my shoulder. I felt him steady me, though until that moment, I did not know I was shaking, and after that moment, I no longer felt his hand. I was unsteady on my feet, so I sat on my throne. My eyes were focused on the doorway through which she would appear. She. Who would she be? *For the love of Deenah*, who would she be? My gaze was so trained on the doorway that, soon, I could not see anything.

Darkness was before me, then light—white light entering through the door and carrying with it a rainbow of colors. My rainbow. My colors. They separated from the white light and wrapped themselves around my body. The purple wrapped itself around my head, raising it higher. The red lifted my feet and guided me to walk forward even though I could not see even one step ahead until the colors released me. And then, . . . first I heard, and then I saw. I heard a song—a prayer.

"Praise Yah, praise Yah, my god and the god of my mothers. Praise Yah, praise Yah, my god and the god of my fathers."

The voice singing was soft, quiet, sweet, loving. The singer paused for just a moment to breathe. *Yhhhh. Whhhh.* Then she continued.

"God of my mother Sarah, god of my father Abraham. God of my mother Rebekah, god of my father Isaac."

She was my kinswoman. I knew this, for the guards had called her an Israelite woman. I should not have been surprised, yet my heart fluttered to hear a prayer so similar to the one I had recited so, so many times.

"God of my mother Leah, god of my father Jacob."

I saw her then. I don't know whether my eyes had been closed or open before, but they were open then. I gasped, and her prayer halted. "Deenah." Her name was breath leaving my lips. No sound, just breath. "Deenah," I said again, looking in her eyes, her body so close I could touch her. I hadn't dared to dream of this moment. One more time, I said her name, "Deenah," and then Zafenat Paaneakh, the vizier of Egypt, was gone, and the boy who was Joseph embraced the girl who was Deenah, and I wept and wept. I wept into her dark hair, wept into the weaving of Leah, wept into the smell of my homeland, wept until, when I thought I had shed all my tears, I found that I was on the floor, embracing her legs with my head resting at her knee.

She pulled me to my feet, and I saw that her face was streaked with tears as well. Her face also showed the signs of her determination to see me. The fast had made her skin cracked and her bones sharp. *But soon*, I thought, *she would eat.* We would eat together, and she would look the way My Deenah had looked. "Let us eat," I said.

"I must praise Yah," she replied. "I must thank Yah, the god of my mothers and fathers, for bringing me to this day, to you." And so, she began her song of praise again. Her song was as lovely as any bird's—lovelier. She took my hands in hers and kept her eyes on mine as she sang:

"Praise Yah, praise Yah, my god and the god of my mothers. Praise Yah, praise Yah, my god and the god of my fathers. God of my mother Sarah, god of my father Abraham. God of my mother Rebekah, god of my father Isaac, god of my mother Leah, god of my father Jacob."

She paused ever so briefly. She blinked her eyes and sang another line, one that I had unknowingly interrupted her from before.

"God of my mother Deenah, god of my father . . . Joseph."

The girl spoke more. She spoke of Deenah. I didn't hear most of it. I couldn't hear. I learned the story later from Atsu, whom I had repeat it to me several times until I could tell it as if I remembered it myself.

"Deenah, daughter of Leah," she began, "had a heart full of adventure. She had grand ideas and courage to act on them. She was playful and loving. Most of all, she loved Joseph. One day, she was taken from her beloved, and eight days later, her new life with the prince was stolen, and she became fierce."

Her singsong voice changed when she reached the word *fierce*, but then it went back to the calming lilt it had carried before, and she continued the gentle song.

"Everything she had was taken away, but she was given something new. Deenah, unmarried, bore a daughter. The girl looked like a child of the tribe of Jacob, not like the prince, so her life was spared. Leah told everyone the baby was a daughter of Asher, a twin girl born to his wife right after a boy. Deenah became the girl's nurse and raised her."

The girl paused her story song and moved herself back. When she did, it was as if I had awoken and could now see and hear again. I saw her prostrate herself, arms pointing toward me, forehead on the cool ground of the palace floor. When she lifted her head, she said, "I am called Serrah, daughter of Asher. But my mother, Deenah, called me Blue, and I am the daughter of you."

I still could not say any words. After a short silence, she continued. "My mother told me of the dream you had when I entered her body. The dream of the white birds and the blue one."

"She didn't laugh at me when I told her my dreams," I said.

I helped her up—helped My Daughter to stand. I had to believe her words that she was not Deenah, though my eyes kept telling me otherwise.

"Where is your mother?" I asked. "Where is Deenah?"

My Daughter looked down at her hands. Before a sound could exit her mouth, I yelled: "No! No! Do not even tell me!" I could not bear to hear the details of her death or her marriage to someone else, or whatever else befell her. I could not handle one more stab. I would continue to think of Deenah when I saw the moon and not have any horrible thoughts replace that image.

I sat on the floor beside this beautiful girl. I imagined that if I saw myself at that moment, I would not think I was looking upon a grand ruler. But neither would I think I looked like Joseph. The Joseph that had known Deenah had worn a long tunic of blue and white and gold. The Joseph that Deenah had known was loved by his mother and grandmother and auntie and should be loved by his daughter. I looked at My Daughter. I opened my fists. I breathed her and the moment into me. *Yhhhh*. She did the same. *Yhhhh*. Together, we breathed ourselves into each other. *Whhhh*.

"What shall I give you?" I asked her. "Anything. Name anything in all of Egypt, and you shall have it. You shall have it."

"I wish to have you, Father. I want to stay with my father. I wish to stay with you."

I was overjoyed! "Are you married, girl, . . . daughter, . . . Serrah, . . . Blue? Does your husband await your return?"

Her eyes turned down in sadness again, but only for a moment. "No," she said. "I am not. Like my mother, I had a love that I was not allowed to marry. He is already wed. He called me Blue like my mother, Deenah. And my grandmother, Leah. And my mother's grandmother, Rebekah. Though I am known in Israel as Serrah, daughter of Asher, I would rather be known as Blue."

I looked into her eyes, her mother's eyes. The eyes that had looked at me as a playmate when we were little, the eyes who had watched me practice my scribing. The eyes that had seen me pass her in running races when I finally became faster than her, and the eyes that had gazed into mine when our worlds became one. I could not say no to the girl with Deenah's eyes.

"You shall stay with me," I said, "with your father."

In that very moment, I walked away from my duties as vizier. I walked away from My Pharaoh, from the beggars, from my position as Second-in-Command. Oh, of course, I knew as I was doing so that it would not be forever. It was only because I was in that position that I could walk away from it. But for My Daughter, I would do so, however brief it may be.

It was one glorious week. We spent our days walking through the palace and our nights, feasting. Blue enjoyed leading the way through the hallways and passages even though she did not know where they would end up. I enjoyed watching her slide her feet along the marble walkways and dance down the steps. I enjoyed it when her eyes grew wide with wonder at each meal and then closed with appreciation as she took in the smells before the tastes. Most of all, I enjoyed listening to her singsongy voice as she told me stories from her life in the land of Israel.

"My mother told me many things about you," she said. "Like how she could run faster than you to Grandfather's tent and how handsome you looked in your blue and white tunic. And she told me that you helped our tribe by talking to Yah. And she said that you had once taught her to write her name in the dust. Of course, she told me all about the cinnamon. And she told me about how you two laughed and laughed about the elephants. My mother really loved elephants."

I imagined Deenah telling My Daughter these stories in their tent before falling asleep, just as My Mother had done with me. But Blue said it hadn't been like that. "My mother was usually quiet in the tent, though not always. But if she were outside preparing food or spinning—if her hands were busy with a task—those were the times when she was most interested in telling stories. Usually, she told me and Benno stories about you since we were the ones who were too young to have any memories of you and since we were so often together, and always curious."

"What else did she tell you?" I asked.

"Well, she told me of Shechem, of course, of how she wanted to live in the city, in the palace, but how her brothers came and ruined that. I didn't like her to tell me that story because whenever she did, she drifted into silence for days afterward. But, of course, Grandmother Leah and Grandmother Rebekah told me stories too. I did love their stories! But my grandmothers and Bilhah and Zilpah, and even my auntie, were all so much older. I wished I had girls to tell my own stories with."

"Auntie?" I asked. "You knew Deborah?" But how could that be? She had not known My Auntie, of course, but had given the name to little Emunah. My Daughter had lived a life where the littlest sister had become the auntie. What a world!

"But, of course, I know of your auntie," she added, "from stories about her and from her scrolls."

"You have read The Scrolls of Deborah?"

She laughed. Her laugh sounded just like Deenah's! How had My God created such a treasure twice? "No," she said. "I don't know how to read. Emunah read them to us. Grandmother Rebekah wanted to hear them again." That day, I taught My

Daughter how to write her name and mine. Because I was not a shepherd boy, but a rich man, we practiced on shards and scraps of papyrus until she could do it perfectly. She then painted our names side by side on the wall of my chamber. My Daughter would be there with me even when she was gone.

Eventually, I needed to return to my duties as vizier, and, therefore, Blue needed to return to the Israelites in Goshen. But to my surprise, she didn't want to go. "There is nobody there for me, Father. I want to be with women like my mother was, like you were, like even I was when I was a young girl. The women who called me sister always did so with resentment, for they knew I was not their sister. And I am old enough to marry. What if one of my uncles wants me to wed his son?"

I could not let her near Shimon and Levi. They had ruined Deenah's life, and I would not let them ruin the life of her daughter that resembled her so greatly. The life of My Daughter. I reassured her. "You do not need to go back." I called my guards in. "Take this girl to the harem," I said. "And leave instructions that nobody shall call for her. No man shall request her or go to her, not even the pharaoh. Anyone who protests this shall speak to me. She shall live in the harem from now on."

We embraced, and then I watched the guards escort her out of my chamber. Now, she would be safe. My Daughter. Deenah's daughter. Our daughter would be safe and happy—I would make sure of it. At every harvest moon, I called for her. I asked her needs and, when she had some, I filled them. But mostly, she asked for nothing, and she never asked to go back to Goshen.

CHAPTER 29

The famine ended, and My Pharaoh ruled over more land than any pharaoh had before him. That was my doing. When the Egyptians came to me hungry, I traded them grain for their land and their service. Thus, it became My Pharaoh's land, and they, My Pharaoh's serfs. I continued to be rewarded with more honor, more prestige, and more goods. In addition, with My Sons coming to learn from me regularly, My Daughter safely in the harem, and My Tribe prospering in the fields, I was more pleased than ever with my position in Egypt.

In my youth, I had told everyone that one day, I would rule over My Brothers, and even My Father. I had told them that for one reason only: because Elohim had told me. They had doubted me, but now we all saw. And now that My Father was in Goshen, I could help him prosper, for this was why Elohim had brought me to rule this land: to keep them alive during the famine and help them increase in number and wealth. And I had delivered. I had given all of that to My Father and more.

Before his death, My Father gave me a gift that I could not receive from my position as vizier. When I learned that his days were numbered, My Sons and I went to see him. Although they had honored their grandfather with a visit upon his arrival in Egypt, his eyes were dim, and he no longer recognized or remembered them. But he was pleased when I told him they were the sons that My God had given me, here, in Egypt.

"I never expected to see your face again," he said to me, "and now, my god has even let me see your children. Praise Elohim, who has given me life, sustained me, and allowed me to see this day." He beckoned My Sons to him, and they went. He hugged and kissed them, and we both wept. Then he placed his hands on their heads to bless them: his right hand on Efraim, and his left on Menasse.

"Wait, Father," I said, "Menasseh is the firstborn."

"Yes," he agreed, but he did not correct his hands. Instead, he went on to tell me that both My Sons would be great, but the younger, more so than the older. Efraim would become not only a nation, but a group of nations—as would I, on that day, for My Father took My Sons as his own and gave them both inheritance equal to Reuben and Shimon, increasing me from being as one son of his to the worth of two. More tears streaked my cheeks as he publicly acknowledged my value.

My Sons dutifully and respectfully received their blessing from My Father:

"May the God before whom my fathers Abraham and Isaac walked faithfully, the God who has been my shepherd all my life to this day, the Angel who has delivered me from all harm—may He bless these boys. May they be called by my name and the names of my fathers Abraham and Isaac, and may they increase greatly on the earth. In Your name will Israel pronounce this blessing: 'May Elohim make you like Efraim and Menasse.'"

My Sons kissed his hand and thanked him. When I bent over his bed to do the same, he pulled me down to him in an embrace. "My son," he said, "I loved your mother so. I should not have buried her where I did. I should have taken her to the Cave of Makhpelah to be buried with Rebekah and Leah. I'm sorry, my son. I'm sorry." I did not know whether I could forgive him this or not. But what followed showed me he was not asking my forgiveness, but my mercy.

"I am about to die, but Elohim will be with you and return you to the land of your fathers. There, I give to you one more land than I gave your brothers." I would get the double portion of the firstborn. For a moment, I felt sad for My Brother Reuben, but only a moment, for I was truly the firstborn of My Father and his beloved, the woman who was meant to be his first wife. This had always been known. Now, finally, it would be shown in my inheritance. But then, My Father said the extra parcel of land I was to receive was Shechem, and I had so many thoughts at once that I almost could not breathe.

I wished Atsu were there. He would steady me. The land that Shimon and Levi had pillaged? The land on which My Brothers had slayed Deenah's husband? The land on which blood had been spilled and mixed with her tears? The same place where My Father had sent me as a sacrifice to My Brothers who were still jealous over my rightful and esteemed position as shown by my blue and white cloak? Was this good? Did I want this land?

My questions did not matter. The question that My Father seemed to be asking was this: Will the gift of this land comfort me and persuade me to do his bidding? For along with his gift, there was a request, one that was partially pleading and partially commanding. "If I have found favor in your eyes," he said, looking into my eyes, "then put your hand under my thigh and swear that you will show me kindness and faithfulness. Do not bury me in Egypt, but when I rest with my fathers, bring me out of Egypt and bury me where they are buried."

In accordance with the old customs of my homeland, My Promised Land, I put my hand under his thigh and took the oath. "I will," I said, for in My Father's presence, I was not the ruler of the mightiest land, wherein I could create by my command, but a dutiful son, ready to do the bidding of My Father.

I parted with My Father for what I thought was the final time. However, even after presenting me with my inheritance and My Children with their blessings, he lived longer. I saw him once more.

On what truly was his final day, My Father called all his sons to gather around him for blessings. Reuben, the true firstborn no matter how much My Father loved me, kneeled to the right of My Father's head. Benjamin, the youngest and the new beloved, kneeled to the left of My Father's head. In between the two of them, the rest of us brothers knelt according to our age. As I was feeling old pangs of jealousy and disappointment arise in my stomach, My Father reached for my hand, and I was calmed.

I looked around My Father's bed at the men who knelt beside him. The little boys who used to so confidently refer to themselves as young men were not far from their own ends of days. Reuben, Shimon, Levi, and Judah had seen the sons of their grandsons born. Certainly, their days were numbered. Yet they still gathered around the patriarch with more respect than I had ever seen anyone show to My Pharaoh in all his years of ruling Egypt.

"Reuben," My Father called.

"I'm here, Father."

Though My Father's eyes were dim and his strength nearly gone, he turned his head in the direction of the voice.

"Reuben, you are my firstborn; you are my strength and the beginning of my manhood, superior in rank and superior in strength. Unstable as water, you will no longer be superior. . . ." My Father was angry at Reuben for a secret he had with Bilhah. He did not say what. But as he continued to talk, I was reminded of the young man who'd always had a smile for me. Reuben was accepting, and even welcoming. Our lives had been different from the first day until this day, but we shared the bond of firstborn sons of our mothers. He told me stories and did his best to teach me.

Reuben had said he would always come back for me. Indeed, he had, so many years after throwing me into the pit. Had he pulled me out of there, surely, I would have been killed by My Brothers sooner or later. Instead, I became the ruler I was destined to be. As My Father finished speaking to Reuben for the final time, blessing him and also chastising him for his unholy behavior over the years, I could not help but feel compassion for My Brother and also wonder if any good would come of his transgressions with Bilhah.

"Shimon and Levi are brothers," My Father said, moving on to the twins. They had put me through so much pain as a child, nearly ending my life on more than one occasion. And yet, they were My Brothers. But I was pleased to hear My Father not condoning their behavior. What might have become of my beloved Deenah had they not acted so violently? I had no fond memories of these two, nor did I choose to make any once they had arrived in Goshen. Distance was my friend and my protector. At least My Daughter was now safe from them.

"Judah," My Father called out.

"I am here, Father," Judah replied. His beard had been all white for many years. I caught a glimpse of him rubbing it and didn't know whether he was doing it out of habit or because he knew I was looking. His hair and his body looked too old to receive a blessing for the future, but his eyes were shining bright, and his heart was fully present.

"Judah, your brothers will praise you. Your hand will be on the neck of your enemies. Your father's sons will prostrate themselves to you." I was proud to have such a brother. Lifetimes ago, this sturdy man had taught me how to use a slingshot. He had shown an interest in my learning. He had been kind to me my entire life—a life that he had saved. He had showed me what it means to be strong, honest, wise, responsible, and a leader. And even with all my years as second-in-command, it was clear to me that he was the more natural leader.

I sat a little taller with the pride I felt to have been taught by Judah and the happiness I felt for him as My Father continued the blessing. "The rod will not depart from Judah. . . . " I saw a tear drop from Judah's eye and roll silently down his cheek. Truly, I could not think of a man alive, neither in the north or all of Egypt, neither commoner nor royal, who was more deserving of being a leader. I wiped away a tear of my own that had escaped my eye and remembered that at the beginning of my life, it had been Judah who had told me it was okay to cry, so I let the next ones flow unimpeded.

When My Father had finished the blessing, Judah prostrated himself and kissed My Father's hand. My Father, then, slowly raised that hand and brought it to Judah's cheek. Though he surely felt the age and wisdom present in the long beard, he looked like he was lovingly stroking the cheek of a young boy, a son who had pleased him.

Zevulun, Issachar, Dan, and Gad received their blessings. I hoped My Father's thoughts and his breath would still be full and clear enough to bless me when my time came.

My Father closed his eyes for a long time. I could see how effortful each inhale was. I began to match my breathing with his, hoping that the air filling my body would still fill his as well. At least for a little longer, I hoped that he would not pass without being able to pass along his full blessings. I began to move my lips in prayer, "Please, God of My Father Jacob, Jacob who has served You for his whole lifetime, please allow him to complete his thoughts and his blessings. Please. Please."

"Asher."

Asher quickly sat by My Father's side. "From Asher will come rich food; he will provide delicacies for the king." My Father stopped talking and went back to his breathing. The breaths were shallow and far between. Asher brought My Father's fingers to his lips and respectfully kissed them before stepping aside.

"Naftali."

Oh, Naftali. He was always quick to bring joy and lightness with his flute. "Naftali is a gazelle-like messenger. He delivers healing sayings." Even in that moment, Naftali pulled his flute from the pouch in his cloak and played soothing sounds that brought a smile to My Father's face as well as to mine—and to all of My Brothers'. Looking around this circle of men surrounding our father, I, for perhaps the first time, felt a connection to them all. We'd shared a past, and we'd shared memories of challenges and memories of joy. I had been separated from this for most of my life. Even when we hadn't been in different territories, we had been in different worlds, yet there were still things we'd shared, and now, those things danced on the music of Naftali's lips. By the time he finished the tune, we were all blanketed in peace.

"Joseph, my son." As My Father called me, my whole body awakened from the inside out. My skin became covered in prickles of anticipation. Would he trust me the way he trusted Judah? Would he treat me as the firstborn of My Mother, as the son who'd been replaced by a younger favorite, or as one of so many sons that they could hardly fit around him? I breathed deeply to calm myself as I took My Father's hand and brought it to my lips even before he began speaking.

"I am here, Father," I said. "I am here."

"A fruitful son is Joseph, a fruitful son at the spring; daughters walk on the wall. . . ." For many days, I was deeply saddened to have missed My Father's final words to me. Yes, this is true. I had not heard them when he'd spoken them. The first words from his mouth had brought visions of My Daughter, dancing as the blue bird of song and joy, along with My Auntie Deborah, flying as the wise bee from flower to flower, creating beauty everywhere she goes. I thought of Deenah and My Mother, who were walking love.

Following these four women, I saw myself in human form, but younger and distant from the land of Egypt. And even as I saw myself as such, I knew it wasn't me because I, in that moment, had no form. I was my essence wrapped in all the colors as I had been on only a few special occasions before. Wrapped in that light, I felt pure peace and joy even though I was conscious of sitting at My Father's deathbed. And because I was sitting at his deathbed, I wrapped him in this blanket of color and felt him breathe me into him while I was still above him.

It was only as My Father finished blessing me and called for My Brother Benjamin that I returned to my body—that of an old man. A powerful, respected—revered, even—old man who was also a boy saying a final goodbye to his past. At that point, I realized I had missed My Father's last words to me, and I dropped my head. Although, I quickly changed my posture back to that of a grateful son and proud ruler so that My Brothers would not suspect, *I* knew that I had not heard, and for that, I shed an extra tear as Benno received his blessing. My Little Brother was called wolflike, and all I could think was that I didn't know this man at all. Though we shared both a father and a mother, those were the only things we shared.

Once My Father had finished the blessings, he called us all to listen to him. With great effort and little sound, he charged us for the final time: "I am about to be gathered to my people. Bury me with my fathers in the cave in the field of Ephron, the cave in Canaan in the field of Makhpelah near Hevron, in the cave that Abraham had bought along with the field as a burial place from Ephron the Hittite."

All of us, except Benno, had been to that very cave when My Grandfather Isaac had been buried there. We knew well, oh, so well, the story of Abraham buying that cave. Elohim had promised him the land, yet he had lived there for years as a stranger. Elohim promised the land would belong to his descendants, yet for so many years, he'd had none. In all that time, Abraham had still trusted Elohim, and waited. Until, finally, on the fateful day that he did not slay My Grandfather, his beloved wife died. It was in that full sorrow of losing Sarah that he—we—got the land he'd been promised. Abraham would not allow his beloved wife to be buried in a place he couldn't return to. Her burial place had to be on his own land. And so, he paid four hundred silver pieces for the land and the cave, even turning down the very same when it was offered as a gift to make sure that it was clear that the land was his.

It had been the first land he'd owned. And now, here we were, living in the land of Egypt. All of us. Every last one of us. Surely, My God had sent us down here to live and not die, but we mustn't stay. Even though we'd lived here and prospered, we mustn't stay. We must live and prosper in our land. My Father's words reminded us of this. Even if he wouldn't see the prosperity in the land, his bones would be there when it happened.

After a long pause, Judah reassured him. "We know the cave, Father. We will take you there."

But My Father went on. "There, Abraham and his wife Sarah were buried; there, Isaac and his wife Rebekah were buried; and there, I buried Leah."

With the mention of their mother's name, her sons dropped their heads in mourning. I could not find anger or jealousy in my heart for them. Yes, their mother had gotten a proper burial place while mine had been hastily laid to rest on our travels. But still, they'd had to say goodbye to their mother, and I have nothing but compassion for someone who has been through such sadness.

"We will lay you beside her," I assured My Father.

"The field and the cave in it were bought from . . ."

My Father's pause was long, longer than any of the others. We all waited expectantly, sure that he couldn't be done, that he was just resting and gathering strength to speak. I felt My Brothers beside me, but I felt others in the room as well. All those whom My Father had named had gathered: Abraham, Sarah, Isaac, Rebekah, and Leah. Oh, how beautiful and noble and light they all looked! Oh, how happy I was to see My Grandfather and My Grandmother again! Leah took My Father's hand, and he whispered his final words as she stroked his fingers: "the Hittites."

My Grandmother gently placed a hand on her son's eyes. I saw his lips part as he took a shallow inhale, *Yhhhh*, breathing in Elohim, and a long exhale, *Whhhh*, returning his whole self to his god. And when his exhale was complete, he had joined hands with Leah and My Mother, who had appeared to accompany him even though he would be in a different resting place. My Mother looked as soft and as beautiful and as loving as I had remembered her all these years. She did not look at me, nor at Benno. She was just as the others, barely perceivable light, . . . and then, gone.

My Father's hand turned cold in mine. None of us moved. We sat—twelve men surrounding the thirteenth, who was the first, each of us deep in our own thoughts, yet all of us together—for a very long time.

CHAPTER 30

My Pharaoh never withheld anything from me in his time of need, neither information nor opportunity. The same was true when my time of need came along. Upon hearing of My Father's death, he called me to his chamber. I left My Father in the skilled hands of my servants and physicians so that they could embalm him, then went to My Pharaoh.

"Zafenat Paaneakh, I shall declare this a time of mourning for the people. For the forty days of embalming and the seventy days of weeping, your father shall be treated as well as any member of my court. After which, when his body is ready, he shall have your choice of tombs."

I prostrated myself in gratitude. After having brought him to nearly immeasurable riches, I knew I deserved such an honor. Even so, his kindness toward me in my time of sorrow brought me to my knees. Would he extend the kindness and allow me to return to My Promised Land with My Father? Would he be willing to release me to my inheritance and replace me with a new advisor?

"Thank you, Mighty One," I said. "My Father, your servant, wished to have his bones buried in the land of Canaan. It was his wish to not disturb your court or take a tomb built for another. It was his final wish that we return him to the land where his father is buried, and he made me swear an oath that I would bury him there."

"Very well, then. You shall take my chariots and my servants and seventy elders to mourn with you and escort your father. A man's final wishes should be honored."

So, I was to bring back his chariots and servants. I was to return to Egypt. Still, I prostrated myself once again and began to back away from his chambers, stopping only when he called after me. "Zafenat Paaneakh."

"Yes, My Pharaoh."

"Will you ask for your bones to be buried in your homeland?"

There were two answers to this: the true one and the permitted one.

"My Pharaoh, I was merely a lad when I arrived in Egypt, and I have grown up here. This is where I have served you. This is my homeland. I would not want to be anywhere that you are not."

He was satisfied, and I was free to exit his presence, though not his service.

A LIFETIME HAD passed since I had been north. In all my travels to survey the land and secure the food, I had avoided it intentionally. My desire to return to the land of My Fathers was outweighed by my desire to avoid the land of My Brothers. I had known we would all meet again in Egypt even though I hadn't known when, but I felt safer having that reunion in a place where I was in command.

Now, for the second time in my life, I was traveling to My Land. This journey could not have been more opposite than the trip from Haran. That the movement was northbound this time was the simplest of the differences. Even the flatter landscape of traveling along the richer route by the shore, instead of trekking through the mountains as we had when I was a boy, was a mere trifle of a change.

And this time, I was not a boy, but a man. Not any man, but a ruler. Not any ruler, but the vizier of all of Egypt. I sat in my chariot, blocked from the sun, blocked from the wind, and blocked from My Brothers. And yet they were there, and I was aware of it, for every one of them had come and many of their sons had as well. Only the youngest ones stayed back, suckling with their mothers. On my first trip, even Tirzah and Emunah, still suckling, had left Haran. But, of course, we were never to return to Haran. We would not leave babies behind. Soon, we would be back in Egypt. My Pharaoh ensured that, even though I had told him I would return. By having the women and babies stay behind, he knew I would have to come back to him.

Returning to the hills of Hevron with My Brothers felt much like seeing the eyes of the crocodile peering over the river water. If I stayed long enough, something would happen. And I would not enjoy it. Although I did feel safe with Atsu by my side. Even though he was my official permanent guard, with his age, two younger guards were always with us. I never felt in danger on the journey, but I never felt comfortable either. We kept our peace during the travels, but perhaps it was only because we'd kept our distance until we arrived at the Cave of Makhpelah.

My Father had made a point of showing us that he and his brother had united to give their father a proper burial. I would not disgrace Israel by doing any less.

"Brothers," I said. Some of the men looked in my direction. I had one of my servants bring me a barrel to stand on so that I might be better seen and heard among the crowd. "My Father buried Isaac here in this cave. . . ." I paused. Reuben was shaking his head. Why? "Our father," I corrected. Several men stopped their chattering and gave me their attention then. "Today, we will bless his memory by laying his body beside that of his parents. It is only right that his two firstborn sons carry him in."

Reuben and I entered the cave with lamps. We found stones etched with the names of Abraham, Sarah, Isaac, Rebekah, and Reuben's mother, Leah. We buried My Father, our father, beside Leah, and I spent the rest of the afternoon etching a stone with his two names: Jacob and Israel. As the sun was setting, I entered the cave alone and placed the stone at My Father's head. As it touched the ground, a warmth radiated through it and then through my body.

As I walked out of the cave, I felt that it was not my feet taking me out but rather that I was being pulled, as I had been pulled out of the pit when I'd been sold. But I did not find My Brothers outside conspiring to sell me. I found the camp quiet, everyone having already retreated into their tents. The only presence outside other than myself was the full moon beginning to rise in the sky.

The full moon had risen every month in Egypt, but it was different to be beneath it in the land where I had first learned to love it. And I did love the moon. How had I not realized that? No women had come on this journey north. And none of the women who had taught me to celebrate under the moon were with me. I hummed the moon song quietly to myself.

> Sister, Mother, Daughter and Friend,
> You shine with love from beginning to end,
> We give you our hopes, our dreams, and our pain,
> You keep them safe, until we meet again.

I had sung that song so many times, but I hadn't known that I loved her. Had she loved me all this time too? To the surprise of the servants who had prepared my tent, I chose to sleep outside that night. I stared at the full moon until my eyes finally closed, and I slept with the same thrill, peace, and exhaustion that I had felt after the moon dances so long ago.

CHAPTER 31

Shortly after our return to Egypt, I received word that Levi died. I would not miss him. I could not miss him. I had hardly seen a glance of him for most of my life, and when I had, as a child, I'd suffered at his hand. Still, it was an odd feeling to have one of My Brothers dead. Within the year, it was not one but three, for Reuben and Shimon had both been suffering since the long journey to bury My Father and had finally taken their last breaths. All three of these brothers were buried in the land of Goshen under the watchful eyes of their children and their children's children.

Perhaps I was expected to be sad that My Brothers were dying. My tears were not shed for them, though, but for Atsu. It was his bedside that I had sat beside on his final days. It was his coffer that I had filled with gifts that would go to his wife and children and grandchildren in the following days. And it was his absence that had brought a wail from my throat and left a shadow of sadness beside me for the rest of my days. He was the brother I had grown up with and missed the most.

One warm morning in the Season of the Inundation, my guard entered my chamber with a message. It was a scroll sealed with the symbol of a lion and had just been delivered as the sun began to shine. I unrolled it and looked at the writing. It was well formed and clear. The characters were Egyptian and made by someone who had learned well.

"A message for Zafenat Paaneakh, from Judah, son of Israel. Your wise counsel is requested. Your servant will come and speak at your feet in the palace if you will give him the honor. Or you are welcome in my humble field, which you have provided, at your earliest convenience. May Elohim continue to bless you and keep you."

It was the morning after the new moon, my now regular meeting time with My Grandchildren. They would soon enter to arrange the pillows on the floor so that they could listen to stories for the day. Both Menasseh and Efraim had requested that I continue this tradition with their sons. I agreed to do so on the condition that they would tell their children stories as well. And so, on the mornings after the moon was full, My Sons told their children stories as I had done, and the mornings after the new moons became mine.

Judah had never sent for me, and My Grandchildren had never been to Goshen. I decided, therefore, that we would embark on an adventure together. I would tell them of the story of walking from Haran to Hevron when I was young like them while we walked together to Goshen. I laughed aloud to myself. My old bones could not walk such a distance. But I had my guard prepare a chariot, and I would tell them of my journey as we rode across the beautiful land of Egypt.

We found Judah standing tall in the grass, watching over sheep as he had done every day of his life since My Father had first taken him into the fields. He was an old man now, still with a slingshot on his belt and with a staff that was tall and commanding. I was glad that this was the first glimpse of a shepherd that My Grandchildren would ever see. He would forever be the picture of that word for them.

As I dismounted from the chariot, My Brother laid his shepherding crook on the ground and bowed low before me. I stared at his staff, then looked at the one I held in my own hand. Mine was not worn wood, but polished gold. It was inlaid with pearls from far-off seas and had a chain on top that held a polished sapphire, smooth and round and just the right size for my hand to hold. Not only that, but I could unhook the sapphire at my whim if I were more in the mood for an emerald or a ruby or an onyx, for I had a box only for precious handles in my chamber. And yet, for a moment, I envied Judah's simple, worn, familiar staff. I let my eyes go back to My Brother and signaled for him to rise. When he did, he put his hand on my shoulder. It felt like My Father's hand there: heavy, strong, confident, approving. The children looked on in silence.

"This is My Brother," I told them. "He is wise and honest and the leader of the Children of Israel. You may kiss his hand."

As they did, from oldest to youngest, I continued to talk. "You see this staff that he holds? You can see that it is worn smooth from his hand, from many years of shepherding. He uses it to direct stray sheep back to the flock. And on his belt, you can see something very special. That is a shepherd's slingshot. He uses it to protect his flock from anyone or anything who would try to harm them."

I had never had the chance to be a shepherd, but I was proud to show off this little bit of knowledge to My Grandchildren. "Perhaps," I said, "perhaps Judah will teach you how to use it as he once taught me when I was a child."

Judah laughed. "Joseph, I believe I could still hit a coyote between the eyes if I had to, but I would need to rest for weeks afterward from the effort. But look just there in the field." I followed his gaze to see a tall boy watching the sheep not far away. "He is an excellent marksman and can teach these children many things."

Judah called the boy over, and he came skipping and smiling.

"Yes, Uncle."

"Do you know who this man is?" Judah asked, referring to me.

"No, Uncle."

"This is Zafenat Paaneakh."

The boy bowed before me. He was almost a young man. His hair had not yet coated his chin, but it would soon. His voice had not yet dropped completely to the depth of a man, but it was trying. His feet were sturdy and planted on the ground as if they were as unmovable as tree roots, though I had just seen him move with the agility and joy of a gazelle. His hands reminded me of the hooves of a gazelle as well. Although he had all five fingers, they were joined together in pairs on each hand, with only his thumbs being separate. This created the illusion of a thumb and two wide fingers on each hand. Upon standing again, the boy looked at the children, their garb, and their proximity to me, and he bowed to them.

"You needn't bow before them," I said. "They are My Grandchildren. What is your name, boy?"

"Sir, my name is Amram, son of Kehat."

"Amram, son of Kehat, like these children, you must certainly have a grandfather. What is his name?"

"Yes, sir," he said. "I had a grandfather, and he has died. His name was Levi, son of Israel."

I looked at Judah with an unspoken question. My body nearly shook with fear for My Grandchildren. What had I done to bring them here, into a situation where they may be tortured by a son of Levi?

"Joseph," Judah said, continuing to address me by my childhood name, "Amram is a master with the slingshot. He is also a scribe. It was his hand that wrote the message you received from me."

"A student and a shepherd? Both?" This was quite impressive already, even without his strange hands.

"Yes," Judah said. "I am very proud of this boy. And I would not be so foolish as to endanger the grandchildren of the second-in-command of all Egypt. Nor," he continued, "would I want to bring any sorrow to my brother or his seed." And then I saw him stroke his gray beard with his thumb. I didn't know that this would be the last time I would see him do that. I just knew I trusted this man, this brother. My thumb rose to my own bare chin in consent, and I turned to the children.

"You will have a very special day today, indeed. If you listen to Amram intently, and follow his words well, you will learn to use a slingshot. Would you like that?"

"Yes, Grandfather!" they chorused.

"Very well. You may do so."

To my great surprise, I left My Children, the very babies who had come forth from the loins of Menasseh and Efraim, in the hands of a son of Levi, and Judah and I walked to sit in his tent. As we did so, he told me more about the boy.

"Amram is a fine shepherd. The finest. He is able to anticipate the needs of his flock with his skillful awareness of all the surroundings. Furthermore, because he has lived his whole life with those fingers of his tied together, he knows what it is to rise above challenges. While others mocked his appearance, he learned to do everything they could do, only better. He is strong, like Levi, but without the rage. His tongue is tied to the bottom of his mouth. This makes him slow of speech, and he has become an attentive listener. Only when he has heard all the details of a problem does he open his mouth and share a few words. Few, but wise."

We sat on cushions in the shade of Judah's tent and drank barley beer and ate sweet dates together. The tastes of my childhood. When we finished, My Brother told me the reason for requesting my presence. "Joseph, as Amram wrote for me in the message, I have asked you here because I require counsel. I am the head of this tribe now. We have grown and prospered here under the arc of your generosity. We are numerous, fulfilling the prophecy that our grandfather Abraham received. Within our tents, there are tens of people—and even more ways of doing things.

"Even with just twelve sons, our father's hands were full of responsibilities. Now, each of our brothers has sons and grandsons. The shepherds argue, the women compete, the babies wail, and the children run amok, all at once. While at the same time, there are many great ideas, innovations, and celebrations."

Judah sighed and paused for a long while before continuing. "Joseph, it is an honor to be the head of such a fine tribe. It is a responsibility that I fully accept with pride and commitment. I always have." I nodded my acknowledgment of this truth. "But as our tribe grows, I wonder if, perhaps, I should be doing something differently. You are second only to the king. You lead a people much larger than this little tribe. Brother, please, can you help me? For the sake of our father Israel, can you advise me?"

I noticed myself sitting a little taller on the cushion. I noticed the gray hair of Judah's long beard. If I had a beard, it would surely be gray as well, but I had never seen that gray, and my clean-shaven face looked years younger than Judah's. I felt, at the same time, like the adoring little brother and the adored king. The little brother in me did not know what to say, but the ruler I had become did.

"Judah, you will not always be liked, but if you find yourself a confidant and a teacher, you may always be steady. Stand with me now. Lift up your eyes to our homeland. We cannot see the hills we came from, but you know they are there. Have faith in Elohim; Elohim is the source of your help." We stood shoulder to shoulder and looked to the hills in silence for a long while, and we breathed in the way of our ancestors. *Yhhhh. Whhhh.* I had breathed that way so many times, but countless years had passed since I had done so with one of my own tribe.

"Joseph," he said when our bodies had relaxed and our thoughts had cleared, "we are only nine brothers now, and I am an old man. You have given us the choicest land that Egypt can offer. It is second only to the land that Elohim gave our father. With your generosity, we have become great in number here, survived the famine, and prospered—prospered so much, in fact, that our flocks bump into one another and our kinsmen quarrel.

If we had more grazing land, though, each man with his own hills and valleys and tents for his own sons . . ."

I cut him off. I could not bear the thought of losing them once again. "You are the head of this tribe," I told him, "but I am the head of Egypt. My Pharaoh will not allow my body to leave this land with my breath still in it. It was you who sent me down to this land. Brother, I ask you, do not leave me here. Take me back with you, even if it is only my bones. You are old, but My Pharaoh is older. His days are numbered, and thus, so are mine. It won't be long now. Don't leave without me."

Judah bent his head in respect, and I acknowledged him in the same way. Then I signaled to my chariot driver to bring my ride. He collected the children and came to get me. Amram had gotten a ride—his first—on the way. He had a broad smile on his face that he did not hide when he stepped down from the chariot. Judah clapped his hand on the boy's shoulder. For a moment, Amram's eyes sparkled blue and green before going back to brown, all the while showing admiration for the uncle who admired him.

Before entering my chariot, I paused for a moment to breathe in My God, here, with My Brother. And together, we breathed all that we were in that moment back into My God. Then I reached to the top of my staff and unhooked the sapphire handle that was there. "Here," I said to Judah, "you may use this." He looked at it, puzzled. "You do not know what it is, do you?" He admitted that he did not. "This is a gift from Elohim. Elohim gives us gifts all the time. Sometimes they are in the form of dreams, sometimes they are in the form of healthy sheep, and sometimes they are in the form of a wise woman or a loving brother or a mild grandson of an unruly man." I clapped my hand on Amram's other shoulder. "Sometimes," I continued, "they are even in the form of being thrown into a dark pit or sold as a slave. All things are gifts from Elohim, but it is our job to figure out how to use them."

My brother placed the sapphire on the hook of his staff, winding the chain around twice so that it would hold fast. We watched as the sunlight sent blue sparks through the gem, and Amram lifted his fingers to touch them gently. Then My Brother bowed on the ground at my feet. He got up slowly, as a man with knees and ankles so old does not arise quickly from the ground. But when he embraced me, I felt that he still had every bit of power that I remembered. I felt safe in his strong arms and knew our tribe was safe in his capable hands.

CHAPTER 32

Judah did indeed outlive my Pharaoh, which means that he is outliving me, of course. I am happy for him, though I did try to extend my own life. When My Pharaoh called me in to his deathbed, he shared with me many words of praise and gratitude. But even while swelling with pride in the job that I'd done, I was not able to listen to his words well, as I was planning my request to end my service.

When he granted permission for me to speak, I addressed him with great praise also. "My Pharaoh, you have been a mighty ruler; your legacy shall live on in these lands forever. Surely, the gods are pleased and will welcome you with open arms. . . ."

I did not have a chance to say any more, for he began to speak again, and I could not speak above him. "Zafenat Paaneakh, it was you who earned me my riches, my stature, and my honor. I will need you beside me in the next world to do the same." I bowed before him and placed my head on his signet ring. It would be according to his command.

That night, I called for My Sons, Menasseh and Efraim, for My Brother Benno, and for My Daughter, Blue. I had a feast prepared for us. I was eager to see these loved ones one last time, and yet I also found that, with my foot about to cross the threshold to the next world, I was eager to see the ones who awaited me there as well.

Though I had thought of My Mother every day since her death, it was not until My Father's death that I imagined we would one day be reunited. To be with her again, and My Father, my beloved Deenah, and my honored grandparents brought me a peaceful sense of longing for my death that replaced the disappointment I had held only moments before. A curiosity was quickly added. Would I see My Son Soaf? Hold him? My tiny baby sister Levav? I imagined reuniting with Atsu in his secure embrace and reassuring smile. I had buried Ah-seenat years earlier, in a respectful and opulent tomb, but I had not missed her. At the thought of seeing her again, I wondered whether it could be as pleasant as things had been before we'd separated. And what about My Brothers who had already died? Would Shimon and Levi torture me even in the next world? Would My Auntie help protect me from them and teach me about the world to come? Would Katib train me? Would I need to report to My Pharaoh each day?

I was lost in these questions and so many others when Menasseh and Efraim were escorted into my chamber. My Sons had grown into Egyptian men, important Egyptian men, sons of the vizier. They each had children and grandchildren of their own and important roles in the court. Their bodies were shaved clean, their skin was oiled and shiny, and their short tunics were woven with gold. They had grown up in this land and its ways. They knew well the law that when My Pharaoh died, I would be called to go with him. They came to see me for one last time, always knowing that the one last time would come. They were stoic and poised, as if they had been trained for this very moment.

But they were also Israelite men. The stories of my homeland and the addition of the tribe of Israel into the land of Goshen had been important events in their lives. They knew they would one day inherit the promise of Elohim, and with me no longer on the throne, they knew that Elohim would have more to offer them than Egypt. They were ready to claim their inheritance of their own parcels of land.

When they entered, they each bowed to the vizier of Egypt, then embraced their father. My Sons had become old men. I imagined them leaving this life and returning to the land from which I had been sold so many years ago. Lifetimes ago. I thought of them in our traditional tunics, not with Leah's weaving, for she was long gone, but in something similar. I wondered whether their faces would be adorned with gray hair when they got to the north or whether there would still be a few dark ones in there. I took them each by the chin and laughed.

Benno came in next. His beard was long and gray. He and My Brothers had kept the old ways. My Litte Brother looked like My Father: old, poised, strong, distinguished. We had seen each other only two other times since his arrival in Egypt—when My Father had died, and when we had buried him. But he had prospered. I had seen to that. They had all prospered thanks to my help, and they would go back to the land of My Father with much greater wealth than they had arrived with.

Benno fell on my neck, and we wept.

"Brother," he finally said, "I have heard talk that you are to be buried along with the pharaoh. But have you not told him of the cave that our father Abraham purchased in Hevron? Have you not told him of our traditions, that his are not ours?"

Before I was able to answer him, Blue was brought to the chamber. She still looked exactly like Deenah to my eyes. Her hair was still dark, her skin still smooth, unwrinkled. All her teeth were in her mouth, and she walked like the young person she appeared to be. Only her garb was different.

Benno also gasped and exclaimed, "Blue?"

She ran to him and buried her face in his shoulder.

"I thought you were dead," Benno said. "You left and never returned. I looked for you, Blue. I looked everywhere. The others helped. I thought that surely you were dead—or worse—and so I decided . . . hoped . . . you must be dead. You look exactly the same. But, . . . but, . . . is it really you?"

"I am not dead," she said. "Benno, I have missed you terribly. I have missed our jokes and the funny snorting sound you make when you laugh. I have missed your shoulder to cry on. And not just you—I have missed everyone. I have missed the lentil stews with the flavorings of home and the familiar smell of the sheep. I have missed hearing them bleat when agitated and smelling their wool woven as womb-like tents of my youth. And the funny thing is that I didn't realize how much I missed all those things—any of those things—until this very moment. Until seeing you. I have been happy."

"But where have you been, Blue?" My Brother asked My Daughter. "Why do you look . . . so young? You don't look any older than when I last saw you. My grandsons have taken brides, and you look like you could be one of them."

"Oh, Benno," she said. "You have grandsons. I have missed so much. I don't know why I look like I do. The women in the harem—for that's where I've been all these years—the women, the oilers, they oil my skin, and it becomes soft and supple. I don't have to look after the sheep or draw water."

"You've been in the harem?" he interrupted. "Like, . . . like, . . . Hallel?" Hallel had been sold to the pharaoh by Lot, and I would not have My Brother compare me to such a man.

"Of course not," I nearly yelled. "Yes, in the harem, but not like Hallel. My Pharaoh may have kept nothing from me, but I did not do the same. I kept My Daughter from him. I put her in the harem so she would be safe, unharmed by any man who would see her beauty and desire her, including My Pharaoh. He never knew she was here. He was never able to call for her. And I see she has thrived."

"Yes, I have risen to a position of great respect," she confirmed.

Benno spoke next. "Blue, it has been so long. Please, please stay beside me." He reached his hand toward her, and she took it.

I took My Sons by their hands and began walking. Blue and Benno followed. I released their hands only when I placed my right hand in the center of the wall, onto a large onyx stone with wheat carved into it, and pushed. The stone went into the wall, revealing a latch that unhooked a door that could not be noticed until opened. I took a lamp and led them down the path that was the direct entrance to my burial hall.

Of course, when I would be buried, I would be paraded the long way, outside, in front of the people. But I wanted them to know this entrance. It was a short walk. We stood in the center of the hall. It was dimly lit but clearly ornate. The walls were painted white and covered in words of praise. There were jugs of jewels and wine and clay sculptures of all sizes and forms. The most important parts, of course, were the jars that would soon hold my entrails and the sarcophagus that would soon hold my mummy. After admiring all of this, we turned around and walked back to my chamber.

The banquet had been prepared and waiting for us even before they'd arrived. It was time for it now. The food was eaten in silence, but I'm certain they enjoyed it. How could they not? The food included the freshest melons, the choicest meats, the most fragrant breads, and the sweetest dates. Even My Sons, who had grown up in the palace, accustomed to plenty, were impressed by the opulence of this meal. When the table was cleared away, I rose and spoke.

"I have proven myself a leader, and so it is clear that I would have been able to be the one to lead the Children of Israel out of Egypt. But My Pharaoh will not allow it, and so I know that My God does not wish this. Elohim will bring you a new leader who will bring you up from this land and take you to the land promised to Abraham, Isaac, and Jacob. When your days of mourning me are completed, and you are led out of Egypt, take me with you.

"I have spent most of my life in Egypt, but I was a son of Jacob first and will always remain an Israelite. Thanks to me, My Father's tribe has grown and prospered in this land and will leave as a wealthy nation. I have arranged it all. Only I cannot go with you while living. I shall never see My Land again. Elohim has blessed me with grandsons to live on that land. When my embalming is complete and the days of mourning are fulfilled, My Grandsons will go to that land and take their babies who have played upon my knees with them. Swear to me that they will also take my bones and bury them in my inheritance. Swear this to me."

They promised me, and I knew I would go back. Before parting, I gave them each a gift. I invited them to choose anything they wanted from my chamber. It would all go into my tomb in the morning, but as I was the one who did the accounting, there would be no punishment for missing pieces. Until the morning, everything there was mine to do with as I wished, and it was my wish that my family take any of my riches to become theirs.

My Brother Benno chose my wine goblet. He let out a light laugh. "You gave me your goblet before. This time, I shall take it for myself." He embraced me and stood beside Blue. I could see him encouraging her to choose something, but she remained quiet.

My firstborn son, Menasse, stepped forward and slowly walked around the chamber. He lifted a few items, then set them back down. He came back to me and asked, "Father, may I choose anything? Anything at all?" I confirmed that he could. With my permission, My Son took my signet ring from my finger and placed it on his own. I had not expected this, but I would not retract my word. I chose a different ring to wear in its place, a ring that was pure gold and had the shape of a bee on one side and a flower on the other. I embraced My Son for the final time.

Efraim, who had closely watched his brother and who had taken time to consider his choice while Menasseh was choosing, walked directly to my chest of silver spoons. He opened the lid and gently stroked each one. There were seventeen. I knew without recounting. After all, I had put them there. I wondered which he would choose. But after careful consideration, he closed the lid and took the entire chest. "For myself and my children," he said. "I will tell them the story of the seventeen spoons and the people that they are. Were. I shall tell them of Joseph: the boy, the vizier, the Israelite." I stood as tall and pleased as on any of the proudest days of my life. I took my boy in my arms and held him one last time.

I looked to My Daughter. "Come, choose anything you like."

"All I ever wanted was you," she said. "My mother spoke of you with stars in her eyes and honey on her tongue without even knowing who you had become. I wanted to know that man. You gave me that," she said, "and so much more than I ever could have imagined."

I embraced My Daughter until My Brother spoke. "Blue," Benno said, "choose something. Perhaps you're right, but you won't get another chance. Choose something for later. Later, your father will be gone, the father you waited so long for." His voice was quiet, and he held her hand.

I watched as her eyes took in my chamber and then as her feet brought her across it. She placed her hand on the wall where the name she had written so long ago was still as vibrant as she was.

"Father," she said, "I would like you to write my name on the four corners of your coffin so that I may always be remembered. My full name: Blue, daughter of Deenah and Joseph." I blissfully fulfilled her wish with her beside me. And when I had written her full name four times, I handed her the brush that I had used to do so. As she opened her hand to receive it, I began to see light and colors starting in her palm and filling the room. When I placed my brush in her hand, my coat of colors covered us both. We stood there together for all time.

When My Daughter stepped back, my coat went with her. I bowed my head in gratitude, and she did the same. The four of them left my chamber, and I did not see another person until it was time to be placed in my coffin.

CHAPTER 33

I may have been on my way to my grave, but until I was dead, I still held power. When My Pharaoh died, the others were given the drink and supervised as they swallowed. But when I asked for mine to be in a flask, I could not be refused. And so it was that I laid myself in my wooden coffin; and so it was that I heard the wailing of the Egyptians as I was paraded before them; and so it was that I was awake and aware when my wooden casket was placed into my stone sarcophagus, arms crossed on my chest, one hand closed around a vial of poison.

It was dark in there, of course. The darkness sharpened my hearing, though even that was still difficult. Since I had the privilege of my own burial hall, I came across no men waking from their poison and screaming to be let out. It was rare that it happened, but it did happen. I knew they would be quickly and mercifully killed if so. But I chose to die slowly. I was not used to being commanded, for there was only one man who could order me to do anything—even to die. But I still controlled the timing of my death.

I don't know whether my eyes were closed or open, for the experience was exactly the same. But I opened my mouth and breathed in My God. *Yhhhh.* And with my lips still parted, *Whhhh*, I breathed myself into Elohim, Yah, as My Auntie and My Grandmother would say. I felt that I was breathing them in as well. After all, where could they be that was not a part of Elohim? And thus, a part of me. Like My Father, My Mother, My Grandparents, and My Auntie. Like little Levav and sweet Soaf. Perhaps like Reuel and Qarib by now, and some of My Brothers. And, of course, the best brother of my heart: Atsu.

I continued my breathing. I had breathed for so many years. What a blessed man I was. Since my very birth into the world, even when I had not noticed, I was breathing in My God and my ancestors, my teachers and my loved ones. They had all been a part of me. For 924 million breaths.

And who had shared those breaths with me? Who had taken *me* in? My dear parents, my esteemed grandparents, My Beloved and My Wife, My Brothers and My Sisters, My Sons, My Daughter, My Grandchildren, My People. My *Peoples*—those of My Father and those of Egypt. I was in them. A part of me will always be in them and live on.

As I write these final words, the oil is nearly gone. Once again, I have chosen a date as the last food I shall eat. This one from the storage jug is not juicy and supple like a fresh date. It is dried but still sweet—like I am. Blessed is Yah, who created me like the date: soft in youth, wrinkled in old age, and valuable in both. I am holding the silver flask of poison in my hand. It was molded into the shape of a fish. I chose it for its fine workmanship. I trace the scales with my fingers. I feel the smooth coolness of the metal and think of the water of the very first stream I bathed in, of the great river I crossed by boat in the north, and of the River I lived beside in Egypt. Soon, I will not feel metal, or anything at all, again. Some tears flow from the corners of my eyes. My last feeling of water.

For the final time, I whisper: "Elohim, My God, God of My Father Jacob, God of My Father Isaac, God of My Father Abraham. . . . " For just a moment, I think back to the very first time I spoke to My God, but only for a moment, for I have already done all my thinking. I have already done all my writing. Even if I had unlimited oil, I would not be able to remember every detail of my extraordinary lives. And so, I continue my prayer. I speak to My God for the last time. "My God, the breath that You placed in me is pure. You created it; You formed it; and You blew it into me and have allowed me to keep it for all these years. For all the time that this breath has been in me, I am thankful to You, Elohim, Yah, My God, God of My Ancestors. I praise You for placing this breath in me. *Yhhhh*. And now, I return it to you with gratitude. *Whhhh*."

Thus ends the reign of Zafenat Paaneakh and the life of Joseph, Son of Jacob. I shall now return to my coffin, place the vial to my lips, and drink.

AUTHOR'S NOTE

I didn't plan to write this book. One difficult night in 2018 I couldn't sleep. I decided to spend a few minutes reading a book on my phone—I was sure that would help my eyelids to get heavy and my brain to settle down. The book I was reading was *This Messy Magnificent Life* by Geneen Roth. In the section that came up that night, I read, ". . . an eighty-year-old person takes about 672,768,000 breaths in a lifetime. . . ." And at that moment, I felt Joseph's death come to me.

Numbers in the bible have always intrigued me and I had often felt that the mention of Joseph's death at age 110 was a way of telling the readers that he died before his time (120 being the number that represents a full life). For years I'd thought Joseph was buried with the pharaoh. After all, what (or who) could be more valuable to take to the next life than the man who had overseen all of Egypt?

Although I'd had that thought, I had never envisioned the moment of Joseph's death before the fateful night with the book on my phone. And once I began writing Joseph's death story, most of his life story wrote itself. Sometimes the ideas came faster than I could type them. Of course, some of these ideas had been sitting with me for a while. Just one example is that the key to understanding Joseph's sun, moon, and stars dream was that the numbers correspond to numbers of years—the objects only *seemed* to be the main point. But I had never dreamt about seventeen spoons until I wrote that Joseph did.

Although *Seventeen Spoons* is the second book in The Desert Songs Trilogy, it's the one I wrote first—before I even knew there would be a trilogy. Back when this book was in progress, I was lucky enough to have a handful of enthusiastic and supportive readers who devoured each chapter as I wrote it and met with me on video chat to give me their feedback. At this time, I'd like to thank all of the early readers: Jan, Lori, Naomi, Netta, Patti, Rebekah, Roxanne, Sandy, Shira, Tom, Yael, and Wendy. Thank you.

Thank you to all the readers of the finished form of this book who liked it enough to make the time to leave a review online. I'm so glad to share this story with you and I appreciate that you share it with others.

Sincere gratitude to Ruthie and Ben for letting me use their daughter Levav's name. Ruthie's brave sharing of her moving experience of delivering Levav early and burying her with honor deeply inspired Rachel's birth story in this book.

A shout out to Rick Recht and his song "Halleluyah." I listened to this song on repeat for weeks because I felt that in many ways it expressed how Joseph felt when he was on his way to Egypt. I danced to it and embodied it and then wrote it into Joseph's revelation as he left for Egypt.

As always, it's Shira Gura's songs that permeate this book. Thank you, Shira, for writing the incredible tune to my words in the song "Praise Yah" that Blue sings. And the tune to the lullaby in *The Scrolls of Deborah*. And the tune to a song in *The Song of the Blue Bird* (stay tuned). And for your beautiful tunes to some of the traditional words that are included in The Desert Songs Trilogy because of how much I love singing them with you.

On a different note, I'd like to thank Netta for teaching me how to kill a deer with one arrow (and how not to). Thank you, Netta. No deer or arrows were involved in this tutorial, only words. In fact, many or most, or possibly even all flora and fauna related sections in this trilogy have benefited from your wisdom—as have I.

Of course a huge thanks to my kids who heard and read parts of *Spoons* while it was in the works, and engaged in great discussions with me about breathing and boats and brothers and everything in between. Your enthusiasm means a lot to me.

Thank you also to Raquel and Ellis for all the times you entertained my questions about Joseph during dance carpool. I enjoyed and appreciated your comments and thoughts.

Thank you to my two favorite Josephs: the OG Yosef and My Friend Yosi. You were always destined for greatness. I'm glad I get to come along for the ride.

This book wouldn't be complete without thanking my amazing editors. It was fun to write this book! But sometimes my thoughts moved faster than my fingers could record them coherently. Thank you to the editor I hired before this book had a publisher. Maggie McReynolds, your great questions and attention to detail helped make this book better. When people ask me if I can recommend an editor, it's your name that I give out.

Gina Frangello, you are a gift. Even though *Seventeen Spoons* arrived at your inbox as a "completed" manuscript, working with you felt like a true collaboration of love. Your whole-hearted dive into getting to know the characters and your passionate advocacy for everything that I believe in about this story helped me to open up parts of it in ways that I hadn't before. I'm so excited to continue this journey with you with "Blue."

Thank you to Meghan Rollins Wilson for dealing with my lack, of, knowledge, of how to properly, use, a, comma, and all the other "little" things you fixed that cleaned up this manuscript, making it easier to read. Thank you to Julie, my informal editor of everything at all hours. And thank you to everyone on the Row House team who helped turn *Spoons* into an actual book that people can hold in their hands, listen to with their ears, and read on their devices (including on their phones when it's hard to sleep).

Finally, thank you, Mom and Dad, for being my roots, telling me stories, sticking around long enough to get to hear the first two chapters of *Seventeen Spoons*, and supporting me in your way wherever you are now.

ABOUT THE AUTHOR

ESTHER GOLDENBERG, a Chicago native who has lived in Israel, is an author, educator, and mother of two. Though once a reluctant reader, Esther's innate fondness for captivating storytelling led her to discover a deep passion for writing. Alongside her writing endeavors, Esther remains committed to teaching individuals and groups of all ages, sharing her knowledge and creative insights. In her free time, she enjoys adventures with her children, communal chanting sessions with her neighbors, and the serenity of nature through leisurely walks. *Seventeen Spoons* is the second installment in The Desert Songs Trilogy, which began with *The Scrolls of Deborah*.